To Disguise the Truth

Books by Jen Turano

THE
BLEECKER STREET INQUIRY AGENCY

3

To Disguise the Truth

JEN TURANO

BETHANYHOUSE
a division of Baker Publishing Group
Minneapolis, Minnesota

© 2022 by Jennifer L. Turano

Published by Bethany House Publishers
11400 Hampshire Avenue South
Minneapolis, Minnesota 55438
www.bethanyhouse.com

Bethany House Publishers is a division of
Baker Publishing Group, Grand Rapids, Michigan

Printed in the United States of America

Library of Congress Cataloging-in-Publication Data
Names: Turano, Jen, author.
Title: To disguise the truth / Jen Turano.
Description: Minneapolis, Minnesota : Bethany House Publishers, a division of
    Baker Publishing Group, [2022] | Series: Bleecker Street inquiry agency
Identifiers: LCCN 2021035949 | ISBN 9780764239885 (casebound) | ISBN
    9780764235337 (paperback)
Subjects: LCGFT: Detective and mystery fiction. | Novels.
Classification: LCC PS3620.U7455 T58 2022 | DDC 813/.6—dc23
LC record available at https://lccn.loc.gov/2021035949

This is a work of fiction. Names, characters, incidents, and dialogues are products of the author's imagination and are not to be construed as real. Any resemblance to actual events or persons, living or dead, is entirely coincidental.

Scripture quotations are from the King James Version of the Bible.

Cover design by Dan Thornberg, Design Source Creative Services

Author is represented by Natasha Kern Literary Agency.

Baker Publishing Group publications use paper produced from sustainable forestry practices and post-consumer waste whenever possible.

22 23 24 25 26 27 28   7 6 5 4 3 2 1

For Tammy Dawson Bizzarri

Because rooming with me in college and surviving to tell
the tale was quite the feat, and that type of friend definitely
deserves to have a book dedicated to her!
Thank you for all the fabulous memories!
What a special time we had together.

Love you!

Jen

CHAPTER
One

Considering she'd once shot the man sitting across from her, Eunice Holbrooke was beginning to get the sneaking suspicion her past had finally caught up with her.

Breathing a silent sigh of relief that she'd had the presence of mind to throw on not one but three weeping veils that morning, Eunice peered through the dark crape of the veils at the few notes she'd taken before she lifted her head.

"From what I understand," she began, speaking in a breathy voice that was not her usual voice at all, "you're here because you'd like to hire the Bleecker Street Inquiry Agency to locate a missing person. Is that right so far, Mr. . . . what did you say your name was again?"

"Arthur, Arthur Livingston."

Hearing him speak a name that had plagued her for seven long years sent a frisson of something best left uncontemplated down Eunice's spine as she wrote his name in the notepad, not that there was the slightest chance she'd ever forget it, seeing as how she'd put a bullet through his arm. Granted, she hadn't been intending on killing the man, but . . . still. One didn't forget the name of a man one shot.

"My apologies, Mr. Livingston. I was preoccupied with another case and missed your name when you were first ushered into my office."

Arthur leaned back in the dainty chair, his large frame obviously behind the squeak of protest from the chair in return. It was rare for the agency to see many men, which was why Eunice had outfitted her office with feminine furniture, each piece chosen to put the distraught women who came seeking their services at ease. Eunice did keep larger chairs at the ready, but since she'd not had advance warning that Arthur was going to appear in her office, she hadn't had an opportunity to switch out the chairs.

Not that she would have agreed to see Arthur in the first place if she'd been given a choice in the matter. Frankly, he was the last person she'd ever wanted to see again, and not only because she'd once shot the man.

Arthur Livingston posed a danger to her that wasn't to be taken lightly—a danger that revolved around the missing person he was determined to locate. A person she had no intention of helping him find, not when it wasn't in her best interest to do so.

"There's no need to apologize, Mrs. Holbrooke," Arthur said, interrupting her thoughts. "I did arrive without an appointment. Frankly, I was surprised when Miss Judith Donovan didn't hesitate to escort me into your office. I'd been warned it's difficult to secure an appointment with this agency on the spot."

Eunice rolled her eyes, an action that went unseen because of her many veils. "Your arrival into my office was a surprise for me as well. Judith isn't normally the person responsible for manning the front reception room. However, our regular doorman is currently unavailable, which is why she was pressed into service today. I imagine she's at a critical point with her current painting and didn't appreciate the interruption of a potential client breezing through the door. I also imagine she wanted to speed up the interruption by passing you along to me."

Arthur raked a hand through midnight black hair, leaving it decidedly rumpled. "That explains why Miss Donovan greeted me at the front door with a scowl and a paintbrush. Curiously enough, her scowl disappeared when her attention settled on my face. She then smiled at me, said something about my bone structure, and questioned whether I'd consider sitting for an up-and-coming artist."

"Oh . . . no," Eunice muttered, praying Arthur hadn't agreed to sit for Judith because that would definitely complicate her life.

Arthur smiled an easy smile, which seemed completely out of character for the man she'd once known. "No need to worry that I was put out over Miss Donovan's query. Yes, it's unusual for me to find myself confronted by up-and-coming artists, but after I told her I'm only in the city for a few days—a week at the most—and thus have no time to sit for a portrait, Miss Donovan hustled me right into your office."

"I wouldn't relax your guard on the way out. Judith possesses a tenacious attitude when it comes to her work. If she has your bone structure in her sights, she'll probably try to convince you to sit for her again."

"Perhaps I'll use the back door."

"A prudent decision on your part."

Arthur shifted in the chair, causing Eunice to wince when the chair gave a touch of a shudder. "May I assume Miss Donovan doesn't concentrate all her efforts on portraits? I glimpsed an unfinished painting as she was hurrying me down the hallway, and to my untrained eye, it appeared to be a medley of fruit."

Finding it beyond peculiar that Arthur seemed content to engage in idle chitchat, something he'd never done in their past, Eunice tapped her pencil against her notepad. "Judith used to concentrate her artistic efforts strictly on fruit. She's now dipped her toe into the portrait world, although she's chosen abstract portraits as her latest obsession, having been influenced by a specific female artist whose work Judith admires. I believe the painting you saw was the beginning of a portrait of another one of our agents, Daphne Beekman Henderson."

"If what I saw is a portrait of Daphne Beekman Henderson, I would definitely describe it as abstract. Is this the same Daphne who was recently revealed to be the author behind the Montague Moreland books?"

"Indeed she is."

"I'm a great admirer of Montague Moreland books," Arthur continued. "I must admit, though, that I was taken aback when the news broke about Daphne Beekman being the author behind those riveting reads. I could have sworn, given the complexity of the Montague Moreland plots, that they'd been penned by a man."

Any lingering remorse she'd been feeling about shooting the man disappeared in a heartbeat because clearly, lurking underneath the charming demeanor he'd displayed to her thus far, remained a most annoying gentleman. "How disheartening to learn you're still one of those less-than-progressive gentlemen who believe women are incapable of great accomplishments such as penning complex, and need I add, best-selling novels. That makes me wonder why you'd seek out the services of an inquiry agency that's owned and operated by the feminine set."

Arthur's brown eyes narrowed. "What did you mean by *still*?"

It had been inevitable that her jangled nerves would have her slipping at some point, but she hadn't expected that to happen quite so quickly. Eunice readjusted one of her veils. "I simply meant that given your age, which I'm going to estimate to be around thirty, you would have outgrown such an attitude."

"I'm thirty-three, but my age aside, tell me this. Do you make a habit of insulting your clients, Mrs. Holbrooke? Pointing out that I'm not progressive is hardly good for business. I imagine your late husband, Mr. Holbrooke—and allow me to extend my deepest condolences over the loss of him—would have encouraged you to refrain from saying anything controversial that might offend your clientele."

Her fingers itched to pull her pistol from the top drawer of her desk, an itch she staunchly ignored. "Mr. Holbrooke would have never taken it upon himself to school me on matters of business."

"Ah, he was a progressive sort, was he?"

Truthfully, Eunice had no idea if Mr. Richard Holbrooke was progressive because she didn't actually *know* a Richard Holbrooke. She'd only chosen that name for her fictitious late husband after reading a lovely account of a Richard Holbrooke's life she'd seen in the *New York World*, one that had listed his last address as London, far removed from the States. She'd needed a surname that began with an *H* because all of her luggage, which she was loath to part with because it had been a gift from her mother, was stamped *EH*. That was also why she'd chosen the name Eunice for her new first name, believing Eunice to be one of those unassuming names, and unassuming was exactly what she'd needed.

"May I presume that after your husband died," Arthur continued, pulling her from thoughts that were definitely distracting her, "you found yourself in dire straits, which was a mitigating factor in opening up a business that usually isn't run by the feminine set?"

Eunice's lips thinned. "While the state of my finances at the time of my, ah, husband's death is none of your concern, I've never been left in dire straits, and this agency came about years after he, erm, died."

"If Mr. Holbrooke died years ago, may I be so bold as to inquire why you're still garbed in deep mourning attire? I was under the belief that's worn by widows for a year and a day, at which time they can adopt a lavender shade and abandon their veils. You must realize that potential clients find your appearance disconcerting because sitting across from a woman whose face is not revealed is quite a novel and, frankly, unnerving experience."

Given that there was no possibility she could remove her veils in front of Arthur, which would complicate an already complicated situation, Eunice struggled for an appropriate response, smiling when it sprang to mind. "I apologize if my veils unnerve you, Mr. Livingston, but you see, I'm still, even after all these years, grieving the loss of my dear Mr. Holbrooke. I've been known to descend into spontaneous bouts of weeping because of my grief, and, believe me, you as well as other clients would find that weeping far more unnerving than the sight of my veils."

"The sight of a lady weeping has never unnerved me."

"I'm sure that's only because you're accustomed to a certain type of weeping. I assure you, I'm not a dainty weeper. Besides, I've chosen to remain in deep mourning for a reason—that being my deep and abiding love for Mr. Holbrooke. Surely you don't want to encourage me to abandon something that lends me comfort, do you?"

"Of course not. But I've heard that weeping veils have been responsible for widows suffering ill health, occasionally even death." He frowned. "I hope that you're not also continuing to wear deep mourning because you long to join your Mr. Holbrooke in the hereafter."

"I don't have a death wish, for pity's sake, and to ease your concerns, know that I've modified the veils to include a layer of netting, which allows me to breathe easier."

Curiosity flickered through his eyes. "But if you never abandon your mourning attire, you'll never have an opportunity to meet another gentleman and marry again, something I understand most widows are keen to do."

Her pencil began beating a rapid tattoo against the notepad. "Forgive me, Mr. Livingston, but I find myself wondering if you often make it a point to offer unsolicited business advice as well as unsolicited personal opinions to women you've just met."

"In all honesty, no, that's not a frequent habit of mine."

"Then why are you making that a habit with me? Do I strike you as a woman who longs to accept such advice and opinions from unknown gentlemen? Or, better yet, do I strike you as a woman who would tolerate what I can only describe as a condescending attitude toward me on your part?"

"I wasn't being condescending."

"You didn't just try to school me regarding insulting my clients?"

"I don't know why you'd consider my response to that condescending, considering you did insult me."

She winced. "I may have been somewhat short with you, but I assure you, Mr. Livingston, I don't make it a point to insult any of our clients."

"I seem to be the exception to that point."

"I can't argue with that," Eunice admitted. "Nevertheless, allow me to apologize. I certainly didn't mean to offend you. Perhaps if you could refrain from offering any business or personal suggestions from this point forward, I could then refrain from insulting you further."

Arthur's gaze suddenly sharpened on her. "What I'm about to say next isn't a personal suggestion, more along the lines of an observation, but I find myself curious why your voice is changing the longer I converse with you. When I first arrived, you were speaking in dulcet tones, but now you're speaking in a more direct manner with what is clearly a hint of exasperation in your voice."

Calling herself every sort of ridiculous for allowing Arthur to get under her skin to such an extent that she'd completely forgotten to disguise her voice, even though the veils did a somewhat sufficient job of that, Eunice tried to gather her thoughts into some semblance of order, something she rarely had to do since she wasn't a lady predisposed to scattered and errant thoughts to begin with.

It was maddening the way Arthur was currently rattling her, especially when she'd once been adept at holding her own with him. Her thoughts had not gone whizzing every which way during their past encounters, not even when Arthur had taken to pointing out what he felt were flaws in her character, all of which revolved around behavior he believed was less than acceptable for a young lady.

He'd frowned upon her riding astride, took umbrage over the fact she'd preferred wearing trousers over skirts, and certainly hadn't approved of her being armed at all times.

His intolerable attitude had been baffling to say the least because there wasn't a logical reason for him to take issue with her less-than-ladylike behavior, given the casual relationship between them. Arthur had merely come to her home state of Montana at the request of her grandfather, concerning matters of business. However, not long after arriving at Mason Manor, the grand estate she shared with her grandfather, he began taking it upon himself to encourage her to abandon what he'd called unconventional ways.

She was not a lady fond of being taken to task regarding her behavior, which was exactly why she'd abandoned every etiquette lesson her numerous governesses had imparted to her, instead throwing herself wholeheartedly into heated debates with the man.

His reaction to her blunt responses to his suggestions had been downright amusing at first since Arthur evidently hadn't been accustomed to women speaking their minds. He'd rallied quickly, though, voicing his irritating opinions about her behavior with increasing frequency.

She'd never gotten rattled with him during their heated exchanges, but that had evidently changed, probably because the sight of him in her office had left her yearning to flee from the agency as fast as her black leather boots could carry her.

Leaning across her desk, she lowered her voice to almost a whisper. "Being in charge of an inquiry agency does occasionally require me to speak firmly with clients, especially when some of them become overwrought due to their circumstances. I've found that maintaining a dulcet tone is not always advisable."

"I'm not feeling overwrought in the least, nor do I imagine I appear overwrought, which suggests you have an alternative reason for speaking firmly to me."

"Well, quite."

"You might need to expand on that because 'well, quite' doesn't explain why you're obviously exasperated with me. I don't normally incur such a response from ladies."

Unable to help but wonder how the conversation had managed to get away from her so quickly, Eunice drew in a steadying breath. "I was being purposefully vague just now because I was hoping to avoid insulting you again, but if you must know, I spoke firmly to you because *you* insulted my dear friend Daphne Beekman Henderson, which then left *me* in a foul mood."

"I did no such thing."

"Did you or did you not state that you were incredulous to discover Daphne is the author behind the Montague Moreland mysteries?"

"I don't know if I used the word *incredulous*."

She gave an airy wave of her hand. "Perhaps you said you were taken aback, which amounts to the same thing. Nevertheless, I took that as a grave affront to Daphne that then, I'm afraid, resulted in a brief lapse into temper on my part, which escalated when you questioned the reasoning behind why I'm an inquiry agent."

"I would think you'd take my incredulity or my being taken aback regarding Daphne's books as a compliment, since I believe her talent rivals most gentlemen writers."

"There's nothing complimentary about that sort of drivel," Eunice shot back, wincing when she realized she was once again speaking in less-than-dulcet tones. She immediately returned to her notes, attempting to get a temper that didn't seem to want to cooperate in check. "But since we're unlikely to agree on your position on whether you complimented Daphne or not, why don't you explain to me why, when you evidently have such a dismal view of women, you've decided to seek out the services of this agency, a question I recently voiced, but one you have yet to answer."

"I don't have a dismal view of women."

"Allow us to respectfully disagree about that."

Arthur began drumming his fingers against the arm of the chair. "Obviously you and I are suffering from a misunderstanding regarding my views of women, but to answer your question, my younger brother Chase encouraged me to seek out your agency. He's been keeping abreast of your success through the local newspapers. When I told him how urgent it was to locate the missing person I mentioned to you, he suggested I have your agency look into the matter."

"Why not use the Pinkertons? They're an agency that employs

mostly men. You'd probably have more confidence in male agents solving your case over female ones."

"I hired the Pinkertons years ago to look into this matter. They were unsuccessful."

She stilled. "Are they still on the case?"

"I'm afraid not. They ran out of leads years ago."

Her lips began to curve. "How . . . unfortunate."

"Indeed, but I'm hoping your agency will be more successful. From what my brother told me, the Bleecker Street Inquiry Agency has seen success where the Pinkertons have not."

Realizing there was nothing to do but get Arthur out of her office as quickly as possible, especially when it was becoming abundantly clear he was determined to hire her agency to solve his case—something that wasn't going to be a possibility—Eunice cleared her throat and hoped Arthur would be reasonable about what she was about to say. "While it is true that we've solved many cases since we opened our doors, I'm afraid your case doesn't sound as if it would be a good fit for this particular agency."

"Why not?"

"Because it's been cold for years. It's highly unlikely we'll be able to uncover any new leads regarding this missing person of yours. With that said, I believe now is where I bid you adieu and wish you well in your quest." She rose to her feet. "If you'll follow me, I'll see you to the door, and the back door at that, which will allow you to get on your way without being waylaid by Judith and her desire to sketch your prominent cheekbones."

CHAPTER
Two

It was difficult to resist a sigh when Arthur didn't so much as budge from his chair.

"I'm not bidding you adieu just yet," he said. "Your reason for refusing my case is flimsy at best, and I'm getting the distinct impression there's another reason why you don't want to take me on as a client."

Eunice released the sigh she'd been resisting. "I was hoping to avoid getting into that because you'll probably take it as another insult. So, to voice this as gently as possible, we're very selective about the cases we take on. Yours isn't a case we'll want to consider."

"That explanation is flimsier than your first one."

"Well, then, how about this? We're a small agency and have more requests than we can handle. And because your case seems next to impossible to solve, we won't have enough agents to investigate it for you."

"Try again because you haven't even heard the details of my case. Yes, it's been years since the woman I'm searching for has been seen, but I would think that would pique your interest, not diminish it. I also have to think that, if you were able to solve my case, it would be a distinct feather in your cap, something I'm sure your agency could then use to secure future clients."

"This would be so much more pleasant if you'd simply accept my decision and take your leave."

When Arthur remained firmly in his seat, Eunice moved back to her chair and settled into it. "Fine, since you're obviously going to be persistent about the matter, the main reason behind my decision is this. You and I are already at odds with each other."

"What does that have to do with anything?"

She gave a flick of a black-gloved hand. "It has everything to do with my decision because we believe in working closely with our clients, something I'm convinced I'm not going to enjoy doing with you."

"You don't need to enjoy me to take on my case."

"Oh, but I'm afraid I do expect to enjoy being in the company of clients." She brushed a piece of lint from her sleeve. "I imagine that's because I'm a woman. Women, I'm sure you'll agree, tend to dissolve into unexpected fits of pique, or worse yet, fits of the vapors, when our tender sensibilities are roused. That would certainly happen if I had to frequently encounter your less-than-progressive attitude."

"Business has no room for tender sensibilities."

"Yet another reason our agency is *not* the agency to take on your case."

Eunice swallowed a laugh when Arthur's eyes turned darker than ever, a clear sign he was becoming frustrated with what he had to realize was a valid argument voiced on her part.

Her amusement disappeared in a flash, though, when his gaze sharpened on her. "I'll pay you triple your normal rate."

It took a great deal of effort to hold back a snort.

Arthur had once remarked to her, after he'd lectured her about the inadvisability of traveling into town in trousers, and after she'd changed the subject and launched into how Mr. Jasper Green was reluctant to consider her grandfather's offer to purchase the man's farm, that he firmly believed anything could be bought if the price was right. He'd then said that if Eunice's grandfather upped his offer to where it was downright irresistible, Mr. Green would eventually sell his farm. Annoyingly enough, Arthur had been right about that, as her grandfather had purchased the farm not long after that discussion. But Arthur was sadly mistaken if he thought she'd take on his case simply because of his irresistible offer, because she wasn't motivated by money.

Yet even without that type of motivation, and even though she'd presented a valid reason why she didn't believe working with him was a good idea, she was coming to the realization that she might need to tread carefully. Arthur was obviously determined to hire the Bleeker Street Inquiry Agency to find his missing person, and a determined Arthur was not a man to tangle with if at all possible. He hadn't made an impressive fortune because he lacked intelligence, nor because he gave up easily. Clearly, if she dismissed him too rapidly or overplayed the flighty, feminine role too dramatically, his pesky curiosity assuredly would be further aroused. A curious Arthur was not something she wanted to deal with either, because it could very well lead to the rapid end of the comfortable life she'd built for herself in New York if he caused her to slip up again and say something she shouldn't say or, worse yet, inadvertently disclose something that would lead him to realize exactly who she was.

Her mind whirled with possible responses, and she settled on the one that seemed the least likely to arouse his suspicions. "That's an intriguing proposition, Mr. Livingston, but you see, I'm not the only one at the agency who decides what cases we take on. I have two partners and will need to consult with at least one of them before any determination about your case is made. With that said, I believe this is where we discontinue our conversation. You may then return at some point during the week to set up an actual appointment with the agency. I'd suggest you set up that appointment now, but you'd have to go through Judith and that could very well see her hounding you to agree to sit for your portrait."

Arthur leaned back in his chair, causing it to squeak again. "I'm afraid leaving doesn't work for me, Mrs. Holbrooke. Time is of the essence. I have a week at the most to complete my objective, but besides that, I get the feeling that if I were to leave now, I may very well find no appointment times are available when I return to set one up."

"What an interesting conclusion you've derived from my suggestion."

"And accurate, if I'm not mistaken."

"Perhaps."

He blinked. "I wasn't expecting you to be quite so blunt about the matter, but with all of that out in the open now, where do you suggest we go from here?"

Eunice was spared a response she didn't have readily available when there was a hard rap on her office door before it opened and Daphne Beekman Henderson breezed into the room in a flutter of expensive fabric, her delightful afternoon gown designed by their very good friend Monsieur Phillip Villard. Daphne's cheeks were flushed and her eyes were sparkling, a direct result, no doubt, of spending the morning at the literary salon she attended with her husband, fellow author Herman Henderson.

The sparkling disappeared in a flash when Daphne's gaze settled on Arthur, and she came to an abrupt stop.

Large gentlemen had always made Daphne uncomfortable. And even though she'd married a gentleman who was larger than most men, and even though she'd been seeing some success with keeping her nerves under control when it came to large gentlemen in general, the sight of Arthur Livingston, who'd risen to his feet, left Daphne frozen on the spot, her green eyes enormous behind the thick lenses of her spectacles.

"I beg your pardon, Eunice," Daphne began. "I was unaware you were interviewing a client." She began backing her way toward the door. "If you'll excuse me . . ."

Realizing that Daphne was about to make a speedy exit because the sight of Arthur could very well lead her to a fit of the vapors, Eunice rose from her chair. A sliver of remorse slid over her at what she was about to do, but she really had no choice in the matter. Daphne was the interruption she desperately needed, and if she allowed her friend to flee, well, there was a good possibility that Arthur would uncover her secret—one that would see his missing person case solved without her doing so much as lifting a finger to get to the bottom of the matter.

She bustled to Daphne's side and took hold of her arm. "What a timely arrival on your part, Daphne," she began, pretending not to notice that Daphne was still trying to edge her way toward the door. "I was just telling Mr. Arthur Livingston that I always consult with one of my partners before the agency agrees to take on a case, and here you are . . . one of my partners."

Daphne stilled. "You rarely—"

"Mr. Livingston and I have already had a discussion about you," Eunice interrupted before Daphne could blurt out the fact that Eunice rarely consulted with Daphne or their other partner, Gabriella Goodhue Quinn, about what cases the agency took on. "I'm certain you'll be delighted to learn he's an admirer of your Montague Moreland books."

It was not a surprise when Daphne went from trepidatious to remarkably delighted in the blink of an eye as she cast a smile Arthur's way. "How lovely to learn you enjoy my work."

Arthur returned the smile. "Indeed I do, and I was just telling Mrs. Holbrooke that I believe your work compares favorably with notable male authors of the day."

Daphne's eyes flashed with temper as she turned to Eunice. "I'm getting an inkling as to why you wanted to consult about this case with me."

"I thought you would."

Daphne returned her attention to Arthur. "How kind of you to tell me that my work compares favorably with noted male authors. Goodness, but compliments like that do leave my little female heart all aflutter."

Arthur raked a hand through his hair, leaving it more disheveled than ever. "Please do not say that you're taking what I believe was a compliment as an insult because, believe me, that was not my intention."

"I'm sure it *wasn't* intentional, considering you want to hire the Bleecker Street Inquiry Agency," Daphne said coolly. "With that said, *as* a partner, I'm already convinced it wouldn't be a good idea for us to take up your case, as we here at the agency normally expect to enjoy working with our clients."

"That's exactly what I already told him," Eunice said.

"And it's reasoning I find rather faulty," Arthur argued. "I cannot believe that some of the clients you've taken on before me—or at least the ones connected with the New York Four Hundred—are enjoyable to work with."

Daphne tilted her head. "I suppose that is a valid point, but you see, dealing with a disagreeable society lady is completely different than dealing with a contrary gentleman. Contrary gentlemen tend to make women nervous. I don't imagine you'd enjoy spending time with nervous inquiry agents who often happen to be armed." She smiled a tight smile. "Nerves and firearms really shouldn't go hand in hand."

For the briefest of seconds, Eunice was certain Arthur was going to concede the point and take his leave, until he crossed his arms over his chest and began considering Daphne in a very calculating fashion. "I've clearly made a grave misstep today, one I'm sure I can't remedy with a simple apology, so allow me to present my case a bit differently." He took a step forward. "You, Mrs. Henderson, are known for penning mysteries with unusual twists and turns. I assure you, the mystery I need solving is incredibly complex and would certainly provide you with fodder for a future book."

To give Arthur credit, as a strategy it was brilliant because Daphne's eyes began brimming with curiosity.

"I suppose it wouldn't hurt to hear a few particulars about your case," Daphne said before Eunice could do more than settle the tip of her pointy black boot directly on top of Daphne's delicate afternoon slipper, earning a rather guilty look, along with a touch of a grunt, from Daphne in return. However, before Daphne could revoke her invitation, Arthur was settling an encouraging smile on her.

"As I've already told Mrs. Holbrooke, I'm interested in procuring the services of your agency to locate a missing person. It's a complicated case, one that stymied the Pinkertons, and it's rife with intrigue, danger, and a person who has been missing for over seven years—and there is an unsolved murder at the center of everything."

It was almost impossible to hold back a groan when Daphne raised a hand to her throat. "A missing person *and* an unsolved murder?"

"Indeed, and if that's not enough incentive to at least listen to the details of my case, know that I've also offered to pay your agency three times your usual fee."

Daphne turned to Eunice. "It really *wouldn't* hurt to hear the particulars of his case."

"You just said you were convinced we shouldn't take him on as a client," Eunice pointed out.

"But he's willing to give us three times our usual fee."

"Which is not enough of an incentive to convince me we should look into his case."

The wide smile now residing on Arthur's face suggested the man smelled victory in the air. "What if I not only pay three times your usual fee but also include a two-thousand-dollar bonus as an added inducement to take on my case?"

Daphne gave the sleeve of Eunice's black mourning gown a tug. "Two thousand dollars would be quite the inducement."

"We're not going to take on Mr. Livingston's case merely because he's offering us what amounts to a bribe."

"He called it a bonus, and, again, it wouldn't hurt to hear what he has to say. It does sound like an intriguing case, and you can't tell me you're not at least a little curious to hear more."

Truth be told, Eunice *was* more than a little curious to hear what Arthur had to say regarding the missing person and the murder that had occurred, especially given that she was involved with both of those incidents. She was also curious to learn why he was willing to part with a substantial amount of money to secure the services of the Bleecker Street Inquiry Agency.

Even though her instincts were screaming at her that lingering in Arthur's company was not a good idea, she gave a nod of her veil-covered head, which had Daphne directing her full attention to Arthur.

"If you'd be so kind as to resume your seat, Mr. Livingston, we'll then get down to business."

After everyone was settled, Arthur turned a charming smile on Daphne, one he'd never turned Eunice's way. "What would you care to know first?" he asked.

Daphne straightened from rummaging around in the large bag she was never without, brandishing a notepad and pencil. "Let us begin with the basics regarding this missing person and then we'll move on to the murder. Who is he, and he's been missing for, was it seven years?"

"It's a she, not a he, and yes, she's been missing for a little over seven years." Arthur reached into his pocket and pulled out a folded-up piece of parchment.

Trepidation began swimming through Eunice's veins when Arthur got to his feet and smoothed the parchment out on Eunice's desk, gesturing for Daphne to take a closer look. "This is Miss Eugenia Howland, the missing woman. I had an artist create this flyer from a painting that hangs in Eugenia's home in Montana. As you can see, she's an unusually beautiful woman, possessed of very light blond hair and eyes that are a unique shade of blue. I'm of the belief that those distinctive features will eventually lead to a resolution concerning her disappearance."

It really came as no surprise when Daphne's mouth gaped open as she peered at the image staring up at her from the desk, an image Daphne was all too familiar with considering it just happened to be an image of Eunice.

CHAPTER
Three

"And isn't this unexpected," Daphne finally muttered, a response that Arthur was certainly not going to construe as a normal response to the picture of Miss Eugenia Howland that Daphne was continuing to gawk at.

"Is something amiss?" Arthur asked, stepping closer to Daphne, which had Daphne's head snapping up before she snatched up the picture of Eugenia, moved across Eunice's office, and took a seat on a divan upholstered in a soft shade of pink, apparently needing to put distance between herself and Arthur in order to process the unexpected situation at hand.

Daphne didn't speak a word for an entire minute as a myriad of expressions crossed her face. But then she pushed her spectacles back into place and squared her shoulders. "Forgive me, Mr. Livingston. I assure you nothing is amiss. I fear my imagination as a writer has come into play because Miss Eugenia Howland's face is exactly the inspiration I've been searching for of late. I've begun writing a new heroine who possesses an unusual appearance, and"—she gave the flyer a wave—"this woman fits my heroine to a *T*. There's something mesmerizing about the lady's eyes." She slid a look Eunice's way. "Why, I don't believe I've ever seen that shade of blue before *in my entire life*."

As far as acting abilities went, Daphne's attempt to convince Arthur she'd never seen the lady in the flyer before was somewhat amusing, although, thankfully, Arthur didn't seem to realize Daphne's dramatic denial was a tad overdone for the occasion.

"I specifically chose a flyer done in color to draw attention to Eugenia's hair and unusual eyes, although I do have a photograph I can share with you." Arthur fished a small metal frame out of his pocket and moved to hand it to Daphne. "I took this from a mantel in Eugenia's home, and it could very well lend you some inspiration for a future character as well, given that it's a picture of Eugenia sitting on her beast of a stallion, Wyatt. He's a horse that's not what one expects a young lady to ride, which lends insight into Eugenia's unconventional attitude, Mrs. Henderson, and—"

"Please, call me Daphne."

Curiosity swirled in Arthur's eyes. "Do you normally encourage your clients to address you by your given name?"

When Daphne began looking like a deer in the lantern lights, Eunice sat forward. "We often encourage an informal atmosphere here, Mr. Livingston. It makes our clients feel more comfortable as they disclose unseemly matters."

"Does that mean I should begin addressing you as Eunice?"

"No. But to return to your case, which is why you're still here, what else can you tell us about Eugenia? Where was she last seen, why do you believe she went missing, and why, pray tell, do you need to find her?"

"Excellent questions, Eunice," Daphne said, seemingly having gotten herself composed enough to where she was ready to reengage in the conversation. She returned the flyer and photograph to Arthur, then sat down in the chair she'd recently abandoned, flipping her notepad to a blank page. She began writing in it, pausing a moment later. "Tell me everything you know about Eugenia, beginning with who she is and when she was last seen."

"Would you like the official version of Eugenia, or would you rather hear the truth?"

"There's more than one version?"

"I'm afraid so. There are also more twists to this case than one would think possible. I'm hopeful the complexity of Eugenia's story will intrigue you enough to agree to look into what actually happened to her, not the official version that's been bandied about for years."

"I'm certain I speak for both of us when I say we're already intrigued," Daphne returned. "I'd like to hear both versions, the official and the truth, but only after you give me the basics of who Eugenia Howland is."

"Fair enough," Arthur said, settling into his chair, which sent that chair wobbling again. "The first important thing you need to know is that Eugenia is the only grandchild of the late James W. Mason of Butte, Montana."

"James W. Mason, as in the copper mogul?"

"One and the same."

"Not something I was expecting to hear," Daphne muttered before she frowned. "But how did it come about that you're involved with searching for the granddaughter of a man who was rumored to be one of the wealthiest men in America at the time of his death?"

Arthur rubbed a hand over his face. "It's complicated, but I'll start with this—I struck up a business relationship with James W. Mason after meeting him at a gathering of the country's most prominent mining investors about eight years ago. After we enjoyed a dinner together, James invited me to his home in Montana."

"Why?" Daphne asked, flipping to another blank page.

"He said he was interested in having me merge my copper mines with his. I was only twenty-five at the time and had only been investing in mines for a few years, but James thought I was on my way to becoming a formidable force within the industry. He believed a business merger would be beneficial to both of us."

Eunice stilled. "Merging as in forming a business partnership?"

"That's what I thought at first," Arthur returned. "It quickly became evident, though, that James was more interested in a merger through marriage with his granddaughter, Eugenia."

Eunice's breath caught in her throat, but she was spared a response to what was definitely an unexpected development when Daphne sat forward.

"Shall I assume the reason behind Eugenia's disappearance had something to do with this marriage merger between the two of you, Mr. Livingston?"

"Please, call me Arthur, but no, that's not why Eugenia disappeared. Truth be told, I'm not certain she was aware her grandfather had marriage in mind pertaining to the two of us."

"Perhaps she discovered her grandfather's plan, didn't care for it, and felt compelled to disappear to avoid marriage."

"While there's no question Eugenia and I frequently locked horns, and I had doubts she'd agree to marry me even if James had been able to convince me to court his granddaughter, I believe her disappearance was a direct result of James W. Mason being murdered."

Daphne's pencil dropped to the ground, which she ignored. "If I'm remembering correctly, the newspapers wrote that James W. Mason died of an unfortunate accident with a pistol, an accident that was self-inflicted."

"That would be part of that official story I mentioned."

"I see," Daphne said, retrieving her pencil and putting it to immediate use before she lifted her head. "I also see that you weren't exaggerating when you claimed this is a complicated case. With that said, I'm now going to ask you to repair to the receiving room. Obviously, your case *is* exceptionally complex and will certainly demand many working hours to solve. I need to confer with Eunice before we waste your time with additional details because we may not be able to devote the time needed to do justice to your case."

"Have you forgotten that I'm willing to pay exceedingly well for all those hours needed?"

Daphne gave an airy wave of her hand. "Not at all, but it would hardly benefit our reputation if we were to neglect cases we've already taken on. As a businessman, I'm sure you can understand the importance of caring for a reputation."

"Indeed, but as a businessman, I also respect the value of profitability. It would be unwise for your agency to reject my case simply to take up cases that won't help your bottom line nearly as much as my case will."

Irritation flashed through Daphne's eyes. "True, but Eunice and I will also need to discuss the advisability of taking on a case where we'll frequently be subjected to a condescending attitude toward the feminine set. It's rather disconcerting to find myself being lectured by you on profitability, as if my feminine mind is incapable of grasping the nuances of profitability in the first place."

"I wasn't being condescending."

"That's debatable, and we can debate that right now if you'd like, but I assure you that will not benefit you in the least, especially when it's all but certain it will have mine and Eunice's feminine emotions rising to the occasion."

A blink of an eye later, Arthur was rising to his feet. "Since the bluntness I'm known for in the business world is not helping my argument of why you should take on my case, I believe it may be best if I just hie myself off to the receiving room to await your verdict."

"A sensible decision on your part," Daphne said, rising to her feet as well. "I'll accompany you and see you settled with a nice cup of tea and plate of scones. A tasty snack should keep you occupied while Eunice and I debate the merits of your case. Fair warning, though, it may take us a while to come to an informed decision." With that, Daphne headed for the door, Arthur trailing after her.

"And while you get him settled, I'll pull out our calendar to see what cases we currently have on the books," Eunice said, even though the second Daphne and Arthur disappeared, she rushed for the agency's nearest door and barreled toward the Holbrooke boardinghouse, which was only five houses away.

Bursting through the back door moments later, she drew in a much-needed breath of air as Alma Kozlov, cook for the boardinghouse, but more importantly, a woman who knew all about Eunice's past, looked up from where she'd been assembling a pie.

"Goodness, Eunice, whatever is the matter?" Alma asked, dusting flour off her hands as she stepped away from her worktable. "You never use the back door."

"I didn't have time to run around to the front, but I have something of the utmost importance to tell you—Arthur Livingston is at the agency, looking to hire us on to locate, I jest you not, Eugenia Howland."

Alma sat down on the closest stool available to her. "Arthur Livingston wants you to find, well, you?"

"Yes, he does, which is an odd circumstance to be sure. But because he's still at the agency, I need you to make certain that when Ivan returns, he remains out of sight until Arthur takes his leave."

"Wouldn't it be better if I sent Ivan straight over to the agency? Arthur could pose a danger to you if he discovers who you are."

"Ivan can't show his face because Arthur will certainly recognize him as well as remember that Ivan was my bodyguard. Being an annoyingly astute gentleman, I don't believe it'll take Arthur long to figure out that the widow Eunice Holbrooke is actually the woman he's searching for."

Alma snatched up the morning newspaper and began fanning her face with it. "I'll watch for Ivan, but should I begin making preparations for us to disappear again?"

"That might be premature. Besides, I have no desire to pick up and leave New York City to reinvent myself again. But there's no time for me to say more. Daphne is undoubtedly bursting with questions for me, and I won't have much time to explain my story to her, not with Arthur currently cooling his heels in the receiving room."

She gave Alma's arm a reassuring squeeze before bolting out of the kitchen, the odd thought coming to her that given the amount of physical exertion she was currently doing and what with how her breathing was more labored than usual, she might need to increase her daily activities, especially if Arthur couldn't be convinced to give up his desire to hire the agency, which would mean she'd need to go on the run again.

CHAPTER

Four

Slipping through the back door, Eunice made her way as quietly as possible into her office, finding Daphne pacing around the room.

"I suppose it's too much to hope that you have a doppelgänger who goes by the name of Eugenia," Daphne said after Eunice plopped down in the nearest chair, flipped her veils up, and dashed a handkerchief over a face that was now perspiring.

"I'm afraid it is."

"Then you *are* Eugenia Howland?"

"I am, but I didn't murder my grandfather, if that's what you've been thinking."

Daphne rolled her eyes. "Well, of course you didn't. But tell me everything as quickly as possible because I didn't get the impression Arthur Livingston is a patient man."

"He's not, so . . . my story, the condensed version." Eunice dabbed her forehead again. "I *was* Miss Eugenia Howland for the first twenty years of my life, which I spent in Butte, Montana. There is no Mr. Holbrooke, and I *am* the only grandchild of James. W. Mason. The *W*, if you're curious, stands for Wyatt, a name he abhorred. Also, I didn't run away because my grandfather wanted me to marry Arthur. I was oblivious to that plan, although Arthur does play a role in why I disappeared."

"Didn't Arthur say you were sitting on a horse named Wyatt, a name your grandfather apparently abhorred?"

"Of everything I just disclosed, I wasn't expecting you to zero in on that, but yes, I named my horse Wyatt because I was annoyed with my grandfather at the time we acquired the horse." Eunice shook her head. "I'd picked out a delightful mare by the name of Clover at a horse auction, but instead of purchasing Clover, my grandfather had Wyatt delivered instead." She shuddered. "From the moment I met that brute of a horse, we were at odds. Grandfather refused to return the horse, hence the reason behind the name." She smiled. "I thought naming him after my grandfather was the least I could do to show Grandfather how put out with him I was, not that it swayed his decision. He insisted I keep the beast because he wanted me to overcome what he said was an irrational fear of the horse."

"Your grandfather sounds charming."

"Charming is not a term anyone ever used to describe Grandfather. He was a self-made man, a tyrant at heart, and he didn't believe in coddling me, expecting me to comport myself like the grandson he didn't have instead of the granddaughter he did." Eunice tucked her handkerchief into her sleeve. "But because time is short, I'm going to jump to the day my grandfather died. I wasn't supposed to be on the estate that day. Instead, I was to be at the train station, where I was scheduled to take the ten o'clock train bound for New York City. After arriving in New York, I was then supposed to board a ship bound for England, where I would begin an extensive tour of Europe."

"That sounds lovely."

"And I'm sure I would have thought the same if I'd been given the opportunity of time to plan and then anticipate a grand tour. Grandfather arranged the trip on the spur of the moment, which was odd, especially when he'd refused to allow me to take a grand tour with my mother before I reached my majority."

"Why didn't your grandfather want you to take a tour with your mother?"

"He thought my time would be better spent learning the mining business, something he'd begun to focus on when I turned fourteen and he fired my governess and hired a tutor for me instead. The tutor was a dreadful and exacting man by the name of Vincent Wagner. Vincent was relentless in teaching me everything there was to know about copper mining. He idolized my grandfather, catered to his every whim pertaining to my curriculum, and even took to having me travel into the mines with him and Grandfather so that I could see different mining techniques." She scratched her nose. "I loathed those trips into the mines because when Grandfather wasn't with me, his miners weren't what anyone could call respectful. Grandfather, however, wouldn't hear of my abandoning my mining studies, not when he'd made it clear he was going to have me take over his company."

"It seems to me from what Arthur disclosed," Daphne began, "that your grandfather had a change of heart about that. Perhaps your grandfather sending you off on a tour had something to do with that decision or . . ." Her eyes went distant for a moment before she nodded. "Perhaps it had something to do with Arthur not being keen to court you. Maybe your grandfather thought he'd have more success talking Arthur into that courtship if you weren't underfoot."

"That would be one odd way of convincing a gentleman he was well suited with a lady, but . . ." Eunice frowned. "Why would you think Arthur wasn't keen to court me?"

"He said, and I quote . . ." Daphne flipped through her notepad. "'I had doubts she'd agree to marry me even if James had been able to convince me to court his granddaughter.'"

A trace of disgruntlement slithered up Eunice's spine, one she tried to ignore.

"I find it curious," Daphne continued, "that Arthur would have needed convincing to court you. I would think, given that you weren't hiding yourself underneath layers of veils back then, that you were in high demand. You're a very beautiful woman."

Eunice smiled. "That's very kind of you to say, but in all honesty, most of the gentlemen in Butte did not try to procure my affections. Frankly, men have always found me peculiar."

"Because . . . ?"

Eunice's lips twitched. "You lived in the boardinghouse with me for years. I wouldn't think my peculiarity needs explaining. However, if you haven't noticed, I'm far too direct, I've been dressing in spooky widow's weeds for seven years, and before that I preferred trousers over skirts, and I'm more proficient with weapons than most gentlemen are. I'm also almost always in the company of Ivan, whom my grandfather hired as my bodyguard years ago. He taught me how to box, a sport that's not considered acceptable for women, but one I excel in, something Ivan made sure everyone in Butte knew."

"Ivan's your bodyguard?" Daphne shook her head. "And here I've been thinking the two of you were siblings."

"Ivan looks nothing like me."

"He has blond hair."

"And Gabriella and Nicholas both have dark hair, but that doesn't make them siblings, and thank goodness for that since they're married."

"A fair point."

"Indeed, but we seem to be getting distracted from what matters most—that being my grandfather's murder."

"We're not distracted at all," Daphne countered. "This is what's called backstory, and I need it to fully comprehend your story."

"And I'll fill in more of it later, but Arthur is waiting to hear our decision, which is obviously going to be a resounding no to taking on his case."

"It would be an incredibly easy case for us to solve."

"True, but considering there's a possibility Arthur believes I killed my grandfather, I can't reveal my identity to him, not when that could very well see me behind bars."

Daphne's mouth dropped open. "Good heavens, and here I've been concerning myself with your backstory when clearly this is something we should have discussed right from the start. Why would Arthur believe you killed your grandfather?"

"Because he found me at the scene of my grandfather's murder, or more specifically, leaning over my grandfather's body." Eunice scratched her nose. "I should also mention that there is a possibility, although I don't believe it's a strong possibility, that Arthur killed my grandfather and tried to set me up to take the fall."

"If either of those two things are true, we're going to have to get Arthur out of the agency as soon as possible because he's a distinct threat to your well-being . . . but not until we get some answers from him."

"I don't think we should question him further. I say we simply tell him we consulted our caseload and we currently have too many cases on the books."

Daphne rolled her eyes. "But then we won't know if he thinks you're a murderess, or if he's a murderer. However, because you're obviously far too close to this case, I'll take over the responsibility of asking him the majority of questions. You may simply sit at your desk, looking intimidating." She consulted her notepad and frowned. "Before we fetch Arthur, though, why might he think you murdered your grandfather, or better yet, if he did the deed, how would he be able to frame you for it?"

"He overheard a fiery argument my grandfather and I had the night before Grandfather died."

Daphne's hand flew across the page of her notepad as she scribbled away. "An argument I'm going to assume you had because you were trying to get your grandfather to change his mind about your grand tour?"

"It wasn't that I was trying to get him to change his mind— because Grandfather never changed his mind. I was merely trying to get him to tell me *why* he was sending me away. He refused to do so, which left me furious with him and not stingy with telling him exactly how furious I was. Arthur overheard part of our argument. I felt guilty the next morning over our contentious exchange, which is why I, of course, decided to seek Grandfather out and bid him a proper good-bye before I set off on my grand tour.

"Grandfather always began his day on the target field, where we often repaired together to practice our shooting skills. The field was located about a mile from the main house, and knowing I'd be stuck on a train for days, I decided to walk to the field, telling Ivan to meet me with the carriage in thirty minutes so I'd have plenty of time to make my scheduled train departure."

Eunice settled into the chair. "I knew something was wrong when I reached the field. I didn't see Grandfather at first, but then I caught sight of him on the ground. When I reached him, I found him lying in a pool of blood, a pistol lying two feet away from him. At first, I thought he was dead, but then he stirred and opened his eyes when I leaned over him." She took a second to get her thoughts in order. "He then, if I'm remembering correctly, reached out and took hold of my hand when I told him I was going for help, telling me there was no time for that nonsense because he knew he was not long for this world. He then said that someone shot him, but he didn't see who.

"Grandfather, even suffering from a bullet, was an astute man, and after he caught sight of a pistol that hadn't been on the ground when he'd gone to reset his targets, realized someone was trying to involve me in the shooting."

Daphne frowned. "He realized that because of a pistol?"

"The pistol was mine. It's a very distinctive pistol, silver with an inlaid handle of mother-of-pearl and my initials carved into it, but a pistol I hadn't packed for the trip, preferring to take a smaller derringer pistol that fit nicely in my reticule. Grandfather knew as soon as he saw it that someone was trying to, at the very least, frame me for his murder. That's why he did the one thing I never imagined him doing—he urged me to flee from Mason Manor and continue on with my grand tour, believing that tour would keep me safe as well as foil the attempt to frame me for his murder since I wasn't supposed to be on the estate that day."

Daphne tilted her head. "But since you *were* supposed to be on your way to the train station at the time of your grandfather's death, it seems odd that someone would try and frame you."

"No one except Grandfather, Ivan, and Alma—who is more to

me than simply the Holbrooke boardinghouse cook—knew I was going off on that tour. We'd not had any visitors that week, not even family members, although I believe Grandfather had something to do with that. He was notorious for letting our relatives know he wasn't receptive to guests in any given week, and when not a single relative came to visit after Grandfather disclosed my grand tour plans to me, I thought he might have wanted to keep them away from the house in case I prevailed upon them to intervene on my behalf, not that I would have expected my relatives to do that. We were not what anyone would call close."

Daphne bent over her notes again. "Perhaps your grandfather knew danger was stalking him, hence the reason for your spur-of-the-moment trip. And perhaps he also had concerns that the danger might be coming at the hands of one of your relatives, hence the reason for not being receptive to their visits over the days before he died."

"I've thought the same thing during the past seven years. And when you take into account the rather cryptic last words Grandfather said to me, there's little doubt that he was aware he was in danger."

"What did he say to you?"

"After he told me to flee from Mason Manor, he asked me to not think poorly of him if some truths of the past were ever revealed to me. He said something about chickens coming home to roost and then added a bit about trying to atone for the sins of his past by finally doing right by me. Before he could expand on that, though, he took his last breath."

"It must have been difficult to watch your grandfather die," Daphne said quietly. "I'm sure it was also difficult for you to not get concrete answers from him, although it sounds to me as if there could be a strong possibility that if Arthur didn't kill him, one of your relatives is to blame. Is there any particular relative who stands out as a more likely suspect than another?"

"I'm afraid not."

"Which means a suspect list is going to be lengthy. But since we can't question your relatives yet, tell me how Arthur fits into all of this."

"He appeared on the target field not long after Grandfather died. My first thought, of course, was that he'd shot Grandfather. My second thought was that he was coming for me next. That's why I grabbed the pistol someone had left by my grandfather, leveled it on Arthur, and when he didn't so much as slow his advance toward me—I shot him."

"You shot Arthur Livingston?"

"I'm sure you would have done the same."

"No, I would have fainted on the spot. What happened next?"

"Arthur fell to the ground, but I didn't shoot to kill, merely to slow him down, and my shooting him definitely did that. I then raced back toward the house, Ivan intercepting me when I was about halfway there. I jumped into the carriage that was to take me to the train station, telling Ivan and Alma, who was going with me on the tour to lend me companionship, everything that had happened. We decided I should heed Grandfather's last words and continue on with my tour, and that's what we did—although I didn't actually end up on that tour, deciding to stay in New York instead."

Daphne looked up from her notepad. "You didn't mention your mother being in the carriage to go on tour with you."

"Because she wasn't, but now is not the time to get into that sorry story. I mentioned to you a few months back that my mother left me without a word, and she did that when I was only seventeen, so clearly she wasn't around at the time of my grandfather's death."

"Unless she was on bad terms with your grandfather and came back to settle with him on that target field."

"My mother is a challenging woman to be sure, but I doubt she would have tried to frame her only daughter for her father's murder."

"An excellent point." Daphne wrote something down and frowned. "So, you, Ivan, and Alma got on the train, went to New York, and . . . ?"

"We decided to stay, thinking it would be easy to lose ourselves in the vast number of people who live in the city. I bought the boardinghouse because it was an unassuming building, and we needed a place to live. We also decided to take in boarders to hide behind a cloak of authenticity. Alma took on the role of boardinghouse cook, and Ivan continued as my bodyguard, although everyone living in the boardinghouse simply thought he was there to look after all the ladies, which he was to a certain extent. It's been his mission the past seven years to keep me safe and out of sight, hence the reason behind his disapproval at times with my running an inquiry agency."

"Can't say I blame him for that," Daphne said. "But returning to your story, how convinced are you that Arthur murdered your grandfather?"

"Not very, to tell you the truth. Arthur never struck me as the type of gentleman capable of shooting a man in cold blood."

"I'll still question him about the matter and see if I can ferret out the truth," Daphne said. "But even if he didn't murder your grandfather, he's a danger to you. You were, after all, at the scene of the murder, and you shot Arthur, a guilty reaction if there ever was one. He might be holding a grudge about that and might have decided it's past time you were held accountable." Daphne rose to her feet. "But there's only one way to find out why Arthur's determined to find you and that's to hear him out. Here's hoping his story sheds some light on your case, light we can then begin using to solve the mystery of your grandfather's death."

"I didn't say anything about solving my grandfather's death."

"I know, but with my knowing about your past now, there's little chance that I'll be content to leave well enough alone. You've been hiding under your dreadful widow's weeds for far too long, and in my humble opinion, it's time to uncover the truth—which will then hopefully allow you to abandon your disguise and get on with the business of living a life out of the shadows."

CHAPTER

Five

Being a man of business, Arthur was used to being the object of unflinching stares directed his way during meetings with fellow men of business, many of whom were known as ruthless robber barons. Interestingly enough, he'd never once felt uneasy under the gazes of those men.

Being on the receiving end of an unwavering stare coming from Miss Judith Donovan, however, left him feeling decidedly disconcerted. It also left him wondering if he should abandon his desire to hire this particular agency to locate the exceedingly difficult-to-track-down Eugenia Howland because, frankly, nothing about his time at the Bleecker Street Inquiry Agency was going according to plan.

Unfortunately, because he'd given his word to Mr. James W. Mason that he would make certain Eugenia's best interests were looked after if James ever found himself incapable of personally seeing after those interests, he was going to have to see his decision through and hope the ladies of the agency would decide to take on his case.

Truth be told, having Eugenia send a bullet through his arm had not exactly left him keen to honor his word, but given the dire circumstances that were now unfolding in Montana, he felt compelled to locate her once and for all and was willing to embrace any means to discover her whereabouts, even if that meant hiring an inquiry agency that didn't seem all that interested in securing his business.

"Would you mind if I took the liberty of sketching your face while you wait for Daphne and Eunice to reappear?" Judith asked, causing Arthur to blink back to the unsettling situation at hand, that of being watched far too intently by a lady who was apparently still determined to document his bone structure.

He summoned up a smile. "While I'm not opposed to your sketching me, Miss Donovan, I'm not sure you'll have time to make much progress. Surely Daphne and Eunice, or rather Mrs. Holbrooke, as she told me she prefers to be addressed, will be out soon to tell me what they've decided."

Judith gave a wave of a paint-stained hand. "It won't take me any time at all to sketch you, but did Eunice really tell you she prefers to be addressed as Mrs. Holbrooke?"

"Why do I get the distinct impression you find that surprising?"

"Because it is," Judith said before she rushed over to a table, snatched up a sketchpad and pencil, sat down in a chair, and, without another word, began sketching away.

Shifting on the hard-backed chair to get comfortable, which earned him a narrowing of the eyes from Judith, Arthur stilled and struggled to think of something to say that might have the awkward atmosphere that had settled around them dissipating.

"Have you been painting long?" he finally asked.

"Only about three years. My darling aunt left me a bequest in her will that allowed me to escape the dull life on my family farm and pursue my passion for the arts."

"How delightful."

"Quite." With that, Judith returned her attention to his face again, scratching her nose with the end of her pencil. "Could you possibly try to soften your expression, Mr. Livingston? I have a certain look in mind that I'd like to capture on paper, but I need you to look more approachable."

"I'm not certain how I'd do that."

"Perhaps you could think of something dreamy."

"I'm not really a dreamy sort of gentleman."

"I'm sure you could summon up a dreamy look if you put a bit of effort into it. Simply settle your thoughts on whichever young lady has garnered your attention, or perhaps you could think of your wife if you're married."

"I'm not married."

"Then think of whichever lady captures your interest the most, and do not tell me you don't know any ladies of interest. A handsome gentleman like yourself is probably in high demand. Choose one of those ladies, concentrate on her, and for heaven's sake, wipe that grimace you're now sporting off your face."

"I imagining I'm grimacing because I'm quite unused to being asked to summon up a dreamy look."

"Be that as it may, it lends you a most unpleasant air, and unpleasant is not the look I'm striving to capture." She lowered her pencil toward her sketchpad. "Why don't you close your eyes? That may help you drum up an image of an appealing lady."

The last thing Arthur wanted to do was to close his eyes to conjure up an image of a lady because the lady who would most assuredly appear was not a lady he enjoyed dwelling on, not after she'd toyed with his affections and then callously tossed him aside and married another man.

"You're not very good at taking direction, are you?" Judith asked, releasing a dramatic sigh. "You're still grimacing, and you've yet to close your eyes."

"Has anyone ever told the ladies at the Bleecker Street Inquiry Agency that you're a rather assertive lot?"

"Daily, but if you'd like me to discontinue my assertive attitude, close your eyes and conjure up an image of an alluring lady."

Realizing it would be far easier to close his eyes and deal with an image of Melinda Jarvis—known to her intimates as Mitzi, and known to everyone else as Mrs. Thomas Gibson—Arthur closed his eyes, opening them a split second later when an image not of Mitzi but of Eugenia Howland pounced into his thoughts.

He shook his head ever so slightly, but the image of Eugenia stayed with him, something that left him feeling more disconcerted than Judith's stare had done.

Granted, it wasn't completely unreasonable Eugenia would pop to mind, given that he was on a mission to find her, but having her pop to mind after Judith suggested he conjure up an image of a lady who captured his attention was somewhat disturbing.

Yes, Eugenia Howland was the most beautiful young lady he'd ever seen, which was saying something because Mitzi had been declared an incomparable when she'd made her debut. And yes, there might have been something about Eugenia that had fascinated him, given that she never shied away from speaking her mind and engaging in unlikely conversations with him.

However, because he'd had a specific plan for his life, and courting a lady who wasn't a member of the esteemed New York Four Hundred hadn't been part of that plan, he'd striven to avoid thinking of Eugenia as a fascinating and alluring young lady, even though he'd occasionally been unsuccessful with that. When she had invaded his thoughts, though, he'd taken to being more argumentative with her than ever, even though her responses to his argumentative state always resulted in rousing debates that, quite frankly, impressed him.

Judith narrowed her eyes at him. "You've now taken to scowling, which is worse than a grimace and has left me with nothing to conclude except that you're suffering from lady problems."

"I'm not suffering from lady problems."

"Your expression says otherwise."

Arthur ran a hand over his face. "Perhaps it might be best if we chose a different topic to distract me from my supposed grimacing."

"It's not supposed grimacing. You *are* grimacing."

"Be that as it may," Arthur said through teeth that had taken to clenching, "what say we try another tactic to stop me from grimacing? Maybe you could answer a few questions about the agency, especially since I don't believe I'll be getting any answers to the many questions I have from Daphne or Mrs. Holbrooke anytime soon."

"Your case must be complicated, because I've never known Eunice to take so long deliberating whether she wants to accept an assignment."

"I was led to believe the partners always confer about cases, but now I find myself questioning whether that's actually true."

Judith abandoned her sketching. "And now you're looking suspicious, which is not a look I wanted to capture either."

The thought flashed to mind that his day was not unfolding in any way, shape, or form the way he'd envisioned it.

Judith cleared her throat. "How about if I tell you something else about the agency, something that's not suspicious in the least—my role here. I design all the signage our agency uses as well as manning the reception room when there's a need."

"You don't work on cases?"

"I have not as of yet because I'm very consumed by my art. But I have been trying to convince Eunice to allow me to put my artistic talents to greater use for the agency, using those talents to paint flyers of suspects or missing people we've been hired to locate." Judith frowned. "She doesn't seem keen to act on my offer, believing my fondness for abstract portraits may not be a good match for flyers."

Judith nodded to a painting that was hanging on the opposite wall, one that sported brightly colored yet clearly undefinable shapes. "I've been inspired to paint abstract portraits because of the lady who painted that masterpiece. That particular painting is a self-portrait."

Arthur eyed the painting for a long moment. "How would you know that's a self-portrait? It looks like a collection of rectangles and squares to me, although I can discern an eye in the very middle of the piece."

"Self-portrait is written on the back of the canvas."

"Ah, well, that was helpful of the artist to include that. And while the painting does have a certain intrigue, I believe Mrs. Holbrooke is quite right in that an abstract depiction of a missing person might not be of much help with locating that person." He reached into his pocket and withdrew his flyer. He unfolded it and handed it to Judith. "I had this drawn up by a local artist out west. It's an illustration of the lady I need to find. Perhaps it'll give you a better idea of what flyers are expected to look like."

Judith smoothed the flyer out on top of her sketchpad, her eyes widening. "Good heavens," she whispered.

"Is something the matter?"

Judith blinked, pulled her attention from the flyer, then darted another quick look at it before she shuddered. "There's, ah, nothing the matter except that, well, having seen this flyer, I have to question whether I, ah, have the skills needed to produce flyers the agency will find helpful."

Given that Judith was now looking everywhere except at him, Arthur was getting the distinct impression she wasn't exactly being truthful. He sat forward. "You haven't seen the lady in that flyer, have you?"

"And who *is* this lady you're searching for?" Judith countered, her gaze settled on something past his shoulder.

"Eugenia Howland."

Her attention snapped back to him. "I've never met a Eugenia Howland before in my life," she said, using the flyer to fan a face that had turned rather red. "Have you noticed how warm it's becoming in here?"

Before he could point out that the room was somewhat chilly since it was early fall and a storm was rolling in, the front door to the agency burst open and a lady stumbled into the receiving hallway.

"I need to speak with an agent immediately," the lady said as she rushed into the room, sights set on him. The next thing he knew, she was holding on to his hand for dear life. "I'm afraid the most dreadful thing has happened. My sister Helen, or rather Mrs. Clement Mills, is missing—well, not really missing. It's far worse than that." The lady drew in a ragged breath. "I have cause to believe her wastrel of a husband has seen her committed to the Blackwell's Island Insane Asylum, an asylum that serves indigent women and supposedly only takes charity cases." She gripped his hand harder than ever. "My sister is far from indigent, which begs the question how she was able to get committed there in the first place, but know that I'll pay anything to see her released."

Arthur frowned. "Is there a possibility your brother-in-law had your sister committed because she's been showing symptoms of mental instability?"

"Helen isn't insane," the lady snapped. "She merely made the colossal mistake of being too vocal about how Clement spends her fortune. He's her second husband, you see, twenty years younger than she is. And even though I told her it was madness to marry the man last year because he only wanted her fortune, she was smitten and refused to listen to reason."

"If I may offer a word of advice, ma'am," Judith said, setting aside her sketchpad. "In order to secure your sister's freedom, the doctors at the asylum may want to speak to you about her mental state. It will hardly bode well for securing your sister's release if you mention things like madness or a refusal to listen to reason."

The lady blinked. "Good heavens, you're right, which means I was also right about securing the services of this agency, since I never considered that anything I say might hinder my sister's release." She released Arthur's hand. "I'm Mrs. Harold Eastman, and I'm imploring you, sir, to agree to get my sister out of that asylum. I can't bear to think about Helen languishing in the bowels of that dreadful place."

Arthur shot a look to Judith, who was no longer paying them any attention because she'd picked up her sketchbook and was adding something to it. Realizing he was evidently on his own, he returned his attention to Mrs. Eastman. "I'm sorry to learn of your distressful situation, Mrs. Eastman. I'm Mr. Arthur Livingston, but I believe you're under the false impression I'm an agent at this agency, which I must hasten to inform you I'm not. I'm here as a potential client."

Mrs. Eastman frowned. "But you look exactly as I would expect an inquiry agent should look, right down to the air of danger about you."

"Mr. Livingston does, indeed, possess a dangerous air, but he's not an agent here."

Glancing to the door, Arthur breathed a sigh of relief as Daphne swept into the room, not stopping until she reached Mrs. Eastman's side. "I'm Mrs. Henderson, one of the partners at the Bleecker Street Inquiry Agency, but you must call me Daphne, Mrs. . . . ?"

"I'm Mrs. Eastman, dear. But aren't you a little young to be an inquiry agent?"

"Not at all," Daphne said. "In fact, my age was responsible for my being a confirmed spinster until I married my husband a few months back. However, that has nothing to do with your case. Allow me to see you settled in one of our offices. I'll then get an agent to take down the particulars of what sounds like a very troubling situation."

"I'll see her settled," Judith said, tucking her sketchpad under her arm before she bustled to Mrs. Eastman's side and took the lady's arm. She sent Arthur a rather weak smile. "I'm afraid duty calls, Mr. Livingston, so I won't be able to finish sketching your remarkable cheekbones." With that, she tugged Mrs. Eastman into motion and all but barreled out of the room, leaving Arthur with the distinct impression she'd offered to see after the lady because she wanted an excuse to remove herself from his company.

The burning question left in her wake was why.

CHAPTER
Six

Before he could remark on Judith's speedy exit, Daphne gestured for him to follow her before she strode out of the room. Unwilling to annoy her by lingering about the reception room, dwelling on Judith's odd behavior, he hurried to catch up with her, following her into Eunice's office a second later.

He smiled when he took note of a large chair that hadn't been in the office before.

"I thought you'd be more comfortable in a chair better suited to your size," Eunice said from where she was once again seated behind her desk, her many veils still covering her face. "I trust your time in the receiving room wasn't too bothersome?"

"Judith Donovan stared at me for the first thirty minutes, then proceeded to sketch me, apparently unable to resist the lure of my face," Arthur said as he settled himself into a chair that was decidedly more comfortable.

"I did warn you she's rather determined when it comes to her art."

"And yet you left me in her company for over forty minutes."

"That was unavoidable, but it doesn't appear as if you've suffered any lasting effects. I will apologize, though, for leaving you languishing for so long. Daphne and I had much to discuss."

"And that discussion led you to realize you have additional questions for me?"

"Indeed."

"I can't claim to be surprised. It's not as if I gave you many details about my situation before I was shown to the receiving room."

"A missing person, along with an unsolved murder, was enough to go with at first," Eunice said. "But in order to truly decide if we'll have time for your case, some pressing questions sprang up between us." She inclined her head in Daphne's direction. "Daphne's jotted down some notes."

"Too right I have," Daphne said, flipping through her notepad. "The first question I need to ask is this—you said that Mr. James W. Mason was murdered. How do you know this?"

"Because he'd been shot, but James wasn't the type of man who'd accidentally shoot himself, because he knew his way around a weapon."

"And yet I distinctly recall that all the articles in the newspapers stated that's exactly what he did."

"I might have convinced the coroner who examined the scene, as well as James's body, that he'd been cleaning his pistol and had, unfortunately, discharged it by accident."

"And this coroner didn't question your story?"

"Not when I'd made a point of dropping James's pistol beside him in a way that looked as if he'd dropped it as he fell to the ground."

"Why would you have set up a scene that disguised the truth?"

"That almost sounds as if you're asking me if I murdered James."

Daphne abandoned her notes and caught his eye. "Did you?"

He held her gaze for a moment. "I'm curious what your reaction will be if I say I *did* murder James because, if you've neglected to realize, you are two women alone, in the company of a man you believe possibly capable of murder. You could have just put your lives at stake."

A blink of an eye later, Arthur found himself staring into the barrel of a pistol Eunice was leveling on him, held in a steady hand.

"I assure you, Mr. Livingston," Eunice began in a voice no louder than a whisper, "our lives are not at stake, but yours could possibly be, unless you answer the question. If *you've* neglected to realize, Daphne has also brought out her pistol, and while she has developed some skills, she's still somewhat unreliable with a weapon. Why, she's been known to pull the trigger by accident, and because she's sitting remarkably close to you, I doubt you'd want that to happen."

Arthur glanced to Daphne, who was holding a tiny derringer pistol in a hand that was trembling just the slightest bit. He refused a shudder and returned his attention to Eunice.

"My apologies. I should have known that inquiry agents would be prepared to deal with a would-be murderer, which I'm now going to emphatically state I'm not. That means you can lower your weapons, or better yet, put them away before someone *does* get shot."

"The only one who'll get shot is you, and to be clear, I won't be stowing away my pistol. I'm a practical woman at heart, Mr. Livingston, and that practicality tells me you could be a threat. If I decide that's no longer the case, then, and only then, will I lower my weapon, although I'll keep it easily accessible. Women alone cannot be too careful these days."

Unable to help but wonder how his time at the Bleecker Street Inquiry Agency had unraveled so spectacularly, Arthur inclined his head. "Fair enough, but to reiterate, I did not kill James."

"Then how did you come to discover his body?"

"I was staying at Mason Manor, and James had a maid deliver me a message that morning, asking me to join him on the target field at eight sharp."

"Why?"

"I assume because he wanted to revisit the discussion we'd had the night before, not that I know that for certain since James was dead when I arrived on the target field."

Daphne cleared her throat. "Was there anyone else on that field when you arrived who could verify your story?"

"Eugenia Howland was there, but she's, of course, missing. That means there's no way to verify my account, but I assure you, I would hardly seek out the services of an inquiry agency if I were the guilty party in James's death. Seems to me that would be opening myself up for questions I wouldn't want to answer."

"Unless you've decided that by seeking out our services you'll be distracting us from your culpability in the matter," Eunice said before turning to Daphne. "You may want to stow your pistol for now, Daphne. Your hand is shaking like mad, and it'll be safer for everyone involved if you don't try to concentrate on holding your pistol *and* asking questions at the same time."

"Thank goodness," Daphne said, slipping her pistol into the large bag currently at her feet. "It would hardly do the agency's reputation any good if I were to accidentally shoot a potential client." She returned to perusing her notes. "If you're to be believed, Arthur, and you did not shoot James W. Mason, could you have possibly set up that scene because you thought Eugenia murdered her grandfather and decided to conceal her guilt for some yet undisclosed reason?"

"An interesting question since I did think Eugenia killed her grandfather at first."

"Because?" Daphne prompted.

"What else was I to conclude after I arrived on the field and discovered Eugenia leaning over James? At first glance, I thought he'd suffered some manner of attack, such as from his heart, but then when Eugenia turned to me, I realized she was splattered with blood. I then noticed her very distinctive pistol on the grass beside her. At that moment, I thought she'd shot her grandfather, that belief increasing when she snatched up the pistol and pointed it at me. When you add in the fact that I overheard Eugenia and James engaged in a heated exchange the night before, it was the most logical conclusion to draw at that time."

Eunice sat forward. "What happened after Eugenia leveled her pistol on you?"

"She shot me."

Daphne jotted something onto her notepad. "I suppose I can understand why you came to the conclusion she murdered her grandfather after shooting you."

"On the contrary. Her shooting me is exactly why I realized she *wasn't* responsible for her grandfather's death."

"I'm afraid I have no idea how you'd come to that conclusion," Daphne said. "If someone shot me, I'd definitely be suspicious about their motives."

"And normally I'd agree with you, but Eugenia Howland is an expert marksman, or rather, markswoman. If she'd been intending to kill me, I wouldn't be sitting here now. However, instead of shooting to kill, she merely put a bullet through my arm, missing all essential parts, which I assure you, she did on purpose. I'm assuming she did so because she probably thought that *I* killed her grandfather and was planning to kill her next."

"What happened after she shot you?"

"The force of the bullet sent me on my backside. I simply stayed on the ground for a long moment, bracing myself for another attack from Eugenia, which didn't come."

"I thought you said you'd decided she wasn't a murderess."

"I didn't decide that right away." Arthur frowned. "Have you ever been shot, Daphne?"

"No, but I did have a knife pulled on me when we were investigating the Knickerbocker Bandit case."

"And while you were being held at knifepoint, did you make any conclusions or decide anything of worth?"

"I can't say that I did."

"Because it wasn't the moment for thinking. It was the same for me, but after I realized Eugenia had fled the scene, my mind kicked into gear, and that's when I decided that she'd not shot me because she'd killed her grandfather but because she'd been desperate to get away from me."

"Did you go after her?" Eunice asked.

"I was intending on doing exactly that until I began considering the situation in more depth. It seemed suspicious to me that Eugenia's very distinctive Colt revolver had been on the scene. She had once told me that her Colt pistol, while custom made for her, was too showy, and she didn't care for the way it performed. She instead preferred her Smith & Wesson Model 3 revolver or a small derringer that was easily hidden in the pocket of the trousers she enjoyed wearing."

Eunice, to his surprise, returned her pistol to the desk drawer and then settled back in her chair. "I've decided you're not a threat, Mr. Livingston. But don't relax your guard. I assure you I won't hesitate to bring my pistol out again. With that settled, back to your story. You decided the scene was suspicious, and . . . ?"

"Someone was trying to frame Eugenia. She is a grand heiress, after all, and if someone shot James because of his money, the best way to get to that money after he was dead was to either kill Eugenia or to frame her for the deed, as it's likely a judge would render Eugenia's right to her fortune invalid if she were convicted of her grandfather's murder.

"That's when I decided to stage the scene. I wrapped up my arm, retrieved James's pistol from his jacket pocket, and arranged it to where it looked like he could have dropped it if he'd shot himself. I then made my way back to the house, slipping in through a side door so as not to be seen. After I changed out of my bloody shirt, I headed out of the house again, making certain the staff knew I was on my way to meet up with James. I returned to the house a short time later, telling everyone there'd been an accident."

"And no one realized you'd been shot?" Daphne pressed.

"It was merely a flesh wound. The bullet took off a bit of skin from the side of my arm, and I hate to admit this, but it was a brilliant shot on Eugenia's part, especially considering she had to have been in a distressed state after finding her grandfather dead."

"It was kind of her to be so brilliant with her shot."

"It would have been kinder if she'd refrained from shooting me in the first place."

"Well, quite." Daphne bent over her notes again. "You said you were on the target field because James asked you to meet him there. Can you say more about what you think he wanted to speak to you about?"

"I thought he wanted to further discuss the promise I'd given him the night before, one that had me agreeing to look after Eugenia's best interests if the circumstance arose where he was unable to do that."

Eunice leaned forward. "He made you promise to look after her best interests?"

"He did, although I was reluctant to agree. I knew there was a chance that promise would be followed by a request to marry his granddaughter, a request I wouldn't have been keen to grant. However, with that said, there was something different in his eyes when he made his appeal, something . . . desperate. James was not a man who ever pleaded with anyone, but that's what he was doing with me, which is why I relented and agreed to look after his granddaughter."

"Why didn't you want to marry Eugenia?" Daphne asked.

Arthur frowned. "I don't believe that has any relevance to the case."

"But it would appease my curiosity," Daphne said.

He felt the oddest inclination to laugh. "You're very persistent, I'll give you that. But I'm afraid your curiosity will have to stay unappeased because I have a feeling you'll take exception to my reason for not wanting to marry Eugenia. That will hardly encourage you to take on my case, and speaking of my case, dare I hope I've now given you enough information to where you realize that finding Eugenia Howland is a worthy cause?"

"We still have a few questions," Eunice said, rising from her chair to move beside Daphne. She took Daphne's notepad from her and flipped through the pages. "Ah, here's a good one. Why do you believe Eugenia could be in New York City?"

"I'm not convinced she is, but the only lead I have was given to me from the Pinkertons seven years ago. They discovered that Eugenia had arrived in this city, but that she never boarded the ship she was scheduled to take to England. I'm hoping she decided to stay here."

Eunice returned Daphne's notepad before she moved behind her desk again, her weeping veils rustling as she settled into her chair. "Have you considered that she may no longer be alive? Perhaps whoever killed her grandfather caught up with her and took care of her once and for all."

"That's a worthy consideration, except I doubt the culprit behind James's murder was able to track Eugenia down. She has access to a large trust fund that can see her well hidden."

"How do you know she had access to a trust fund?"

Arthur shrugged. "The Pinkertons learned of it from her grandfather's banker. They then learned she'd accessed the money in her account after she landed in New York City, withdrawing all her money from that bank. She probably opened a new account at another bank under an assumed name, but the Pinkertons never discovered what that name was or what bank she may have used. The trail of Eugenia Howland went cold from there."

Daphne ruffled through her notepad, skimmed down a page, and lifted her head. "But why try to find Eugenia now? Or better yet, why do I get the impression there's a sense of urgency to your search, even though she's been missing for years?"

"Her relatives have decided to have her declared dead and are pursuing a presumption of death case. They intend to do that on Eugenia's birthday, which is only a few weeks away. That's why I need to find her within the week so that I have enough time to get her back to Montana before she's declared dead."

"Couldn't you simply advise the proper authorities that you have reason to believe she's alive?" Daphne asked.

Arthur shook his head. "It's not New York City, Daphne, it's the Wild West. It won't be difficult for the Mason family to promise future windfalls to the officials who can make death certificates appear at will as well as look the other way if a shred of evidence other than Eugenia in the flesh is produced."

"An unusual twist to Eugenia's story to be sure," Daphne said. "But tell me this—has the Mason family received information that suggests Eugenia is dead? Better yet, where do they think she's been all these years?"

"The last word they received years ago about Eugenia was that she was in Europe," Arthur said. "And before you ask, I was the one who told them about her European tour as well as made up a somewhat plausible excuse as to why that tour had been kept hush-hush. I believe I told them James planned the trip as a surprise birthday present and didn't want anyone in the family to ruin the surprise."

Eunice muttered something about it being a surprise the Mason family would have bought that, but before he could ask her what she meant, Daphne sat forward.

"Didn't they question why Eugenia hadn't returned home from her tour? Grand tours don't often span years."

"They didn't question her absence because I told the family that she never received the telegram I sent to intercept her in New York before she boarded the ship bound for England, one telling her James had died. About a month after his funeral, I was asked by James's brother to stay in Montana to help manage the mines until James's estate could be organized. I then arranged to have a telegram supposedly sent from Eugenia to Mason Manor, stating that she learned of her grandfather's death in a newspaper article."

"How were you able to do that?" Daphne asked.

"I told you, it's the Wild West. You can arrange a lot of questionable things if you have money to do so."

"Did this telegram say anything else?"

"I don't remember the exact wording I used, but it lent the impression Eugenia was so distraught about James's death that she wasn't sure when, or if, she'd be returning to Montana."

"And Eugenia's relatives never questioned her decision to stay in Europe?"

"Not at all. In fact, after they received that telegram, a few of them moved out of their respective homes and into Mason Manor, which is one of the largest and most impressive houses in Montana."

Eunice crossed her arms over her chest. "No wonder they readily accepted that telegram. But if they've already been enjoying some of Eugenia's inheritance, why have her declared dead now?"

"I believe that decision is a direct result of what geologists uncovered on the old Green farm James acquired not long before he died. Turns out that farm is a hotbed for copper—and not just any copper, but copper that's thirty percent purer than most of the copper mined in this country. There's a general belief that the land will yield the biggest copper strike this country has ever seen, which is why Eugenia's great-uncle, Raymond Mason, put the word out that the family is interested in selling Mason Mines. There's a lot of interest from investors, and from one gentleman in particular—a D. H. Loring, who is pushing the family to sell Mason Mines to him. He's offered a price they're hesitant to refuse, which is why they're determined to have Eugenia declared dead as soon as possible."

Daphne lifted her head. "Should I assume Eugenia is the sole heir to her grandfather's estate?"

"She's not the sole heir. James left a percentage of his assets to his daughter, Georgette, although she hasn't been heard from in years either. He also left monetary bequests to his other relatives, which were substantial, although nothing in comparison to Eugenia's fortune. I believe the Mason family has held that against Eugenia and are now determined to get what they think is their fair share of the family fortune by having her declared dead."

"May I assume they're going to have Eugenia's mother declared dead as well so they're the only remaining living relatives?" Eugenia asked.

"Of course. They're resolved to not leave a chance that their claim on the estate could be challenged."

"Savvy of them," Eunice muttered. "But tell me this, Mr. Livingston, why are you involving yourself once again in Mason affairs? Yes, you apparently gave your word to James Mason that you'd look after his granddaughter, but it's been seven years. Surely you can't believe he'd have expected you to honor your word after she disappeared on you."

"I don't believe there's a statute of limitation on a man's word. And because I became aware of the plan to rid Eugenia of her inheritance, I have no choice but to find her and see after her best interests. I certainly can't stand by and allow her inheritance to be stolen from her."

"And while I have to admit that speaks well of your character," Eunice began, "tell me this. Was there anything else you gave your word to James about before he died?"

"In the spirit of full disclosure, yes. As I mentioned, he seemed desperate to me that last time we spoke. To ease some of his desperation, I finally promised him, and rather reluctantly, that if circumstances demanded it, I would marry Eugenia to keep her safe."

Silence descended over the office for a long moment until Eunice sat forward. "Should I assume that means if you locate Eugenia you're no longer reluctant to marry her?"

"Oh, I'm still reluctant considering the contentious relationship Eugenia and I shared, but I don't see how I can look after her best interests *without* marrying her."

"Hmmm," Eunice said before she rose to her feet. "I believe I've heard enough, so this is where our interview ends."

Arthur rose to his feet as well. "Because you've heard enough details about the case and are going to take it on?"

"We will not be taking on your case."

"Why not?"

"Because your arrogance apparently knows no bounds."

"Arrogance? What arrogance?"

She drew herself up, looking more than formidable in her black widow's weeds. "You just claimed it'll be in Eugenia Howland's best interest to marry you but not once have you mentioned how Eugenia may feel about a marriage to you. It seems, at least in your mind, to be a foregone conclusion that marriage to you is her best option, and that is arrogance at its finest."

"There are other reasons marriage to me will be in her best interest. I simply haven't gotten to them yet."

She held up a black-gloved hand. "I have no desire to hear those reasons. I'm sure they'll be questionable at best, just as I'm sure you won't mention a word about how marriage to Eugenia would benefit *you*. The law is clear in this country about what happens to a lady's inheritance when she marries. It goes to her husband. If you're correct about the amount of copper lying under that old farm, Eugenia would become the majority owner of the largest copper venture in the country. If you marry her, you'll have full control over that copper, along with the rest of Eugenia's fortune."

"I never said I wouldn't benefit from a marriage to Eugenia," Arthur countered.

"True. You merely neglected to say anything at all about the matter, presenting your case as if you're going to be doing Eugenia a great favor by taking her as your wife. Again, arrogance at its best. With that said, allow me to bid you adieu and caution you to never darken our doorstep again."

Before Arthur could think of a suitable response to salvage a situation he'd lost complete control of, Eunice retrieved her pistol from her desk and strode his way, the black train of her widow's weeds swishing over the floor. She reached his side in the blink of an eye, and without a by your leave, gestured with her pistol toward the door. A second after that, she marched him out of the Bleecker Street Inquiry Agency while not speaking another word to him, leaving him standing alone on the stoop as she shut the door firmly in his face.

CHAPTER
Seven

"Out of any possible solution to the Arthur Livingston situation, your going undercover as an inmate at Blackwell's Island Insane Asylum is the worst option available."

Eunice pulled her attention from the window of the carriage that was trundling its way toward the East River, where she would then board a boat bound for Blackwell Island. She settled her gaze on Ivan Chernoff, her bodyguard and best friend. He was sitting directly beside her, looking decidedly irritable as he raked a hand through his short blond hair.

"We've been over this, Ivan, numerous times. My going undercover is the perfect solution. Mrs. Eastman is desperate to see her sister regain her freedom, and I was very moved by Mrs. Eastman's distress and felt compelled to take matters into my own hands since Gabriella and Nicholas, who would have been the best suited to take on this matter, are out of town on another case. Besides, I need to make myself scarce from the agency until Arthur leaves the city in a few days, a week at the most. That's why it makes perfect sense for me to be the agent to go undercover."

"Except that there's no reason for you to make yourself scarce in the first place. You seem convinced that Arthur doesn't believe you murdered your grandfather, nor does it seem as if he did the dastardly deed. It's ridiculous for you to place yourself in a situation I'm convinced you're ill equipped to handle."

Eunice batted away a veil that was obscuring her vision. "There's every reason for me to avoid Arthur because I fear if I see the insufferable man again, I'll be hard-pressed not to shoot him. If that happens, I'll certainly find myself behind bars since Arthur probably won't forgive a second shooting quite as easily as he forgave the first one."

"I don't recall you saying Arthur forgave that first shooting," Agent Cooper Clifton said from where he was sitting across from her.

Switching her attention to Cooper, a Pinkerton agent who often worked in conjunction with the Bleecker Street Inquiry Agency, Eunice frowned. "Hmmm. . . . Now that I think about it, Arthur didn't actually say he'd forgiven me. But because he's determined to marry me, he must not be holding too much of a grudge, although I could be wrong about that, which is another reason I should avoid him."

Cooper tilted his head. "Even if he's not holding a grudge, I don't understand why you'd be tempted to shoot the poor man again. Most normal women would view his determination to marry you as a compliment."

"Eunice is not what anyone would consider normal," Ivan muttered, earning a swat from Eunice and a snort from Miss Ann Evans, a fellow inquiry agent who was sitting beside Cooper.

"Eunice is perfectly normal," Ann said. "And I for one understand exactly why she longs to shoot Arthur. No lady wants to hear that a gentleman has decided to marry her for her own good. Honestly, what *could* that man have been thinking?"

"I'm sure he thought he was casting himself in a favorable light. Most people, gentlemen and ladies alike, believe looking after a lady's best interest is what a gentleman is supposed to do," Cooper said.

"Which is a valid point," Ann said as she sent a rather flirty smile Cooper's way, something she did often whenever she was in his company. "Eunice might have considered him more favorably, though, if he hadn't implied he was going to be doing her a favor by marrying her."

"That right there is exactly why my trigger finger has turned a bit twitchy," Eunice said, settling back against the seat.

Cooper winced. "Perhaps it *is* a prudent decision for you to remove yourself from the city until Arthur leaves town. I may not currently feel compelled to disclose your identity to the Pinkertons, even though they were once hired to find you. But if you shoot Arthur, who was once a Pinkerton client, I'd not only have to disclose your identity but also arrest you."

"I would expect nothing less."

Ivan crossed his arms over his chest. "You're not going to shoot Arthur again, even if he may have presented his argument about why he wants to marry you somewhat clumsily. There's a distinct possibility his clumsiness was a direct result of your being contrary with him from the moment he stepped foot into your office as well as a result of what sounds like you and Daphne teaming up against him."

"I was thinking along those same exact lines," Cooper said before Eunice could argue against that nonsense. "And, to add my two cents' worth, have you considered there's a possibility that Arthur changed his mind about marrying you because he decided you were an intriguing woman, something that perhaps took him seven years to figure out?"

Eunice rolled her eyes. "Arthur never once lent me the impression he found me intriguing. Besides, he admitted he'd not been eager to court me when Grandfather first broached the topic."

"But again, that could be because he found you're more of an acquired taste, and perhaps he's come to the conclusion you've aged to perfection—like fine wine," Cooper said.

"I've never cared for wine."

"You're missing the point," Cooper returned. "You also seem to be forgetting that Arthur told you numerous times that his quest to locate Eugenia stems from the word he gave to your grandfather. An honorable man should not be dismissed lightly."

"I never said one should take an honorable man lightly, but I'm certainly not going to disclose my identity to Arthur simply to allow him an avenue to honor a promise I knew nothing about and don't have any intention of helping him keep. If I need repeat this again, we're talking about a gentleman who seems to believe he'll be doing me a favor by marrying me."

"If you ask me," Ivan said, "his decision to marry you could almost be considered a favor, since Arthur knows after spending two months in your company how contrary you can be."

Eunice caught Ann's eye. "Is it my imagination or does it seem as if they're taking Arthur's side in this?"

"Gentlemen do tend to stick together," Ann said, settling a frown on Ivan even as she gave Cooper's knee a pat. "But because both of you are annoying Eunice by defending Arthur, which is odd because he clearly made some grave missteps in presenting his case, what say we change the subject for now? Eunice is about to embark on a delicate mission, and the last thing she needs is to descend into an annoyed state before we reach the asylum."

"I don't know why she's annoyed with us," Cooper said. "We're simply trying to explain why Arthur may have changed his mind about marrying her. But speaking of Arthur yet again . . ." He returned his attention to Eunice. "I'm curious how it came to be that the two of you were always at odds with each other. From what I uncovered about him when I did some digging yesterday, society finds him to be the consummate gentleman who never has a harsh word to say to anyone."

Eunice blinked. "Arthur's a member of society?"

"You didn't know that?"

"How would I know that?"

"You're an inquiry agent. You have the resources available to investigate people. You've also been hiding from Arthur for the past seven years. It seems peculiar you've never attempted to gather any information about the man."

"I've tried not to dwell on my past."

"Which was clearly not a very logical decision because your

past has caught up with you and left you flat-footed in the process. But since you apparently don't know anything about Arthur, he's a member of *the* Livingston family, one of the most esteemed families within society."

Ann tucked a strand of red hair that had escaped its pins behind her ear. "I've encountered a Benjamin Livingston when I've traveled in society with the ladies I'm a companion to, but I've never been introduced to an Arthur Livingston."

"That's because he's rarely in town," Cooper said. "He's a second son, his older brother, Benjamin, the Livingston you've encountered, being the heir to the Livingston business interests, which are extensive. From what I uncovered yesterday, society was astonished when Arthur left New York at the ripe old age of twenty-one, turning his back on the role everyone expected him to take up—that being a gentleman of leisure."

"Arthur never struck me as a man who'd be comfortable living a leisurely life," Eunice said. "I have to admit, though, that learning he's from a New York Four Hundred family does explain much about him." She smiled. "It's little wonder he took exception to my less-than-ladylike behavior back in Montana. It's doubtful he ever encountered ladies like me amidst the New York elite."

"It's doubtful most gentlemen have encountered a lady like you," Ivan muttered.

She couldn't resist giving Ivan another swat, earning a grin from him in return before she caught Ann's eye. "Since it's only a matter of time until Ivan and Cooper join forces against me again and begin waxing on about Arthur and his honorable intentions, what say we concern ourselves with the case we're about to undertake." She glanced out the window. "We're almost to the dock, which means we should go over our plan one last time. I doubt we'll be able to talk much as we're making our way across the river to Blackwell Island on the ship that transports patients there."

Ann readjusted the white nursing cap she was wearing before she reached into her satchel and pulled out letters written by physicians, which would get Eunice admitted into the asylum. "Our first order of business after we arrive on the island is for me to escort you to admissions, where I'll present these letters stating you're insane." She tossed another flirty smile Cooper's way. "Did I mention how impressive I found it that you were able to procure these letters on such short notice?"

Cooper returned the smile. "You have not, but even though I adore impressing you, I have to admit that procuring those letters wasn't much of a feat. The two doctors I approached have their practices in Five Points and have known me for years, since I grew up there. Once I explained that I was working a case, they were only too happy to provide me with letters declaring Eunice mentally unfit, because it's never a bad thing to have a Pinkerton owe you a favor."

Eunice blew out a breath. "Frankly, I'm not sure it was in our best interest that you were able to procure those letters so rapidly. We might have needed that additional time if Arthur doesn't leave the city for an entire week, because Ann and I could very well locate Mrs. Clement Mills today. I can't imagine it'll take us much time to see her released since she's been unjustly committed, which means after we deposit Mrs. Mills at her sister's house, we'll then need to find another place for me to lie low until we know for certain Arthur's departed for Montana again."

Ivan flipped open a small notepad that detailed their plan and frowned. "I don't think you're going to need to worry about that because I'm not convinced it's going to be easy getting Mrs. Mills released." He glanced at his notes. "There are approximately forty-five to fifty women housed on every floor, with a total of over sixteen hundred patients housed in the asylum. I doubt it'll be easy to run Mrs. Mills down, especially when I don't believe the asylum allows their patients to have free roam of their buildings. You're probably going to be stuck on whatever hall they assign you to, and the odds of Mrs. Mills being assigned to that same hall are slim to none."

"But that's where Ann comes in. Everyone will be told she's been sent as my personal nurse because her presence calms my fits of weeping. I'm sure the other nurses won't care to deal with that all the time, especially when I'll make certain to add in some loud wailing as well. Ann can then graciously offer to fill in where needed when she's not attending me, which will gain her access to other floors."

Ivan narrowed his eyes. "Ann should not leave your side. You don't have much experience in the field, and having you take an undercover role in an asylum is not an ideal foray into fieldwork."

"I've worked in the field before," Eunice countered. "If you've forgotten, I was of great assistance to Gabriella as we dealt with that dog-napping case."

"Assisting with a dog-napping case is not the same as going undercover in an asylum, where it's rumored that women committed there are mistreated."

"Then I suppose it's fortunate I'm well-equipped to handle myself."

Cooper frowned. "What does that mean exactly?"

"It means I can box and handle a knife, pistol, and slingshot with ease. And not that I'm proud of this, but I wouldn't be above hair pulling if someone tries to harm me."

"You can box?" Ann asked.

"She's actually quite good in the ring," Ivan admitted. "She's got a right hook that leaves a mark."

Cooper's eyes widened. "You've been in the boxing ring with her?"

"I'm the one who taught her. We box several times a week."

Ann wrinkled her nose. "But I've never seen you and Eunice box before, and I live in the boardinghouse."

Ivan waved that aside. "Eunice bought an old warehouse on Greenwich Avenue about six months after we arrived in the city. She didn't want to let her skills go rusty in case whoever murdered her grandfather came looking for her. We also take our pistols out to a practice range a few times a week, but not the one the agents use down by the Battery."

Cooper settled a frown on Eunice. "It almost sounds as if you've deliberately not allowed anyone at the agency to learn about your skills, which is odd since you asked me to begin those physical exertion and weapon classes months ago."

"It would have been tricky to explain why a widow knows how to knock a man out with a single punch," Eunice said. "Now that you're aware of my skills, though, and the ladies know my secret, I'll be more than happy to lend my fighting expertise to your lessons. I'm sure many of our agents will enjoy learning how to box."

"Indeed we will," Ann agreed, sitting forward and looking out the window. "But additional talk of boxing will need to wait. We've arrived at the docks."

After the carriage pulled to a stop a moment later, the door opened and Elsy Evans, Ann's sister, who was dressed as a male coachman and was the agency's main driver when she wasn't working her other position as a paid companion, stuck her head into the coach. She held out her hand to her sister, and after Ann stepped from the carriage, Eunice followed, her gaze settling on a group of shabbily dressed women standing on the dock, waiting to board a rather derelict-looking boat.

It did not escape her notice that there were three policemen standing close to the women, having been hired, no doubt, to make certain the potential new inmates didn't cause trouble on the boat ride to the island.

"I'll have to say good-bye for now from here," Cooper said, retreating back into the carriage. "That's Officer Bockert over there, and he knows me." He caught Eunice's eye. "Ivan and I will follow you on another boat, just as we planned. We'll be able to gain entry to the asylum, although it'll be tricky for us to get inside the buildings since we're supposed to be new groundkeepers. But at least we'll be on site."

"I'll come looking for the two of you at some point," Ann said. "But we have to go. They've begun boarding."

Eunice readjusted her veils, gave a few experimental sobs, then turned to Ivan, who was looking more concerned than ever. "Don't look so worried. I can take care of myself, and besides, I have every confidence Ann and I will be perfectly fine."

CHAPTER
Eight

Four hours later, Eunice was convinced they were going to be anything *but* fine.

Shifting on a bench that was incredibly uncomfortable, Eunice glanced to the three women sitting beside her, wishing there was something she could do to alleviate the worry stamped on their faces.

From the moment she and Ann had disembarked from the horrid boat that had taken them across the river to Blackwell Island, Eunice had realized this case might be far more difficult than she'd been expecting.

For one, she'd not been anticipating that the head nurse would immediately balk at allowing Ann to remain by Eunice's side. Instead, she'd insisted Ann hie herself off to hall number eight to assist with getting the inmates from that hall into a bath. Ann, having no choice but to comply, took her leave, whispering to Eunice that she'd be back soon, and hopefully with the news that she'd managed to locate Mrs. Mills.

Ann's departure had left Eunice in the care of Nurse Grady, a hard-looking woman who didn't seem to have a compassionate bone in her body. Nurse Grady had rounded up the three other women who'd been on the ship along with Eunice and marched them through an entrance hallway that was cold, uninviting, and didn't do a thing to put a person at ease. Nurse Grady then ushered them into an equally cold and sparsely furnished waiting room, where they were told to sit on the hard bench and wait for the arrival of a doctor who would do an initial assessment on each of them.

When Eunice had stated the obvious—that she'd already been given an assessment by two other doctors—Nurse Grady had taken her roughly by the arm, shoved her onto the bench, and ordered her to keep quiet. As an obvious incentive to obey that order, the nurse gave Eunice's arm a hard pinch, one she took as a warning that there would be repercussions if she didn't comply with the nurse's orders.

She'd never been fond of people who used their power for intimidation, which was exactly why, after Nurse Grady quit the room, she'd begun to question the three women left with her instead of keeping quiet. Their stories were more than disheartening.

Tillie Turney was a woman of about thirty, who'd been at Bellevue hospital for an entire month, recovering from an exhaustion illness she'd procured while working in a shirtwaist factory. She'd had no idea she was being sent to an insane asylum, nor did she show any sign of mental instability. But here she was, terrified to think that she may soon find herself committed as an insane woman, her terror only increasing after Nurse Grady told her she'd need to resign herself to her plight, since it was rare any patients were ever released.

Mrs. Edmund McGuinness was another woman who didn't appear to have lost her wits, but when questioned about why she was at the asylum, Mrs. McGuinness merely shrugged and said her husband had been responsible for having her deemed insane after she couldn't control her anguish over the death of their infant daughter four months before. After disclosing that, Mrs. McGuinness had not spoken another word, sitting stiffly on the bench as tears trailed down her cheeks.

The third woman waiting with Eunice was Louise Schanz,

or at least that's what Eunice thought she said her name was. The woman spoke not a word of English, only German, and seemed completely bewildered by her surroundings. When she'd tried to ask Nurse Grady questions in German, the nurse had dismissed her out of hand, claiming the woman was obviously demented, even though Eunice was convinced the poor woman simply couldn't make herself understood because she didn't speak the language.

Unfortunately, when Nurse Grady reentered the room and Eunice suggested it might be prudent to have an interpreter summoned, the nurse gave her another pinch and quit the room again, returning a minute later in the company of the doctor they'd been waiting on for hours.

Trepidation mixed with a great deal of curiosity flowed through Eunice when Nurse Grady called her name, or rather called out Eunice Hickenbottom, the name she'd decided to assume, and told her the doctor would examine her now.

Readjusting her veils so they covered her face again, even though Nurse Grady had insisted she lift them over her head upon arriving at the asylum, Eunice followed the nurse into the room, finding the doctor sitting behind a desk, watching her as she sat down in the chair Nurse Grady shoved her toward.

"This is Dr. Franklin. He's to give you an examination. After that, you'll join the women you'll be sharing a floor with." Nurse Grady bent closer to Eunice's ear. "Do what the doctor tells you, or you'll suffer the consequences from me." With that, she straightened and marched out of the room.

"Remove your veils" were the first words out of Dr. Franklin's mouth after Nurse Grady shut the door.

Eunice squared her shoulders. "I'd prefer to keep them on."

"That's not an option, nor will it be an option for you to remain in your widow's weeds. All the patients are given the same skirt and blouse, and Nurse Grady will see to that later today." Dr. Franklin rose to his feet, moved directly next to her, and yanked the veils from her head, not bothering to take out the pins that secured them to her hair, which resulted in a bit of her hair being pulled out.

"That was hardly necessary," she snapped, a complaint the doctor ignored as he tilted her head back.

"I thought you'd be older," he said slowly.

"I hear that a lot."

His eyes narrowed on her face. "The doctors who initially examined you wrote that you're suffering from acute melancholy as well as female hysteria. They also mentioned that you rarely speak, but that doesn't appear to be the case now."

For the briefest of seconds, Eunice considered feigning a bout of weeping but reconsidered that as curiosity got the better of her. From what she'd gathered through things Nurse Grady had said, it was next to impossible to get released from the asylum after one was committed. With that in mind, she decided she was going to behave as she normally did—sane and without a whiff of female hysteria about her, if only to see if that made any difference with the doctor's diagnosis.

"I'm afraid the physicians who examined me didn't allow me the opportunity to speak, but I assure you, Dr. Franklin, I'm rarely without words."

"I'm sure that'll change after you've been here for a week or two."

The sheer arrogance of his tone made Eunice's hands clench, but before she could contemplate wiping the man's smile from his face with her fist, he bent closer to her.

"Stick out your tongue."

"I beg your pardon?"

"Your tongue. I need to examine it."

"What possible reason could you have for examining my tongue?"

"That's not for you to question."

"It is when it's my tongue and I see no plausible reason for you to examine it. My mental state is at issue, not my tongue."

When Dr. Franklin took hold of her face in a grip that was certain to leave a bruise, Eunice forced a hand that was completely clenched to relax, telling herself that she would be no help to Mrs. Mills if she punched the doctor and found herself carted off to a place in the asylum called the Lodge.

That section, according to one of the policemen who'd been on the boat, and whom Ann had decided to chat up to gather information, housed the most violent of patients, or those predisposed to suicide. The policeman had also mentioned that those unfortunate patients, when allowed outside to get fresh air, were tethered together with a rope, quite like one would do when taking a dog for a walk.

Having no desire to end up in that ward, which definitely would impede her search for Mrs. Mills, Eunice stuck out her tongue, earning a nod from Dr. Franklin before he looked at her tongue and wrote something down on a notepad.

"It's just as I feared," he muttered.

"What is?"

"You're demented."

"You can tell that from my tongue?"

He didn't bother to answer as he began probing her head with his fingers before he stepped back, picked up a gas lamp that was on a table beside him, then told her to look directly into the flame.

Her curiosity about the exam had her looking into the flame, trying hard not to blink at the bright light that was all but blinding her as Dr. Franklin peered into one eye and then the other. Shaking his head and clucking his tongue, he then pulled out a measuring tape and started taking measurements of her head.

He set the tape aside as Nurse Grady reentered the room.

"Your verdict on this one?" Nurse Grady asked.

"Mad as a hatter."

Eunice drew herself up. "I most certainly am not."

Dr. Franklin ignored her as he took the paper Nurse Grady was holding out to him, set it on top of his desk, and scribbled something on it. He turned to Eunice. "You've now been officially committed to Blackwell's Island Insane Asylum."

"And the reason for that?"

He exchanged an amused look with Nurse Grady. "Further proof the poor thing is delusional." He caught Eunice's eye. "You're insane, my dear. Your fits of acute melancholy and female hysteria have damaged your mind to where I'm afraid there's little hope you'll ever recover."

"I don't feel at all melancholy at the moment, nor am I displaying any symptoms of female hysteria," she couldn't resist pointing out.

Dr. Franklin's brows drew together, but instead of responding to what was clearly a rational statement, he sent Nurse Grady a jerk of his head. "See that she gets taken immediately to one of our private rooms. I fear she's soon to suffer from a hysterical fit, given her obstinate attitude, which may pose a danger to the other inmates. I'm not yet convinced she belongs in the Lodge, but time will tell. Hopefully, spending the rest of today and tonight alone will see her in an improved state, her hysteria aided by a day of complete quiet. You may include her with the general population tomorrow."

"A well-thought-out decision on your part, Dr. Franklin." Nurse Grady stepped next to Eunice and took hold of her arm in a grip that was so tight there was little doubt Eunice's arm would soon be sporting another bruise, one to match the bruise from the pinch. After sending Dr. Franklin a smile, Nurse Grady dragged Eunice out of the room, down a hallway, up several flights of stairs, finally stopping in front of a door that had number 28 stamped on it.

"You'll be staying here," Nurse Grady said, pulling out a ring filled with keys from a chain around her waist and opening the door. She shoved Eunice into the room. "You'll not be served dinner, which will hopefully go far in seeing you stifle your ridiculous questions and observations from this point forward. If you refuse to do so, I assure you that you'll find yourself at the Lodge come tomorrow. Believe me, you won't enjoy a stay there, especially not when that lovely hair of yours will need to be shorn off to spare it being pulled out by some of our more violent inmates."

Thirty seconds later, the door slammed shut, leaving Eunice all alone and wondering, not for the first time, if Ivan had the right of it and she didn't have the experience needed to maneuver her way through a case that was in no way, shape, or form anything like she'd been expecting.

CHAPTER
Nine

"I see you're still in a morose frame of mind, although I'm not surprised, given that you managed to get yourself tossed out on your ear from an inquiry agency that doesn't enjoy a reputation for abusing potential clients in such an amusing manner."

Refusing a sigh, Arthur turned toward the library door and watched as his younger brother Chase bounded into the room, the cheerful smile on his face doing nothing to banish the morose frame of mind Arthur was actually in at the moment.

Chase, the baby of the family at twenty-three, was possessed of an unusually sunny disposition, which meant he was brimming with good cheer more often than not. That trait was decidedly annoying when the person being subjected to all that good cheer was perfectly content to descend into bouts of moroseness every now and again.

"I didn't get tossed out of the agency, merely shown the door in a forceful fashion," Arthur said as Chase settled himself into a chair.

"You told me Eunice Holbrooke brandished a pistol at you two days ago, propelled you out of the agency, then slammed the door in your face. If that's not being tossed out on your ear, I don't know what is."

"She overreacted."

Chase laughed. "You may keep telling yourself that, brother, but considering you told her that you were going to marry Eugenia Howland for that lady's own good, I think her reaction was warranted." He shook his head. "What were you thinking?"

"I was thinking it was best to be truthful, and there's nothing untruthful about it being in Eugenia's best interest to marry me."

"I imagine Eugenia might have something to say about that. From what you've said about the time you spent with her, I got the impression the two of you shared an acrimonious relationship. Acrimonious isn't exactly a state most women long to pursue, especially when it pertains to marriage."

"Eugenia is practical to a fault. If, or rather, when I find her, I assure you, she'll agree with my decision because she'll need a strong man by her side to help her reclaim her inheritance. Her relatives are determined to see that inheritance divided between them, and they're not going to take kindly to Eugenia depriving them of millions."

"Your presence would assuredly come in handy, but marrying her seems a little over the top." Chase shook his head. "You've been a consultant for the Mason estate ever since James Mason died. If you ask me, taking on that consulting position was acting in Eugenia's best interests while she's been gone. I would think the most logical path forward would be for you to continue in a consulting capacity, which will spare you marriage to a woman I've never gotten the impression you like."

"I never said I disliked Eugenia."

"You told me the two of you argued all the time."

"True, but that's mostly because I might have, or actually did, go out of my way to provoke her."

Chase crossed one ankle over the other. "That seems quite unlike you. The brother I know has always been solicitous to the feminine set and wouldn't try to provoke anyone on purpose. Why did you do that?"

"Because James Mason made it clear that he was anxious to see a union between me and his granddaughter. From the moment I caught my first glimpse of Eugenia, I knew that a union between us wasn't going to be possible."

"You knew that from a first glimpse?"

"She was a disaster, covered in mud after having taken her beast of a stallion out during a storm. She'd apparently allowed her stallion his head, or perhaps he did that all on his own, which was why she was drenched after barreling over a field that was inches deep in water." Arthur frowned. "Come to think of it, though, the mud might have come about because her horse threw her after jumping a hedge. She was a little sketchy about the details."

"You knew she wasn't a lady you'd marry because she was muddy?"

"No, I knew she wasn't the lady for me because she was wearing trousers and men's riding boots, and when her grandfather introduced us, she held out her hand and shook mine with a firm grip I wasn't expecting. She also left a great deal of mud behind while doing so, something any other young lady of my acquaintance would have been mortified to discover she'd done. Eugenia didn't bat an eye. She merely dug a handkerchief out of her pocket, handed it to me, then told me I was welcome to keep it, quite like a gentleman would have done after extending a hanky to a lady."

"She sounds delightful."

"Eugenia *does* have a certain charm about her, but she was absolutely not the type of lady I'd decided at that time to marry, as she didn't fit the requirement of being an incomparable and moving easily within society. Nevertheless, I wasn't eager to annoy James and flatly refused to consider his suggestion of forming an alliance with his granddaughter because the lure of becoming a partner with him was too much to resist. That's why I decided to convince Eugenia I was a complete and utter boor. I had the sneaking suspicion she wasn't a lady who suffered boors, and it turns out I was right about that."

"But you didn't dislike her?" Chase pressed.

"I suppose there were moments, when she'd fire back retorts

that were hot enough to scorch my face, that I wasn't overly fond of her. But, not that I would admit this to Eugenia, I actually enjoyed a great deal of the banter between us, especially when we'd talk about books. She was very well read, although she didn't allow her grandfather to know that. He didn't believe reading anything but financial statements or the latest mining journals were worthy of a person's time. Eugenia, however, adored the written word, especially dime novels, which, I have to admit, I'm fond of as well."

Chase rubbed his jaw. "Forgive me if I'm off the mark, but it sounds to me as if Eugenia Howland might be perfect for you."

"She's not perfect for me, but I believe we'll rub along nicely once we marry."

"Not that I want to point out the obvious, but Eugenia has no idea you deliberately set out to make yourself disagreeable. That means there's a very good chance she holds you in disdain."

"I'm hopeful she'll find my disclosure about my boorish behavior amusing, but even if she doesn't, Eugenia is pragmatic. And yes, she was unconventional, but she has a keen understanding about her grandfather's business, acquired from James W. Mason himself as well as a tutor possessed of an engineering degree, Mr. Vincent Wagner. Because she's so knowledgeable about copper mining in general, she'll realize what an asset I'll be to her, what with the success I've found in the industry. In all honesty, I think marriage between us is a logical decision for both of us."

"How is that a logical decision for you?" Chase asked. "You've spent over the past decade building up a mining empire, done so, at least according to Mother, because of a desire to leave your mark on the world. Part of that future centers around marrying an incomparable from society, a longing I'm relatively certain came about due to what happened between you and Mitzi thirteen or so years ago. From what Mother has also disclosed, you're determined to sweep back into society as a copper mogul and assume a high-level position within society, with your incomparable bride by your side."

Arthur slouched into the chair. "I don't think I care to continue on with this conversation, especially with Mitzi now being introduced into it. You're my little brother, barely wet around the ears, and as such, I don't believe you have the experience needed to counsel me on matters of marriage or women in general."

"I've always been old for my years, and I spend countless hours counseling men and women when I volunteer at a mission in Five Points." Chase smiled. "You would not believe how adept I'm becoming at understanding the workings of the feminine mind after so many women have disclosed the difficulties they're having with the men in their lives."

"People from Five Points feel comfortable disclosing problems to you, a member of the New York Four Hundred?"

"My society status has little bearing on the work I do at the mission. Besides, everyone just wants someone to lend them a sympathetic ear, which many people don't have available to them."

"Huh" was all Arthur could think to say to that before he frowned. "Since when do you volunteer at a mission?"

"Since I graduated from Harvard and came into the trust fund Grandfather Livingston left me." Chase smiled. "I tried to convince Father and Benjamin that I'd be up for learning the family business, but they didn't seem all that keen to have me join them. Benjamin went so far as to remark that my constantly smiling face was certain to cost him important business negotiations. With my being denied a place in the family business, I was at loose ends. There's only so many society events a gentleman can attend, unless said gentleman agrees to become one of those gentlemen who can lunch, like Grandfather Brevoorts. And while Grandfather appears to enjoy that lunching status, I have no interest in spending my days surrounded by aging matrons. So, I decided to do something useful with my life."

"You could always try to make use of that degree you got from Harvard."

Chase's eyes twinkled. "I knew it was only a matter of time before you broached that topic, since you're often pointing out how you put your engineering degree to immediate use after you graduated. You'll be pleased to learn that I *am* putting my English degree to use these days because I'm teaching English courses at the mission. We're currently reading Charlotte Brontë, and after Charlotte, we're moving on to Shakespeare."

"That's a diverse reading list."

"Diversity helps people at the mission learn English. Most of them don't have a strong grasp of it, but reading fiction seems to help."

"Shakespeare will certainly confuse their grasp of the English language we actually use today."

"I didn't think of that, but it is an interesting point." Chase settled back in the chair. "But returning to you, I'm curious how you came to change your mind about marrying Eugenia Howland, and if it was a result of also changing your mind about marrying an incomparable?"

"It's not that I changed my mind regarding my original plan. It's more that I don't have another choice in the matter. Given the dire situation unfolding with Eugenia's relatives, the only way for me to honor my word to James is to marry Eugenia, even if I have to abandon my desire to marry an incomparable." Arthur tapped a finger against his chin. "Perhaps I should have mentioned to the ladies at the agency that I was willing to put aside my own dreams to look after Eugenia's best interests. That might have had them regarding me in a more favorable light."

Chase released a snort. "No, it wouldn't have, because not only have you decided to marry a woman simply because you gave your word to a man long deceased, you're doing so with what can surely be construed as a reluctant attitude. That hardly suggests the two of you will enjoy an amiable marriage." He folded his hands over his stomach. "The Bleecker Street Inquiry Agency is run by progressive women. They're not the type to want to see any woman coerced into a marriage that seems, even to me, more beneficial to you than it could ever be to Eugenia."

"You know, Mrs. Holbrooke mentioned something very similar to me right before she escorted me out of her agency."

"She clearly took issue with you, probably because she concluded that the only benefit Eugenia might get out of marrying you is that you're willing to help her regain control of her inheritance. But it's *her* rightful inheritance. It's not as if her relatives can make a claim against it after she turns up alive—if she turns up. Besides, it sounds to me as if Eugenia's a take-charge sort of lady. That means, after you inform her of her relatives' dastardly intentions, there's the distinct possibility she doesn't need your assistance at all. You, on the other hand, would be gaining access to an enormous fortune if a marriage were to take place, because owning Mason Mines would propel you to the very pinnacle of mining industrialists."

"Eugenia would be getting far more than simply my assistance by marrying me. She'd be getting protection from someone who may want to kill her."

"Someone wants to kill her?"

Reminding himself that no one except his grandfather Brevoorts knew about the murder of James W. Mason, or the reason behind Eugenia disappearing, he sat forward, taking a few minutes to fill Chase in, but only after he got Chase's solemn word that he'd not breathe a word about what was disclosed to anyone. When Arthur was done, Chase got to his feet and began pacing about the room.

"If I'm understanding correctly, there's a chance Eugenia might believe you murdered her grandfather, although you believe it's a small chance, and yet you think she's going to agree to marry you? Have you lost your mind?"

"I'm sure I can convince her I wasn't responsible for her grandfather's death. After that, I'll then convince her that I can keep her safe."

"You just told me she left Montana in the company of her bodyguard, Ivan something or other. Seems to me a bodyguard would be more than up for the task of keeping Eugenia safe."

"A bodyguard is not the same as a husband."

Chase retook his seat. "A valid point, since a bodyguard can be sent away at night, whereas Eugenia would be stuck with you—

something she might not be keen about, especially if underneath her practicality is a lady who wants to marry for love."

"Eugenia never struck me as a romantic at heart. I doubt she's ever harbored any longings for love."

"Most people long for love."

"I don't."

Chase waved that aside. "That's because your heart was broken at a tender age. However, there's absolutely no reason for you to close yourself off to the idea of marrying for love. Why, I would suggest that instead of pursuing Eugenia Howland—if you can even find her—you try your luck at discovering love during the New York Season. I'm sure somewhere amid all the young ladies out this year is someone you could fall in love with. And if you embrace that charming attitude you usually adopt with the ladies, one you apparently abandoned while dealing with the Widow Holbrooke, I'm sure some eligible young lady out there will fall in love with you in return."

"Did someone mention a widow, and if so, may I dare hope her mourning days are soon to be behind her?"

The sound of a cane thumping on the wooden floor heralded the arrival of Arthur's maternal grandfather, Mr. Lloyd Brevoorts, into the library. Lloyd paused right past the threshold, gesturing with his cane to Chase, who abandoned his chair and strode to his grandfather's side. When he tried to take hold of Lloyd's arm, though, Lloyd gave him a bit of a whack with the cane.

"I'm not ancient, boy," Lloyd barked, earning a grimace from Chase in return.

"I was merely trying to help you across the library, something I assumed you wanted me to do when you waved your cane my way."

"You were sitting in my favorite chair," Lloyd said as he thumped his way to the chair Chase had vacated and sat down. He immediately leveled an expectant eye on Arthur. "The widow?"

Arthur grinned. "One would think with all the widows you're already squiring around town that you wouldn't have the time or interest in becoming acquainted with another one, Grandfather.

And before you argue that point, know that Mrs. Holbrooke is not a woman you'd find enjoyable. She's argumentative and exceedingly forthright, and I didn't get the impression she's old enough for you, although I can't be sure about that because she never removed her mourning veils while I was in her company."

"She sounds feisty. Your grandmother, God rest her soul, was feisty. I enjoy that quality in a woman."

"Feistiness is one thing, but Mrs. Holbrooke keeps a pistol at the ready, and she seems to know how to handle it."

"A take-charge type of lady appeals to me as well," Lloyd said, his lips twitching before he gave Arthur a thorough looking-over. "It doesn't appear you've actually suffered another shooting, which means this Widow Holbrooke has a sense of restraint about her, which is another stellar characteristic in my humble opinion, and good thing for that. Your mother was beside herself after she learned you were shot, what was it now—at least seven years ago?"

"Mother wouldn't have known I'd been shot if someone, that being you, hadn't walked in on me when I was changing my bandages after I returned to New York and decided to inform her of what was really only a minor injury done to my arm."

Chase hauled a chair right next to Arthur's and sat down. "You told me you were accidentally shot while trying to intervene in a heated fight between two of your miners."

"I wasn't very well going to admit that I'd been shot by Eugenia Howland, and on the very day her grandfather died."

"How can you honestly think that a woman who shot you is going to want to marry you?"

"What's this about marriage?" Lloyd demanded.

Chase crossed his arms over his chest. "Arthur has decided to marry Eugenia Howland, if he can find her, something he's been unsuccessful with. His luck is unlikely to change, now that he's apparently annoyed the ladies of the Bleecker Street Inquiry Agency."

"I've merely suffered a *misunderstanding* with that agency. I'm sure I'll be able to remedy that just as soon as I muster up the courage to talk to Eunice Holbrooke again."

Lloyd leaned forward. "Eunice Holbrooke being that feisty widow you were talking about?"

"The one who threatened me with a pistol two days ago, yes."

"Sounds to me, if the lady brought out a pistol, that you suffered more than a misunderstanding," Lloyd said. "What did you do to incur her wrath?"

"I didn't do *anything* wrath-worthy." Arthur blew out a breath. "The animosity she immediately turned my way was peculiar to say the least. And if she'd not taken an immediate dislike to me, I'd have likely verified by now that an agent employed by the agency might have seen Eugenia around the city at some point."

"Why do you say that?" Chase asked.

"Because Miss Judith Donovan, one of the agents—or at least I think she could be considered an agent even though she spends her days painting instead of doing investigation work—had a very interesting reaction to the flyer of Eugenia I showed her. She claimed her look of astonishment was a result of being artistically inspired by Eugenia's face, but I think she's seen Eugenia before. Unfortunately, before I could press her on the matter, a client stumbled into the room, mistook me for an agent, and demanded I get her sister, who'd been unjustly committed to Blackwell's Island Insane Asylum, released."

Lloyd exchanged a smile with Chase. "I feel the distinct urge to visit this inquiry agency simply for the drama that happens there."

"Indeed," Chase agreed. "It would have been amusing to see Arthur's reaction to being mistaken for an inquiry agent." Chase turned one of his bright smiles on Arthur. "You do make a most intimidating impression on most people, and I bet if you were to visit the asylum, they'd release that woman to you with few questions asked."

"I'm not traveling to Blackwell's Island Insane Asylum to seek the release of some woman's sister."

"It might have Eunice Holbrooke keener to take on your case if you take the burden of this case off of them."

"From what little I know of Eunice Holbrooke, my interference would more than likely have me facing the end of her pistol again."

Lloyd laughed and thumped his cane on the floor as he stood. "I'm going to have to meet this woman." He settled an amused expression on Arthur. "Speaking of ladies, though, I'd keep that idea about marrying Eugenia Howland quiet for now. Your mother is hopeful you'll agree to stay in the city for the Season. She's been whispering in the ears of fellow society matrons that it's past time you found a bride."

Arthur rose to his feet. "Which is exactly why I should tell her I'm determined to marry Eugenia before society gets in a dither over learning another eligible gentleman may be on the marriage mart soon, even if that gentleman happens to be a second son."

Lloyd exchanged a glance with Chase. "Sounds like your brother is still holding a grudge over what happened with Mitzi years ago."

"I just broached the subject of Mitzi breaking his twenty-year-old heart when she turned down his proposal of marriage, but he deftly avoided the subject." Chase shook his head. "That means he's still harboring sensitive feelings about that matter."

"I'm not a man prone to sensitive feelings, and Mitzi didn't break my heart, just wounded it," Arthur argued. "She did, however, do serious injury to my pride when she told me she found me lacking because I was a second son with only reasonable prospects. Since she then announced to society the very next day that she was marrying Mr. Thomas Gibson, a firstborn son and heir to the Gibson millions, I was placed in the unenviable role of rejected suitor, since I'd been foolish enough to let many of my friends know that Mitzi and I would one day be married." He caught Chase's eye. "And that right there is why I wouldn't have expected to find love if I were still intending to pursue an incomparable. Ladies who earn that particular title, quite like Mitzi, are not searching for marriages of love, but marriages of advantage."

"A rather harsh conclusion for all the ladies in society," Chase returned. "You've gotten incredibly cynical over the years."

"He has at that," Lloyd said. "But since we're hardly likely to get him to change his attitude, I'd like to return to the subject of Eugenia Howland." He caught Arthur's eye. "I highly doubt she'll agree to marry you, but I think she needs to be found so you can apprise her of the situation in Montana. If anything will convince her to return to claim her inheritance, it'll be learning her relatives want her declared dead." He frowned. "Do you have a clear idea of when they were going to have that happen?"

"I believe they were intending on making it official on Eugenia's twenty-eighth birthday, which is only a few weeks from now."

Lloyd rubbed his chin. "That really doesn't leave much time, which is why I suppose I'm going to have to offer you my assistance in the matter of the Bleecker Street Inquiry Agency."

"What kind of assistance?"

"I'll use the same charm that has charmed more than one society widow, which may convince them to hear you out instead of shooting you when you arrive on their doorstep again." Lloyd smiled. "I guarantee that five minutes after making the acquaintances of the ladies of the Bleecker Street Inquiry Agency, they will offer to take on your case, if only to show their appreciation of my charming nature."

CHAPTER
Ten

"It's a good thing you didn't place a bet on charming the ladies of the Bleecker Street Inquiry Agency within five minutes, Grandfather," Arthur said, pulling out his pocket watch. "We've now been sitting in the receiving room for thirty-seven minutes. Add in the notion that Miss Elsy Evans barely took our names before she disappeared down the hallway, and I'm afraid there's little chance your charm is going to have any effect on these particular ladies, given that they don't seem interested in speaking with us."

Lloyd waved that aside. "I'm sure all the agents are merely busy with other cases. You mark my words, as soon as we're ushered into an office, we'll be in business."

"Or an agent is going to appear, pistol in hand, if they've been told Arthur is persona non grata," Chase muttered before he turned back to the painting Judith Donovan had claimed was the inspiration behind her decision to paint abstract portraits. "Is it just me, or does this painting resemble a very unusual goat to either of you?"

"It's a self-portrait of the woman who painted it," Arthur said, stowing his pocket watch away. "The artist goes by the name of Etta, although I have no idea who that is because Judith Donovan got distracted with my cheekbones and stopped talking to me."

He stepped up next to Chase and took a moment to peruse the portrait. The longer he looked at it, though, the more certain he was that he'd seen the artist's work before, but before he could figure out where he'd seen an Etta painting, the sound of the front door opening and footsteps tapping across the wooden floor distracted him.

Miss Judith Donovan, who had a smear of yellow paint on her cheek with a green smear traversing the length of the apron she was wearing, skidded to a stop the moment her gaze settled on Arthur. "Mr. Livingston, what rotten timing—or rather, ah, pleasant surprise to see you here."

Arthur's brow quirked. "Rotten timing?"

Judith winced. "Pardon me?"

"I thought I heard you say rotten timing."

Judith gave a wave of a paint-spattered hand. "I'm sure I didn't mean to say that out loud, but since I apparently did, it's, ah, rotten timing because I wasn't expecting to find potential clients in the waiting room. I'm only here to fetch my sketchbook and then dash back to the boardinghouse because I left my paints out. That means, if you'll excuse me, I have to dash." Without allowing him a chance to respond, Judith spun on her heel and raced out of the room.

"That went well," Chase said as he took a seat. "I don't believe I've ever seen a lady flee from you before."

"I suppose it's not very grandfatherly of me to admit that I found that amusing, but that was very amusing indeed," Lloyd said, his eyes twinkling. "I had a feeling with you back in the city that life would turn more exciting than the teas I normally attend." His eyes turned wistful. "I was hoping to at least enjoy a nice canter in Central Park today. But since you left Wyatt in Montana for some unknown reason, and your mother doesn't seem to believe my leg has healed enough for me to ride a horse yet, I'll have to content myself with this trip to a very unusual agency to appease the longing I've been feeling for an honest-to-goodness adventure."

Arthur frowned. "I left Wyatt in Montana because he's responsible for the damage done to your leg. I didn't want to risk having you decide to have another go on him by bringing him with me to New York again. You're eighty-two years old. A man your age has no business getting on a horse like Wyatt."

Lloyd waved that aside. "You're beginning to sound exactly like your mother, which is not a compliment. She's been lecturing me for months about the inadvisability of riding Wyatt, but you can bet your last dollar that I'll be having another go on him. He and I were just about to get to an understanding when I fell off him."

"You didn't fall off him. Wyatt tossed you off, so the only understanding you can get out of that is the notion that he didn't want you to ride him in the first place."

Before Lloyd could argue that point, Chase sat forward. "That photograph you carry around of Eugenia Howland—isn't she sitting on a horse named Wyatt?"

"She is, and before you ask, it's the same horse," Arthur said. "One of Eugenia's relatives, Mr. Raymond Mason, got nipped by the beast not long after Eugenia left town. Raymond decided he was going to sell Wyatt to a horse factory, and since I didn't think Eugenia would appreciate her horse being slaughtered, I bought him. Raymond is Eugenia's great-uncle, being James Mason's younger brother, and he didn't hesitate to sell me the horse, perfectly content to take my money for something that didn't actually belong to him."

"Maybe we should tell the ladies at this agency that," Lloyd said. "They may feel more charitable toward you if they learn you saved Eugenia's horse."

"Couldn't hurt."

"But don't mention that you left Wyatt back in Montana, presumably in the care of people who wanted to send him off to a slaughterhouse," Chase added.

"I left him in the care of Miss Hazel Mason, James's youngest sister. She likes Wyatt, and oddly enough, Wyatt tolerates her."

"How old is this Miss Hazel Mason?" Lloyd asked, his eyes

sparkling. "Or better yet, how is it that I've never made her acquaintance when I've come to visit you in Montana?"

Arthur wasn't certain if he should laugh or shake his head. "Hazel is probably seventy, and you haven't met her because she spends a lot of time traveling around the West, searching for unique items to put in the new businesses she's been responsible for opening in Butte. However, before you get any romantic ideas, she's a confirmed spinster and happy to embrace that state."

"That's because she hasn't met me," Lloyd said right as Miss Elsy Evans strode into the room.

"Forgive me, gentlemen, I fear time got away from me. How may I be of assistance to you today?"

Arthur rose to his feet. "We're here to speak with Eunice Holbrooke."

"Oh, that's unfortunate, Mr. . . . was it Livingston?"

He was relatively certain, given the time they'd been left to cool their heels in the receiving room, that Miss Elsy Evans knew exactly who he was. But because he didn't want to chance having her pull out a pistol if he voiced that accusation, he summoned up a smile. "That's right, Miss Evans. I'm Mr. Arthur Livingston. This is my grandfather, Mr. Lloyd Brevoorts, and this is my brother, Chase Livingston."

"How delightful to make all of your acquaintances," Elsy said, beaming a smile all around, her attention settling on Lloyd. "And Mr. Brevoorts, I believe we've met before. I'm—"

"Mrs. Derbyshire's companion," Lloyd finished for her with a charming smile as he limped his way closer, took hold of her hand, and kissed it. "How lovely to see you again, Miss Evans. I had no idea you worked at this inquiry agency."

"It's lovely to see you as well, Mr. Brevoorts, and yes, I hold down more than one position."

"I imagine being a paid companion to the society set gives you incredibly helpful access to gossip around the city, gossip that must come in handy with solving some of your cases."

Elsy wagged a finger Lloyd's way. "That's classified information, although it's exceptionally astute on your part to suggest such a thing. But allow me to deftly change the subject and say that Mrs. Derbyshire speaks very highly of you, although"—Elsy leaned closer—"a word of caution. She's currently, shall we say, put out with you. It seems you told her your leg was bothering you last Thursday during a luncheon at Mrs. Fish's residence, which was why you couldn't escort her while she did a bout of shopping on the Ladies' Mile after the luncheon. Mrs. Derbyshire has since learned you went driving in Central Park with Mrs. Manchester that day."

Lloyd's smile dimmed. "How . . . unfortunate."

"Indeed. Mrs. Derbyshire was so put out with you that she may have shredded the lovely note you penned her the day before, the one where you proclaimed your deepest admiration for her."

Lloyd winced. "Do you imagine Mrs. Derbyshire may become less put out with me if I explained to her that I went driving with Mrs. Manchester because I knew it would not be as taxing as shopping would have been on my poor, yet-to-be-completely-healed leg that was recently broken—in two spots, mind you."

"I don't know if that *would* soothe Mrs. Derbyshire's annoyance with you because I'm relatively certain she would have been perfectly content to abandon her shopping to go driving with you." Elsy took hold of Lloyd's hand. "If I may offer a word of advice?"

"I'm all ears."

"Mrs. Derbyshire is partial to daffodils. You may want to send her a lovely bouquet as well as an invitation to drive through Central Park at your earliest convenience."

"I'll pen her an invitation later today."

Elsy gave Lloyd's hand a pat. "You might also want to consider paring down the list of widows you squire about town." She shook her head. "While these ladies present themselves to society as kind and gentle souls, they're nothing of the sort. Your welfare may be placed in serious jeopardy if they band together."

Lloyd gave Elsy's fingers a kiss. "Thank you, my dear. I appreciate your candor since your advice may spare me another broken limb, were I forced to flee through the city from an angry mob of widows." He arched a brow Arthur's way. "You won't mind if I tag along with you to Montana and stay for a month or so, will you? That should be plenty of time to allow tempers to cool, while still allowing me time to enjoy a good portion of the Season when I return to the city."

"If I don't locate Eugenia Howland, I'll have no reason to stay in Montana and will only be there to pick up Wyatt and make sure there's no pressing business matters to attend to with Mason Mines."

"Then I say it's of the utmost importance for us to locate Eugenia with all due haste." Lloyd turned another charming smile on Elsy. "That's actually why we're here, my dear. Arthur apparently made a muck of matters when he met with Eunice Holbrooke and Daphne Henderson two days ago. I'm here to rectify any misunderstandings that may have occurred, so would you please tell Mrs. Holbrooke that Mr. Brevoorts is here to speak with her?"

"Eunice is not here."

"When is she expected to return?" Arthur asked.

Elsy narrowed her eyes on him. "Suffice it to say, she's unavailable for the foreseeable future."

Given the less-than-pleasant tone Elsy was now using with him, there was little doubt that Chase had been right and Arthur was, indeed, persona non grata.

"And isn't that simply a shame Mrs. Holbrooke is unavailable," Lloyd said, another charming smile on his face. "But what about Mrs. Herman Henderson? I would adore meeting her in person because she's one of my favorite authors."

"And while I'll be certain to pass along your praise to Daphne, I'm afraid she isn't here either." Elsy smiled a sweet smile, which Arthur wasn't buying for a minute. "I'll be sure to leave a note for Eunice and Daphne, telling them of your visit today. If they want to continue discussing the Eugenia Howland case with you, I assure you they'll send a note in return."

"That would be lovely," Lloyd said. "But if it wouldn't be too much of a bother, we wouldn't mind waiting in this lovely receiving room until one of them returns. As luck would have it, we don't have anything of a pressing nature on our schedule today."

When Elsy didn't immediately dismiss his grandfather's suggestion, instead sending Lloyd a somewhat exasperated look, but one that also held a touch of resignation in it, Arthur thought he detected a sliver of victory in the air, which disappeared in a flash when Judith came striding into the room, her sketchbook under her arm. She sent Elsy a rather telling arch of a brow, an arch that was met by a look of disbelief from Elsy in return.

"I thought we agreed it would be for the best for you to return to the boardinghouse, and through the back door," Arthur heard Elsy mutter under her breath.

"You were floundering."

Instead of responding to that, Elsy took hold of Judith's arm and began heading out of the receiving room. "If you'll excuse me, gentlemen," she said over her shoulder, "I need to have a word with my associate."

"You better do something—and quickly," Lloyd whispered. "They're getting away."

"Miss Donovan, I have a few minutes to spare if you'd like to finish sketching my face" was all Arthur could think to call out, which, to his surprise, had Judith shrugging out of Elsy's hold and spinning around.

"What a lovely offer, Mr. Livingston, and—"

"Absolutely not," Elsy said, taking hold of Judith's arm again and giving her a tug.

"There's no need to worry. I'll be fast," Judith said. "Two minutes is all I need, and I've been dying to have another go at sketching his eyes. I'm afraid my first attempt didn't give me the results I wanted."

"Two minutes may very well be two minutes too many."

Judith ignored that as she bustled toward him, gesturing to a chair that was placed by the window. "If you would be so kind as to sit there, I'll get right to work."

Delighted with this unforeseen turn of events, Arthur took a seat right as Judith plopped down on the rug, plucked a pencil from the back of the bun she'd fashioned at the nape of her neck, then turned her attention to his face. "If you'll recall, Mr. Livingston, the last time I sketched you, I was hoping for a dreamy look. I hope you'll be more cooperative about that today."

A sense of impending doom began descending over him because he knew if he couldn't summon up a dreamy look, there was every chance Judith would show him the door before he could ask her about Eugenia.

He closed his eyes, summoned up an image of his favorite dish, which was lobster in a bisque sauce, and opened his eyes, finding Judith considering him closely.

"Dreamy enough?" he finally asked.

"It's not, well, a romantic type of dreamy. More along the lines of how people look when they're savoring a favorite dish."

Arthur shot a look to his grandfather, who sent him a barely perceptible nod before he cleared his throat and stepped toward Judith.

"We haven't been introduced, but I'm Mr. Lloyd Brevoorts, and that strapping young man over there is Mr. Chase Livingston, Arthur's brother. Not that Chase will mention this because it embarrasses him, but there have been many artists scrambling to sketch *his* face over the years, something to do with how symmetrical his features are."

As a strategy to keep Judith in the room, it was brilliant, even though Elsy obviously didn't think so, given the look of horror on her face as Judith immediately set her sights on Chase. She pulled another chair next to Arthur and waved Chase forward. "If you don't mind, Mr. Livingston?"

"It would be my pleasure," Chase said, sitting down as Judith plopped down on the floor again and began sketching.

After everyone got settled, Lloyd settled a smile on Judith. "If we could return to the topic of Mrs. Holbrooke and Mrs. Henderson," he began. "While I understand that your agency may not be comfortable telling us where they are, I don't believe it would hurt to let us know when they'll be back."

"I would hazard to guess they won't be back anytime soon," Judith said before she settled a frown on Arthur. "Your brother has adopted the look I'm trying to achieve with you. If you could muster up the same look, I'd appreciate it."

Arthur shot a look to Chase, knowing he'd never in his entire life had such a pleasant, and yes, slightly dreamy expression on his face. "Perhaps you should concentrate on Chase's face for now."

To his relief, Judith turned her full attention to his brother and began sketching as Lloyd directed a determined eye Judith's way.

"When you say they won't be back anytime soon," Lloyd began, "does that mean they won't be returning until later this afternoon, or did you mean they might not return today at all?"

A grunt was her only reply to that.

Lloyd's brows drew together, probably because he wasn't accustomed to ladies grunting at him. He squared his shoulders and turned to Elsy. "I must thank you again for your wonderful advice regarding the widows. And because it does seem prudent for me to escape the city soon, I wonder if you could at least give me a time frame on when Mrs. Henderson or Mrs. Holbrooke may be returning to the agency."

Elsy rubbed a forehead that had apparently begun to ache, and no wonder. Being the object of gentlemen intent on answers had to be somewhat taxing on a person. "I have no idea when Eunice will return because she's working on a case. As for Daphne, she's currently under the weather, so it's questionable as to when she'll be returning as well."

Lloyd began tsking under his breath. "I'm very sorry to hear that Mrs. Henderson is under the weather. It's been my experience that ladies enjoy being taken soup when they're in that condition. I imagine she would appreciate the soup my daughter's cook makes. It's chicken based but not too heavy, and I swear it's made me feel right as rain after eating a bowl or two of it."

Elsy stopped rubbing her forehead. "You're a very charming

gentleman, Mr. Brevoorts—perhaps too charming—and that was a lovely offer. However, I wouldn't encourage getting within a mile of Daphne right now. She was tossing up her accounts yesterday morning in a manner that suggests she's probably not feeling up to visitors yet."

"She also isn't in town because her husband insisted they travel to their Hudson estate so that Daphne wouldn't be tempted to join Eunice on her undercover mission," Judith added, looking up from her sketchpad and blinking somewhat owlishly at Elsy when that lady let out a snort.

"I believe your two minutes are up, Judith," Elsy said with a less-than-discreet nod toward the door. "You did mention you were concerned about the paints you left out, so . . . ?"

Judith gave Chase's face a final lingering look before she shut her sketchpad and sighed. "I suppose you're right, so off to the boardinghouse I go. If you'll excuse me, gentlemen?"

Arthur rose from the chair and offered Judith a hand up from the floor. "I'd be more than happy to return tomorrow to sit for you again, as would Chase."

Judith's eyes began to gleam, but before she could agree to his offer, Elsy had her by the arm again. "You told me you have an art class tomorrow, the one you're looking forward to because the topic centers around abstract portraits." Elsy gestured to the Etta painting hanging behind them. "I'm certain you'd miss having an opportunity to discuss abstract artists with your artist friends."

Judith gave a rather reluctant nod before she frowned. "I almost forgot. I was going to take that painting with me tomorrow." She turned to Arthur. "Would you mind being a dear and taking it down for me? I only recently brought that painting from the boardinghouse to hang here as a source of inspiration for me when I attend to the receiving room. I hung it higher than I normally would so I could see it to advantage, but I'm afraid I'm not tall enough to get it off the wall without a ladder."

Wanting to keep in Judith's good graces for as long as possible, Arthur moved to the painting, considering it for a moment as he decided how best to get it off the wall without damaging it. A second later, and from out of nowhere, an image of another painting flashed to mind, done in the same abstract fashion.

Pieces of the puzzle regarding the odd behavior he'd received from the ladies of the Bleecker Street Inquiry Agency began falling into place.

He turned and arched a brow at Judith and Elsy. "Before I take my leave or take this painting from the wall, I'd like to know how your agency has possession of a painting done by an artist whose work I've just now recalled was hanging in a house in Montana—Eugenia Howland's house, to be exact."

Elsy blinked. "How extraordinary that an Etta painting would also be hanging in Eugenia Howland's house."

"And far too coincidental, if you ask me." Arthur returned his gaze to the painting as another thought began forming in his mind, one he'd not contemplated until just then and certainly couldn't ignore. He turned to Lloyd. "I'm afraid I may be a complete idiot because—"

The rest of his sentence was interrupted when a lady barreled into the receiving room, her hat askew and her cloak buttoned improperly.

"I've come for an update," the lady declared, stopping when her attention settled on Arthur. "Oh, it's you. Are you here for an update on your case as well?"

"Mrs. Eastman," he said, presenting her with a bow. "How lovely to see you again, and no, I'm not here for an update, not exactly."

"Then you won't mind if I ask these ladies for a report before you finish whatever business you have here, will you? I fear I've been in a dither all morning wondering if any progress has been made with locating my sister."

Arthur frowned. "The agency took on your case?"

"Indeed, and Mrs. Holbrooke is personally seeing to the matter." Mrs. Eastman turned to Elsy. "Have you had any word from her yet? Was she able to gain entrance to Blackwell's Island Insane Asylum?"

As Elsy began looking horrified again, Arthur couldn't hold back a smile since the perfect solution to his problem had presented itself in the form of Mrs. Eastman.

He inclined his head to Elsy and Judith. "Ladies, it's been a pleasure, but now I believe it's time for us to take our leave."

"But we don't have any answers to the questions we've asked," Lloyd said.

"True, but what we do have is Eunice Holbrooke's location, and I've just had a revelation that might explain everything. But I can only prove my revelation is correct by running Eunice Holbrooke to ground."

"That, well, ah, would not be advisable," Elsy sputtered. "Eunice will not appreciate it if you blow her cover, which means you cannot, under any circumstances, try to run her to ground."

"I'm afraid I have no choice but to do exactly that, especially when I believe there could be a good chance Eunice Holbrooke knows exactly where to find Eugenia Howland. In fact, I would think she's been in *very* close contact with her for years."

As Elsy and Judith exchanged horrified looks, Arthur turned to Lloyd and Chase. "Gentlemen, we must be on our way, because Blackwell's Island Insane Asylum awaits us, as does a woman I have no intention of allowing to slip from my grasp again."

CHAPTER
Eleven

"Eunice, thank goodness," Ann whispered as she edged closer to where Eunice was waiting in a long line of women to go into breakfast. "I was just about to contact Cooper and Ivan and ask for their assistance getting you out of that locked room. Thankfully, here you are, but perhaps we should consider abandoning this particular plan and develop another one to get Mrs. Mills released because"—Ann's nose wrinkled as she looked her up and down—"you're a mess."

"I'm sure I've looked better," Eunice said, pulling the tattered sleeve of her mourning gown over fingers that were practically frozen.

"What happened to you? Where are your veils, why's your hair straggling around your shoulders, how is it that you managed to avoid trading in your widow's weeds, and why did you get thrown into isolation in the first place? You cannot imagine my alarm when I learned you'd been locked away."

Eunice patted hair she knew was looking downright frightful. "Nurse Grady forgot to leave me with a change of clothing after she locked me into a room. The nurse who let me out this morning was quite put out about that but not put out enough to where she was willing to fetch me other clothing." She shoved a strand of tangled hair out of her eyes. "As for what happened to my hair, Dr. Franklin tore the veils from my head. I didn't have an opportunity to reclaim my veils or pins before the good doctor—and I use that term loosely—decided I needed time in isolation because I was clearly, and I quote, 'mad as a hatter.' He was seemingly under the belief that time alone would improve my overwrought state, but were I mad, in my humble opinion, that would have only increased the problem, not diminished it."

"I'm not surprised by the doctor's diagnosis," Ann admitted. "I've been speaking with the other nurses on the two floors they've had me working on, and every woman committed here is considered insane, even though a number of the patients I've encountered don't seem insane at all."

"I've gotten that same impression." Eunice brushed some dirt from her sleeve. "I've been wondering if these doctors get paid by the number of patients they have committed or if they're simply grossly incompetent." Eunice shook her head. "However, even though I'd love to pursue the answers to all the troubling questions I have, I vowed last night that I would attempt to not draw further notice, although I'm certain that's going to be difficult if I run across Nurse Grady again. That woman needs someone to take her down a peg or two."

"That someone definitely shouldn't be you. That'll get you sent over to the Lodge for certain." Ann shuddered. "I'm beginning to think Ivan was right and we're not prepared for this case. It never crossed my mind that you'd get thrown into isolation, and I couldn't help wonder what you were doing in there for what . . . eighteen hours?"

"Eighteen hours, thirty-six minutes to be exact. As for what I was doing, I spent the first hour raging against the injustice that had been mounted against me, using the small notepad I'd stuck in my stockings to jot down notes about the ridiculous exam I was forced to undergo. Honestly, Ann, what legitimate diagnosis could possibly be arrived at pertaining to a person's sanity by looking at that person's tongue?"

"I'd be curious to learn the answer to that as well."

"Quite. However, after I realized my temper was getting the better of me when I was jotting down notes about Nurse Grady and her lack of compassion with women who are in a most vulnerable state, I decided I needed a distraction, especially if I wanted to keep my vow of going unnoticed after I got released from my cell. I pulled one of the sandwiches Alma insisted I bring from where I'd stashed it in a pocket in my petticoats, and while I ate it, I took an hour to compose a lesson to teach the children at St. Luke's Chapel the next time I'm asked to fill in for one of the regular teachers."

"I didn't know you taught at St. Luke's Chapel. Frankly, I'm curious as to why anyone at St. Luke's would suggest you teach children. Don't you frighten them half to death with your rather spooky appearance?"

"While I do teach children at St. Luke's, they're not afraid of me because I don't wear my veils when I'm teaching." She smiled. "Reverend Patrick Danford is the one who suggested I teach Sunday school after we became good friends over the past year. He was concerned I was spending too much time beneath my veils as well as too much time on my own, hence the request to teach at his church. He assured me that it would be safe to remove them within the confines of St. Luke's. I couldn't resist that, nor could I resist the opportunity to immerse myself in a house of worship, because my opportunities to attend church were limited in Montana, what with how my grandfather didn't have much use for God."

A nurse suddenly swept past them, stopped, spun around, and settled a scowl on Ann. "That patient isn't appropriately dressed."

Ann waved the complaint aside. "The widow's weeds comfort her, but speaking of comfort . . ." She gestured to the open windows that were allowing a stiff breeze to swirl around the hallway. "Someone apparently thought the day was to be warmer, but I think the patients would be more comfortable if those windows were closed."

"Fresh air is good for the patients."

"True, but many of them might come down with an illness since none of them are dressed for chilly conditions."

Instead of replying to that, the nurse turned on her heel and strode past dozens of shivering women, not stopping until she reached the dining room door. She pulled a large key ring from her pocket and struggled to fit one of the keys into the door that would finally allow the women into the dining room.

"I'm going to have to rethink the Bible verse I settled on for my lesson with the children," Eunice muttered as they began to shuffle forward. "I was considering centering a lesson around a verse from Ecclesiastes—'Be not hasty in thy spirit to be angry: for anger resteth in the bosom of fools.' However, after seeing the hostile environment and blatant disregard for the care of the patients these nurses display, I'm certain my anger is warranted." She shoved another strand of hair out of her face. "Maybe I'll need to find a verse that deals with injustice and how one is expected to deal with injustice in a calm and deliberate fashion."

"It's certainly becoming a trial to remain calm," Ann said, taking all of three steps forward before stopping when another nurse walked out of the dining room and announced that breakfast was going to be delayed, something to do with the tea not being ready. "I hope you're not hungry, because from what I witnessed during the meals that were served yesterday, you're going to find whatever is on the menu to be less than edible."

"Alma sent me with three sandwiches. Although seeing these poor women, I'm feeling guilty for eating them instead of sharing."

"That might have caused a riot." Ann pulled the thin nurse's cape she was wearing close as a gust of wind blew through one of the open windows. "The nurses don't take kindly to any type of insubordination. I witnessed that yesterday while I was assisting patients from hall eight taking a bath. Let us hope we'll be able to get out of here before your hall is called to bathe, because there's only one tub, the water is not changed after a woman is done having water thrown over her and being scrubbed with soap, and towels are in short supply."

"How many women use the same bathwater?"

"The hall I helped with yesterday had forty-six women in it."

"*Forty-six* women used the same bathwater?"

"They did. It's awful, as is the treatment the women receive if they balk at getting into the tub." Ann's eyes glistened with unshed tears. "Some nurses held a woman by the name of Mary underneath the water for at least twenty seconds after she refused to sit down in the tub. I was afraid they were going to drown her and was just getting ready to intervene when they let her up. Needless to say, none of the other patients hesitated to climb into the tub of their own volition."

"Would you have been able to find Cooper and Ivan, had you intervened and needed reinforcements?"

"They've stationed themselves on the side of this building, pretending to attend to the bushes there. They spent the night there, wanting to be close in case you needed them. Ivan was fit to be tied when I told him you'd been locked in a room. He was going to get you released last night but agreed to wait after he learned I was given a cot in a room shared by night nurses on the same floor you were on. That made it possible for me to wander down your hallway every hour to make certain you were safe."

"I was safe unless there'd been a fire. I can't see Nurse Grady taking the time to unlock the door for me if she thought her own life was at stake."

"A disturbing thought, as is the fact that all the patients are locked in at night."

"But if there *was* a fire, how would they get all the women out?"

"I don't think they could, but . . ." Ann stopped talking as the women began inching forward again, a nurse having appeared in the hallway and gestured them into the dining hall. "Before we get parted again, which I'm sure we're soon to be because my services will probably be needed elsewhere, I didn't make any progress locating Mrs. Mills. I tried to question the nurses last night, but when I asked about new arrivals, they told me it's impossible to remember names because there are so many patients here and they change floors all the time."

"Nurse Emerson. Stop chatting and come help us get these women in order," a nurse barked from the doorway. "They're to go in two by two, but clearly that's beyond their mental capacities."

"I think you're Nurse Emerson," Eunice muttered.

"For a moment there, I forgot," Ann said before she hurried forward, helping women form a less-than-straight line and stepping in to intervene after a nurse gave a resounding slap to a woman who'd begun wandering aimlessly.

Resisting the urge to stride forward and give the nurse a slap of her own, Eunice took the arm of a woman who was looking around in confusion, her faded blue eyes widening when her gaze settled on Eunice.

"Do I know you?" the woman asked.

"I've only just arrived. I'm Eunice."

"And I'm . . ." The woman tilted her head. "I'm not sure who I am. Gertrude, maybe?"

"Gertrude is a lovely name, and I'd love to enjoy breakfast with a woman named Gertrude."

"We're having breakfast?"

"Soon," Eunice said as she walked into a dining hall that had a long table traversing the length of the room, with long benches placed on either side of the table. It was a cold and uninviting room, although it was surprisingly clean. Eunice's grip tightened on Gertrude's arm as all the other women started scrambling over the benches, trying to find a place to sit. None of the nurses, except for Ann, were trying to aid the women with finding a seat. Instead, they were gathered at a separate table, many of them calling out suggestions to Ann as she tried to get a woman to sit down.

"A good boxing of the ears might help," one called.

"Or just push her on the bench," another yelled.

Ann ignored them, bending close to the woman to whisper something in her ear, something that had the woman climbing over the bench and taking a seat, folding her hands demurely in her lap.

"Nice to see they've brought on a nurse that isn't quick with her fists," a woman said as Eunice helped Gertrude onto the bench before she sat down beside her.

Eunice shoved another strand of hair out of her face, wishing she'd had the foresight to stick some extra pins in with the sandwiches Alma had given her. "Do the nurses use physical force often?"

The woman nodded. "Thinks it helps them maintain order."

After learning the woman's name was Rose Santana, Eunice glanced around the table, seeing cups with a pinkish liquid, a substance Rose informed her was tea. Next to the tea were small plates with shriveled prunes, bread and butter, and that was it. Unfortunately, with no supervision from the nurses, many patients were grabbing as much bread as they could, leaving some patients without any bread at all.

She took the bread in front of her and handed it to Gertrude, who refused to eat it.

"You'd best eat it yourself," Rose said. "It'll be all you get until lunch, and lunch ain't much better."

"I think I'll just stick with the tea," Eunice said, handing the bread to Rose, who took it and grinned.

"The tea's worse than the bread."

One sip of tea proved Rose right. Setting aside the cup, Eunice frowned. "I take it there's no sugar added?"

"And no salt for any of the food. The nurses take home the salt that's meant for us, but don't say anything about that to them. That'll only earn you a slap and a stay in a room by yourself, or worse yet, a transfer to the Lodge."

At the mere mention of the Lodge, every woman within listening distance shivered.

"I'll be certain to stay mum about the salt. Would it be looked upon more favorably by the nurses if I were to commend them on how clean the dining room is?" Eunice asked.

Rose laughed. "Oh, that's rich, believing the nurses clean." She nodded around the table. "We're the ones to keep it clean, and mark my words, they'll soon have you on your hands and knees scrubbing the floor since you're new. They enjoy breaking in the new patients right from the start. Think it'll keep you in line."

"How delightful." Eunice leaned closer to Rose. "Speaking of new patients, you haven't met a new arrival by the name of Mrs. Clement Mills, have you?"

Rose peered at the patients gathered in the dining room before she nodded toward a woman sitting at the far end of the table. "That's her down there, but what do you want with Helen? She's completely lost her wits, she has, keeps telling everyone she's a woman of means. I told her just last night to stop doing that because she's providing the nurses with far too much enjoyment." Rose sent Eunice a knowing look. "They relish any opportunity to mock us."

Eunice twisted on the bench, craning her neck to get a better look at the woman Rose had pointed out. The lady was sniffling into her sleeve, not eating a bite of breakfast, but that might have been because the woman sitting next to her seemed to have absconded with Mrs. Mills's bread and prunes. She couldn't tell for certain because of the distance that separated them, but Mrs. Mills did seem to resemble her sister, Mrs. Eastman.

"What do you want with Helen?" Rose asked again.

"Ah, well, we shared the same doctor before we got sent here" was all Eunice could think to respond. "He suggested I try to befriend Mrs. Mills, thinking it would lend me comfort in my new environment."

"Why'd you get sent here?"

"I'm apparently suffering from acute melancholy and female hysteria. Why'd you get sent here?"

Rose released a grunt. "I had a disagreement with me landlord. The man said I didn't pay my rent eight months in a row, but I did. He punched me in the nose when I tried to shut the door in his face. I ain't one to suffer nonsense like that, so I punched him back. Before I knew it, I was carted away from my rented room, taken to Bellevue Hospital, deemed insane, and sent here."

"Returning a punch doesn't make you insane," Eunice said. "Have you no one to intercede on your behalf and get you out?"

"Not anyone who'd want to risk being shut up here as well."

As Rose returned to her bread and butter, Eunice returned her attention to Mrs. Mills, who was now hunched down over the table.

Eunice turned back to Rose. "Are the women allowed an opportunity to socialize at any point in the day?"

"Occasionally," Rose said, taking a slurp of her tea. "Sometimes the nurses will have someone play the piano for everyone, and during that time, we can talk to one another. Just depends on which nurse is in charge." She set aside her tea. "It would be nice if we got the piano time every day because it breaks up the hours, but the nurses don't like us gettin' too friendly with one another. They're afraid that'll give us ideas."

"Like escaping?"

"Shh . . ." Rose whispered. "You'll be sent to the Lodge for sure if anyone thinks you're planning to . . .well, you know. The *E* word."

Sending Rose a nod, Eunice spent the rest of mealtime in silence and was less than encouraged to discover that there was to be no socializing after the meal. Instead, all the women were expected to sit in silence on benches that seemed to grow harder by the second, none of them allowed to get up from the bench, even to use the retiring room.

Thankfully, after being made to sit in silence for over an hour, with anyone who spoke getting a swift slap from one of the few nurses who would occasionally walk up and down the table to check on everyone, a woman by the name of Nurse Riley clapped her hands, drawing everyone's attention.

"It's time to clean the hall." She scowled at the room at large. "I would urge all of you to remember what happened to Jane yesterday when she decided to dally instead of scrub the tables." Nurse Riley gestured to a woman sitting on the bench, her arms wrapped around herself and an ugly bruise staining her cheek.

"If you don't want to end up looking like Jane," Nurse Riley continued, "put your back into whatever task you're assigned. I assure you, if you don't, you'll be sorry."

CHAPTER
Twelve

Five minutes later, armed with a bucket and rag, Eunice was on her knees, scrubbing the floor, but making her way one swipe at a time toward Mrs. Mills, who was wiping down the table.

Waiting until she was only a foot away from the woman, Eunice squeezed the water from the rag, ignored that the soap was beginning to burn her hands, and lifted her head. "Mrs. Mills?"

Mrs. Mills stilled before she looked around, her attention settling on Eunice. "Are you speaking to me?"

"Are you Mrs. Clement Mills?"

"I am. How did you know that?"

"I need you to be very quiet as I explain, but know that I've been hired to get you freed from here."

Mrs. Mills abandoned her task and sat down on the bench. "You're here to get me out?"

"I'm going to try."

"Did Clement hire you?" Mrs. Mills asked, her voice trembling.

Eunice refused a sigh. "Forgive me for what I'm about to say, Mrs. Mills, but I have to ask if you're aware that your husband is the one who had you committed here."

Mrs. Mills waved that aside. "I'm not senile, dear. Clement *has* threatened to have me committed before, numerous times. I never thought he'd see his threats through, though, and I'm sure he's realized he's made a dreadful mistake. He may claim I annoy him with my endless chatter, but I know he misses me by now." She leaned closer. "He's a mere thirty years old, and young gentlemen often behave rashly. I fear he got testy when I told him he couldn't continue betting so much on the ponies. My first husband, God rest his soul, believed gambling was the quickest way to lose a fortune. Since I don't want Clement to lose my fortune, I decided to appeal to what I know is an intellectual, if slightly immature, mind and request that he abandon his gambling posthaste."

"Considering you've been committed to an asylum, you may have appealed more to that immature mind than the intellectual one."

"Well, indeed, but because he has now sent you to get me released, Clement has evidently realized how immature and rash his actions were."

"Clement didn't send me. Your sister did."

"Surely not."

"I'm afraid so. Mrs. Eastman recently paid a visit to my inquiry agency and was quite distressed because you'd disappeared. From what she told me, she only discovered your whereabouts after your husband bragged within earshot of your servants about how he'd finally taken care of you once and for all. At first, your poor sister thought he'd taken care of you permanently, until your maid overheard your husband telling one of his friends that if one pays enough, one can make problems disappear into an asylum."

"But surely Clement didn't know he was sending me to a place where indigent women go," Mrs. Mills said. "My husband has benefited tremendously from our marriage, and I would hope he had more consideration for me than to send me to this horrid place that's filled with women not of my social station."

Even though Eunice was quite accustomed to working with some of the wealthiest, and need she add snobbish, people in New York, the idea that Mrs. Mills seemed to be more affronted that she'd been tossed into an asylum that cared for indigent women than over the conditions the poor women were forced to endure set her teeth on edge. Reminding herself that Mrs. Mills had suffered a great shock, Eunice swallowed the retort she longed to make and opted for a gentler response.

"I'm sorry to say, but given Clement's actions, you've married a cruel, immature fortune hunter. And because of the differences in your ages, I have to wonder if it ever occurred to you that he might have ulterior motives when he asked you to marry him?"

"Clement didn't ask me to marry him. I asked him." Mrs. Mills's expression turned wistful. "He was such a dashing gentleman, you see, and very, well, virile, which is why I wanted to make him mine."

"I probably didn't need to know that. Although I suppose it's somewhat encouraging to learn you've at least enjoyed a, ah, robust romantic life with him."

To Eunice's surprise, Mrs. Mills's lip began to tremble. "He's never shown me his virile side. I only assume he has one because he keeps more than one mistress."

Eunice rubbed a now-chafed hand from the harsh soap over her face, stopping mid-rub when an interesting thought sprang to mind. "Are you saying that you and your husband have never spent any intimate time together?"

"We maintain separate bedchambers, even during the one and only trip I've taken with him for our honeymoon."

"But that's wonderful."

"My honeymoon wasn't wonderful in the least," Mrs. Mills argued. "In fact, it was quite dreadful, especially after I sought Clement out to question him about the matter of separate bedchambers and found him keeping company with one of the maids."

Eunice's brows drew together. "And you didn't consider seeking out an annulment from a man who clearly had no intention of making your marriage a proper marriage? Surely you know that a marriage that has never been consummated can be used as terms to seek out an annulment."

"I never said I wanted out of my marriage."

It took a great deal of effort to resist shaking some sense into the lady.

Getting up from the floor, Eunice sat down on the bench and took hold of Mrs. Mills's hand. "I know this is going to be difficult for you to accept, but your husband is a scoundrel. He didn't get you committed here by accident. I believe he had you committed to an asylum for indigent women to alleviate the risk of someone recognizing you, which might have happened if you'd been committed to a sanitorium. Those sanitoriums welcome visitors and have planned activities. One, the Long Island Home for Nervous Invalids, even allows its patients to keep their own gardens, believing gardening relaxes those with troubled constitutions." She gestured around the stark dining hall they were in. "There are no planned activities here, I've yet to see any visitors, and you're treated as a lunatic, mocked every time you tell someone you're a woman of means."

"I am a woman of means."

"Yes, but when you say that in a place like this, you're going to be considered mad, because I imagine it's a very unusual circumstance for a woman of means to find herself here."

"I suppose that is a valid point, but . . ." Mrs. Mills's expression grew wistful again. "Clement is such a handsome man, and I enjoy seeing the envy on ladies' faces when I go driving with him in the city, especially ladies from the New York Four Hundred." The wistfulness disappeared in a flash. "That illustrious group denied my first husband and me entrance into their midst, claiming our money was too new and our manners too common."

Eunice drew in a breath, reminding herself that being overly direct was not going to help the situation, even though Mrs. Mills didn't seem to grasp the gravity of what had happened to her.

"I need to make certain you understand a few very important things," Eunice began. "Your husband bribed someone to get you committed here. He did not intend for you to ever get out. I assure you that he's enjoying the freedom he's discovered since you've been here, and I guarantee you that he will not appreciate that freedom coming to an end. I run an inquiry agency, Mrs. Mills. I've seen things I never thought I'd see. If I get you out of here and you foolishly go back to him instead of seeking an annulment, he'll take steps to get you out of his life again—perhaps permanently."

Mrs. Mills's gaze sharpened on Eunice. "You believe he might have me killed?"

"I don't believe that's a stretch on my part because your death would allow him to spend your fortune however he sees fit."

"But . . ."

"Have you two decided to abandon your chores and have a nice leisurely talk instead?"

Turning on the bench, Eunice found Nurse Grady standing before her, a scowl on her face as she looked at Mrs. Mills before switching her attention to Eunice, her eyes narrowing to almost slits as she looked Eunice up and down. "Why are you still wearing those ridiculous widow's weeds?"

Eunice lifted her chin. "You didn't provide me with a change of clothing yesterday, and the nurse who let me out of my prison cell today couldn't be bothered."

"The nurse I had this morning wouldn't help me with my hair," Mrs. Mills said, giving her hair a pat. "She then called me 'Her Highness' and—"

"Shut. Up," Nurse Grady snapped before she followed her words with a resounding slap across Mrs. Mills's face.

The unwarranted attack on a defenseless woman left Eunice seeing red, any thought of remaining inconspicuous disappearing in a flash as she rose from the bench. "That's quite enough, Nurse Grady."

"What did you say to me?"

"I said, enough."

A second later, Nurse Grady lunged for her. It was only due to the reflexes she'd honed from her time spent boxing with Ivan that she was able to avoid the fist swinging her way.

Darting away from the bench, Eunice arched a brow. "You don't want to hit me. Unlike the other women incarcerated here, I assure you I'll hit back and it'll hurt."

Nurse Grady's face began to mottle. "How dare you speak to me in such a manner." She snapped her fingers and a group of nurses began to advance Eunice's way. "You've just earned yourself a place at the Lodge."

Eunice pushed up her sleeves. "I don't believe I'd care to visit the Lodge. In fact, I've had enough of this place. I've found what I came to find, and if I have to use force to get you to step aside, so be it."

It came as little surprise when Nurse Grady didn't bother to address a single thing she'd said and instead, snapped her fingers again, which had the rest of the nurses heading her way.

As the first nurse reached her and grabbed hold of Eunice's hair, instinct kicked in, as did every lesson Ivan had shared about how to handle oneself while in the midst of a brawl. It took a mere ten seconds to see the nurse flat on her back. Eunice's lips began curving into a less-than-amused smile when another nurse immediately stepped forward, that nurse's eyes flashing with temper as she brandished a fist that was already clenched.

CHAPTER
Thirteen

"Forgive me for keeping you waiting, Mr. Livingston," a gentleman wearing a dark suit said, stepping into the room where Arthur, Lloyd, and Chase had been escorted after telling a nurse they were at Blackwell's Island Insane Asylum to pay a visit to their dear friend Eunice Holbrooke. "The new patients I was examining were difficult cases. It took me longer than expected to assess their degrees of insanity. I'm Dr. Franklin."

"It's a pleasure to meet you, Dr. Franklin," Arthur said, rising to his feet to shake the doctor's hand. "We won't keep you long. We're merely here to visit Eunice Holbrooke."

Dr. Franklin moved behind a cluttered desk and took a seat as Arthur sat down as well. "I don't recall admitting a Eunice Holbrooke, but I see a great number of new patients on a daily basis. However, before I question you further about your friend, I find myself curious about your name. You wouldn't happen to be a member of *the* Livingston family, would you? The ones who own a good portion of New York City—along with the Astors, of course?"

Even though Arthur had striven hard to make a name for himself, avoiding the association with his illustrious family whenever possible so as not to receive preferential treatment because of their high standing in society, given the gleam residing in Dr. Franklin's eyes and given that he needed the doctor to cooperate with him, Arthur didn't hesitate to nod. "Collin Livingston is my father." He glanced to Lloyd. "This is my maternal grandfather, Mr. Lloyd Brevoorts, along with my younger brother, Chase Livingston."

Dr. Franklin's gaze sharpened on Lloyd. "Brevoorts, as in the railroad Brevoorts?"

"Guilty as charged, although my eldest son took over the running of our company years ago."

Dr. Franklin returned his attention to Arthur. "I must say that I'm tickled to have all of you in my office. It's not every day we see members of the New York Four Hundred—or ever, in fact. I've been hoping that would eventually change because we're sadly lacking in funds, and yet the need for our asylum as a place to house the poor has been growing at an alarming rate."

"I'd be happy to have a conversation with you at a later date pertaining to philanthropic endeavors," Arthur said. "However, that discussion will need to wait until after we speak with Eunice Holbrooke."

"I'm sure a visit with your friend can be easily arranged," Dr. Franklin said. "But as I mentioned, I'm unfamiliar with that name. Would you happen to know when she was admitted?"

Lloyd cleared his throat. "There's a possibility Eunice may be using a different name, but she would have been admitted within the last"—he glanced at Arthur—"two days?"

"I would say that's likely."

"Why would she be using a different name?" Dr. Franklin asked.

"Because she's suffering some manner of mental incapacity" was all Arthur could come up with to respond, breathing a sigh of relief when Dr. Franklin didn't argue the point but nodded instead.

"A diseased mind is difficult to comprehend at times, and identity confusion does occasionally come into play. Nevertheless, it'll be difficult for me to know what patient you want to see if you don't know the name she's using here. What does she look like?"

Since he hadn't actually seen Eugenia for seven years, and he wasn't exactly certain of his conclusion that Eunice was Eugenia, it was going to be slightly problematic to provide the doctor with an accurate description. "Eunice is a little difficult to describe . . ." He paused before inspiration struck. "But I imagine she would have arrived in widow's weeds and her face covered by veils."

Dr. Franklin brightened. "Ah, I know exactly who you're looking for now. She arrived yesterday, but I can't recall her name." He turned toward the door. "Nurse Kroener," he called, "would you bring in my files from yesterday?"

A moment later, a nurse hurried into the room, files in hand. She set the files on his desk, a blush staining her cheeks when the doctor sent her a warm smile.

"Was there a specific file you wanted to see, Doctor?"

"The widow. The one who was examined yesterday."

"Ah yes, the widow," Nurse Kroener said. "She was an extreme case, and I was in full agreement with you and Nurse Grady for sending her off to isolation."

Arthur frowned. "Why was she sent into isolation?"

"She was suffering from a severe mental episode," Dr. Franklin said as Nurse Kroener began riffling through the files, pulling one out and flipping it open.

"Indeed she was," Nurse Kroener agreed. "I was outside the door while she was being examined, and she was very belligerent and questioned the doctor relentlessly, especially when he asked to see her tongue." She pulled out a file and flipped it open. "Eunice Hickenbottom is her name, and she was diagnosed as suffering from acute melancholy, delusions, and female hysteria."

"And some of that diagnosis was derived from an examination of her tongue?" Arthur asked, his question left unanswered when another nurse hurried into the room, looking rather flustered.

"Forgive me, Doctor, but I have two women just outside the door. They're asking to see a patient by the name of Eunice Hickenbottom. I've told them it's not visiting hours yet, but they're demanding to speak with someone in charge."

Dr. Franklin glanced to Arthur. "How interesting that one of our patients has so many people wanting to visit with her today."

Arthur was spared a response when two women came barreling into the room, two women he wasn't exactly surprised to discover were none other than Miss Judith Donovan and Miss Elsy Evans. He *was* surprised, though, over how disheveled they looked as well as being remarkably wet. He rose to his feet, drawing Elsy's notice.

She narrowed her eyes on him. "Mr. Livingston, I bet you weren't expecting us to be dogging your heels."

"Well, we weren't dogging his heels fast enough, since we missed the ferry to the island," Judith said, pulling a soggy handkerchief from her sleeve, which she used to dab at water dribbling down her face, smearing a streak of yellow paint still on her cheek. "Because we missed the ferry, we were forced to hire the only boat available, which turned out to be a sailboat—or more of a dinghy, really—with a sail I could have sworn was made out of a bedsheet and captained by a boy who couldn't have been more than ten years old."

"He told me mid-crossing he was nine," Elsy said. "Bless his heart, he tried to give us a smooth sail over the river, but after the wind sprang up, we were in direct danger of capsizing."

"Danger we wouldn't have had to face if you, Mr. Livingston, would have waited for Eunice to return instead of running her down while she's—" Judith stopped talking, shot a look to Dr. Franklin, who seemed somewhat bewildered, then turned her attention to Lloyd. "With all that said, and since we did manage to survive a perilous ride across the river, I'm sure you'll agree, Mr. Brevoorts, what with you being such a chivalrous sort, that Elsy and I should be the ones to speak with Eunice first."

"I'm beginning to understand why their agency is so highly recommended," Chase muttered, coming over to stand behind Arthur's chair. "That was a brilliant move, appealing to Grandfather's chivalrous nature."

"You're supposed to be on my side," Arthur muttered back as Lloyd took hold of his cane and limped his way over to Judith and

Elsy, making a big to-do about kissing their soggy hands before he smiled.

"If it were up to me, my dears, I'd be happy to stand aside and allow you to speak with Eunice Holbrooke, or Hickenbottom, or whatever she's calling herself today, but I'm merely here as an observer."

Elsy rolled her eyes. "I expected better of you, Mr. Brevoorts, but I suppose you can be forgiven, because you're likely somewhat overwrought over the idea you may soon be run out of town by an angry horde of widows" She turned and sent Arthur a remarkably sweet smile, paired with a delicate arch of a brow.

It was difficult to swallow a laugh because clearly Elsy Evans had decided to turn on the charm for him, as she smoothed back hair that was currently a disaster due to their rough crossing of the river and then even went so far as to wring her soggy-gloved hands together, quite as if she were a damsel in distress.

He wasn't buying it for a second.

"I believe it's only right to allow Dr. Franklin to decide who gets to visit with Eunice first," Arthur said, earning scowls from Judith and Elsy, which deepened when Dr. Franklin nodded at Arthur.

"Because you, Mr. Livingston, arrived before the ladies, it seems only fair that you should be allowed to speak with Eunice first. I'm somewhat confused, though, why all of you need to speak with the widow. She's mad as a hatter and isn't going to be much of a conversationalist."

"Which is exactly why *we* should be allowed to visit with her first," Judith exclaimed before Arthur could respond.

"And why is that, Miss . . ."

"Donovan. And this is Miss Evans, and the reason is . . . ah . . . we need to speak with Eunice first because I'm afraid these gentlemen are going to press her about a missing person named Miss Eugenia Howland, which could very well leave Eunice, ah, Hickenbottom in a more despondent state than ever."

"Who in the world is Eugenia?" Dr. Franklin asked. "And why

does it seem like there are so many names beginning with *E* being tossed around right now?"

Arthur stepped forward. "It does seem as if there are numerous ladies sporting *E* names in our conversation, Dr. Franklin. But if we could return to the pressing business at hand, since you've decided it's only fair for me to speak to Eunice first, I'd like to see her now."

"Absolutely not," Judith said, moving to block the doorway. "That's not fair in the least, not when, ah, well, *family* should be permitted to see her before casual acquaintances."

"That was some impressive improvising there," Chase said under his breath.

Before Arthur could agree, Dr. Franklin frowned. "You're family?"

"Indeed." Judith shot Arthur just a touch of a triumphant look before she turned a remarkably innocent smile on Dr. Franklin. "I'm her daughter."

"Brilliant," Chase muttered as Dr. Franklin's gaze sharpened on Judith.

"How interesting for you to claim you're her daughter. You're far too old for that role."

"How would you know that?" Judith demanded. "You told us she's mad as a hatter, so if she told you her age, I doubt she told you the truth."

"I saw her face."

"She took off her veils?"

"Not voluntarily."

"I'm sure she wasn't happy about that," Judith murmured before she actually resorted to fluttering her lashes at the doctor. "As for my being too old to be her daughter, you're right about that. I should have been more specific and said that Eunice is my stepmother."

Dr. Franklin frowned. "But you told me you're Miss *Donovan*. If she's your stepmother, she would have married your father, whose name would have been Hickenbottom, or perhaps Holbrooke.

Unless you're saying that Eunice is neither Hickenbottom or Holbrooke but Donovan instead."

Chase inched closer to Arthur. "He's more astute than I gave him credit for. It'll be interesting to see how she gets out of that one."

Arthur grinned, his grin fading when Judith got a determined look in her eye right before she gave an airy wave of her hand.

"Donovan is my stage name. I'm an actress."

Lloyd chuckled as he stepped next to Arthur. "I'm sorry, but I think they deserve to see Eunice first. They're very impressive, not to mention quick on their feet."

Any response Arthur was going to make died on the tip of his tongue when yet another nurse sprinted into the room, looking frazzled.

"Dr. Franklin. Come quick! A patient has gone completely mad and is causing mayhem with the nurses. The other patients are becoming agitated, and—"

Dr. Franklin didn't wait to hear what else the nurse had to say because he was already bolting out of the room, the nurses right after him.

"We should follow them," Elsy said, turning on her heel and dashing with Judith after the doctor.

"What do you think the chances are that those two are off to locate Eunice while everyone's distracted?" Chase asked.

"Relatively high," Arthur said as he headed for the door, Chase right behind, Lloyd calling out that he'd catch up with them at some point.

Reaching a staircase, Arthur took the steps two at a time, keeping Elsy and Judith in his sights. He'd almost caught up with them when a nurse came sprinting down the stairs, coming up short when she spotted Elsy and Judith. "Dining room, hall seven. She's in trouble. I'll be back with reinforcements." With that, the nurse sprinted into motion again, barely giving Arthur and Chase time to get out of her way as she flew down the steps.

"Is it my imagination or did that nurse bear an uncanny resemblance to Miss Elsy Evans?" Chase asked as they surged up the stairs again.

"She did, and I wouldn't be surprised if the woman that nurse was talking about is Eunice."

Reaching a landing, Arthur turned to the right and ran toward the shrieks coming from an open door at the end of the hallway, suggesting that the patients were indeed becoming agitated.

He rushed through the door, finding it next to impossible to move farther into the room because his path was blocked by a group of women dressed all the same, their attention settled on something at the far end of the room, something that was having them cheer loudly.

Seeing a gap in the women against the wall to his left, he headed for it and began edging his way along the wall, stopping at the sight that met his eyes once he cleared the throng of patients who'd begun to chant something that sounded like "One more down, one more down."

Five nurses were standing in a line ten feet in front of him, their concentration centered on a lady dressed in black, her back turned to him as she advanced on another nurse who was edging backward, probably because of the bucket the lady was wielding like a weapon.

In the blink of an eye, the lady in black, who was most certainly Eunice Holbrooke, knocked the woman to the ground, not waiting to assess the damage she'd done to the woman before spinning around to face the other nurses.

As Arthur's attention settled on Eunice's face, he blinked, and then blinked again as time slowed to a stop because he'd been right after all.

Eunice Holbrooke was none other than Eugenia Howland, the woman he'd been searching for.

Her distinctive blond hair was straggling about her shoulders, but she wasn't letting that stop her as she sent a nurse who'd rushed forward and grabbed hold of her arm tumbling to the ground. Her lips curved into a smile that was downright terrifying as she set her sights on the four nurses still left standing, which should have sent those nurses, if they'd been sensible, running from the room.

It soon became apparent the nurses weren't possessed of much sensibility because one of them, a bulky woman wielding a club, began inching Eugenia's way. Striding into motion, Arthur stepped around Dr. Franklin, who was merely gawking at the scene unfolding in front of him, and moved directly for the nurse wielding the club. He came to an abrupt stop when Eugenia's attention swung to him and then, quite unexpectedly, she rolled her eyes.

"Honestly, and here I thought my day couldn't possibly get worse, but evidently I was wrong about that," she called out even as she swung the bucket back and forth. "If you haven't noticed, Arthur," she continued, quite as if she were not in the midst of a brawl, "this is hardly the moment for any type of reunion. I'm a touch occupied right now."

With that, she swung the bucket in a wide arc as the nurse wielding the club began to advance more rapidly, seemingly under the mistaken belief that Eugenia was currently distracted.

The peculiar thought sprang to mind that there was something impressive about a woman who could converse and wield a bucket like a weapon at the same time.

Pushing what was a rather ridiculous thought aside, given the circumstances, Arthur took a single step toward Eugenia, stopping again when she glared at him.

"I thought you might be in need of my assistance," he called.

She tilted her head and considered the nurse who was still heading her way. "And ruin my fun? I think not."

CHAPTER

Fourteen

"Get ahold of yourself, Dr. Franklin. You're supposed to be in charge here. I suggest you remember that and get busy trying to gain control over what is clearly a descent into complete chaos."

Turning, Arthur found his grandfather limping determinedly toward Dr. Franklin, the sight of the distinguished gentleman with the silver-handled cane causing the patients who'd been cheering for Eunice, or rather, Eugenia, to turn their attention away from the drama and settle it on Lloyd.

His grandfather didn't seem to notice the attention as he reached Dr. Franklin's side, giving the doctor a nudge toward the three nurses who'd taken to circling Eugenia.

"Have at it, Dr. Franklin," Lloyd said. "Seems to me your nurses are having difficulty with that woman." He glanced to Arthur. "Were you right? Is she Eugenia?"

"She most definitely is Eugenia."

"How wonderful, although given the situation, it's concerning at the same time." Lloyd returned his attention to Eugenia, who was now assuming a boxer's stance, having lost the bucket when she used it to whack the club out of her previous attacker's hand. "Not that this is probably the moment, but it's little wonder you've changed your mind about marrying an incomparable from society. Eugenia Howland puts all those young ladies to shame. Why, there's no other way to describe her except as magnificent. She's clearly possessed of unusual spirit, and spirit, my dear boy, makes a lady incomparably fascinating."

Arthur found he couldn't disagree with his grandfather's assessment because . . . she was magnificent. She was also still apparently fearless because there wasn't a smidgen of fear on her face as she stared down what most ladies would see as daunting odds.

The last time he'd seen her, she'd been twenty years old and had been beyond beautiful—not that he'd allowed himself to consider her beauty often. He'd had a distinct plan back then, and courting an unconventional lady from Montana hadn't been part of that plan, even if he occasionally found her stubborn streak and dry wit compelling.

She was no longer a young lady, but the years had been kind to her. In fact, she was more beautiful than ever, even dressed in a black gown that was tattered and torn, with her hair tangled and a streak of dirt marring her cheek.

Eugenia had been self-assured when he'd first become acquainted with her, but now, taking on a throng of angry nurses, it was clear she'd become more confident, and—

Arthur snapped out of his thoughts when a thud echoed around the room, a direct result of Eugenia sending a nurse who'd been trying to take her by surprise on her backside.

"Only three left," Eugenia said cheerfully, rolling up her sleeves and gesturing with her fingers for the three nurses left standing to come her way.

Instead of beginning an immediate advance, those nurses looked to their fallen contemporaries, many of whom were nursing swollen lips, bleeding noses, and obviously aching heads, then turned on their heels and dashed out of the room.

"Looks like you've won the battle, Eugenia, which is wonderful because obviously you and I have a few matters we need to discuss," Arthur called, taking a step toward her but freezing on the spot when he noticed her hand was clenched into a fist again.

"I don't go by that name these days, Arthur. I've become rather fond of Eunice," she returned. "As for us having a discussion, I don't believe I'd enjoy that, especially not when I know that talk will center around your ridiculous ideas about marrying me."

"It seems I may have not been accurate regarding my diagnosis of that woman after all," Dr. Franklin said, stepping up beside Arthur. "Her mind is obviously far more diseased than I realized because only a diseased mind causes a person to change their names at whim."

"I don't change my name at whim," Eugenia, or rather, Eunice, called.

"I beg to differ because you seem to go by quite a few different names," Dr. Franklin returned. "Most sane people are content to travel through life with only one name."

"Unless you're a woman and marry," Eunice shot back. "Then your name changes, and if you're widowed and then remarry, well, your name changes again. Hardly a whimsical situation in my humble *and* sane opinion."

Arthur caught Dr. Franklin's eye. "She seems remarkably capable of presenting a valid argument, which suggests she's not insane."

"I don't need you pointing out the obvious for me, Arthur," Eunice snapped.

He felt the distinct urge to laugh as he turned to her. "How delightful to discover you're still as contrary as ever."

She dusted her hands off. "I've always thought my contrariness was one of my most stellar qualities. Perhaps you should rethink your determination to marry me for my own good because my contrariness has only increased with age. And before you bring up that nonsense about honoring your word to my grandfather, he never should have asked that of you without first seeking my opinion. I assure you, if he'd told me he had you in mind to marry me, I would have nipped that in the bud straightaway."

Arthur opened his mouth, but before he could reply, Dr. Franklin settled a frown on him.

"Surely I misheard and you're not considering marriage to this woman, are you?"

"It's a long story, and I'd rather not get into it with you, especially not when there's other matters to settle, such as getting Eunice released."

Dr. Franklin's eyes widened. "My dear Mr. Livingston, she can't be released. She's mad."

"Mad as a hatter, in your words," Eunice corrected. "Frankly, I found that to be insulting because it's a mocking term and shouldn't be used to describe your patients."

"I'll thank you not to tell me how I should speak about my patients," Dr. Franklin all but spat before he began looking around the room, his gaze sharpening on a nurse who was pushing herself off the floor while holding a handkerchief to her nose. "Nurse Grady! I trust you'll soon have this situation well in hand?"

Nurse Grady bobbed her head as she wove her way unsteadily to a table, grabbing hold of a medicine bag from underneath a chair. She began riffling through it, pulling out a vial a second later. "Won't be long now, Dr. Franklin. Morphine has a way of subduing even the most troublesome patients."

"Now see here," Arthur began, "I won't stand by and allow you to drug her, and—"

He stopped talking when he realized he was speaking to Dr. Franklin's back. Dr. Franklin was moving toward a group of at least ten nurses who'd just entered the room, all of whom were carrying very intimidating-looking batons.

Arthur didn't hesitate to surge into motion, striding toward Eunice and being joined by Elsy and Judith, both of whom looked as if they'd run into some difficulties since entering the dining room because their clothing seemed more disheveled than ever and Elsy was missing her hat.

"A patient decided Judith and I were her daughters," Elsy said before he could ask what happened as she smoothed a hand over hair that refused to be tamed. "She didn't like that our clothing was damp and tried to remove it for us."

"It was very sad," Judith added. "Until the woman realized we weren't her children and started boxing our ears for misleading her."

"This is a very disturbing place," Arthur said as they reached Eunice's side and he caught her eye. "Still hesitant to accept my assistance?"

To his surprise, Eunice shook her head as she glanced at the brigade of nurses advancing their way. "I think the sheer size and number of those nurses coming for me may be more than I can handle on my own, so I'll thank you in advance for your assistance. Know, though, that accepting your assistance does not mean I'm going to marry you. And before I forget, and while I'm thinking about it, and have thought about it for years, I am sorry I shot you. I'm sure that wasn't a pleasant experience for you."

Before he could do more than blink over the unexpected apology, Eunice turned to Judith and Elsy. "Should I ask why you're here?"

"I would think Arthur Livingston's presence at the asylum is explanation enough," Judith said. "His presence is mostly my fault, but I'll explain that later. We've got more important matters to worry about, such as making certain they don't succeed with using that morphine on you."

"We certainly won't allow that to happen," Lloyd said, limping up to join them, Chase by his side. Lloyd presented Eunice with a bow. "I'm Arthur's grandfather, dear, Mr. Lloyd Brevoorts, but you may call me Lloyd, or, better yet, Grandfather."

Eunice dipped into a perfect curtsy. "How lovely to meet you, Lloyd."

Lloyd's eyes began to twinkle. "Too soon for the grandfather business?"

"I'm not certain what your grandson told you, but if he's mentioned marriage, know that it's never going to happen."

"Ah, now that sounds like a challenge." Lloyd turned a smile on Arthur. "I like her. She'll obviously give you a time of it, but I have the feeling she'll be well worth the effort."

"Is this really the moment, Grandfather?" Arthur asked, eyeing the nurses who'd stopped their advance and were now huddled together, whispering furiously.

"No need to worry those nurses will get near you with that morphine, dear," Lloyd said, giving Eunice's arm a pat and lifting his cane with his other hand. "I've got a concealed blade in this lovely piece that I won't hesitate to use."

Before Eunice could do more than smile, Nurse Grady began walking toward them, resolve in her every step. She suddenly faltered, though, when two men came sprinting across the room. They stopped in front of Eunice, and Arthur recognized one of the men as Ivan Chernoff, Eunice's long-time bodyguard and a man one wouldn't want to cross—ever.

Before Arthur could even acknowledge Ivan, though, Eunice stepped forward, Ivan moving to stand on one side of her and the second man moving to stand on the other.

"I believe, Dr. Franklin, that it should now be obvious I'm not going to be subdued," Eunice began. "I'm also not going to be locked away in this asylum for the rest of my life, nor examined by any other doctors with questionable qualifications."

Dr. Franklin drew himself up. "I do not have questionable qualifications."

"I beg to differ," Eunice returned in a voice dripping with ice. "You proclaimed me insane after your examination, and yet I didn't even bother to assume a mentally challenged attitude."

"You were sent here for a reason," Dr. Franklin argued. "Besides that, I wasn't the only one to proclaim you insane. You were deemed insane by physicians who examined you and realized it would be safer for society if you were locked securely away in this asylum."

"I'm sure you'll find this distressing, but I got admitted to this asylum on my own accord with the assistance of that man." Eunice nodded to the gentleman standing to her right. "Agent Cooper Clifton of the Pinkerton Agency arranged to have two physicians provide me with letters that allowed me admittance into your asylum."

Dr. Franklin gave a tug of his tie. "What is a Pinkerton man doing here?"

"He works in tandem with the Bleecker Street Inquiry Agency, of which I'm a partner. We were hired by a woman to find her sister, Mrs. Clement Mills." Eunice nodded to where two women were crouched underneath one of the long tables, peering over a bench. "I was successful in locating Mrs. Mills, and with that task completed, I intend to depart from your horrifying establishment without any obstruction by your nurses." She gave a flick of her hand toward the nurses. "Now would be the time to instruct those women to escort the other patients back to their rooms for a nap. I'm sure this has been quite the emotional day for many of them."

"But it's bath day," Nurse Grady said, drawing Eunice's attention as well as her temper, given the way her eyes had begun flashing.

"The last thing they need is to be tossed into a cold bath, one where the water isn't changed after each woman bathes."

"The water is changed," Dr. Franklin argued.

"No, it's not," Eunice said. "Although how interesting to learn you didn't know that, Dr. Franklin. I imagine there's much you don't know about what goes on here. I'd be more than happy to have you visit me at my inquiry agency, where I'll tell you all about the atrocities that I've learned occur behind the very doors of an establishment that houses the most vulnerable of our population— one you've been entrusted to protect and treat, something you and the other members of the staff have failed to do."

"I don't appreciate your tone, Mrs., er, Hickenbottom. You should tread carefully. I am the one who can see you released from here, or not."

Eunice crossed her arms over her chest. "You don't have a form with Eunice Holbrooke on it, which means I'm not a patient here, so you have no reason to hold me." She lifted her chin. "And I'll be taking Mrs. Clement Mills with me when I depart because she shouldn't be here either. You should know that your nurses have taken to mocking her because she's been claiming to be a woman of means, but Mrs. Mills *is* a woman of means. That right there begs the question of how she got admitted here in the first place." She turned to Agent Clifton. "I'm sure the Pinkertons would be interested in uncovering how that occurred. Given what her husband has been bragging about to his cronies, it's obvious he paid someone a very large bribe to get her committed here."

"I'm sure nothing as untoward as a bribe was involved pertaining to Mrs. Mills's admittance into Blackwell," Dr. Franklin said, giving his tie another tug. "Nevertheless, I feel compelled to point out that there are many sanitoriums in the city that cater to the upper crust that accept . . . donations, if you will, from family members of patients to assure they're given only the best of care. That could have been the case with this particular patient—her husband deciding to make a, ah, donation on her behalf to ascertain she received special attention from us."

Eunice shot a look to Mrs. Mills, who was still underneath the table, her white and drawn face suggesting she'd not been pampered in the least. "I'm sure Mrs. Mills will be more than happy to speak with you about the special attention she hasn't received here, if there was a donation made to assure she was well taken care of. As for the sanitoriums you mentioned that cater to people of means, yes, donations are often made, but you and I know those donations rarely ascertain patients receive extra care."

As Nurse Grady sidled up to join them, still clutching the vial of morphine, resignation flickered through Dr. Franklin's eyes. "You won't need to be taking that patient back to her room, Nurse Grady."

"Why not?"

"Because I'm here under false pretenses," Eunice snapped before Dr. Franklin could respond. "You also won't need to escort Mrs. Mills back to her room because she'll be coming with me as well as"—she shot a glance to the woman crouching underneath the table with Mrs. Mills—"Rose Santana. She doesn't belong here either."

It came as no surprise when Dr. Franklin began to sputter.

"That's out of the question. You can't tell me you're simply going to take Mrs. Mills with you, nor will I release, ah . . . I can't recall her name, but you're not taking that other woman merely because you decided she doesn't belong here. You're hardly an expert on the matter of insanity."

"I'm probably as much, if not more, of an expert than you are, Dr. Franklin," Eunice said coolly. "I spend hours speaking with women at my agency, and that has given me great insight into their mental capacities. Unlike you, who seem to believe that looking at a woman's tongue and then prodding her head is a sufficient enough examination to understand the workings, or lack thereof, of her mind."

"I'm not releasing her."

Eunice turned to Ivan. "I'm going to need to borrow your pistol."

Ivan's brows drew together. "Absolutely not. Shooting the doctor, no matter that he probably deserves it, will only land you out of this prison and into another one."

When Eunice held out her hand in response, Arthur swallowed a laugh, realizing an intervention was certainly needed. He, of all people, knew Eunice was perfectly capable of shooting a man if she felt so inclined.

He turned to Dr. Franklin. "I would encourage you to agree to Eunice's demands. But to give you more of an incentive to do that, allow me to remind you of our recent conversation in which you proclaimed how interested you were in having the New York Four Hundred become involved with this asylum. I assure you that you'll not enjoy the type of involvement you'll soon see from them if I allow society matrons to learn what kind of care is not being given to the patients residing here."

Dr. Franklin narrowed his eyes on Arthur. "That sounds like a threat."

"I would call it more of a promise."

Dr. Franklin gave another tug of his tie before he glanced at Rose Santana, who was still crouching underneath the table with

Mrs. Mills. "May I assume that promise wouldn't materialize if I allow those two women to leave the asylum?"

"You may."

"And you'll give me your word as a gentleman on that?"

"Of course."

"Then it's done. You can take Rose as well as Mrs. Mills." Dr. Franklin's gaze lingered on Rose as he smiled. "I have little doubt that I'll be seeing that woman again since she is, indeed, insane."

With that, Dr. Franklin turned on his heel and strode from the room, not bothering to assist the nurses as they cleared the room of patients, all save Eunice, Mrs. Mills, and Rose Santana, who was looking somewhat incredulous, as if she couldn't believe her good fortune.

"May I suggest we remove ourselves from this asylum before the doctor changes his mind, or before that nurse takes it upon herself to deliver that dose of morphine to you simply out of spite?" Ivan asked, taking hold of Eunice's arm.

"An excellent suggestion, Ivan," Eunice said, giving his arm a pat. "All things considered, though, I think this turned out far better than I was expecting it to when I got ambushed by those nurses. I'm now convinced I'm perfectly suited to fieldwork and intend to do more of it in the near future."

"And I'm convinced this debacle, for lack of a better word," Ivan argued, "proves the last place you belong is out in the field. You're fortunate you're not currently drugged and on your way to the Lodge. It was sheer luck that this has turned out so well, although I believe you might owe Arthur a word of appreciation because he did get Dr. Franklin to allow all of your releases with that clever threat."

"You're probably right." She turned to Arthur. "Before I do that, though, know that I'm less than pleased that you somehow uncovered my identity. However, since there's nothing to be done about that now since the genie's out of the bottle, allow me to thank you for helping me in what certainly turned into a concerning situation. Your arrival was timely, although I'm not in agreement about you giving that horrid doctor your word that you wouldn't get society involved in this institution. Society wields substantial influence with politicians who could be persuaded to intervene here, which would go far in improving the life of the patients."

He inclined his head. "I'm sure I should probably apologize for the way I handled the revealing of your identity, but I'm afraid because time is of the essence that you left me no choice in the matter. And while I was happy to be of assistance to you, I'm relatively certain you would have handled yourself well with those other nurses. However, I believe you may still be a little harried from the brawl you just enjoyed because I would think you'd understand exactly why I gave my word to the doctor."

"Since you seem keen to honor your word anytime you give it, all I understand is that you've allowed the doctor to continue running this institution in a way that's hardly acceptable."

"I've done no such thing. Yes, *I* gave my word, but my grandfather and brother didn't give theirs." He smiled. "I assure you, the New York Four Hundred will soon be apprised of the horrors transpiring here."

"Hmmm . . ." was all Eunice said to that, although she did send him just a hint of a smile, which he took as a somewhat encouraging sign. She then tugged Ivan into motion while Judith and Elsy hurried to Mrs. Mills and Rose Santana, taking hold of their hands and leading them toward the door.

Arthur fell into step behind Eunice, Lloyd and Chase joining him.

"This has certainly been more of an adventure than I was anticipating," Lloyd said.

"I have a feeling more adventures may await you in Montana," Chase said.

Eunice stopped in her tracks. "Why would Lloyd be going to Montana?"

"Grandfather wants to accompany us back to Montana because, well, that's a story in and of itself," Arthur began. "I didn't think you'd object to his company because Grandfather has a few private Pullman cars at his disposal, which means we'll be traveling to Butte in style."

"I'm not going back to Butte."

He swallowed a sigh. "Of course you are. Your relatives are going to have you declared dead and then sell Mason Mines to D. H. Loring. After they do that, and after they get their hands on your inheritance, you'll have a difficult time retrieving your fortune."

"And while it galls me that my relatives are so greedy, I have no intention of returning to Montana. Yes, it's a lot of money, but the trust Grandfather set up for me when I turned eighteen has grown through sound financial investments through the years and is large enough to where if my relatives abscond with my inheritance, I'll be able to live a more-than-comfortable life without it."

Storm clouds began gathering in Eunice's eyes. "That means there's no reason for me to hie off to Montana or, heaven forbid, marry you. And while I appreciate your diligence in trying to see after my best interests as well as your assistance with this horrid asylum situation, I'm going to absolve you of your promise to my grandfather, and as soon as we breach the walls of this institution and get off this island, bid you good-bye once and for all."

CHAPTER

Fifteen

"You can't simply absolve me of my word to your grandfather because it suits you," Arthur said, causing Eunice to falter the slightest bit before she climbed into the carriage she'd left waiting for her while she'd deposited Mrs. Mills at her sister's house, settling herself on the seat beside Judith.

"Of course I can," she returned. "It was simple, and I'll say it again—I, Eunice Holbrooke, absolve you of any promises you made to my grandfather, especially the ones concerning seeing after my best interests and marrying me for my own good."

"And that way of thinking works both ways because I, Arthur Livingston, reject your attempt to absolve me of my promise. A gentleman's word is directly tied to his honor, and honor cannot be dealt with in such a willy-nilly fashion."

Eunice tucked a strand of rather dirty hair behind her ear as the carriage jolted into motion. "There's nothing willy-nilly about it. I'm giving you a way out of what has to be an unenviable position. You never once lent me the impression you longed to marry me. Case in point, you told me and Daphne you weren't keen to court me in the first place. If you're unaware, marriage is an entire step beyond the whole courting business."

"I had my reasons for not wanting to court you back then."

"Reasons I'm sure that centered around my inability to adopt a demure and expected demeanor and around my preference for wearing men's trousers."

"You don't seem to have that trouser preference these days."

"It would have been hard to blend in as a widow if I'd chosen black trousers instead of skirts."

"Does that mean you'll return to wearing trousers once you're back in Montana?"

She threw up her hands. "You're tenacious, I'll give you that, but I'm not returning to Montana. And not that I should have to point out the obvious to you, Arthur, but finding you in my carriage after depositing Mrs. Mills at her sister's house seems to be a tad stalkerish on your part."

"I told him you wouldn't be pleased," Ivan said from where he was sitting next to Arthur on the opposite seat. "But since his carriage left him behind, I didn't feel right leaving him standing outside since it's begun to rain. He did, after all, assist you at the asylum."

"A little rain never hurt anyone." Eunice caught Arthur's eye. "Besides, if you haven't noticed, I'm not in the proper emotional state to engage in what will clearly be a tumultuous conversation with you. I spent a day and a half in an insane asylum, and if that wasn't bad enough, I just had to leave a weeping Mrs. Mills in the care of her sister, even though Mrs. Mills still seems to think her dastardly husband isn't that dastardly and longs to return to him. It took a great deal of effort to resist shaking some sense into the lady, although I'm relatively certain Mrs. Eastman will not hesitate with any shaking that needs to happen to keep her sister from returning to a reprobate. With all that said, I'm in desperate need of a bath, a nap, and a decent meal. I assure you, you won't enjoy what I have to say next if you keep pressing me about returning to Montana right now."

"Would you be more agreeable to discussing the matter after you've had a bath, nap, and a decent meal?"

"Probably not."

Arthur's lips began to curve. "Which is not surprising and means, since I have the sneaking suspicion you'll disappear again to avoid further conversations with me, I'm now going to chance your ill humor and continue to press you about Montana."

"I don't want to talk about Montana. But because there's little likelihood that you'll spend our ride through the city in silence, I *will* talk to you about something else." She leaned forward. "How did you figure out my identity, how did you find me in the asylum, and better yet, why did you track me down? You could have blown my cover."

"Tracking you down was unavoidable because you were obviously going to great lengths to avoid me."

"For good reason, since I'm the woman you wanted to hire the agency to find."

"Well, quite, but you would have made everything much easier on yourself if you would have simply tossed up your veils after I explained the situation at the agency. Clearly I'm no threat to you, but since you didn't disclose your identity, I had no choice but to take the unusual step of seeking you out at the asylum. And, to address the business of blowing your cover, you did that without any assistance from me."

Judith cleared her throat, wincing as she looked to Eunice. "Not that this speaks well to my skills as an inquiry agent, but I'm to blame for Arthur learning you were undercover at the asylum. Granted, I wasn't actually the one to tell him where you were—Mrs. Eastman did that. And then Elsy and I tried to convince him he'd come to the wrong conclusion about who you were, but he skedaddled out of the agency before we were successful with that."

Eunice's brows drew together. "I thought we'd agreed you'd avoid the agency until Arthur left town."

Judith's shoulders slumped. "I left my sketchpad there. But I did think about not going to retrieve it for an entire hour before I gave in to the longing to fetch it. And not that you'll understand this because you're not an artistic sort, but I needed my sketchpad because I've begun an oil painting of Arthur's face. I wouldn't have been able to make much progress if I didn't have the sketches to work from." Her shoulders slumped another inch. "It was horrible luck on my part that I just happened to dash into the agency while he was waiting in the receiving room. It went downhill fairly quickly from there, especially when after I escaped from the receiving room without divulging anything, I made the poor choice of returning to the room because I thought Elsy needed help dealing with Arthur."

"You're doing an oil painting of me?" Arthur asked.

"Pretend he didn't ask that question, Judith," Eunice said. "We don't have time for a lengthy dissertation on your plans for that painting right now. Instead, we need to discuss exactly how he was able to track me down because we'll need to devise a better plan in case a similar situation arises in the future. We can't very well have random clients running us to ground while we're out on assignment."

"I'm not a random client," Arthur argued. "I highly doubt anyone else would ever have to go to the lengths I went through to locate you."

Eunice shrugged. "We at the Bleecker Street Inquiry Agency believe in learning from our mistakes, and having you locate me while I was out in the field was a mistake if there ever was one. The identity I've been diligent with hiding for years has also been revealed."

"And wouldn't have happened if you'd listened to me months ago when I voiced objections to the inquiry agency for exactly that reason," Ivan said.

"I know, Ivan," Eunice said, blowing out a breath. "And you should glean a great deal of satisfaction from learning you were right. However, I was becoming stifled by the restrictions I'd placed on myself over the past seven years, and the agency lifted the ennui I'd been experiencing because of them. I now have a noble purpose to pursue, which is one of the reasons why I won't be returning to Montana." She glanced to Arthur. "I have a business to run."

"You have two business partners who I'm going to assume are capable of running the agency in your absence."

"You met Daphne. Did you really get the impression she'd be good at seeing after the more mundane aspects of the business, such as billing and scheduling?"

"An excellent point, but you do have another partner, Gabriella."

"Who is currently off on a case, one that centers around a young lady who foolishly decided to run away with the family butler. The last telegram I had from Gabriella and her husband said they were in Florida, so there's little hope she'll be back in time for me to get to Montana by my birthday, the date you told me the family was going to have me declared dead." She turned to Judith. "You may continue with your story. I believe you stopped at retrieving your sketchpad, which led to your encounter with Arthur."

Upon concluding her side of the story five minutes later, Judith released a dramatic breath. "Clearly I failed miserably today and fully expect you to toss me from the rank of inquiry agent, even though I don't do much inquiry work."

Ivan sat forward and settled a rather un-Ivan-like smile on Judith. "No one is going to toss you from the inquiry agency. You weren't solely to blame for the debacle that happened today. Truth be told, it sounds to me as if you handled yourself magnificently under what can only be described as the most daunting of circumstances. You did, after all, take it upon yourself to dash off to Blackwell Island with Elsy, and that right there shows your dedication to the agency as well as your concern for Eunice. Although it might be best if you don't man the receiving room again."

"Judith doesn't enjoy manning the receiving room in the first place," Eunice pointed out as a blush began staining Judith's cheeks right as she and Ivan began staring at each other in a way that was definitely going to demand further contemplation at a later date, especially when Ivan's cheeks turned a bit pink as well.

"Should we step out of the carriage?" Arthur asked.

Eunice's lips curved. "If it wasn't moving, I would say yes."

"Why would you want to get out of the carriage?" Ivan asked, pulling his gaze from Judith to settle a frown on Eunice.

"It's getting a little warm in here."

Ivan shot another glance to Judith. "I suppose it is. But if we could return to Judith's role at the agency? I'm in full agreement that she doesn't belong in the receiving room and should instead be given tasks that are more suited to her delightful artistic nature."

Eunice's nose wrinkled. "What tasks would those be?"

"I'll have to think further on that, but I'm sure we can find something for her to do, perhaps even allow her to try her hand at creating flyers of victims or suspects."

Judith raised a hand to her throat. "I'm not certain I'm up for the task after seeing the flyer of Eunice that Arthur has in his possession."

"And I'm convinced you'll rise to that challenge magnificently," Ivan argued. "I've seen the bowls of fruit you've painted, and the apples look so realistic that I find myself longing to take a bite out of them."

Arthur suddenly coughed behind his hand, although Eunice was relatively certain it was an attempt to disguise a laugh.

She couldn't say she blamed him because, obviously, things were taking a turn for the interesting within the closed confines of the carriage.

"I never knew you'd given my fruit paintings much attention," Judith said in a breathy voice as her cheeks turned pinker than ever.

"I've stared at them for what must be hours."

Eunice found herself hard-pressed to not ask the carriage to stop because she was now in danger of laughing as well, what with how she was trapped in a carriage with two people who seemed to be in the midst of a romantic interlude, or perhaps experiencing the eye-opening moment where they'd apparently begun to realize there was some type of spark between them. She cleared her throat and struggled to think of something to say that would break the peculiar atmosphere now settled around them.

"If you're concerned, Judith, that you'll be leaving us in the lurch if you don't occasionally man the receiving room, you shouldn't be," Eunice said as a burst of inspiration came to her, though her statement did nothing to interrupt the moment between Judith and Ivan.

Eunice cleared her throat again. "I've had the most brilliant idea of who we can hire to become our permanent receptionist."

That didn't earn her so much as a blink from the lovestruck couple.

Arthur settled a grin on her. "And who would that be, Eunice?"

She resisted the inclination to grin as well. "Rose Santana, Arthur, and thank you so much for asking."

"You're very welcome, and I have to say that Rose Santana *is* a brilliant idea. As we conversed on the ferry ride across the East River, she struck me as a very formidable woman. In fact, I bet if she'd been manning the reception room earlier today, I wouldn't have made it past the front door."

"Then I'm definitely hiring her."

"Surely you wouldn't tell her to turn me away, would you?"

"Without a second's hesitation. But if you really consider the matter, there's no reason for you to call on me again. You wanted to find me to apprise me of the situation unfolding in Montana. I've now been found and apprised, so you may consider your job done."

Arthur immediately took to looking grumpy. "My job isn't done since I'm not comfortable accepting your decision to turn your back on your inheritance without more discussion about the matter."

"But what more is there to discuss? I don't want to return to Montana, nor do I want to marry you. End of discussion."

"We need to discuss the extent of the inheritance your grandfather left you in his will."

"I imagine he left me at least a twenty-five percent stake in his holdings, dividing the rest between my mother and his vast assortment of relatives and friends."

Arthur shook his head. "You're wrong. He made special bequests to numerous people, that money taken from his incredibly large bank account, but he left you seventy-five percent of Mason Mines as well as his house and lands, the remainder of the funds in his bank accounts, and the entirety of his stock portfolio."

"I would have thought he'd leave all that to my mother."

"Why? He was obviously grooming you as heiress apparent, until he changed his mind because you're a woman, hence the reason behind his inviting me to Montana. I think he was hoping he'd get us married off well before he died, and if he'd been successful with that, he would have known that your fortune would be in good hands because I do know a thing or two about mining. Truth be told, it's because of me that geologists were brought in to survey the old Green farm."

Her eyes widened. "If that's the case, then it seems to me that it's your fault my family wants to have me declared dead. I imagine the lure of increased profitability for Mason Mines was too much for them to resist."

Arthur rubbed a hand over his face. "I didn't actually consider that."

"Well, you should have. It's your fault, and . . ." She smiled. "That actually makes me feel better for some reason."

"I have no idea why that could be, but returning to your grandfather's will, he left your mother twenty-five percent of Mason Mines and a bequest of ten million dollars."

Eunice blinked. "That's a nice chunk of change."

"The twenty-five percent of the company is far greater than ten million, considering that Mason Mines is worth over one hundred million dollars—and that's without the Green farm being mined yet."

Curiosity had Eunice sitting forward. "The business was worth seventy million seven years ago. How did it increase so rapidly with no clear leader at the helm? I find it difficult to believe that Great-Uncle Raymond was capable of taking the business in hand, let alone getting it to thrive without my grandfather guiding him."

"On the day of your grandfather's funeral, Raymond asked me to manage the business. He was, at that time, seventy-five years old and knew he wasn't capable of taking up the reins for such a vast enterprise. Because I'd given your grandfather my word to look after your interests, I didn't hesitate to agree to Raymond's proposition."

"Did Uncle Raymond have you assume the role of president of Mason Mines?"

"He kept that title for himself, though it's just an honorary title because he doesn't have anything to do with the copper mines."

"And you agreed to that?"

Arthur shrugged. "I've been well compensated for running the mines—or for 'consulting,' as Raymond calls it. I negotiated a deal with Raymond where I get a percentage of any profits I'm able to make."

"That could have been a bad decision on your part if the mines didn't yield a profit."

He smiled. "I was determined that wasn't going to happen."

"What percentage did you negotiate?"

"Twenty-five percent. And since Mason Mines has seen a thirty-million-dollar profit since I began consulting, that's—"

"Seven and a half million dollars."

"And that you were able to calculate that on the spot suggests you're a businesswoman at heart."

"It merely suggests that I had a more than capable tutor—Mr. Vincent Wagner, if you remember him. He drilled me endlessly about profit margins, different types of ores, and the most up-to-date managerial practices used in the mining industry."

"And because you've had that extensive mining education, I would imagine if you don't return to claim your inheritance, you're always going to wonder if *you* could have increased profitability at your grandfather's mines. That's something I'm sure your grandfather would have expected you to do. In case you've forgotten, I saw firsthand the relationship you shared with him, and even though he was the worst kind of tyrant, you held your own with him, which was something he respected."

"I'm immune to guilt, Arthur, and it's not well done of you to try and use the complicated relationship I had with my grandfather as a way to get me to return home."

"I thought it was worth a try. I'm beginning to run out of ideas."

"I would think you're actually out of ideas at this point. But to return to our earlier conversation, how were you able to achieve that level of profitability at Mason Mines in such a short amount of time?"

"The fact that you're curious about that suggests to me you're not completely opposed to returning to Montana."

She settled back into the seat. "We'll have to agree to disagree."

"You realize age has not diminished how incredibly annoying you can be, don't you?"

"Something that seems to be a mutual problem between us, so . . . ?"

Arthur shrugged. "Increasing profitability wasn't difficult. I realized from the moment your grandfather gave me a tour of one of his most productive mines that profitability could be significantly increased if steps were taken to improve the conditions in the mine. After I took over managing the mines, I began to put new and stringent safety guidelines in place, while also increasing the miners' pay and shortening their hours. We saw an immediate increase in productivity and word got out about the higher pay, which means Mason Mines is never without enough miners these days."

"Grandfather would have fought you tooth and nail about increasing wages."

"I'm sure he would have, but he would have been wrong since my theory about increasing productivity and profitability through better conditions and better pay for the miners was on point."

"I'm beginning to understand why Grandfather brought you to Montana," Eunice admitted. "You obviously know what you're about when it comes to mining, which is why Grandfather should have simply brought you on as a partner instead of trying to convince you to marry me."

"That's what I thought he intended when he extended me an invitation to visit him. It wasn't until I reached Montana that I learned he had something else in mind." He smiled. "To say I was taken aback when he broached the matter is an understatement. He was adamant about having me join his family through marriage, though, which was why I might have . . ."

"Might have what?" Eunice pressed when Arthur simply stopped talking.

"It doesn't matter now" was all he said. "What does matter, though, is getting you back to Montana. I gave my word, Eunice, and my word means everything to me. I cannot honor that word if you don't at least show up in Butte to prove you're still alive."

"Can't you just go in my stead? I can send you with a letter, proving I'm still breathing."

"I don't think that'll be enough to convince your great-uncle Raymond. There's a lot of money at stake that your relatives intend to divide amongst them."

"Then I suppose I'll have to learn to live with their actions because I'm not returning to Montana."

"You're being unreasonable about this, and I have no idea why."

"It's complicated."

Arthur considered her for a long moment, a less than reassuring gleam flickering through his eyes before he sat forward. "What about your mother?"

"What about her?"

"You mentioned seven years ago that even though your mother had run off unexpectedly, never to return, you still adored her and understood her erratic behavior, since that behavior was brought about when your father died before you were born."

"Your father died before you were born?" Judith asked, pulling her attention from Ivan, the length of time the two of them had continued staring at each other more than telling.

"He did," Eunice said. "And I'm afraid Mother never recovered from his death, telling me on a few occasions that my father had been the love of her life and she never intended on marrying again."

Arthur frowned. "Do you know if she inherited any money from her late husband?"

"He was a younger son, and I'm not aware that he had much money to his name." Eunice blew out a breath. "From what I've been told, Grandfather was furious at Mother for marrying a man a month after she met him while attending finishing school in New York. Grandfather immediately concluded my father was a fortune hunter, and I don't think he was all that perturbed when my father died after suffering an unexpected illness."

"But if your mother didn't inherit money from her late husband," Arthur continued, "she should at least be told about her inheritance and that it's at risk."

"Allow me to admit that as a strategy, that was an exceptional one, Arthur. However, I have no idea where my mother is and haven't seen her for ten years." Eunice settled a smile on Judith, who was watching her with sympathy in her eyes. "And there's no need to look distraught about that, Judith. My mother was not what I'd consider attentive, so even though I adored her, I never depended on her. With that said, though, I do like to have reminders of her around, which is why I didn't balk when you brought that painting of hers into the agency to use as inspiration while you manned the reception room."

Judith raised a hand to her throat. "Your mother is Etta—the artist who inspires me the most?"

"She is. But again, I have no idea where she is, nor am I going to devote time to look for her."

"What if I were to tell you that you don't need to spend any time at all searching for her because . . . I know where she is," Judith said.

"What?"

"Etta is often the topic of conversation when I'm with my artistic friends." Judith smiled. "It just so happens that one of those friends had the privilege of staying at the artist colony Etta formed. He then very kindly gave me the address to that colony, but I've yet to work up the nerve to visit." Judith's eyes flashed with excitement. "I wouldn't be nervous at all, though, if you were with me, and if you'd allow me to go with you when you reunite with your mother."

"I have an agency to run. I don't have time to travel right now."

"But it won't take long at all to reach your mother's artist colony because it's right on the river—a short drive from Daphne and Herman's Hudson estate."

Arthur rubbed his hands together. "And how convenient is that? Why, it's as if the stars have aligned, and those stars are telling us that we should travel to the Hudson as soon as possible, which means you need to clear your calendar so we can leave tomorrow morning at the latest."

"Not that you're going to want to hear this, Eunice, but after listening to your diatribe against Arthur for the past hour, complete with complaints about his character, his handsome face, and the way he makes you long to punch him, I'm left wondering if the contentious relationship both of you share is something entirely different than a clash of two strong personalities. You seem to bring out unusual emotions in each other—exasperation and irritation, just to name a few. But curiously enough, I'm beginning to think that you enjoy your exchanges with Arthur, which is quite telling."

Eunice stopped smoothing out the skirt of her black traveling dress and settled her gaze on Daphne, who was sitting on a lovely chaise by the window of her Hudson home, her feet tucked underneath her and her ever-present notepad on her lap.

"I'm not certain I understand what could possibly be telling about my exchanges with Arthur," Eunice said, even though she knew exactly what Daphne was suggesting. Quite frankly, she'd been contemplating that very thing ever since she'd parted ways with Arthur the day before, telling him in no uncertain terms that he wasn't going to be accompanying her on her trip to reunite with her long-lost mother.

Truth be told, it might have been prudent to have him with

her to explain the intricacies of her grandfather's will and vast holdings, but she'd made an on-the-spot decision not to spend additional time in his company because . . .

Arthur Livingston, even with his propensity for irritating her on a minute-by-minute basis, was far too appealing for his own good.

It seemed absurd, the idea she found him appealing, but when she'd seen him standing in the dining hall of Blackwell's Island Insane Asylum, ready to jump in and assist her with an angry mob of morphine-and-baton-wielding nurses, her heart had given a most unexpected lurch.

She'd actually been thinking that perhaps Dr. Franklin had the right of her after all and she was a bit mad because it was sheer madness to find Arthur Livingston so appealing.

Granted, there were valid reasons why she found Arthur appealing, such as his intellect, his ability to make a profit because of innovative practices that most mining industrialists never would have considered, and the way his eyes crinkled at the corners when he smiled. She also found his determination to honor his word to her grandfather somewhat appealing as well because a man of his word really *wasn't* to be taken lightly.

What wasn't appealing about him, though, was his refusal to completely discard the idea of a marriage between them, although he hadn't told her they were going to get married—probably because he didn't want her to shoot him again.

But even with him not voicing that idea, she knew he still believed it was a viable option, which it most certainly was not because who wanted to marry a man who'd not spoken a single word of affection, let alone attempted any physical acts of affection, such as holding her hand or kissing her?

She had a feeling Arthur Livingston would know his way around a kiss.

And that, right there, was the crux of her problem with Arthur.

While she'd occasionally—both in the past and since they'd reconnected—considered kissing and Arthur in the same breath, she was relatively certain that he hadn't considered kissing her at all, what with the practical way he'd broached the marriage idea as if it were merely one of his business ventures and needed to be treated as such.

It was disheartening, knowing she might be the means to an end, one that would allow him to honor his word to her grandfather while also reaching the very pinnacle of mining success. He was apparently willing to pursue those means until the "I do's" were exchanged, which meant he was far more like her grandfather than she'd realized.

Yes, she'd loved her grandfather, even with him being cantankerous and a bit of a tyrant, but she didn't want to be romantically drawn to a man with similar characteristics. That meant she needed to stay far removed from Arthur, no matter that he made her heart lurch in a most annoying and unexpected manner.

Arthur's appeal and her decision to resist that appeal had been exactly why after she'd bid him good-bye the day before when they'd reached the Holbrooke boardinghouse, she'd traveled directly to Daphne's home on the Hudson. Well, after she'd taken a bath to rid herself of the stench of the asylum that had clung to her like a winter cloak.

There was no question that Arthur was going to be annoyed with her when he arrived at the boardinghouse today and found her missing once again, instead of waiting for him to accompany her to the Hudson River Valley.

It was also not in question that he wasn't going to be amused when he discovered that Judith was not around either. The unanimous decision had been made that Judith would accompany Eunice to Daphne's house because there'd been a definite risk with leaving her behind in the city. Even Judith had admitted there was a chance she'd disclose the classified information of directions to Georgette's artist colony if the right questions were asked, something Arthur was capable of doing.

"You do remember that I solve mysteries for a living, don't you?" Daphne suddenly asked, pulling Eunice from her thoughts. "That means I've now pondered what was an evasive response to

150

my original statement and have concluded that I'm correct and that there is more between you and Arthur besides the fact the two of you argue all the time. I believe both of you might go out of your way to annoy each other, and I think it's a sign of the romantic tension neither of you have admitted is occurring between you." Daphne settled a knowing look on Eunice. "Your arguing can almost be considered a courting technique, albeit a rather peculiar one."

"Arthur and I are not courting. If you've forgotten, he was quite vocal about his reluctance to that idea when my grandfather broached the matter with him seven years ago."

"True, but as I was convalescing here on the Hudson after tossing up my accounts the other day—and for every day since—I was wondering what was really behind his reluctance. I get the distinct feeling there's a story there."

"One that will have to go unread because I have no intention of seeing Arthur again."

Daphne gave an airy wave of her hand. "If you believe Arthur is going to return to Montana without you, I think you're in for a rude awakening. And not that we've discussed the matter of your grandfather's murder, but you simply can't allow his murderer to not be brought to justice." She flipped through her notepad. "I've been jotting down a few notes concerning the murder, and I've been wondering if it could possibly have something to do with that farm—the one with all the copper. What if there was someone else who wanted to purchase that land but your grandfather acquired the land first?"

"An interesting theory, and one I've never considered because I didn't know at the time of Grandfather's death that Mr. Green's farm was such a highly prized tract of land. You may be on to something, but again, I'm not interested in returning to Montana to solve the case, as I've said now numerous times."

"You could send another agent or two out to investigate for you, although that's not going to solve the problem of proving you're alive." Daphne tapped her pencil against her notepad. "You could always have a sworn affidavit filled out, proclaiming you alive, which would spare you a jaunt to Montana as well as allow you to maintain control over your inheritance."

"I thought about that, but what you need to understand is that the Wild West is run differently than New York." Eunice pulled a black glove over her hand. "Arthur told me that my great-uncle Raymond was left a bequest from my grandfather, which means he has the wherewithal to bribe someone to have me declared dead. He could also use the tempting bait that he's going to be coming into a large windfall if I *am* declared dead in order to encourage someone to make a sworn affidavit disappear."

"I could probably get enough fodder from what sounds like a delightful family to get me through an entire series of new books."

"I'm sure you could, but given your bouts of tossing up your accounts, I'm going to assume there's no possibility of you traveling to Montana to seek out that fodder for the foreseeable future."

"An excellent point."

Eunice arched a brow. "That's it, an excellent point? You must know I was fishing for a more definitive response."

"I'm a mystery writer, Eunice. I believe in building up a sense of anticipation." Daphne turned to the window and peered out. "And to increase that sense of anticipation, I now find myself spared from a more detailed response because there's a carriage trundling up the drive." She pressed her nose directly against the glass. "It looks like Elsy, and, yes, that's Phillip sitting beside her on the driver's seat. He's hanging on for dear life because Elsy is attempting to steer the carriage around the half circle that leads to the front vestibule."

"I'm surprised Phillip was agreeable to letting Elsy take the wild curve in your drive, but I'm incredibly concerned to see them here. Judith and I took the ferry up the Hudson last night because Elsy was scheduled to attend an early brunch with Mrs. Paxton today, making her unavailable to drive us last night."

Daphne fished her shoes out from under the chaise, then waved Eunice on as she settled back on the chaise and began lacing herself into her shoes. "You should go see what's happened. I'll be down in a minute."

Telling Daphne to take her time because she was suddenly looking a little pasty, Eunice made her way down a curving staircase to the first floor, then headed through the front door that was already being held open by Jeffries, Daphne and Herman's recently hired butler. After sending Jeffries a smile, she made her way down steps that led to the drive as Elsy jumped lightly to the ground, Phillip Villard shaking his head as he jumped down after her.

"I was going to assist you," Phillip said, tugging his well-tailored jacket that sported a crisp white pocket square into place as he settled an exasperated eye on Elsy.

"And I would have let you assist me if you hadn't annoyed me by waxing on for the last thirty minutes about the personal appointment you had yesterday with Miss Penelope Griffin and her mother," Elsy shot back. "Everyone knows Penelope is a diamond of the first water, and I didn't particularly care for the way your eyes lit up as you were speaking about her."

"That explains why you refused to hand over the reins, even on the tricky parts of the drive," Phillip muttered. "But to address your accusation, if my eyes did light up as I was talking about Penelope, it was only because she's destined to become a leader within society after she marries Mr. John Lathom. That means attention will always be on her, which then means attention will be on her gowns, most of which I designed."

"A pretty excuse if there ever was one, but I'm sure you wouldn't be so keen to accept an excuse like that from me if my eyes lit up when I was talking about another gentleman." Elsy tucked a strand of red hair behind her ear before she readjusted the top hat done up in a deep shade of purple and set her sights on Eunice. "Ah, Eunice, I bet you weren't expecting to see us today."

"I wasn't, nor was I expecting to overhear what was clearly an argument," Eunice said, stepping close to Elsy and giving her a kiss on the cheek.

Phillip bustled up to take hold of Eunice's hand and placed a kiss on it. "Elsy and I weren't arguing."

"Her expression suggests otherwise," Eunice said.

Phillip glanced to Elsy, who was scowling back at him, and winced. "Perhaps you're right, but to address what I know is concern on your part, we're not here because of any horrible news, although I do have news that Ann made me promise to impart to you straightaway so I don't forget."

"Clement Mills has been arrested for attempting to hire a killer to murder his wife," Elsy said before Phillip could get the news out of his mouth.

"I was supposed to tell her."

"You were dawdling about the matter, so now she knows." Elsy took a step closer to Eunice, which had Phillip removing himself a safe distance away from both of them, probably due to the scowl still on Elsy's face. "Cooper decided to have a little chat with Clement after all of you returned from the asylum because he had a feeling Mrs. Mills wasn't convinced she should stay away from him. When Cooper arrived at the Mills's residence, Clement was just leaving, so Cooper decided to follow him. Turns out Clement had an appointment in Five Points with a known assassin for hire. Clement had received a note from his wife that she was out of the asylum and apparently decided to take care of his wife once and for all. Cooper positioned himself close to the men in the pub where the meeting was taking place and overheard everything. As soon as money changed hands, Cooper arrested both men."

"Which will keep him away from Mrs. Mills for the foreseeable future," Eunice said. "Hopefully, his decision to hire an assassin will be the straw that has Mrs. Mills seeking out an annulment."

"I should hope so," Elsy said. "It was very inconsiderate of her husband to try to kill her, and no woman should tolerate inconsideration in a man." She glanced to Phillip, released a sniff, then stalked toward the back of the carriage.

Phillip frowned as he watched her walk away. "She really is out of sorts today because I don't believe hiring a killer to murder one's wife can be considered inconsiderate. It's more along the lines of vastly deranged."

"Elsy wasn't talking about Clement Mills."

Phillip blinked. "You don't think that was aimed at me, do you?"

"It was definitely aimed at you."

"How concerning," Phillip said, glancing to where Elsy was now glancing up at the trunks that were strapped on the back of the carriage. "But now is hardly the moment for me to figure out what I've done to annoy my dearest Elsy because I'm sure you're wondering what we're doing here."

"I must admit I am curious."

"We're here because I, and with the full support of your fellow agents, have decided to take you in hand."

"What?"

Phillip gestured to the black traveling gown she was wearing. "You're a mess, my dear. I'm here to change all of that." He smiled. "You may think of me as your fairy godfather, come to spruce you up before you go off to see your mother."

"I don't believe I'm in need of a fairy godfather."

"Oh, you are," Phillip countered before he began walking around her, sizing her up. "When I get done with you, you'll look like a princess right out of a fairy tale."

"What is it with you and fairy nonsense today?"

Phillip settled a stern look on her. "Surely you don't want to reunite with your mother after all these years looking like"—he made a sweeping gesture with his hand—"that."

Eunice tucked a strand of hair that had come undone from her chignon behind her ear. "I don't look that bad, Phillip, and besides, I haven't seen my mother in a decade. And while it is true that I didn't search for her over the years, and true that I may hold a slight bit of animosity toward her for disappearing on me without a word, it doesn't feel right for me to delay a reunion because I need a new wardrobe, something that would take weeks to have done up for me."

"Perfectly understandable. Which is why I've taken it upon my-self to create an entirely new wardrobe for you." He turned and gestured to the trunks Elsy was still considering. "It's all there in those trunks, all seven of them."

"How were you able to create a new wardrobe for me? You've never taken down my measurements, nor could you have created a wardrobe in a day. You're good, Phillip, I'll give you that, but not that good."

Phillip brushed a piece of lint from his shoulder. "But it's be-cause I am that good that I was able to create a wardrobe for you, although not overnight. As for your measurements, I have an eye for ladies' figures. I sized you up months ago when I was design-ing a new line because I knew there would come a day when you were going to need to abandon those hideous widow's weeds and embrace a new and improved you. To my delight, that day has finally arrived."

Eunice opened her mouth, but before she could get a word out, Elsy stalked up beside Phillip and settled a glare on him.

"You have an eye for ladies' figures?"

Phillip's brows drew together. "I'm a dressmaker, Elsy. I'd be less than competent at my job if I didn't have an eye for figures. Dressmakers are supposed to create dresses that flatter a lady and her curves, which means I need to be acquainted with those curves so I can design my dresses accordingly."

When Elsy released a sniff and stalked off for the carriage again, Eunice shook her head and leaned closer to him. "Not that I enjoy involving myself in anyone's personal affairs, but I believe Elsy's annoyance is directly tied to your attention to other ladies. You might want to think about how to apologize to her for that, and I wouldn't suggest that apology include anything in it about ladies and their curves." She gave his arm a pat. "I'll go arrange for some footmen to help with all those trunks, and you, my dear friend, should go and make amends with Elsy."

Leaving Phillip mumbling something about having no idea what he was supposed to be amending because it wasn't as if he ogled anyone's curves, Eunice climbed the steps and reentered the house, finding Daphne walking toward her down the hall.

"Did something happen at the agency?" Daphne asked when she reached Eunice's side.

"Nothing concerning, but . . ." Eunice stopped talking as she considered Daphne. "Do you know you're a rather unusual color of green, and—"

Before Eunice could complete the sentence, Daphne spun around and dashed toward a powder room that was at the end of the hall. Knowing Daphne would hardly care to have someone hovering outside the door, Eunice made her way to the library, picking up the Jane Austen book she'd been reading the night before and settling into a chair. Five minutes later, Daphne trudged into the room, clutching a wet cloth in her hand, which she immediately dabbed over her forehead once she took a seat.

"Are you all right?" Eunice asked.

"I knew I shouldn't have had that heavy soup for lunch, but since I feel queasy again even mentioning soup, distract me by telling me why Elsy and Phillip are here."

"Phillip has decided to take me in hand," Eunice admitted, setting aside the book. "He seems to believe he's about to turn into my fairy godfather."

Daphne's eyes began to twinkle. "How delightful, and it's about time." She looked around. "Where are Phillip and Elsy?"

"They're still outside because they're in the midst of a spat."

"I imagine it's because he's been delaying proposing to Elsy, wanting to create a magnificent occasion for her that she'll never forget. He obviously doesn't understand that by delaying his proposal and by keeping Elsy in the dark about the reason why, Elsy is now wondering if he's reconsidering their courtship, which, in turn, has left her feeling put out with him."

"She told you that?"

"I'm a writer, Eunice. People don't have to tell me much for me to get a picture of what's happening in their lives. Given that Elsy has turned grumpy of late, which is out of character because she's the most cheerful of all of our inquiry agents, it's clear she's begun to question whether Phillip has any intention of marrying her."

Before Eunice could respond to that, Phillip breezed into the room, Elsy by his side. Given the annoyance still stamped on Elsy's face, it was apparent Phillip hadn't made much of an inroad with settling matters between them.

"Daphne," Phillip exclaimed, heading directly for her and taking hold of her hand. "How charming you look today, although . . ." He began giving her a thorough perusal. "Upon further consideration, you're looking somewhat puny. I would say the almost-jaundice tint you're sporting is due to the color of your day dress, but that green should make you look luminous, given your normal coloring." He tapped his finger on his chin before he smiled. "Ah, but of course. And lucky for you, even though Elsy and I need to return to the city this afternoon because Ann's only available to fill in for Elsy's companion duties today, I'll still have enough time to alter a few of your dresses. I'm sure you'll appreciate having a dress or two that allows you a touch more room for your expanding figure."

"What a thing to say to Daphne," Elsy said with a roll of her eyes. "And from a man who keeps claiming he's an expert on the ladies. No lady wants to hear that someone thinks she may be a little plumper than usual."

"Daphne's not plump because she's been indulging in too much cake," Phillip countered. "She's expecting and will probably be large as a house before too long."

"Honestly, Phillip," Daphne said, crossing her arms over her chest. "You can't simply spit out information like that with no warning. I've been withholding my expectant condition from Eunice as well as everyone else except Herman because I was attempting to draw out the suspense."

Phillip winced. "Oh, well, then please forgive me, but will it make you feel better if I divulge that Gabriella is also expecting so it doesn't seem as if I'm singling you out and only disclosing your secret?"

"Not particularly," Daphne said. "Nor do I believe Gabriella will be thrilled you've taken it upon yourself to blurt out that information. I'm sure she probably cautioned you to keep that confidential when she told you about her condition."

"She didn't actually tell me she was expecting, but when she stopped in at the shop before she left on her latest case, I noticed her dress had been altered." Phillip smiled. "And while Gabriella is more than capable of altering a dress to perfection, I made that particular dress for her and knew she'd let out the seams. Since Gabriella could probably eat an entire goat and not gain an ounce, I realized she was in a delicate way."

At the word *goat*, Daphne immediately dashed for the door.

"I don't believe expectant ladies enjoy the image that's created when someone suggests eating a goat," Eunice said.

"It's an unappealing image, even for those of us not expecting," Elsy agreed. "But goats aside, it is lovely that the agency is going to be getting some little additions within the year. I spent some time as a governess before I became a lady's companion, and I've missed being around children."

"I didn't know you were a governess," Phillip said.

Elsy lifted her chin. "There's a lot you don't know about me."

Phillip took hold of her hand. "Indeed there is, but I'm looking forward to learning everything about you over the next fifty years or so."

Any hint of annoyance disappeared from Elsy's face as she sent Phillip a smile right before they began staring into each other's eyes, quite like Ivan and Judith had recently done.

Unable to decide if she should slip out of the library to give the two lovebirds some privacy or perhaps clear her throat to remind them they weren't actually alone in the room, Eunice was spared either choice when Phillip kissed Elsy's hand and sent Eunice a somewhat sheepish smile.

"Sorry, I fear Elsy and I are being rather rude by ignoring you. What were we discussing?"

"I believe you had mentioned eating goats, an unfortunate choice of words with Daphne, who probably won't return to the room for the foreseeable future, what with how green she was," Eunice said.

Phillip ran a hand through his hair, leaving it standing on end, which was quite an unusual look for him. "I'll definitely be more mindful of my word choices, but I have to wonder with Daphne and Gabriella both being expectant if they'll continue working at the agency."

"We've never talked about the matter before," Eunice admitted. "I suppose that's a discussion we'll have soon, but one thing is now abundantly clear—there's no possible way I can leave the agency to trek off to Montana. I'll need to remain in New York so that the agency can continue operating in an efficient fashion."

"And while I know you've been dying to find the perfect excuse to ignore the situation in Montana, know that I've found the perfect solution for you in regard to managing your agency while you're gone."

Eunice stilled for the briefest of seconds before she forced herself to turn, finding Arthur standing in the doorway. "I wasn't expecting to see you here today."

Arthur smiled. "I'm sure you weren't, but I knew you'd disappear last night, which is why I had Grandfather get Herman Henderson's direction for me." His smile turned into a grin. "I could have come after you last night, but I thought that really would come across as stalkerish behavior, which is why I waited until today to join you."

"How is waiting half a day not stalking me?"

"I'm not sure that it isn't, but I'm here now, and as I've said, I've a solution to your dilemma about the agency. Chase is going to step in for you."

"Your younger brother has experience with managing an inquiry agency?"

"Not exactly, but he's been volunteering at a mission for months. From what I understand, he's very good with speaking to people possessed of horrible problems, something that will come in handy while dealing with potential clients at the agency. He's also good with scheduling." Arthur rubbed his hands together. "So, that's that, and now shall we get on our way?"

Phillip shook his head. "I'm afraid Eunice isn't going anywhere until I say she's ready." He moved up to Arthur and held out his hand. "I'm Monsieur Phillip Villard, and you're Arthur Livingston, the man Eunice fondly refers to as the scourge of the earth."

"She does seem to have a way with words," Arthur said, shaking Phillip's hand before he sent the barest hint of a grin to Eunice. "May I ask why a renowned dressmaker has to say you're ready before we can travel to your mother's artist colony?"

"He's decided to take me in hand."

"And you've agreed to that?"

"I believe I've been overruled."

"How delightful," Arthur said, moving to a chair and taking a seat. "I'll just wait here for you, and . . . Eunice?" He smiled. "Know that I'm waiting with bated breath to see exactly how Monsieur Villard takes you in hand. I have a feeling he's very good at what he does."

"I'm not good," Phillip scoffed. "I'm exceptional."

"Then I imagine we'll soon see some exceptional results."

Eunice narrowed an eye on Arthur. "You realize I never invited you to stay to witness the results of Phillip taking me in hand, don't you?"

He grinned. "Of course, but I have no intention of leaving, so you might as well get on with it. As I mentioned, I'll be waiting with bated breath."

"You're very annoying."

"Now there's a clever retort."

Since she had nothing resembling cleverness at her disposal to say to that, Eunice sent Arthur a roll of her eyes, which only had his grin widening before she spun on her heel and stalked out of the room.

As she made her way down the hallway, though, she couldn't resist a grin of her own, which faded when she realized she *did* enjoy her somewhat contentious exchanges with Arthur, which seemed to suggest that Daphne had been right about Eunice's animosity toward Arthur being so much more.

The question of the hour now was exactly what that so much more actually was.

CHAPTER
Seventeen

Arthur had been looking forward to exceptional, but what Phillip Villard had accomplished with Eunice was beyond exceptional and more along the lines of extraordinary.

Gone were the widow's weeds, replaced with a gown of ivory that showed off Eunice's lithe frame to perfection, while also accentuating curves he'd never realized she possessed. He hadn't allowed himself to linger on those curves, though, as she'd strode into the library because, well, it was Eunice, and she wouldn't take kindly to any lingering on his part.

She'd made it perfectly clear she wasn't interested in him in a romantic fashion, that point proven when Phillip had said she'd described him as the scourge of the earth. But even with her thinking of him as a scourge, he couldn't help but admire her new look, nor could he help that the sight of her walking into the library had left him feeling all sorts of discombobulated.

He'd been expecting some self-consciousness on her part, since he was relatively certain she'd never been dressed in the first state of fashion, but she hadn't seemed self-conscious at all, though her cheeks had turned just the slightest shade of pink when he'd taken her gloved hand and pressed a kiss on it.

In all honesty, the moment his lips had touched her hand, he'd felt heat settle on his face, but she hadn't seemed to notice, although Daphne's gaze had sharpened on him after he'd released Eunice's hand and told her she looked nice.

"I still cannot believe you insulted Phillip by proclaiming I look nice."

Arthur blinked out of his thoughts and discovered Eunice frowning at him from the opposite side of the carriage, Judith sitting beside her.

That she looked more than nice was not in question. She looked beautiful, it was as simple as that, with her hair fashioned in a most becoming style underneath an enormous wide-brimmed hat, a simple band of ivory satin wrapped around its base.

But even though she was now dressed in the first state of fashion, Arthur was beginning to realize that her allure wasn't because of her current style.

It was simply because of her.

"Do you have nothing to say about insulting Phillip because you know that's exactly what you did?"

"I thought saying you looked nice was a compliment."

She waved that aside. "It took Phillip an hour and a half to 'pull me together' as he called it. That type of effort deserves words more descriptive than nice." She shook her head. "Poor Phillip is probably even now trying to figure out how he could have improved my appearance."

"He couldn't have done a single thing more to do that."

Eunice opened her mouth, closed it, opened it again, and then, to his surprise, she grinned. "On my word, Arthur, that might have been the first compliment you've ever extended me."

"That's not true. I distinctly remember telling you once in Montana that you had a very good seat on Wyatt."

She wrinkled her nose. "Considering Wyatt threw me shortly after, I then distinctly remember you saying that perhaps you'd been hasty in stating I had a good seat."

"I only said that because I was annoyed with you for insisting on owning such a beast in the first place."

"I didn't insist on Wyatt. Grandfather did. I loathed that horse, although I have felt guilty over the years because I left him behind when I fled Montana."

"Wyatt's fine, so there's no need for any guilt. I bought him from your uncle not long after your grandfather's funeral."

"Why would you buy a horse with such a questionable temperament?"

He shrugged. "It was either that or your uncle was going to send him to the slaughterhouse. Since I didn't think you'd want Wyatt dead, no matter that he seemed to have the habit of unseating you often, I decided to step in and rescue him for you."

Eunice smiled. "That was very kind, Arthur. Thank you."

The sight of her smile left him feeling somewhat befuddled, until Ivan cleared his throat in a rather telling way. Shaking his head in the hopes of removing all befuddlement, Arthur returned her smile. "Would you find it kinder still if I gave Wyatt back to you?"

She shuddered. "No. He's yours now, and good riddance. May I dare hope he's better behaved for you than he was for me?"

"We've come to terms, although he can turn ornery when one least expects it. He threw my grandfather six months back, which resulted in Grandfather breaking his leg. That's why I didn't bring Wyatt to New York."

"Wyatt's questionable temperment is exactly why I told my grandfather I didn't want anything to do with the beast. However, my grandfather was rather ornery as well and insisted the sight of me riding such a horse would have the miners respecting me more."

Arthur stilled. "I wasn't aware James made a habit of taking you into the mines."

"It was a habit I wish he'd never taken up, but considering he was, at one point, going to turn Mason Mines over to me, my going into the mines was never up for debate. I started going with him when I was about seventeen." She shook her head. "My mother was fit to be tied about that, and she and Grandfather had a heated argument over the matter."

She smoothed a hand over a wrinkle in her skirt. "I didn't hear their entire conversation, but Mother was livid about Grandfather placing me in a dangerous situation—not simply danger from the mine, but the miners themselves. Before I could hear Grandfather's response, though, my great-aunt Hazel caught me eavesdropping at the door. She hustled me out of the house, lecturing me for a good hour about how unladylike eavesdropping was. She then apparently felt guilty for lecturing me, as was often the case with Aunt Hazel, and took me into town to buy me a new dress and have an ice at the General Store." Eunice fiddled with a button on her glove. "When we returned home, Grandfather informed me that Mother had left in a huff. I wasn't too concerned about that because she often went off for a day or two after she and Grandfather fought, but this time she never returned. I've not heard from her since."

"It must have been difficult having your mother leave you like that," he said.

"Mother and I were never close," Eunice said. "I've always believed she saw my father every time she looked at me. From what little she told me about him, he was the love of her life, and I was a reminder of a love she no longer had. She seemed content to let Grandfather raise me, which was why I was surprised she stepped in about the mining situation. Clearly, the argument with Grandfather was a deciding factor in her decision to leave me, but I don't care to discuss this matter further." She blew out a breath. "I'm soon to find myself face to face with her for the first time in over ten years, and it'll hardly be a pleasant reunion if I concentrate on the hurt she inflicted on me by leaving without a word." She turned her attention to a small watch dangling from a chain on her wrist. "It shouldn't be much longer now. Herman said the artist colony was only a forty-minute carriage ride from his home."

A moment later, the carriage turned onto a side road and then slowed to a stop. It rocked as someone jumped off the driver's seat, and then one of the Henderson groomsmen appeared, holding his hand out to Eunice, who took it and stepped from the carriage.

Arthur joined her, frowning as he looked at a wrought-iron gate that rose a good ten feet into the air, complete with spikes on the top that were clearly there to dissuade intruders. The iron gate was flanked by hedges that were at least ten feet high as well and ran as far as the eye could see. Given the heavy chain and lock wrapped around the gate, it was obvious that gaining entrance into the artist colony was going to be trickier than expected.

"I'm getting the distinct impression Etta doesn't care for unexpected guests," Judith said, coming to stand beside Arthur and pointing to a sign that was sticking out of the hedge. "Seems rather ominous."

"'No Trespassing or Risk Imminent Death,'" Arthur read out loud, his lips twitching. "Not exactly a warm welcome and does leave me wondering if we should return to Daphne's, send a telegram, and then await your mother's response before we try to pay a call on her again."

"I'm not going to delay this reunion by taking time out to send a telegram," Eunice said. "We'll find a way through the hedge."

"But what about the risk-imminent-death business?" Judith asked.

"While Mother is better with a pistol than I am, which means imminent death could be possible for strangers gaining access to her artist colony, she's not going to shoot me, her one and only daughter. With that said, though, perhaps I should go through the hedge alone. She'll recognize me straightaway, whereas she might get a little quick with her trigger finger if she catches sight of the rest of you before she sees me."

"Your mother knows who I am," Ivan pointed out. "Which means I'm going with you."

"And I'm not staying behind," Judith said, speaking up. "If you've forgotten, I'm an inquiry agent, and it seems to me that an inquiry agent shouldn't be left cooling her heels while an investigation is unfolding."

Eunice rubbed a hand over her face. "An excellent point." She looked up at the foreboding wall of green in front of her. "But there's every possibility that we won't find a hole in the hedge, which means we're going to have to climb over it."

Judith lifted her chin. "The hedge won't pose a problem for me because I, unlike you, have been forced to avail myself of Cooper's thrice-weekly physical exertion lessons. I assure you, scaling a hedge won't be difficult for me. I'm also very good at dodging. Cooper recently decided we had to participate in dodging-the-ball exercises that have left me fleet on my feet because the ball we use in that exercise is heavy and smarts if it hits you. That means I should be able to dodge a bullet if your mother turns a little aggressive with her pistol."

"Dodging a bullet is not the same as dodging a ball," Eunice pointed out.

"Which I'm sure Judith knows," Ivan said, sending a warm smile Judith's way. "But she really has excelled at those physical exertion lessons. I can attest to the fact she's mastered climbing, so I'm in full agreement that she needs to come with us."

Eunice threw her hands up. "Fine. Since I'm evidently outnumbered, everyone can go over the hedge. But if Mother starts shooting at all of you, you'll have no one to blame but yourselves." With that, Eunice headed off along the hedge, Arthur, Judith, and Ivan hurrying to catch up with her.

"Aren't you curious why Etta's outfitted the perimeter of her artist colony like a fortress?" Judith asked.

"I'm sure she has her reasons, although you should know that Mother was never addressed as Etta. She signed her paintings that way because my grandfather didn't want anyone to know that his daughter dabbled in the arts."

"Dabbling in the arts is an insult to your mother's talent."

"I can't argue with that," Eunice said before she stopped and eyed a hedge in front of her. "This one seems a little shorter." With that, she stepped closer, took hold of a branch, and began climbing.

"How surprising that Eunice can climb so easily," Judith said, shading her eyes with her hand as she watched Eunice's progress.

"I was under the impression she avoided physical activity since she refuses to participate in Cooper's exertion lessons."

"She only refused to do that to avoid questions about her athletic abilities," Ivan said, positioning himself directly underneath Eunice in case she fell. "She's actually climbs a rope four or five times a week in the warehouse where we box."

Judith sent an unexpected flutter of lashes Ivan's way. "I've always longed to learn how to box."

Arthur wasn't exactly surprised when Ivan and Judith immediately began staring at each other in a rather flirty fashion, which had him nudging Ivan out of the way since, clearly, the man was far too preoccupied to catch Eunice if she fell.

"Before you promise Judith you'll teach her how to box, Ivan," Eunice called, "remember that it's highly unlikely you'll be comfortable doing that, not when there's always the possibility you'll unintentionally hit her." She reached for a limb and pulled herself up a foot before she glanced down, catching Arthur's eye. "Ivan once tried to discontinue our boxing lessons after his fist glanced over my cheek."

"I didn't sleep for a week after that accident," Ivan said, pulling his attention from Judith to send Arthur a wince. "The only reason I agreed to continue boxing with her was because she was the only grandchild of one of the wealthiest men in the country, and she needed to learn how to handle herself in a fight if anyone ever tried to abduct her and she wasn't able to get to a weapon."

"No, you agreed to continue boxing with me because I threatened to trot down to the local boxing gym and hire a few men to spar with me."

"That might have been another reason," Ivan muttered as Eunice stopped climbing and sent Arthur a nod.

"I'm going over," she called. "Be mindful of the branches on your way up. They're prickly."

A second later, Eunice disappeared over the top of the hedge, and a second after that, the distinctive sound of a pistol rang out.

Eighteen

Eunice dropped lightly to the ground, shaking out the folds of her skirt as Georgette Howland strode toward her, pistol in hand. She was wearing, unusually enough, a brightly colored robe, her blond hair assembled in a messy knot on top of her head, secured with what seemed to be two paintbrushes.

"You might want to put the pistol away, Mother," Eunice said, tipping back the brim of her hat. "I didn't tear a hole in an afternoon gown I adore to be shot before I've had a chance to speak with you."

Georgette stopped in her tracks, tilted her head, and tucked the pistol in a holster that was hanging low on her hip. "Sunshine, is that you? My goodness but this is a surprise. I thought you were one of those annoying society ladies who like to come snooping around. You should have let me know you were coming. I would have opened the gate and left my pistol in the house."

"While it's somewhat bewildering why you'd believe a society lady would climb a ten-foot hedge, I didn't let you know I was coming because I only recently learned your direction and wasn't expecting to encounter what amounts to a fortress upon my arrival."

Georgette gave an airy wave of a hand. "I was forced to take extreme measures to maintain my privacy after some society members who have their spring homes on the Hudson began making a habit of driving onto my land because I have lovely views of the river. It was quite annoying to find ladies and their gentlemen strolling about my yard as if they had every right to do so. Nevertheless, when I scared some fashionable ladies in an open carriage by shooting a rifle into the air, the local police paid me a visit and threatened to arrest me if I ever did that again. So, I added the iron gate, spikes, and additional hedges, and painted a threatening sign." She smiled. "I'm pleased to report that I no longer get pestered by sightseeing members of the New York Four Hundred."

"Since you operate an artist colony, one would think you'd want to cater to those darlings of society since they're known to enjoy patronizing artists."

"A reasonable point, but I've never been one who enjoys the patronizing attitude that comes with patrons of the arts. But since I doubt you're here to listen to me wax on about society members, why don't you—"

Before Georgette could finish her sentence, Arthur dropped to the ground, which had Georgette whipping out her pistol again and training it on him.

"I see you weren't jesting about your mother being a tad aggressive with her pistol," he muttered as he raised his hands in the air. "There's no need for alarm, ma'am. I'm with Eunice."

Instead of lowering her pistol, Georgette cocked it. "Who, pray tell, is Eunice?"

Arthur blinked. "Oh, well, that's a bit of a story in and of itself, but for the sake of expediency, since you are holding me at pistol point, Eunice is actually Eugenia, although she doesn't go by the name Eugenia these days."

Georgette's only response to that was to quirk a brow in Eunice's direction.

"It's a long story, but I changed my name to Eunice as well as changed my last name to Holbrooke—and not through marriage, mind you, if that was going to be your next question. I'm not married."

"And here I was hoping that the delectable and dangerous-looking man claiming he's with you was making that claim because he's, well, *with* you," Georgette said as she stowed her pistol away again. "But tell me this, Sunshine, why in the world would you have gone through the bother of changing your name? Better yet, if you didn't care for Eugenia, why would you have changed it to an even duller name?"

"Eunice isn't dull, but as for why I chose it, I'm very fond of my traveling trunks that are stamped *EH*."

"We'll have to agree to disagree about the dullness of your new name, but . . ." The corners of Georgette's lips twitched. "The luggage explanation makes perfect sense because beautiful luggage cannot be overrated. With that said, though, I still adore the name Sunshine, so I'm certain you'll understand if I continue to call you that over Eunice." She turned to Arthur. "You're looking rather confused, dear. If you're unaware, my daughter's middle name is Sunshine. I've always called her that, not having a fondness for the name Eugenia."

"If you weren't fond of the name Eugenia, why would you name your daughter that?"

"On account of my father's demands, of course. He was adamant about naming my daughter after his mother, and because Father could be unpleasant when thwarted, I agreed to his demand but then chose Sunshine for her middle name." She smiled. "I derived a sense of satisfaction every time Father shuddered when he heard me calling her Sunshine."

"You did seem to relish annoying Grandfather," Eunice said. "But speaking of names, I fear I'm neglecting my manners. I've yet to introduce you to Arthur. Mother, this is Mr. Arthur Livingston. Arthur, my mother, Georgette Howland."

"It's a pleasure to meet you, Mrs. Howland," Arthur said, presenting her with a bow.

"Please, call me Georgette. But what a pity that it appears you and Sunshine aren't romantically involved. I have a feeling you would have made a delightful addition to the family."

Arthur's eyes twinkled. "How kind of you to say, but I'm relatively certain your daughter wouldn't agree with that. She finds me annoying as well as far too opinionated."

"Does she now?" Georgette asked, the gleam flickering in her eyes more than a touch concerning.

"Don't read anything into that, Mother," Eunice began. "And for heaven's sakes, don't consider turning your attention to any matchmaking plots. Yes, I'm sure you're disappointed to learn your one and only daughter is a confirmed spinster, but you lost the right to meddle in my life when you left me without a word ten years ago."

Georgette released a sigh. "I suppose it was too much to expect that my disappearance wasn't going to be broached straightaway. May I assume you're annoyed with me about that disappearance?"

"Annoyed would be putting it mildly."

"Then I should probably fortify myself with a nice bracing cup of coffee before we discuss the matter further. I have a feeling our conversation is going to be somewhat . . . prickly." She gestured toward a dirt path. "Shall we repair to my humble abode?"

"We need to wait for our other companions, who I'm sure will be tumbling over the hedge any second now. But while we wait, and since you don't want to delve into your disappearance without coffee, allow me to turn the conversation to something noncontentious." Eunice smiled. "You're looking well these days, although the robes are a different style for you."

Georgette smoothed a hand down the front of a robe that was a mixture of blue, red, purple, and vivid splashes of orange. "I think the style suits my artistic nature, and besides, I've never been good with a needle and thread. Robes are far easier to make than fitted dresses."

A sense of unease tickled the back of Eunice's neck. "Why would you make your own clothing?"

Georgette shrugged. "Funds are limited for me, my dear, and

making my own clothing is preferable over going naked, although there is a case to be made that strolling around naked could be quite pleasant if it's an overly warm day."

"And here's where I remove myself to a safe distance to allow the two of you some privacy," Arthur said as he all but sprinted away, not stopping until he was underneath a large maple tree with vibrant red leaves, one that was well away from her mother.

Eunice fought a grin. "I see you still have a propensity for saying whatever pops to mind."

"I probably should have resisted the word *naked*, but it's always amusing to see what a gentleman will do when faced with the unexpected. Your gentleman chose to flee, which was probably a wise choice on his part."

"He's not my gentleman."

"So you keep saying, but wherever did you meet him? Was it while you were on your extended European tour?"

"How did you know about my tour?"

Georgette shrugged. "I sent a telegram to Uncle Raymond inquiring about you. It must have been seven years or so ago. Well, I actually sent the telegram to Aunt Hazel, wanting to circumvent Father, but Uncle Raymond was the one to reply to it. He told me you were taking an extended tour of Europe and weren't expected home for the foreseeable future."

"What else did Uncle Raymond tell you?"

"Nothing of any consequence. It was a telegram, which doesn't allow for an excess of words. I sent him a return telegram, telling him he could find me in New York if he ever needed to contact me. I assumed he'd pass that information on to you once you returned. Since I never heard from you, I concluded you didn't want to talk to me."

"Did Uncle Raymond mention anything about Grandfather?"

"No, but I wouldn't have expected him to. It's not as if the family wasn't well aware of the relationship I didn't enjoy with Father. Uncle Raymond obviously knew I wasn't fishing about for an update, so didn't give me one."

"That's too bad."

Georgette quirked a brow. "Should I take that to mean Father's dead?"

Eunice quirked a brow right back at her. "I wasn't expecting you to be so blunt about the matter, but yes, I'm afraid he is. He died years ago. Uncle Raymond should have let you know that, no matter if he thought you wanted an update or not."

"It's not as if I didn't have an inkling he might be gone by now, Sunshine. He was elderly, after all, and in all honesty, I've even said a few prayers for his soul every now and again when I attend church." She frowned. "Was his death a result of a heart ailment? I always said his temper was going to see his heart give out in the end."

"It wasn't his heart."

"An accident?"

"He was murdered."

Georgette's eyes widened the slightest bit. "Murdered? Good heavens, that's rather troubling, although . . . I can't claim to be surprised, given how many people despised him. Who was behind the dastardly deed?"

Before Eunice could respond, a shriek sounded behind her, followed by the sight of Judith plummeting to the ground. Ivan dropped down beside her a second later, lending Judith assistance as she got unsteadily to her feet.

"May I assume these are the companions we've been waiting on?" Georgette asked, her hand hovering over her pistol.

"They are, so don't shoot them," Eunice said. "This is Miss Judith Donovan, who is an admirer of your paintings, and you already know Ivan."

Georgette beamed a smile Judith's way. "How delightful to learn you enjoy my work. I'm Eunice's mother, Georgette Howland."

Judith opened her mouth, but all that came out was a bit of a squeak, suggesting she'd been struck all but mute over finding herself face to face with a woman she considered an artistic icon.

Georgette didn't seem to notice the unusual reaction, because she'd turned her attention to Ivan. "Ah, Ivan. Why am I not surprised to find you're still in the company of my daughter." She frowned. "Did you know your cheek is bleeding, dear? You've got a trail of blood running down it, and I'm afraid it's soon to stain your jacket."

Ivan fished a handkerchief out of his pocket, dashed it over a cheek that was, indeed, bleeding, and narrowed his eyes on Georgette. "I wouldn't be bleeding all over the place if I'd not been forced to scale your hedge. We're fortunate none of us suffered more than a few scratches, but with that out of the way, allow me to say that you're looking well, Mrs. Holbrooke. The years away from Montana seem to have agreed with you, although I fear I must point out that those years took a toll on your daughter."

Georgette frowned. "I wouldn't think wandering around Europe would have been taxing on either of you."

"We weren't touring Europe," Ivan said shortly, earning a blink from Georgette before she turned to Eunice.

"There's evidently a story there. And while I'd dearly love to delay the inevitable conversation you and I must have, shall we finally repair to the house? I baked a lovely cake earlier today to go along with the coffee. It may be just the thing to assist with softening a talk I'm sure neither of us will enjoy." Georgette turned and began striding down the dirt path, slowing to look over her shoulder a second later. "Be aware that you may encounter some of the resident artists. They're an eclectic group, and two of them tend to take people aback at first. Mr. Dodger Barstow is a brilliant watercolorist, but he makes a habit of wandering around the grounds wearing a Viking helmet and billowing capes done up in bright shades of puce. He's also prone to badgering anyone who possesses what he calls *a face* to sit for him." She settled a smile on Arthur. "He won't be able to resist your face, so you may want to avoid him."

"See? I'm not the only one who believes you have a face," Judith mumbled, turning pink when Georgette directed her attention her way.

"Are you an artist as well, dear?"

When Judith immediately turned from pink to bright red, Georgette shot a quirk of a brow to Eunice, who sent her a smile in return.

"As I mentioned, Judith is an admirer of your work. I fear she may be a bit awestruck with you right now, so returning to your artists. You mentioned there were two we should be aware of—Mr. Dodger Barstow and . . . ?"

"Ah yes, Mr. Grover Cropsy. He's usually with Dodger, and you'll be able to spot Grover straightaway because he's been experimenting with unusual mediums of late. He'll likely be covered in mud from our pond, which I'm afraid tends to make him look like a swamp monster. But don't be overly alarmed. He's relatively harmless." With that, Georgette turned and headed down the path, Eunice breaking into a trot to keep her mother in sight.

"That is not how I was hoping an introduction to your mother would go," Judith said, trotting up to join Eunice.

"I'm sure you'll do better with her once we reach the house."

"I would hope so. Do you think she noticed that I've been verging on a fit of the vapors?"

"That would have been difficult to miss."

"How unfortunate," Judith said, dashing a hand over a forehead that was smudged with a streak of dirt from her plummet to the ground. "She's exactly how I imagined, though. Eccentric, quirky, and it's obvious you got your looks from her because she's breathtakingly beautiful."

"I imagine if you let her know you think she's breathtakingly beautiful, she'll not remember a thing about how tongue-tied you just were."

Judith's lips curved, and without another word, she dashed away to join Georgette, clearly intent on launching into a touch of flattery that would hopefully go better than their limited interactions had gone thus far.

Judith's spot was soon taken by Ivan, who watched Judith until she disappeared around a turn. "There's something quite adorable about seeing Judith so delighted by this opportunity to meet your mother. And this has nothing to do with how adorable Judith is, but before I get completely distracted, did you catch the part where your mother said she baked a cake?"

"I did, which has left me feeling decidedly uneasy. Mother never knew her way around a kitchen, and when you add in the fact she's also making her own robes due to limited funds, I'm finding myself apprehensive about hearing her story."

"A word of caution, though, Ivan," Arthur said as he joined them. "You might want to refrain from mentioning her robes since that could very well have her launching into the benefits of traveling around her artist colony naked again." He shuddered. "Not exactly something I expected to hear today."

Ivan grinned. "Georgette always did enjoy shocking people by saying the most unexpected things. She once drew me aside about a year after I became Eunice's bodyguard to tell me in no uncertain terms that I was to keep any, and I quote, 'manly thoughts' about her daughter in check."

"I remember when she did that," Eunice said. "I had to sit her down and tell her that although you were technically my bodyguard, you were like the brother I never had, so there was no reason for her to worry that the two of us were going to run off together."

Ivan stopped in his tracks, causing Eunice and Arthur to do the same. "You never told me you think of me as a brother."

"I assumed you knew."

"I suppose I did at that, but that's the nicest thing you've ever said about me. I consider you to be the sister I never had, albeit a very opinionated and difficult sister to keep alive at times."

She grinned. "I imagine it has been difficult to keep me alive at times, but as your opinionated honorary sibling, allow me to give you some sisterly advice before we get to the house. Mother is certain to pick up on the flirtation you and Judith seem to be enjoying. If you don't want her to embarrass you by remarking on it, you may want to curb the flirting, at least until we get back on the road. With that said, though, you've not mentioned a thing to me about your interest in Judith."

Ivan tucked his handkerchief away. "I wasn't allowing the, ah, affection I've felt for her for some time to become known because my job has been to keep you hidden. But now with everything coming out in the open, I might have time to perhaps turn my attention to some, er . . . courting, if, ah, Judith returns the affection I hold her in."

Guilt was swift.

Ivan had been by her side for years, seeing after her life and never once complaining about what a toll it might be taking on his life. She'd been a poor friend to him by not realizing that living undercover for all these years had robbed him of much.

She laid a hand on his arm. "You should have told me the job of seeing after me was more taxing than I knew."

Ivan gave her hand a pat. "It's hasn't been taxing, Eunice. It's been my pleasure keeping you alive, and you seem to be forgetting that I've been well compensated for doing that. Now, though, with the possibility that you may soon be able to live a more normal life, I may not need to be with you all the time. However, now is not the moment for us to worry about any of that. Your mother is your priority right now. You need to learn why she left you, and she needs to be told about her inheritance."

Moving into motion again, they rounded a curve in the path and discovered a two-storied farmhouse nestled in a grove of trees, painted an unassuming white with black shutters, and sporting a wraparound porch with brightly colored rocking chairs. The house had an air of general neglect Eunice hadn't been expecting, which only increased when she got closer and realized the white paint was peeling in places.

Striding up the steps and into the house, Eunice followed the sound of Judith's voice, who'd evidently recovered her ability to speak. She soon found herself in a large rectangular room that had splashes of color everywhere, the walls adorned with too many paintings to count, not all of them done by her mother.

The furniture placed around the room looked comfortable, if well-worn, the threadbare state of the upholstery brightened with colored pillows.

"Make yourselves at home," Georgette said as she gestured to a stone fireplace. "If anyone is feeling chilly, feel free to build up a fire. I'll be right back. I just need to fetch the coffee and cake." She turned to Judith. "Would you care to assist me?"

Given the expression on Judith's face, it seemed as if Christmas had come early.

"Georgette never struck me as the farmhouse type," Ivan said, walking around the room, his gaze traveling over the paintings on the wall. "But the eclectic grouping of artwork certainly suits her." He frowned. "I don't remember seeing a lot of paintings hanging on the walls at Mason Manor."

"That's because Grandfather only allowed Mother to hang a few of her paintings around the house, not wanting any guests to get the impression Georgette wasted her time on frivolous pursuits."

"Your grandfather was such a charming man," Georgette said, pushing a teacart into the room. "Heaven forbid he would have ever used any of his vast fortune to promote the arts in Butte, something that would have lent our small place in the world a touch of sophistication." She tucked a stray strand of blond hair behind her ear. "He never balked at spending his fortune on things I found unnecessary, though, such as the boxing ring he built after he decided you would benefit from learning that rather uncommon sport for a woman."

"I know it's an unusual sport for the feminine set," Eunice began, "but boxing has served me well over the years. Case in point, I was able to hold my own against a few nurses in an insane asylum."

Georgette's eyes filled with what almost seemed to be horror. "And here I've always held fast to the notion that Father would never turn against you, but I was wrong about that, wasn't I? He sent you off to an asylum for some infraction you probably didn't even know you committed, and then, if I'm not mistaken, allowed everyone to believe you'd been off taking a nice European tour."

A sliver of dread began weaving its way through Eunice as she took a step closer to her mother. "Grandfather never had me committed, but given the look of terror in your eyes, I now fear he may have very well done something dastardly like that to you."

CHAPTER
Nineteen

As a hundred questions whirled through Eunice's mind, Georgette released a sigh of what sounded like relief. "Thank the good Lord your grandfather didn't have you committed," she began. "For a moment, I was worried I'm destined to win the Most Horrible Mother on the Planet Award because I never came back to rescue you. I need to state here and now, though, that the reason for not coming back has nothing to do with the selfish attitude you know I possess." She bit her lip. "Not that I've made great strides with my selfishness, but that particular trait was not the reason I never returned to Montana or why I went away in the first place. However, before I get into my disturbing story, we're going to need coffee—and lots of it."

Once everyone had settled around the room with a cup of coffee and a piece of cake, Eunice took a seat beside her mother on a faded settee that sported bright red and purple pillows. "Are you ready to tell me what happened?"

Georgette set aside her cup. "I'd prefer to never revisit those dark days again, but you deserve to hear the truth." She began tapping her toe against the carpet, quite like she'd often done in Eunice's youth when she was gathering her thoughts. "I didn't voluntarily leave you ten years ago, although I'm sure your grandfather made up a whopper of a story to explain where I'd gone."

"He said you were in a huff after the argument I heard you having with him about taking me into the mines."

"You heard that?"

"Not all of it because Aunt Hazel caught me eavesdropping and whisked me out of the house. When I returned, you were gone." Unexpected tears suddenly stung Eunice's eyes. "I was certain you'd return within a week at the most, but you never came back, nor did you send me a letter telling me where you were."

"I sent you letters, but I knew they'd never reach you." Georgette reached for her coffee, took a sip, then set aside the cup again, probably because her hand had taken to trembling. "I was livid with your grandfather for taking you into the mines. I knew without your even telling me the vile things you overheard those miners saying about you that they were dangerous. Your grandfather, however, wouldn't listen to reason. He told me you were tough enough to handle what he said was 'men being men' talk, and that he knew they'd do nothing more than talk because they valued their jobs. I argued that his confidence in his miners was misplaced and said I wasn't willing to take the risk of having one of those men harm you simply because he was being obtuse about the matter."

"I imagine Grandfather didn't appreciate being called obtuse."

"That's putting it mildly." Georgette blew out a breath. "I eventually told him enough was enough. That even though I'd allowed him to raise you with little input from me, I wasn't going to stand aside and watch him put you in direct danger. You were only seventeen. You should not have been expected to take on the responsibility of learning everything about Mason Mines, nor should your grandfather have contemplated putting you in charge of those mines in the first place."

"So Grandfather *was* intending on having me take over for him?"

"He was, but we'll revisit what happened with you in regard to the mines after I finish my troubling tale." Georgette reached for her cup again, took a sip, and frowned. "I've come to realize that the mistake I made that day was telling your grandfather I was going to take you away and never return. I should have simply done it—taken you away without a word in the middle of the night. He, of course, flew into a rage, telling me I had no right to take you away, that you were his heir apparent. He grew more enraged when I pointed out you were an heiress, not an heir, and besides that, you were my daughter, which meant I had every right to take you away from his madness, because that's what I decided it was . . . sheer madness.

"I left him standing in the middle of his office, raging against me with words I'm glad you didn't overhear. I went to my room and pulled a traveling trunk from my wardrobe, throwing my clothes into it as fast as I could. I then went to your room, but before I could get a single thing of yours packed, your grandfather was in the room with me, in the company of three of his hired men. Those men tied me up, gagged me, then hauled me to a waiting carriage. They threw me in that carriage, along with my one trunk, and off we went to the train station."

Eunice's stomach lurched. "What happened next?"

"He gave his men instructions to get me out of the country, promising to pay them handsomely if they kept me out of Montana until he summoned me home. Those men became my keepers, one of them always with me as we made our way to England. Your grandfather paid every expense, apparently doing so to alleviate the small bit of guilt he might have felt for having me abducted and taken away from you. I began purchasing pieces of jewelry, intending on pawning it to aid my escape someday."

"I take it you were successful escaping your guards at some point?"

Georgette shook her head. "I didn't need to escape them because your grandfather suddenly stopped sending money. Turns out those guards weren't as loyal to him after their funds dried up. I woke up one morning while we were in Spain, and they were gone. I immediately sold some jewelry for a pittance of what it was worth, but it was enough to buy a ticket on a steamer ship bound for New York. After three long years of being guarded every moment, I was finally free. Once I reached shore, I booked a room at the Fifth Avenue Hotel and dashed off that telegram to Aunt Hazel, although Uncle Raymond somehow got it instead."

Judith raised her hand, quite like she was in a classroom. "Why wouldn't you have sent a telegram to Eunice?"

"Because I knew she'd been lied to about why I left. There was every chance she wouldn't respond to my telegram, so I decided it would be more productive to go through Aunt Hazel. Hazel, out of all my relatives, was always the most sensible as well as the only relative who seemed to care about me. It was unfortunate that Uncle Raymond received my telegram instead, although how that happened is a mystery to me."

"Hazel and Raymond moved out of their respective homes and moved into Mason Manor not long after your father died," Arthur said, sitting forward. "Your telegram probably got forwarded from Hazel's house to the main house and then landed in Raymond's hands. He enjoys maintaining control over family matters these days."

Georgette's nose wrinkled. "It's curious that Father would have left Uncle Raymond the big house because he never cared for his younger brother much."

"He didn't leave Uncle Raymond the house, but we'll get into that after you finish your story," Eunice said.

"The plot thickens," Georgette said before she caught Eunice's eye. "I'm sure you're wondering why I sent a telegram instead of boarding a train for Montana, which is what I'm sure most mothers would have done. But I was afraid. Father was not a man to cross, and I knew that even before he sent me off to Europe. I'd crossed him in the past and it did not go well for me. I was convinced that if I showed up at Mason Manor, he would take steps to get me out of your life again, steps that could very well have had me sent somewhere not nearly as pleasant as Europe." She sighed. "I'm sure you must think that was incredibly selfish of me."

"Not at all," Eunice argued. "It's not as if I don't know how difficult Grandfather could be, although learning he sent you away and lied to me about it does suggest he was more ruthless than I knew. But I don't blame you for not returning to Montana, and besides, I wasn't even in Montana then. If you'd made the trip, it would have been for naught and could have very well placed your life in jeopardy."

Georgette set a hand on Eunice's arm. "Do know that I have felt inordinately guilty about you over the years, although my guilt was assuaged when I thought you were taking an extended tour of Europe. Even being watched by guards, I had been able to enjoy parts of my European tour and hoped you were experiencing all the wonders Europe has to offer. Evidently, you didn't get the opportunity to explore the continents."

"I *could* have traveled to Europe. Grandfather arranged a tour for me right before he died, but I decided to stay in New York. I knew it would be easy for me to blend in with the crowd here and assume the new identity of Eunice Holbrooke—an identity I adopted after I fled from Montana the day Grandfather died."

Georgette considered Eunice for a moment before she leaned forward. "I hate to ask this, but did you flee from Montana because you were responsible for his death?"

Amusement was swift. "What a thing to ask me, but no, I didn't murder him."

"Your grandfather was a reprehensible man, so I had to ask." Georgette's lips curved. "I can guarantee you, if I'd been in Montana at the time of his death, the authorities would have considered me a prime suspect."

"I doubt anyone would have believed you'd kill your own father."

"And I doubt anyone, at least our relatives, would have believed anything otherwise. I didn't disguise how much I loathed the man."

"Because?" Eunice pressed.

"I have my reasons," Georgette said vaguely. "But let us turn our discussion to you. You mentioned you moved to New York, but what have you been doing there over the years we've been parted?"

Taking a moment to refill her coffee, Eunice resettled herself on the settee and then launched into the story of her life, setting aside her cup an hour later when she finally finished.

"So, if I'm understanding this correctly," Georgette began, "one of the main reasons you're here is because our relatives want to have us declared dead, which will then affect our inheritance."

"That sums it up nicely."

"But Father told me he was writing me out of his will."

"Grandfather was notorious for telling people he was cutting them out of his will. He threatened to do that to me after I named that dreadful horse Wyatt."

"He would have never taken you out of his will, no matter his threat, because you, unlike me, were never a disappointment to him," Georgette said. "He never forgave my decision to never marry again after your father died. He longed for a male heir, you see, but when he realized I wasn't going to change my mind, he knew you were going to be his only legacy." She settled back against the settee. "May I assume he left me ten thousand dollars?"

"Why would you assume that?"

"It would be his way of having the last word, his way of showing his disdain for me."

"Because . . . ?"

"It's of little consequence. But whatever he left me, even if it's a pittance, I certainly won't turn my nose up at it." Georgette gestured around the room. "As you can see, I don't live an extravagant life. I sold the rest of the jewelry to buy this farm, and I use whatever money I bring in from my paintings for the upkeep of the house and grounds as well as basic necessities."

Judith raised her hand again. "I would think your paintings bring in a substantial amount."

"And aren't you just a dear girl?" Georgette said with a smile. "Unfortunately, there doesn't seem to be a large market for abstract portraits right now, so I haven't made much money over the past couple of years. I've had to resort to painting some landscapes, something I don't enjoy, to make ends meet at times. I charge my resident artists a minuscule fee to stay here—minuscule because these artists are the picture of the proverbial starving artist—but those fees go toward upkeep for the small cabins the artists live in as well as food for our community meals."

"You feed the artists who stay here?" Judith asked slowly.

"I can't actually let them starve, something that would happen if I didn't provide three meals to them a day." Georgette turned to Eunice. "I'm not telling you the realities of my life to make you feel sorry for me. While it's true I've had to learn how to grow my own food and milk my own cow, which was a terrifying feat but one I eventually mastered, I've found a sense of peace here that I never thought I'd find after your father, well . . . left me. I can also attend church without being berated for my faith, something your grandfather always did, even though he always accompanied your grandmother to church before she died when I was a child. He stopped attending services after her death, claiming he had no use for what he saw as a vengeful God. He only allowed me to attend services during my youth because Aunt Hazel told him the townspeople would look harshly on him if it became known his daughter wasn't permitted to attend church."

Georgette nibbled on a bite of cake. "After I came back to raise you under Father's roof, he often berated me for wanting to attend services, stating that God had certainly not been looking after me since I was a woman alone with a small child to raise. The battles I had with him on any given Sunday eventually wore on me, which is why I stopped attending church often, even though I felt I was doing you a disservice by not providing you with a strong foundation to begin building your own faith upon."

"You don't need to feel guilty about that," Eunice said, taking her mother's hand. "It would have been difficult to constantly battle with Grandfather about church. But there's no need to fret I've not been able to find my own spiritual journey. I've become dear friends with Reverend Patrick Dunford of St. Luke's Chapel.

He's been diligently providing me with guidance concerning all matters of faith."

Georgette gave Eunice's hand a pat. "That puts my mind at ease. If I've learned anything over the years I've been away, it's to rely on my faith. Still, I've been striving this past year to learn to turn my troubles over to God and actually *believe* He'll provide for me. Oddly enough, I asked Him only last night if He could show me how I was going to pay for the roof repairs on some of the cabins. The very next day, you arrive on my doorstep to tell me I have some type of unclaimed inheritance waiting for me."

For the briefest of seconds, Eunice found it rather difficult to breathe.

There'd been a part of her that had been hoping her mother wasn't in need of her rightful inheritance, but clearly that wasn't the case. That meant she couldn't blithely turn her back on her inheritance, not when doing so would affect her mother's inheritance as well.

It also meant that she was going to have to finally, and without hesitation, deal with the truth of why she didn't want to return to Montana.

Forcing breath into lungs that were still somewhat constricted, she rose from the settee and nodded to Arthur, who was watching her closely.

"I believe I need some air. While I'm gone, I'd appreciate it if you'd tell my mother about her inheritance." She summoned up a smile and turned back to Georgette. "You may want to continue sitting down, Mother, because what Arthur's about to tell you definitely means you're not going to have to worry about how you're going to afford those new roofs for your cabins."

CHAPTER

Twenty

There'd not been a single time when Arthur had delivered favorable financial news where the recipient of that news broke down and began sobbing, but that's exactly what Georgette did a mere moment after he disclosed the extent of her inheritance.

"She could use a hug," Judith whispered in his ear as Georgette continued sobbing into a handkerchief Ivan handed her.

"Perhaps you should do the hugging," Arthur said. "I'm not really the hugging sort."

Judith's only response to that was to cross her arms over her chest.

Taking that as a firm refusal to intervene, Arthur joined Georgette on the settee, perching gingerly on the edge of it. Not really knowing what else to do, he gave her what was undoubtedly an awkward pat on the shoulder, earning a snort from Judith in return, which he ignored.

"There, there," he began, which earned him a snort from Ivan, one he didn't appreciate in the least.

"Feel free to step in," he muttered, which only resulted in Ivan moving to look out the window.

When Georgette released another sob, and realizing Judith and Ivan didn't seem inclined to offer their assistance, Arthur took hold of her hand. "You're going to make yourself sick if you continue sobbing" were the only comforting words that sprang to mind.

That earned him a snort from Georgette before she gave his hand a squeeze. "You're not very good at this, are you?"

"I'm afraid no one has ever accused me of being overly comforting."

She smiled a wobbly smile. "No one has ever accused me of that either, or my daughter for that matter. But speaking of Sunshine, where is she?"

"She said she needed some air."

Georgette brushed aside tears that were trailing down her cheek. "Which is usually said when a person has matters to contemplate. May I assume there's something my daughter is withholding from me about claiming our inheritance?"

"I wouldn't want to speak for her, but she seems remarkably reluctant to return to Montana."

"Because she really *might* have killed her grandfather?"

It was Arthur's turn to snort. "Eunice didn't kill James, but perhaps I should go speak with her and find out once and for all exactly what's behind her reticence with returning to Montana."

"Just don't tell her she's going to have to marry you," Ivan said, turning from the window. "If you really understood Eunice, you'd know a marriage of convenience is not something she'd ever entertain. Pressing her on the matter won't have her changing her mind. It'll merely result with you suffering from injured pride—or a broken nose, depending on Eunice's mood."

Arthur rose to his feet. "I'm not a complete idiot, Ivan, even though my initial idea of pursuing a marriage with Eunice does seem rather idiotic now. Truth be told, I forgot how capable she is, and that trait of hers only seems to have increased over the years. However, if she weren't such a competent lady, my idea would have been the most practical solution for both of us—allowing me to honor my word and allowing her to regain her inheritance with relatively little fuss on her part." He frowned. "But what did you mean about if I really understood Eunice?"

Ivan shrugged. "She's far more complex than you know, but that's all I'm comfortable saying. And if she does decide to retrieve her inheritance, I guarantee there's going to be a fuss involved. She's not said much about her relatives deciding to have her declared dead, but you mark my words, she's furious about that. A furious Eunice is not a woman her relatives are going to enjoy seeing come back from the dead." His lips twitched. "I imagine they're going to be in for a rather rough time of it." With that, Ivan moved to join Georgette on the settee, pulled her into his arms, and gave her a soothing pat on the back.

Considering Georgette immediately dissolved into fresh sobs, Arthur wasn't convinced hugging had been the best choice to stop her tears to begin with.

"Since Ivan seems to have the situation well in hand now, what say we go check on Eunice," Judith said, pushing herself to her feet before she took hold of his arm and tugged him toward the door.

"I'm not sure Ivan has *anything* well in hand," Arthur said when Georgette began sobbing in earnest.

"Of course he does. He's very competent." With that, Judith increased her pace, and before he knew it, he was out of the farmhouse, down the porch steps, and standing on a cobblestone sidewalk.

"Was there a reason we just hightailed it out of the house as if we were being chased by a pack of wolves?" he asked.

Judith waved a hand in front of cheeks that were decidedly pink. "I was afraid if I lingered a moment longer, I'd join in with all that weeping going on. The last thing dear Ivan needs is to contend with two distraught women, not that I don't believe he'd rise magnificently to that occasion."

"Why were you in danger of weeping?"

"Honestly, Arthur, I would think that needs no explaining."

"It does if you expect me to understand why you were evidently on the verge of tears."

"Ladies are occasionally overcome with emotion when they witness a gentleman they hold in high esteem behave in a manner that leaves their hearts pitter-pattering." Judith sent him a rather sad shake of her head. "You really should work on your sensitive side, Arthur. Perhaps if you were to allow that side to come out of that dark chasm you apparently call a heart, people wouldn't call you the scourge of the earth."

"The only one to ever call me that is Eunice, and you know full well she only called me that because she wasn't in agreement with my taking her back to Montana."

"She does seem to enjoy thwarting you." Judith gave him a pat on the arm. "You may very well be beyond hope, dear, in the sensitivity department, but I suppose time will tell about that. And with that said, if you'll excuse me? I've just spotted some of the resident artists gathered by the barn, all dressed in Grecian costumes. I'm afraid I can't resist the lure of mingling with fellow creatives, especially when I know that any attempt to help you embrace a more sensitive attitude is surely going to be for naught."

After she gave his arm another pat, Judith darted across the lawn and toward a group of at least ten people who, upon closer inspection, looked exactly as if they'd come straight out of a Greek tragedy. Arthur wasn't surprised when Judith made a beeline for a man wearing a Viking helmet, who seemed to be in the process of posing his fellow artists around a circle of boulders.

That man, a Mr. Dodger Barstow no doubt, welcomed Judith with open arms, as if they'd been friends for years, right before he handed her off to a man splattered with mud. That man, Mr. Grover Cropsy if Arthur wasn't mistaken, immediately handed Judith a pail brimming with something questionable. But since Judith was beaming a bright smile at the man, Arthur didn't feel compelled to intervene, instead turning his attention to where three women were walking out of a henhouse, one of whom turned out to be Eunice.

His lips quirked as he watched her decline a chicken one of the women was trying to hand to her before she caught sight of him, said something to the women, then began striding his way, stopping a few feet away from him.

He grinned. "May I assume I just provided you with a viable excuse to get out of what could have turned into a concerning situation? I distinctly remember you telling me years ago you don't care for chickens."

"I couldn't think up a plausible reason to avoid seeing the chickens those women told me Mother adores, but I was in fear for my very life the entire time I was in that henhouse. Chickens and I have never seen eye to eye, but . . . you remembered that I don't care for chickens?"

"Why do you seem surprised?"

"I didn't think you ever put much stock in our conversations."

"You'd be wrong about that."

Her eyes immediately narrowed. "This isn't some new tactic to convince me I need to marry you, is it?"

He narrowed his eyes right back at her. "You're a remarkably suspicious woman, and this time your suspicions are completely unwarranted."

She considered him for a moment before she bobbed her head. "Good, then I'll apologize for the suspicion. But before you retort with something that may have me calling you a scourge again, tell me how matters went with Mother."

"She dissolved into sobs the second I finished disclosing the extent of her inheritance."

Eunice blinked. "I bet that was an unexpected twist to your day."

"Indeed, and then, when I proved I was less than adept with the consoling business, Ivan took over." He frowned. "I'm not convinced he's all that adept either, because Georgette started sobbing again, although I'm sure it doesn't speak well of my character that I fled from the house, but that was only because Judith hustled me right out of it. Apparently, the sight of Ivan being considerate was leaving her in danger of breaking into sobs as well."

"There is something compelling about a man possessed of a sensitive nature."

"Ivan doesn't strike me as being all that sensitive."

She smiled. "You'd be surprised. Underneath that gruff and

194

dangerous exterior lies a man with a heart that's as soft as a new-born kitten." Her smile faded. "It is concerning that Mother was sobbing, though. She's not a physically demonstrative type and she rarely cries."

"I noticed that the two of you didn't enjoy so much as a single hug when you reunited after a ten-year absence."

"We're not really the hugging type."

"You might want to mention that to Judith at some point. It could spare me another lecture from her on my lack of sensitivity if she realizes you're not a sensitive sort either."

"I never said I wasn't sensitive. I'm simply not comfortable with physical affection, probably because of the house I was raised in."

"I see" was all Arthur could think to say to that, although he didn't really see at all. Frankly, he'd never considered the idea Eunice might be sensitive because she presented herself as a tough-as-nails woman, and . . .

"I'm feeling a distinct need to walk in order to think some things through," Eunice said, interrupting his thoughts. "Would you care to join me? I wouldn't mind some company."

A sliver of unexpected warmth flowed through him. "I'd be happy to join you."

Taking her arm, they began strolling down a dirt path strewn with fallen leaves, a comfortable silence settling between them as they walked, until Eunice stopped and turned to him.

"As hard as this is for me to say, I think I'll have to return to Montana after all. Discovering that Mother is experiencing financial hardships is not something I was expecting, nor can I turn a blind eye to it. Granted, I could give her money from my trust fund to see her well set, but my trust fund is a pittance compared to her inheritance. Given the abuse she suffered at my grandfather's hands, the least I can do for her is get her finances settled, which means I'm going to have to present myself to the family, proving once and for all that I'm alive and well."

She began rubbing her temple. "There's a part of me that wishes I could send Mother off on her own to settle the matter, but I know that wouldn't be fair. The family has already laid claim to the Mason fortune, if only in their minds, and they won't admit defeat easily. Their disappointment will most assuredly have them turning hostile, and Mother has already experienced more than enough abuse at the hands of my family. I won't allow her to suffer more, not when it's in my power to take care of the matter of her inheritance for her."

"Did your family often target Georgette when they were upset or disappointed?"

"My family was held under the thumb of my grandfather, which meant they were often disappointed with their lives in general. Mother was an easy target for them because of how she'd incurred Grandfather's wrath when she married my father. It was quite the scandal, especially with Grandfather convinced my father was a fortune hunter, and the family often took to making snide remarks to Mother about her disastrous marriage."

Arthur frowned. "While I'm aware your family has the ability to act less than ethically at times, I never realized they were cruel."

"My relatives learned cruelty at the hands of a master—my grandfather. I didn't realize until hearing what he'd done to my mother exactly how cruel he was." Her shoulders took to slumping just the slightest bit. "That is why I can't let Mother deal with this inheritance business on her own, even though I vowed seven years ago I'd never return to Montana."

"I have yet to understand *why* you vowed to never return. Surely there's a part of you that misses your home, isn't there?"

"I don't miss much about Montana, and this conversation is starting to make me feel all sorts of queasy," she said, rubbing her forehead again. "Would you mind if we continue walking for a bit? It might help clear my head and settle my stomach."

Having no idea why their talk was making Eunice queasy, although her face did look paler than it had when he'd first joined her outside, Arthur fell into step beside her. They headed through a grove of trees, Eunice seemingly content to not speak at all, her silence continuing even as they hiked over a hill, picked their way down a steep bank, and finally came to a stop when the Hudson River spread out before them.

"How are you feeling?" he asked as she stared out over the river, her expression almost haunted.

"I'll be fine."

"You don't look fine."

Her lips twitched. "Honestly, Arthur, Judith might be right about you lacking a sensitive nature." She sighed. "The walk did help, as does this view of the river. It's certainly beautiful and peaceful here." She released another sigh. "Sadly, I haven't known true peace in years."

Arthur took hold of her hand, surprised when she didn't pull it away from him. "Perhaps if you finally get matters settled in Montana, you'll rediscover a sense of peace."

"Except that returning to Montana comes with a cost I'm not certain I want to pay."

"What cost?"

She returned her attention to the river. "I'm afraid," she whispered.

Of anything he'd been expecting her to disclose, that hadn't been it.

"Afraid of what?"

She turned to face him, and to his incredulity, he saw two large tears trailing down her cheeks. "I'm afraid that whoever killed my grandfather will do the same to me."

"There's nothing shameful about admitting you're afraid, Eunice. There's no question that danger awaits you in Montana. Anyone would be afraid to face that danger."

She withdrew her hand from his and shook her head. "I was raised by my grandfather to be fearless. Growing up, any obstacle that stood in my path I was expected to overcome and grow more confident from the experience. But I'm not merely afraid of returning to Montana—I'm terrified. I watched Grandfather die in front of my eyes and then had to leave everything behind—and on Grandfather's instructions, which terrified me more than you can imagine because he was the bravest man I knew. He all but pleaded with me to get out of Montana as quickly as possible, which showed me, as nothing else could, the danger I was in. The person who murdered Grandfather is the worst type of monster—a faceless creature who has haunted me every day for the past seven years." She dashed fresh tears from her cheeks. "Grandfather would be ashamed of me."

"Your grandfather is the one who told you to flee. He knew the danger you were in."

"True, but I knew he never meant for me to stay away forever. He would have expected me to return to solve his murder, or at least hire someone to solve that murder for me, and then take up the reins of his business—or, rather, marry you and let you move on with Mason Mines. He would be disappointed that I've been hiding from the world all these years, content to ignore what happened in Montana and content to give away my inheritance simply because I'm too frightened to face what awaits me there."

Arthur watched as more tears fell from her eyes and was helpless to ignore her distress. He stepped closer and pulled her into his arms, not letting go when she stiffened.

To his surprise, a moment later, she relaxed against him as a sob escaped her, and then she was burrowing her face into his chest, sobbing so hard her entire body shook.

He had a feeling the sobs were long overdue.

Smoothing a hand down her back, he let her sob without saying a word, simply holding her as she cried herself out. A good five minutes passed before she stepped away from him and lifted her head, her eyes still bright with tears as she scrubbed a hand over her cheek, missing a tear in the process.

He couldn't resist brushing that tear away with his thumb, finding himself leaning closer to her when she caught his gaze and held it for what felt like forever. Her remarkable eyes seemed to darken the longer she held his gaze, but then she blinked and took a step away from him.

"Forgive me, Arthur, I don't know what came over me." She

fished a handkerchief out of the sleeve of her gown and blew her nose.

In all honesty, he didn't know what had come over him either.

For the briefest of moments, he'd felt an almost overwhelming need to kiss her, kiss the tears from her cheeks, and then kiss lips that were far too inviting. Frankly, the sight of her tears left him feeling raw inside, a feeling he'd never experienced, but one that suggested that somehow, and in the very short time he'd been reunited with Eunice, she'd come to mean more to him than he'd understood.

"It's not a crime to cry, Eunice," he said softly.

"My grandfather would have disagreed with you."

"Perhaps, but your grandfather was wrong about many things."

A trace of a smile flickered over her face. "Dare I hope that you've finally realized he was wrong about the two of us marrying?"

"I don't think he was wrong about that. He obviously came to the realization at some point that having you run Mason Mines wasn't a good idea, but he was wrong about not approaching you to get your thoughts on the matter."

Her eyes narrowed. "So you still think we should marry?"

"I didn't say that, but what I will say is this—if you do claim your inheritance, I don't think you should try your hand at running Mason Mines. Mining is a man's business, and I'm not saying that simply because, as you've mentioned often, I'm a less-than-progressive gentleman. I've been involved with copper mining for years. During that time, I've dealt with men who, if I call them uncouth, I'd be kind. I've also dealt with men who use their physical size to get their way. Even though you've proven you can hold your own in a fight, there may come a time when you would be up against men who would overpower you simply because of their size. It also wouldn't be unexpected for these men to intimidate you in more unsavory ways, but I won't get into that because such a conversation would be unseemly."

"I run an inquiry agency, Arthur. I know exactly what you're implying. The reality of what would have been required of me to run Mason Mines is another reason I didn't want to return to Montana. I never wanted to be in charge of the mines. I merely learned everything about mining because Grandfather demanded it of me. He evidently realized it wasn't a good idea to leave me in charge. However, as I've said before, he should have established a business partnership between the two of you instead of latching on to a business-through-marriage idea."

"Out of sheer curiosity, why *are* you so opposed to the idea of a marriage of convenience between us?" Arthur asked. "Many ladies in society procure those types of marriages, and I rarely hear any of them complain."

"And I hear complaints often at the agency from ladies who agreed to marriages of convenience," Eunice countered. "But whenever I considered marriage—and believe me, I considered it often, starting when I was a young girl—I never found myself thinking, 'Hmmm . . . when I reach my majority, I'd really like to secure myself one of those marriages of convenience, the kind that doesn't come with much affection and certainly doesn't leave me breathless or have my pulse beating a rapid tattoo.'"

For the briefest of seconds, Arthur's mind went curiously blank, until things he'd never considered about Eunice snapped into place.

While he'd been coming to the conclusion that Eunice was far more complicated than he'd once thought, he hadn't been close to exactly how complicated she was.

Yes, she was practical, opinionated, independent, exasperating, and apparently possessed of emotions that a normal person experienced, such as fear, though she'd hidden it well. However, she also seemed to be something he'd never contemplated, but something that answered all of the remaining questions he had about why she balked at the thought of marrying him because . . .

Miss Eunice Holbrooke had been disguising a rather large truth about herself under her practicality because she was, if he wasn't mistaken, a true romantic at heart.

CHAPTER
Twenty-One

"This is difficult for me to fathom, but I think I may have just rendered you speechless, something I never thought you capable of."

Arthur snapped out of his thoughts, finding Eunice watching him closely. He smiled. "I fear you may be right about my speechless state because I never imagined I'd hear such a disclosure from you."

"And exactly what earth-shattering disclosure did I make?"

"You're a romantic."

Something interesting flashed through her eyes. "There's no need to sound so incredulous."

"It was a completely unexpected disclosure, so of course I find myself incredulous."

She took a step away from him. "Do you consider me such an odd and unalluring woman that it's unfathomable for you to comprehend that I could possibly long for romance?"

"I never said I consider you odd. Unconventional, yes, but not really, er, odd, and I definitely never said you were unalluring."

She released a snort. "That was convincing. But tell me this, does the reason you thought I was unromantic stem from the fact that I run an inquiry agency, own a boardinghouse, once preferred trousers over feminine attire, can wield a variety of weapons better than many gentlemen, and can hold my own in a boxing ring?"

He ran a hand through his hair, wondering how the conversation had turned so tumultuous, and so quickly at that. "Those aren't exactly normal occupations for a lady. Besides, you've always projected a practical, no-nonsense air, and that is not something one associates with a romantic."

"Women, if you haven't realized, can be practical and romantic at the same time. We're quite capable of more than one emotion because we're complicated creatures."

"I'm certainly not going to argue that you're complicated."

A storm began brewing in her eyes. "I'm not sure you meant that in a positive light."

Arthur's collar began feeling somewhat snug. "I wasn't trying to be insulting. You must realize it would have been difficult for me to know you possess a romantic nature because that's not what you project to the world. You're independent, self-assured, and you possess an education that rivals most gentlemen I know, compliments of Mr. Vincent Wagner. Vincent and I have spoken often over the years, and he's gone to great lengths to brag about the accomplishments you achieved while he was your tutor."

"Vincent was an unreasonable man who expected me to complete what amounted to a college education in mining before I was twenty years old. And before you tell me how impressive that is, know that he was an unrelenting taskmaster because he idolized my grandfather and wanted to impress him through my accomplishments. I once tried to get Grandfather to hire a different tutor for me, but he wouldn't hear of that, believing Vincent was the best to teach me since he had a lofty degree from Harvard. In all honesty, I felt Vincent was rather disdainful about being my tutor, but Grandfather apparently paid him such a handsome salary that Vincent was reluctant to discontinue instructing me."

Wondering how in the world he could salvage a conversation that was going downhill at a rapid rate, Arthur summoned up a smile. "Vincent told me you excelled at your studies, which makes me wonder if there's a part of you—not the romantic part, of course—that could possibly long to become involved, at least to a certain extent, with Mason Mines. We could work together and build something extraordinary."

He was not encouraged when she settled a scowl on him.

"Simply because I admitted I'm a romantic does not mean it would be odd if I professed an interest in Mason Mines."

His collar tightened another notch. "I don't believe that's what I said."

"It was implied."

"Does that mean you have an interest in Mason Mines?"

She released a snort. "Of course not. I was merely stating that it wouldn't be odd if I did, which, again, I don't. I'm perfectly content to run my inquiry agency, something I have no desire to abandon simply because of an inheritance I'm apparently going to have to claim."

He took a casual step away from her. "But you do realize that you're going to have to make some decisions about Mason Mines since you're the majority owner of the company, don't you?"

Another snort was her first response to that. "Disclosing my romantic nature has not had my intelligence diminishing, Arthur. Of course I know decisions need to be made, just as I know that any decisions I need to make should most assuredly be discussed with you beforehand." She caught his eye. "I'm hopeful you'll want to continue on with Mason Mines, although to be clear, that position will not involve any sort of marriage agreement between us."

"I've relegated the marriage idea to the furthest recesses of my mind, where it'll stay forever."

"Wonderful, because I am not any run of the mill romantic, mind you. I'm an incurable romantic."

"What does that mean exactly?"

"It means I want the fairy tale, complete with my own Prince Charming. I also want flowers and sonnets recited to me every now and again, but most importantly, I want the happily ever after."

"You don't really seem like the sonnet-enjoying type. If memory serves me correctly, you enjoy dime novels."

"True, and sonnets aren't my favorite, so perhaps I should have said I want a romance novel read to me." Her expression turned wistful. "I believe it would be beyond romantic to have a gentleman read to me from one of my favorite novels, *Pride and Prejudice*."

"This just keeps getting more and more surprising."

"I also want to find a gentleman who knows his way around a good kiss."

He found himself speechless again because he certainly hadn't expected to ever hear Eunice say that, although there was something refreshing about a woman who spoke her mind.

"I know my way around a kiss," he heard slip past his lips before he could stop himself.

She waved that straight aside. "I'm sure you do, but since you don't seem to view me in a romantic light, telling me you know your way around a kiss is not going to be enough to convince me to consider marrying you, which is why it's good that you've decided to relegate that idea to the remote recesses of your mind."

His lips curved into a smile as he realized he was enjoying himself even though he was in the midst of one of the most unusual conversations he'd ever held with a lady. "What if I offered to read *Pride and Prejudice* to you? Although I have to admit that my preferred Jane Austen novel is *Emma*."

Eunice blinked. "You've read Jane Austen?"

"Her entire collection."

"Why?"

Even though he should have been expecting the question, it still caught him off guard. "Will you be surprised to hear that I read every Jane Austen book because I was trying to impress a lady in my misguided youth?"

Her eyes widened before she took hold of his hand, all but dragged him over to a large boulder, and pulled him down next to her. "I want to hear all the details of what happened with this lady."

"You have never once struck me as someone who'd be interested in what verges on gossip."

"Telling me about a lady from your past is hardly gossip. It's merely one of the stories of your life, and I don't know anything about your youth." She smiled. "I find myself curious about that now."

"I'm not really comfortable disclosing details about that particular incident."

"That's too bad because I've now disclosed two of my best-kept secrets—that I'm afraid and that I'm a romantic. It's your turn now."

"Why does it need to be my turn?"

"Because I'm still distressed over the idea I'm going to have to return to Montana. Given that I've already dissolved into sobs once already—although allow me to say that you did rise to that occasion magnificently and may have a somewhat sensitive nature buried deep down in your soul—I'm sure you want to distract me from my distress to avoid any additional weeping episodes on my part." She smiled. "Besides, you've now witnessed both me *and* my mother descend into a sobbing state, and you surely have met your quota for dealing with emotional women in any given day."

"You don't appear as if you're going to return to sobbing anytime soon."

"Women are complicated, so you shouldn't assume I'm incapable of sobbing again, even if I don't look sad."

"You're looking almost cheerful."

"That's because you're about to tell me a story about a lady from your past. I have a feeling it's going to be quite the story if you read Jane Austen books to impress her."

"You're not going to let this go, are you?"

"You're the one who mentioned that I'm tenacious, so no, I'm not."

"You certainly are tenacious, so I'll tell you my story. But a word of warning—if you're expecting a love story, you're going to be sadly disappointed." He drew in a deep breath. "It all started with Mitzi Jarvis."

Eunice's nose wrinkled. "Is her name really Mitzi?"

"It's Melinda, but her name doesn't have anything to do with my story."

"Of course it does. With a name like Mitzi, I'm already of the belief that she was a charming young lady who was amusing and probably a bit flirtatious."

"You got all that out of a name?"

"I read romance novels whenever possible. The names chosen for heroines always disclose a lot about the characters, and because Melinda evidently decided she wanted to be addressed as Mitzi, it speaks volumes about her character."

"Forgive me, but your theory about names is completely flawed. You chose Eunice as your new name, but Eunice is hardly a name one associates with a romantic."

"Unless I've decided to change the impression that springs to mind when people think of a Eunice."

"The only impression I fear you've changed, what with the way you've been wearing widow's weeds ever since you assumed the name, is that people now must surely believe Eunice is an intimidating name that can be associated with a rather formidable and spooky woman."

"A fair point, but if I decide to abandon my widow's weeds and adopt a first state of fashion on a regular basis, I'm sure my theory will turn sound and people will begin to view the name Eunice more favorably. But we're not discussing me at the moment, we're discussing you. So, returning to Mitzi. Was she from society?"

"She was, and still is for that matter—a leader in the making, to be exact. When I first became acquainted with her, though, she'd not yet made her debut. We met at a dancing class, and I was a few years older than she was. Being a second son, I was expected to attend such events because, well, that's what second sons are expected to do. Mitzi was the star pupil that year, and I was often partnered with her, which caused me to develop affections, if you will, toward her. After I discovered she was partial to Jane Austen novels, I read Jane's entire collection so I'd be well-versed while discussing those books with Mitzi."

Eunice's lips curved. "It sounds to me as if you were quite the romantic in your youth."

"I was an idiot in my youth," Arthur countered. "In hindsight, all of that time reading Jane Austen to impress Mitzi could have been better spent doing something more constructive."

"I now find myself sitting on the edge of my boulder to hear what happened."

"If you're hoping for that fairy-tale ending, as I already warned you, you're certain to be disappointed."

"Since you weren't accompanied by a Mitzi when you traveled to Montana seven years ago, nor did you ever bring her into any of the conversations we shared, I'm not expecting the fairy tale in this particular case."

"You would be right about that because, you see, I was attending Harvard when Mitzi made her debut, and I missed that debut because of exams. Nevertheless, I was convinced she returned my affections, so during winter recess, I repaired to the city to attend one of the most anticipated balls of the Season—Mrs. Astor's ball. I'd decided that was going to be the perfect backdrop to officially speak with Mitzi about courting her and decided to speak with her first before I spoke formally with her father."

Arthur rubbed a hand over his face, not particularly thrilled to relive what had to be the most embarrassing moment of his life. "Mitzi seemed genuinely happy to see me that night, and she even agreed to take a tour of the hallways with me to peruse the famed artwork the Astors have displayed throughout their home. Unfortunately, the moment I took her hand and professed my great admiration for her, Mitzi turned from happy young lady to an appalled one. She then told me in no uncertain terms that she wouldn't welcome the opportunity of courtship with me be-cause . . ." He stopped talking and drew in a deep breath, unable to help but wonder how he could have ever been so naïve.

"Because why?" Eunice pressed.

"Because I was only a second son. She told me I didn't possess the sizable fortune she desired since my older brother, Benjamin, was expected to take over my father's vast holdings."

Eunice gave his hand a pat. "That was incredibly harsh of her."

"Indeed, but it was honest. What made the situation worse, though, was that I had allowed a few of my gentlemen friends to know of my intentions toward Mitzi. Those friends soon realized I'd been unsuccessful in my desire to court her, because her family announced the very next day that she was engaged to Mr. Thomas Gibson, a firstborn son who'd already taken up the reins of his father's real estate empire and was destined to inherit an enormous fortune."

"Ah, the plot thickens. Rejected because of another man."

"You're not exactly making me feel better about the matter."

"But surely you've concluded over the years that Mitzi was obviously not the lady for you. In all honesty, it sounds to me as if she flirted with your affections while knowing all the while that she wanted to marry a more established man about town." Eunice shook her head. "You often see that as a subplot in novels, where the lady who dashed the hopes of the hero comes to regret her decision in the end, while the hero ends up with the lady he was truly meant to marry, usually obtaining some wisdom by the end of the book, such as how wrong he was to believe he was rejected because of some deficiency on his part."

It was rather astonishing how much one could apparently glean from reading a vast assortment of romance novels.

"What did you do to get over what had to be a humiliating experience at the hands of Mitzi Jarvis, who I'm going to assume is now Mrs. Thomas Gibson?"

"I devised a plan."

Eunice gave his hand another pat. "I would expect nothing less of you. May I assume that plan involved abandoning the role you were expected to play as a second son and instead throwing yourself into investing in copper mining, determined to become one of the leading copper mining industrialists in the country?"

"Perhaps I should simply allow you to complete the telling of my story because, yes, that's exactly what I did."

She cocked her head to the side. "Your story would definitely have to include a plan to marry someone Mitzi would see as competition, or better yet, someone who had the potential to upset Mitzi's position as an up-and-coming society matron."

"You really have been reading a lot of romance novels, haven't you, and some with rather surprising plot twists."

"Revenge is not a surprising plot twist, Arthur, and clearly that's what you were planning."

It was rather refreshing to have someone speak so directly as well as derive such an honest assessment of a situation he'd wrestled with for years. Drawing in a breath, Arthur stilled as the thought came to him that Eunice was exactly right and that his plan had definitely come about because of a thirst for revenge—revenge that he'd wanted because a young lady had wounded his male pride and embarrassed him amongst his friends.

He was relatively convinced, now that Eunice had brought it into the open, that plotting out his life in such a Machiavellian fashion, and all because of a wounded ego, was somewhat ridiculous.

"I suppose that does explain some of the lingering questions I have concerning why you were so adamant about not courting me seven years ago," Eunice said. "I'm sure you were determined at that time to marry an incomparable within society, and I certainly didn't fit the requirements for that." She caught his eye. "I'm now wondering, though, if perhaps you made yourself so disagreeable to me because you didn't want to risk having my grandfather dismiss you from entering into some type of partnership with him."

It was extremely disconcerting how easily she was figuring him out.

He winced. "I'm afraid I *was* disagreeable on purpose, and I must beg your pardon for that. It wasn't as if you did anything to warrant my criticism."

"I'm fairly sure you're wrong about that. I mean, yes, I didn't warrant your criticism at first, but after spending only an hour with you, I found it somewhat amusing to deliberately bait you. I may have—or rather, I did—go out of my way to annoy you." She grinned. "I'm normally not quite that argumentative."

"Which is good to know, although I imagine if you decide to return to Montana with me, we'll find something to argue about on the long train ride west."

"I think it's a given I'm going to return to Montana as well as begin doing what I've been doing in New York for almost a year— opening up an investigation into a case that's remained unsolved for far too long."

She blew out a breath. "I'm still terrified to begin investigating Grandfather's murder, but it's becoming clear that until that mystery is solved, I won't find that sense of peace I've been searching for. Someone could still have me in their sights with nefarious intentions in mind, but I don't want to continue hiding underneath my widow's weeds. I'll never find that fairy-tale ending if I don't come out of hiding. That means I have no choice but to return to Montana and try to put the past to rest once and for all."

"I'll be beside you the entire time," Arthur promised as he took hold of her hand. "It'll be easier to help you now that I'm beginning to understand who you truly are. Frankly, I'm getting the distinct impression you've been disguising more truths about yourself than only your identity over the years. Yes, you're an accomplished woman, but you're not nearly as intimidating as you've allowed everyone to believe. Learning you're a romantic, well, it explains much about you, including why it was ludicrous for me to assume you'd blithely agree to a marriage between us."

He got to his feet, pulled her to hers, and smiled before he kissed her hand. "I think this is the part in the story where you and I begin again. I'm Mr. Arthur Livingston. A less-than-sensitive man, or so I've been told, who'd very much like to become better acquainted with you—the real you, the romantic at heart and the woman who has finally found the courage to admit your fears."

She dipped into a curtsy and returned his smile. "I'm pleased to make your acquaintance, Mr. Arthur Livingston, although allow me to say that I think you may be more sensitive than you know. I'm Miss Eunice Holbrooke, proprietress of Holbrooke boarding-house, partner in the oh-so-marvelous Bleecker Street Inquiry Agency, and grand heiress to the Mason fortune."

"It's a pleasure to finally meet you," Arthur said.

"The pleasure is mine, especially since you're no longer de-termined to marry me, although I'm relatively convinced you're not going to suffer the same emotional turmoil from knowing I don't long to marry you as you did with Mitzi, who, in my honest opinion, was a fool."

An urge to pull her close to him and kiss her struck from out of nowhere, but he resisted the urge, especially since she'd just proclaimed herself pleased about his not pursuing a relationship of the romantic kind with her. Instead, he tucked her hand in the crook of his arm, turned her around, and began heading back for her mother's farmhouse.

As they walked, a comfortable conversation sprang up between them, the kind often shared between friends. But even though he knew they were firmly on a path that could lead to a lasting friend-ship, he couldn't help but wonder if friendship was what he truly wanted with Eunice or if he wanted something so much more.

CHAPTER
Twenty-Two

Truth be told, being accompanied to Montana by what amounted to a brigade of armed escorts was going far to alleviate the fear that had been Eunice's constant companion ever since she'd decided she was going to return home to claim her inheritance.

Ann and Judith had insisted on joining her for the journey, both ladies equipped with dainty derringers hidden in their reticules, the daintiness disguising the danger the pistols were capable of, especially since both ladies had made remarkable progress handling pistols in general.

Cooper was traveling with her as well, and in an official capacity. The Pinkertons had been only too willing to agree to work on her case in conjunction with the Bleecker Street Inquiry Agency, knowing that having a hand in solving the murder of a man who'd been one of the wealthiest industrialists in the country would only increase their reputation.

Ivan was, of course, by her side for most of the time they'd spent on the train getting to Montana, going over the list of suspects she'd finally pulled together. He'd taken to reminding her time and again that once they got to Mason Manor, she was never to be without an escort, not that she was keen about going off on her own. Not when someone in Montana could still be biding their time to get rid of her once and for all.

Filling out the people traveling with her were Arthur and his grandfather. Lloyd had been delighted to be included, stating to Eunice that the trip west was exactly what he needed. Apparently, Elsy had the right measure of those widows because they'd banded together, discussed Lloyd and his propensity for squiring more than a few of them around town, and decided they were none too happy with his Casanova behavior.

That Lloyd kept asking her pointed questions about her great-aunt Hazel suggested he hadn't learned his lesson yet. But since Aunt Hazel was more than capable of looking after herself, Eunice was convinced Lloyd was about to meet his match.

As for Arthur, ever since they'd had their discussion at her mother's house, he'd been warmer toward her and definitely not as argumentative. They still shared rousing debates, whether it was politics, social issues, or ideas about what should be done with Mason Mines. More often than not, though, their debates ended in laughter, and a laughing Arthur was, concerningly enough, downright irresistible. He definitely posed a distinct danger to her romantic nature and to her adamant decision about not wanting to entertain the thought of marriage to the man.

Not that she would ever change her mind about a marriage of convenience, but if it *wasn't* a marriage of convenience, well, that was a completely different . . .

"I'm so thankful Lloyd was able to procure private Pullman cars for us," Georgette said, pulling Eunice from her thoughts. "I'd forgotten how lovely traveling in style can be, and it certainly beats how I traveled when I was trekking around Europe." She returned her attention to the canvas she was working on, pulled a paintbrush from where she'd stuck it in her hair, dabbed it in paint, then dabbed the paint on the canvas.

Eunice abandoned the list of possible suspects she'd been looking over and frowned. "I still find it almost incomprehensible that Grandfather was capable of such cruelty toward you. Yes, I knew he was a tyrant, but I never thought he was capable of sending you off against your will to Europe."

"Father was capable of far more than you'll ever know, dear, but if it's all the same to you, I'd prefer not to discuss him. I'm ready to relegate him to my past, although I will admit I'm feeling more charitable toward him because of the inheritance. From what Arthur told me, Father redid his will not long before he died. I've found myself wondering what compelled him to do that as well as wondering if his decision to change his will might be behind his murder."

Eunice's mouth dropped open. "What a brilliant theory, Mother, and one I never considered." She got to her feet. "I need to share that with everyone else." She stepped up to her mother's painting and gave it a long perusal. "Your depiction of Judith is lovely, but I'm a little surprised you've opted to paint her face purple. I thought you were going for realism over abstract."

"It's puce, dear, not purple, and my painting of her is realistic."

"You've painted my face puce?" Judith asked, looking up from the painting she was working on, a smudge of ivory paint on her cheek.

Georgette smiled. "I thought that by using bright colors, any future flyers of potential suspects or missing people we may make for the inquiry agency will stand out on bulletin boards or lamp-posts."

Judith turned the portrait she was painting of Georgette around, one that was a spot-on depiction of Georgette. "And while you may have a point, if you went missing and we posted a flyer made from my painting, there might be a better chance someone would recognize you. The portrait of me, on the other hand, may confuse people because they might take to searching the crowds for a woman with a very unusually colored face."

Smiling as Georgette and Judith launched into a rousing debate about paint color, Eunice moved through the Pullman car she was sharing with Georgette, Judith, and Ann, and reached for the door. She shivered the second she stepped foot outside as the wind from the rapidly moving train swept over her. Hurrying through the door that led to the gentlemen's private Pullman car, she stopped just inside the doorway, glancing around at the well-appointed car Arthur, Lloyd, Cooper, and Ivan were sharing.

Lloyd was currently dozing in a chaise by the window, while Cooper and Ann were watching Ivan and Arthur circle each other, clearly in the midst of a bout of boxing.

"Who's winning?" she asked, taking a step forward.

"They're fairly evenly matched," Cooper said. "Although I'd probably put my money on Ivan because he recently revealed he was a boxer before he took up the position of your bodyguard."

"It's one of the reasons why Grandfather hired him."

Ivan landed a punch to Arthur's middle and smiled. "James attended one of my matches and was impressed with my size and left hook." He settled his smile on Arthur. "That was my left hook, if you didn't notice."

Arthur rubbed his stomach, danced his way around Ivan in a manner that suggested he was comfortable in a boxing ring, then threw a punch, his fist glancing off one of Ivan's arms.

"You weren't concentrating," Ivan said. "And while I know you become distracted anytime Eunice is around, distraction has no place during a boxing match." He stepped back and gestured Eunice forward. "It's your turn. You can spar with Arthur."

Given the look of horror that was settling on Arthur's face, Eunice was relatively certain he wasn't keen to spar with her. And while she wasn't exactly surprised by that, she was surprised by Ivan's distraction comment and couldn't help but wonder if it was actually true, and if so, what it meant.

Normally, at least within the pages of romance novels, whenever distraction situations arose, they were caused because a gentleman found a specific lady intriguing and also found his thoughts lingering on that lady more than he was willing to admit—which always built up the suspense between the chapters.

Feeling a tingle of something delicious travel through her over the possibility that Arthur may find her a little intriguing, Eunice shoved up the sleeves of the delightful walking dress she was wearing and stepped to the middle of the room.

"What are you doing?" Arthur asked.

"Preparing to spar with you, of course, although I have to admit that this gown is going to give you the advantage. I'm afraid Phillip doesn't design gowns that are conducive to boxing."

Arthur glanced at the gown in question and shook his head. "I'm not boxing with you dressed like that, but there's no need for you to rush off and change because I'm not going to box with you at all."

"Because I'm not a gentleman?"

"At the risk of sounding less than progressive, yes. My mother would have a fit of the vapors if she heard I'd taken to boxing with a lady. And even though I've been accused of being a man devoid of a sensitive side, I try to be solicitous of my mother and her expectations for me, which mostly center around my exhibiting proper behavior when I'm in the presence of ladies. My mother would never consider boxing with a lady proper behavior on my part."

"So that means you'll *never* box with me?"

"Do you believe that question even needs to be asked?" he countered with a grin.

The sight of Arthur's grin left her feeling rather fluttery. It was a feeling she'd been having ever since she'd admitted she possessed a romantic nature, that disclosure apparently causing all the walls she'd erected to hide that side of her nature to come crumbling down and leaving her experiencing the most unusual emotions.

"I told you it would be more interesting in this Pullman car, Judith, and it appears I was right about that," Georgette proclaimed, strolling into the car with Judith at her side. Georgette settled a smile on Arthur. "Trying to dissuade my daughter from sparring with you, dear?"

Arthur inclined his head. "I am and find myself delighted you and Judith have joined us because now there's not enough room in here to proceed with a boxing match."

"We're happy to oblige," Georgette said before she strode over to join Lloyd, who was just waking up from his snooze on the chaise.

"You're looking well this afternoon, Georgette," Lloyd said after he straightened his waistcoat and smoothed down hair that was decidedly rumpled. "You also seem remarkably composed, even though we can't be far from our destination now."

Georgette settled herself on the chaise. "After everything I've been through over the years, facing down a crowd of relatives who aren't going to be pleased to find me alive isn't all that daunting."

"Would you have any tips you could share with me so that when I return to New York I won't find facing down all of my widow friends quite as daunting?" Lloyd asked. "From what I've been told, the widows are planning on confronting me at some point over what they call my gentleman-who-believes-in-leaving-no-widow-behind ways."

Georgette laughed. "I suggest you simply muster up a sincere apology, abandon your Casanova ways, and hope for the best."

"I'm not certain a sincere apology will be enough," Lloyd admitted. "Elsy told me that two of the widows I join for weekly luncheons, Mrs. Clark and Mrs. Howland, have declared me, quite like Arthur was declared at the Bleecker Street Agency, persona non grata."

"How unfortunate."

"Indeed," Lloyd said before he frowned. "But speaking of Mrs. Howland, I've just realized that you share the same surname with her. Could it be possible you're related to the Edward Howland family?"

Georgette tapped a finger against her chin. "I suppose that could be a possibility, but I wasn't given the opportunity of meeting many of my late husband's relatives. His family was distressed to learn that their son had behaved so rashly by marrying me after our whirlwind courtship. In fact, the allowance he'd been receiving from his family was cut off and we were forced to live off the monthly allowance my father sent me, although that allowance was soon cut off as well."

Eunice moved to take a seat on a chair next to her mother. "I never heard that story."

"Because I don't care to speak about your father much. I find the topic still incredibly painful even after so many years have passed. He was, after all, the love of my life."

"But how did you and Father survive without an allowance?"

"Since your father died not long after we were both cut off from family funds, I survived by returning to Montana." Georgette took hold of Eunice's hand. "And while I know my decision to return home affected the way you were raised, I thought it would be better to have you raised under my father's roof than in poverty."

"But didn't your late husband's family lend you any assistance after your husband died?" Lloyd asked. "You were expecting his child, after all. I would have thought his family would have wanted to embrace you and their son's unborn child. It seems unusually cruel that they wouldn't have done so."

"I never told them I was expecting." Georgette blew out a breath. "They thought I was a fortune hunter, which was always incredibly bewildering to me since my husband was a younger son—the third son, to be exact. He wasn't expected to take over the family business, nor was he in line for a large inheritance. He did at one time mention a trust fund he'd come into when he turned twenty-five, but he was only twenty-two when we married."

"You could have prevailed upon his family to turn over that trust, which should have rightfully gone to you and Eunice," Lloyd said.

"Frankly, it was easier to simply return home and live under my father's roof instead of prevailing upon those who didn't want me in their family in the first place," Georgette said. "However, this particular topic tends to put me in a gloomy state of mind, and I don't care to be gloomy right now, what with what lies ahead of us." She glanced at a dainty watch that encircled her wrist. "We should be arriving in Butte within the hour." She nodded to Eunice. "Shall we repair to our car to change?"

Even though Eunice longed to question her mother more about her father, she rose from the chair. "Indeed we should. I'm certainly not intending to arrive looking anything less than fashionable, which will undoubtedly throw the family off guard."

"And while I would love to return home dressed in one of my horribly sewn robes just to see their reactions," Georgette said, rising to her feet, "I'm going to wear that delicious gown Phillip made for me."

"Ann and I will join you as well, since we certainly don't want to represent the Bleecker Street Inquiry Agency looking anything but smartly dressed," Judith said. "Besides that, I think I have more than my fair share of paint on me because it's rather tricky to paint while on board a moving train."

"And while the ladies freshen up," Ivan said, rolling down his sleeves, "we gentlemen should go over our plans one last time. I don't want to leave it to chance that we've forgotten anything of importance, because that could very well allow a murderer to slip under our guard and attack when we're least expecting it."

CHAPTER

Twenty-Three

Even though Eunice appeared composed as they stepped onto the platform at the Butte train depot, Arthur thought she might be more on edge than she was letting on, which was why he took hold of her hand as Cooper and Ann went off to secure them hired carriages.

"It'll be fine. We have a plan."

She smiled. "Indeed we do—one where all we have to accomplish is uncover the identity of a murder or murderess, which is no large feat at all, is it?"

"Not with the Bleecker Street Inquiry Agency and the Pinkerton Agency on your case. We'll have a suspect in hand before you know it."

"Or I'll be dead."

He was hard-pressed not to laugh.

During the past two weeks, he'd spent an inordinate amount of time with Eunice, and what he'd discovered was this—she was a delightful mix of practical, whimsy, and dry wit, with her admission about having a romantic nature adding a depth to her he'd not realized existed.

Yes, she was the most independent woman he knew, but she possessed a charm he'd not been expecting, one that drew him in and left him feeling emotions he'd thought had died after Mitzi rejected him out of hand.

Curiously enough, Eunice had suggested he could be a romantic at heart as well, a conclusion he'd denied at the time. However, given how her smile did peculiar things to his heart, and given that he found himself longing to open a Jane Austen book again so that he could read it out loud to her and hopefully make her smile, he was beginning to think she might not be wrong about him and his romantic heart after all.

He knew the resurgence of his romantic nature was a direct result of Eunice, but the problem with that was this—he'd already disclosed his plan to her about amassing a fortune and then marrying an incomparable.

It would be difficult to now convince Eunice he'd had a change of heart about that, as it wouldn't be a stretch for her to believe he'd changed his mind not because of the affection he most assuredly held for her but because she was now one of the greatest heiresses in the country. With that type of wealth, the New York Four Hundred would be only too keen to welcome her into their midst, especially when her fortune was third generation, which made it perfectly acceptable in the eyes of the elite.

"You're not going to be dead," Ivan said, moving up to join them, Judith holding onto his arm. "I've kept you alive all these years, and I have no intention of failing with that now." His gaze darted to the wooden depot building. "Doesn't look like much has changed over the years we've been away. Considering how the mining industry is booming in Butte, I was expecting the train depot to have expanded."

"There are plans underway to give the depot an overhaul," Arthur said. "And while I know this area still looks rough, wait until you see Main Street." He smiled. "It's beginning to look like a street from a progressive city over one from the Wild West."

"How disappointing," Judith said, releasing a sigh. "I was hoping to get some sketches of an authentic Wild West town, complete with cowboys riding in from the trail and perhaps even getting to witness one of those showdowns in the middle of the street that are always written about in dime novels."

Arthur smiled. "Those still happen, Judith, but usually not on Main Street or West Granite. If you travel past those streets, you'll discover a rowdier atmosphere because that's where the majority of miners and cowboys spend their time when they're at their leisure. With that said, I wouldn't recommend you travel to the seedier parts of Butte. Those aren't places for ladies, because there are saloons on every corner, and the men who frequent those saloons aren't known to adopt the best manners."

"We could always stay in the carriage," Judith said.

"Absolutely not," Ivan argued. "If any of those miners would so much as get a glimpse of your beautiful face through the carriage window, there'd be a riot. I can guarantee you all of them would decide you'd make a wonderful wife, and not simply because women are still in short supply in Montana. Believe me, those miners wouldn't be shy about trying to win your favor, and if they were unsuccessful with that, many of them wouldn't blink an eye about throwing you over their shoulder and making off with you."

Judith's face turned pink. "You find my face beautiful?"

"I didn't think that was in question."

As Judith and Ivan immediately began staring deeply into each other's eyes, Georgette moved up to join them, taking Eunice's arm. "This should be an interesting ride to Mason Manor."

"We'll take a carriage without the lovebirds in it," Eunice said before Ivan pulled his attention from Judith and settled a scowl on her.

"You won't be going anywhere—not even in a carriage—without me. Until we uncover who murdered your grandfather, I'm not taking my eyes off of you."

"That may be a difficult promise to keep, what with how your gaze is normally attached to Judith's."

Ivan opened his mouth, clearly to voice an argument to that, but then his lips curved. "A fair point, which means . . ." He turned to Judith. "Would you be overly offended if for the time being we agree to keep a certain distance between us? I'd hate to be so distracted with your loveliness that I neglect my job as Eunice's bodyguard."

Judith's eyes sparkled. "You are a charmer, Ivan. And while I'm sure it'll be difficult to maintain distance between us, Eunice's safety must come before any flirting between us. Besides, seeing as how this is one of my first official cases as an agent with the Bleecker Street Inquiry Agency, I need to prove my worth. I don't believe I'd be successful with that if Eunice were to come to a bad end because you and I were distracted with each other. That means, for now, flirting will need to be set aside, at least while we're on duty."

"Wonderful," Georgette said with a nod to where a few carriages were trundling their way. "And with that settled, it appears our carriages are ready to whisk us off to Mason Manor."

After getting their luggage secured, and then getting Lloyd, Ann, Judith, and Cooper settled into a carriage, Arthur joined Eunice in a carriage with Ivan and Georgette, tapping on the ceiling after he found his seat, which had the carriage surging into motion. They soon found themselves on Main Street, Eunice shifting on the seat to peer out the carriage window.

"You're right. Much *has* changed since I was last here," she said, looking out at a three-story brick building. "Does that sign say Mason Mercantile?"

Arthur nodded. "It does, and you'll find other Mason establishments all the way down Main Street until we reach West Granite. Your family now owns numerous businesses, including a photography studio, an apothecary, a feed store, a candy store, and a dress shop, to name a few." He leaned forward and gestured out the window. "All the sidewalks are now constructed from wooden planks raised six inches off the ground, which helps keeps the perpetual mud from the spring thaw in the mountains out of all the businesses."

"Dare I ask who was responsible for the improvements?" Eunice asked.

"I believe Hazel is behind the majority of the town's renovation. She thought it was past time the Mason family did something beneficial for Butte besides being one of the main sources of employment for the residents."

"I'm surprised Uncle Raymond was agreeable to that."

Arthur grinned. "I believe that might be one of the reasons Hazel moved into the big house with Raymond and his wife, Clarice. Hazel seems unusually adept at badgering, and Raymond probably agreed to her renovation plans simply to put an end to that."

"Hazel was always more cunning than anyone gave her credit for, including my father," Georgette said. "Which is why I believe she belongs on our list of possible suspects, even though I'm not certain she would have had it in her to frame Eunice for my father's murder."

"Speaking of suspects," Ivan began as he pulled a satchel from the floor, riffled through it, and then pulled out a sheaf of papers, "we need to go over our list of prime suspects one last time, just in case we've forgotten anyone." He glanced at the papers. "I'm still convinced that Raymond, James's only brother, seems the most likely suspect, which is why he's at the top of my list. It was well known that he loathed the fact James never included him in the family business, as James believed Raymond lacked business acumen."

"And while I agree that Raymond had cause," Eunice countered, "he's in his eighties now, which means he was in his seventies at the time of Grandfather's death. He's also never been athletically inclined or good with a pistol. I don't know how he'd have been capable of taking Grandfather unaware, let alone shooting him."

"That's a good point," Ivan conceded. "But because Raymond immediately moved into Mason Manor after James died, a house he always coveted, he's still a viable suspect. Envy is a powerful motivator for violence."

"And don't forget Uncle Raymond got his hands on that telegram I sent to Aunt Hazel," Georgette added. "He knew from that telegram that I was staying in New York, but he never reached out to me. Instead, he decided to have me declared dead, which means"—her brows drew together—"perhaps I need to move Howard, Uncle Raymond's son, up on my list. He had reason to resent Father because I'm sure he felt he deserved, being the only male Mason descendant, an important position within Mason Mines, something he was denied."

Ivan wrote something down before he lifted his head. "Does that mean we want to move Howard's wife, Hester, up the list?"

Georgette frowned. "That's hard to say. Hester was always very socially motivated and felt her social ambitions were stifled with my father as the head of the family. He abhorred society and cautioned Hester about the inadvisability of her pursuing what he saw as a frivolous desire to rule Butte society. Clearly, Hester was loathe to procure Father's displeasure, which had her scaling back her social ambitions. I imagine she resented that since she and Howard have two daughters, Doris and Alice, and her inability to climb the Butte social ladder affected her ability to secure advantageous marriages for her girls."

"Did Howard and Hester also move into Mason Manor after James died?" Ivan asked.

Arthur shook his head. "They sold what Hester claims was a modest house on Broadway and moved into Raymond's original house on West Granite."

"It'll be interesting to see how Hester reacts if Uncle Raymond and Aunt Clarice want to move back into their old house after they realize they have no right to Mason Manor," Georgette said.

"I would think Hester would insist Howard build them an even nicer home," Arthur said. "He's become one of the leading businessmen in Butte, building up a tidy fortune he's made through the profits at all the stores the Mason family now owns."

"Where are Doris and Alice living?" Georgette asked.

"With their parents," Arthur said. "Neither is married, much to Hester's chagrin. She has, as I'm sure you won't be surprised to hear, turned into one of Butte's leading society matrons. She hosts numerous events at the Mason house on Granite Street as well as two balls a year at Mason Manor, taking over the responsibility of hosting from her mother-in-law, Clarice. She uses those events to showcase her daughters, but they've yet to settle into wedded bliss."

Georgette frowned. "If memory serves me correctly, Doris and Alice were darling girls, which makes it surprising they'd become spinsters if they've been out and about at all those society events."

"I don't think they lack interested gentlemen, but their reluctance to settle on one of those numerous gentlemen may be a result of the time they spend running the Mason candy store, Doris and Alice's Sweet Shop. It's a highly successful business, and I know they spend a lot of time whipping up new candy recipes." He nodded as the carriage rumbled past a storefront with a green-and-pink striped awning, the glass front window displaying numerous delectable-looking confections. "It's right there."

Eunice considered the shop until the carriage left it behind before she turned to him. "It looks like a delightful shop, and how fun for the town to have access to what I'm going to assume are mouthwatering treats. Perhaps I'll find that I actually like my cousins after all these years, because it sounds to me as if they've turned very entrepreneurial over the time I've been gone, and that entrepreneurial spirit is very likely responsible for their unmarried state."

"Is that why you're still a spinster?" Georgette asked. "You're too busy running your agency to set your sights on any of the gentlemen in New York?"

"I think my hiding underneath widow's weeds has more to do with my unmarried state than any entrepreneurial spirit." She caught Georgette's eye. "However, do not under any circumstances decide you need to turn into one of those matchmaking mothers at this stage of my life. I'm far too old to have you take me in hand."

"It's never too late for a mother to turn an eye toward matchmaking or take a daughter who clearly needs assistance in hand. Besides, it's not as if you're ancient."

"Something mothers always say when they don't want to draw attention to their own age."

Arthur turned a smile on Georgette, who was looking suitably disgruntled. "Don't mind Eunice. I'm sure you know you don't need to worry about your age because you don't look a day over forty."

Georgette's disgruntlement disappeared in a flash. "You are a *delightful* gentleman, and you would have made a *wonderful* addition to the family if you and Eunice had decided to marry, and that's not simply because we know you don't want to murder us."

Eunice laughed. "That's one of the most unusual reasons I've ever heard given for wanting someone to join their family—that they're not out to murder us." She directed her attention out the window again as the carriage veered from Main Street and onto the gravel road that would take them to Mason Manor. "We're getting closer."

Arthur gave her hand a squeeze as silence settled over the carriage, Eunice returning the squeeze a few minutes later when the carriage began to slow and then stopped.

"I'm going to be right beside you," he said after she drew in a deep breath and slowly released it.

"And I'll be on the other side of you," Georgette said before she reached out and took hold of Ivan's hand. "I'm going to need you to hold fast to my arm, dear. I'm beginning to feel butterflies in my stomach. I would hate to give the family something to gossip about if I were to swoon right inside the entrance hall."

"I won't let you fall," Ivan said as the door to the carriage opened.

After Arthur stepped to the cobblestone walkway, he helped Eunice and Georgette out of the carriage, blinking when his gaze settled on the entranceway to the house, the white pillars flanking that entranceway swathed in yards and yards of black bunting.

"Looks as if the family has gone all out to mourn their soon-to-be-declared-deceased relatives," Eunice said dryly. "I find myself wondering how much all that bunting cost, given what can only be described as an impressive display."

"And I find myself wondering if they've moved up the date of your memorial," Arthur said, taking Eunice's arm. "The original plan was to have you declared dead on your birthday, which isn't for two days, and then hold a memorial service that day as well."

"Maybe they're just getting ahead of the service," Eunice said, returning her attention to the house. "It's still as ostentatious as it ever was. Frankly, I always liked the original house Grandfather built when he first moved to town, the one that Howard lives in now."

Georgette rolled her eyes. "Your grandfather would have never been satisfied to stay in that house. Yes, it was the nicest house in town back in the day, but this . . ." She gestured to the house in front of them. "This house, as Father enjoyed telling everyone, cost over two hundred thousand dollars in the early 1860s when he built it. He used to love to tell me what an enormous sum of money that was, but one he made in less than a year back then."

Arthur turned his gaze back on Mason Manor, unable to argue with Eunice's declaration that it was ostentatious, although it wasn't nearly as ostentatious as some of the homes that lined Fifth Avenue in New York. Three stories high and made of red brick, the front steps led to a porch flanked by four white pillars and a double door a carriage could easily pass through. Stained-glass windows were inlaid into the doors, the light coming through those windows making a pattern on the tiled front porch. It made for a lovely welcome for guests and also hinted at the splendors one would find once they crossed the threshold into the house.

"I suppose it's too late for us to jump back into the carriage and flee?" Eunice muttered right as Lloyd, Ann, Cooper, and Judith came to join them, Lloyd moving to take Eunice's hand.

"You'll be fine, my dear. Chin up and remember"—Lloyd waved his cane toward the house—"all of this is yours. You and your mother are not the interlopers here. The members of your family who want to steal this from you are." He tapped his cane on the ground. "And if they prove difficult, also remember that we've come armed and ready to fight."

"Let us hope you won't need to use that nasty blade concealed in your cane," Eunice said before she lifted her chin and linked arms with her mother. With Arthur walking beside her, and Ivan moving to walk on the other side of Georgette, they made their way to the front door that was already beginning to open.

"May I help you?" the butler drawled.

"Seems as if someone got rid of Stanford," Eunice said, arching a brow Arthur's way.

"Stanford left about a year after you did," Arthur said quietly. "That's Mr. Crawford. He's only been on the job about three months, which is actually a record. I believe the butler before him only lasted a month." He leaned closer to Eunice. "They apparently have issues with Mrs. Wagner."

"Mrs. Wagner? As in my old tutor's mother?"

"One and the same," Arthur said. "She's taken on the position of Raymond's personal secretary—a personal favor, or so she told me. Vincent owns a bookstore in town, and Mrs. Wagner was assisting him with running the store but felt compelled to accept the personal secretary position because Raymond told her he was overwhelmed seeing after all the tasks needed to be done to keep Mason Manor running smoothly. Mrs. Wagner, from what I understand, was your grandfather's personal secretary at times."

"Mrs. Wagner started out as Father's nurse years ago," Georgette piped up, "after the carriage accident that killed my mother." She lowered her voice. "Rumor had it she was more than a nurse to Father, which might have motivated him to offer her the position of his personal secretary after he recovered enough to where he didn't need a nurse."

Eunice's eyes turned wide. "Grandfather had a mistress?"

"I don't know for sure," Georgette said with a bit of a shudder. "It's not as if fathers normally discuss that type of tawdry business with their daughters, but it would explain why he purchased her a house in town and paid her expenses for years."

"We're going to have to add her to the list of prime suspects, even though she's not family," Eunice muttered before she turned her attention to Mr. Crawford, who was shifting on his feet, clearly waiting for someone to explain what they were doing there.

Deciding it might be for the best if he explained that, Arthur stepped forward, drawing Mr. Crawford's attention.

"Ah, Mr. Livingston. I didn't see you there," Mr. Crawford began. "I wasn't aware you were expected this evening." He took a step toward Arthur. "I'm afraid you missed the memorial. It was at four."

Arthur frowned. "I thought the memorial was supposed to be held on Eugenia Howland's birthday, which isn't for two days."

Mr. Crawford lowered his voice. "Mr. Raymond Mason changed the date of the memorial because a Mr. Loring is to arrive in Butte a few days earlier than expected."

"Isn't Mr. Loring the man interested in purchasing Mason Mines?" Ann asked, catching Eunice's eye.

"I believe so, which explains why the memorial was moved up, because the family couldn't sell Mason Mines without first doing away with me and Mother. But speaking of the family . . ." Eunice nodded to Mr. Crawford. "May I assume the entire Mason family is gathered here in a united show of mourning?"

Mr. Crawford blinked. "I suppose you could call it that, but if you're here to visit them, I've been given strict instructions that they're not to be disturbed. They're currently gathered in the music room, and—"

Before Mr. Crawford could finish his sentence, Eunice slipped around him and into the house, leaving the butler dithering on the porch.

"It's fine, Mr. Crawford. She's family," Arthur said, stepping around the butler and striding after Eunice, who was already moving down the hallway at a rapid clip.

He followed her past the octagonal reception room that was painted bronze over plaster, then down a hallway with walls that were plastered as well but had been painted with ornate swirls of gold paint. He finally caught up with her as she passed the dining room and headed for the music room, where the sound of laughter and someone playing the piano drifted through a closed door.

Eunice stopped walking and turned to him, her eyes flashing with temper. "I cannot believe the family went through with their plans and held a memorial service for me and Mother."

"I can't claim to be surprised by that since Mr. Loring seems anxious to acquire Mason Mines, something Raymond would want to capitalize on sooner than later."

"We've had so much to discuss of late that I never bothered to ask you who this Mr. Loring is."

"In all honesty, I don't know much about him except that he's a wealthy investor."

"Well, whoever he is, he's in for a disappointment because Uncle Raymond can't actually sell mines he doesn't own."

"I have a feeling the evening is going to be more disappointing to the family once we step into the music room," Georgette said as she joined them. "Is it wrong that I'm looking forward to serving up that disappointment tonight?"

"They've rendered us dead, Mother, so I don't believe anyone would blame you for feeling that way."

As Georgette moved to check her reflection in a decorative mirror hanging on the wall, Eunice surprised Arthur by taking hold of his hand.

"Before I face the family and get distracted by them, I need to thank you for badgering me into returning home. I thought I'd be paralyzed with fear upon entering Mason Manor, but I don't feel afraid at all right now. In fact, I feel somewhat empowered, as if confronting my past and uncovering the truth is something that will allow me to step out of the shadows and live my life unfettered from fear." She stepped up on tiptoe and placed a kiss on his cheek, taking him completely aback.

A second after her lips touched his skin, truth hit from out of nowhere—truth he could never ignore.

For years he'd been pursuing a plan he'd thought made perfect sense, one that would finally allow him to reclaim his pride after

Mitzi Jarvis ground it under her dainty evening slipper. In hindsight, that plan had been directly responsible for why he'd not allowed himself to even contemplate pursuing a courtship with Eunice, because she'd not fit his idiotic desire to court and then marry an incomparable.

Eunice was an incomparable in her own right, and he'd been a fool not to realize that.

Before Arthur could confess about being such an idiot, or respond properly to the chaste kiss she'd placed on his cheek by wrapping her in his arms and kissing her soundly, something he felt a great urge to do, Eunice stepped away from him, her face flushed, probably because Georgette had joined them and was considering both of them with a rather knowing look in her eyes.

Eunice ignored the look as she took hold of her mother's hand. "I believe it's time to make our grand entrance, Mother."

"And I believe you're right, but don't think for a moment that I'll forget what I just saw transpire between you and Arthur."

"I have no idea what you're talking about" was all Eunice said to that before she sent him a bit of a wink, entwined her arm with her mother's, and then together they strode toward the music room with their heads held high.

CHAPTER
Twenty-Four

It was rather surreal walking into a room in a house she'd lived in for the first twenty years of her life and finding it filled with relatives who were laughing and chatting away, not exactly looking as if they'd just held a memorial service for two of their family members.

Her great-uncle Raymond was sitting beside the enormous fireplace, smiling broadly at his son, Howard, while Clarice Mason, Raymond's wife, along with Hester Mason, Howard's wife, were sitting beside the grand piano while Doris and Alice played a duet.

Sitting on the other side of the piano, sipping cups of tea, were Mrs. Wagner and her son Vincent, although why Mrs. Wagner and her old tutor were present at a family event was somewhat baffling, although they might simply be there because Mrs. Wagner was Uncle Raymond's personal secretary.

Standing off by herself and looking out a floor-to-ceiling window was Great-Aunt Hazel, who was the only one dressed in black and who was also the only one looking somber. Aunt Hazel, out of all Eunice's relatives, had been the kindest to her and had tried to console Eunice after Georgette disappeared, always talking her into going into town to enjoy some shopping or a nice cup of tea at a small establishment in Butte.

Giving her mother's hand an encouraging squeeze, one Georgette returned, they advanced into the room, stopping when they were directly underneath a chandelier her grandfather had imported from Paris. Annoyance was swift when Eunice realized no one was paying them any mind at all, everyone so caught up in what they evidently saw as their good fortune that they'd neglected to notice that their good fortune was about to come to a screeching end because the two reasons behind that good fortune had just reemerged from the dead.

Eunice was about to release a whistle to attract everyone's attention when Doris stopped playing the piano and took to gawking at her. It took Alice a mere second before she lifted her fingers from the piano keys and settled a frown on her sister. "We weren't done."

"I'm relatively certain we are," Doris said, jerking her head in Eunice's direction.

One by one, Eunice's relatives stopped talking and turned her way, Howard Mason finally rising to his feet.

"Good heavens, but this is, ah, well, an unexpected surprise," he said, an understatement if there ever was one.

Eunice resisted a sudden urge to laugh. "Howard, how delightful to see you again. I'm sure this *is* a surprise, what with how I believe I've recently been declared dead." She shook her head. "Mother and I heard about the memorial service that was to be given in our honor, and we thought it would be highly amusing to attend the event. Unfortunately, we were under the impression it was to take place on my birthday, which, if you don't know, is two days from now. Sadly, because you held the memorial early, it appears we're late for our own party. May I assume there were many heartfelt stories told about my misbegotten youth as well as more than a few tears shed over Mother's and my demise?"

"Eugenia, Georgette," Aunt Hazel exclaimed, bustling across the room to join them. She pulled Eunice into an unanticipated hug. "How wonderful to find both of you alive and well, although I have to admit it's quite the shock to discover you've somehow risen from the ranks of the dead. Frankly, I feel a distinct need to repair to my room and fetch my smelling salts. I've had to make use of those salts often of late, ever since Raymond showed me your death certificates earlier in the week."

Eunice took hold of Aunt Hazel's hand. "How lovely to discover that at least one of my relatives is delighted to see Mother and me alive, but what was that about death certificates?"

Aunt Hazel nodded to Raymond. "Through a hired investigator, Raymond recently learned that you and your mother had departed to the hereafter. From what that investigator found, both of you died while exploring the wonders of India."

Eunice shot a look to Georgette. "We died together."

"And in India no less," Georgette said. "I imagine that made for a very nice and tidy story."

Aunt Hazel darted a look to Georgette. "Is there reason to believe you wouldn't have been together? According to the report Raymond showed me, the investigator learned that you joined Eugenia in England years ago."

"How exactly did I go about finding her in England?" Georgette asked.

Aunt Hazel blinked. "On account of that telegram you sent to Raymond from New York. He sent you a return telegram telling you Eugenia was off on a European tour, beginning with London."

"Ah," Georgette began. "I must have then hied myself across the Atlantic and joined her."

Aunt Hazel nodded. "According to the report, after you reunited with your daughter, the two of you spent the remaining years traveling the world together—until your deaths, of course."

Eunice cleared her throat. "What a fascinating story, except that I never reunited with Mother in England."

Aunt Hazel's eyes clouded with confusion. "Did you reunite in India, then, where you both unfortunately suffered a dreadful accident that was responsible for your deaths?"

The urge to laugh was almost impossible to resist. "Aunt Hazel, Mother and I aren't dead, which means . . . ?"

"The carriage you were riding in that tumbled off a cliff and tossed both of you from it didn't actually kill you?"

"There was no carriage accident."

"Then why are you supposed to be dead?"

Eunice glanced around the room. "That is the question of the hour, as is why an investigator would create a story about my death that's a complete fabrication. That man would have had to have been paid handsomely by someone to invent a report detailing my death and a whopper of a tale without a shred of truth to it."

"But who would have paid him to do that?"

"I would think the obvious suspect is in this room, someone who would benefit financially from my death."

Murmurs immediately broke out, although Doris and Alice continued gawking at Eunice from their spot on the piano bench.

Eunice returned her attention to Aunt Hazel, knowing out of anyone in the room, Aunt Hazel was the most likely to talk. "Were you aware that the telegram Mother sent years ago was actually supposed to go to you, not Uncle Raymond? She sent it to your former address, not knowing you'd moved into Mason Manor. Evidently it was redirected here, but instead of getting into your hands, Uncle Raymond got it."

Aunt Hazel shot a look to her brother. "Is that true?"

"That was a long time ago, Hazel," Uncle Raymond said. "I fear I don't recall the details of that telegram, but I'm sure I would have mentioned it was addressed to you if that were the case."

Eunice narrowed her eyes on him. "Do you recall that you neglected to mention in your return telegram that you sent Mother that Grandfather had died and that she'd been reinstated in his will?"

Uncle Raymond didn't so much as flinch. "I'm sure I cited James's death, but it was a telegram, so I'm not certain I mentioned anything about her being reinstated in James's will."

"You could have sent a follow-up telegram."

"I assumed she wasn't interested in her inheritance since she never bothered to return to Montana."

"You truly believe Mother wouldn't have been interested in claiming her share of an estate that amounts to millions of dollars?"

"I thought James set up a large trust for her before she left, which was why it was so easy for her to abandon all of us, yourself included, after she and James had that tiff," Uncle Raymond said.

Georgette crossed her arms over her chest. "Father never set up a trust for me, given how he didn't think I was capable of spending my funds wisely. But to return to your neglecting to disclose my inheritance, I wonder if you deliberately withheld that information because you were, even back then, devising a plan to claim my inheritance as your own."

Murmurs immediately struck up around the room again, murmurs that held a distinctly hostile tone. Not wanting the room to erupt into chaos, something that could very well happen at any moment, Eunice released a sharp whistle, drawing everyone's attention.

"I'm sure we'll revisit the issue of the telegrams later, but for now, I'd like to return to that investigator who supposedly uncovered proof of our deaths." She turned to Aunt Hazel. "Do you know how this investigator learned I'd met a grisly end in India? Did he travel there?"

"I believe there was mention about a government contact he used."

"Of course there would be a convenient government contact." Eunice strode across the room, stopping in front of Uncle Raymond. "I'm going to assume you're the one who hired this investigator. And since you're certain to soon claim this has simply been a misunderstanding, albeit one that would have yielded you a vast fortune if you'd been successful, I'm going to have to insist you provide me with the name of this investigator, along with his direction. I also need to see his investigation report and the death certificates."

Instead of responding, Uncle Raymond darted a glance to Mrs. Wagner, who sat forward and settled a warm smile on Eunice.

"First, allow me to say that it's lovely to see you alive and well. And as your great-uncle's secretary, I was privy to the investigator's report. It seemed completely legitimate, which was why I felt comfortable going to the courthouse and obtaining death certificates. There's been a small delay with getting those filed, which is actually a blessing in disguise now, what with how you're not actually dead."

"But obviously, the investigator did not present you with a legitimate report, which means I'm going to need this man's name and address," Eunice countered.

"And I'll be happy to provide you with that information," Mrs. Wagner returned. "It may take me a few days because I've gotten behind on my filing, but that information won't do you much good now. The investigator is no longer in Butte, or Montana, for that matter." She cocked a brow Uncle Raymond's way. "Didn't he say he was going off on a new case in . . . was it Canada?"

Uncle Raymond scratched his chin. "I don't recall, but he was going to be out of the country."

"Hmm" was all Eunice could think to say to that before she nodded. "And am I right to conclude those death certificates were filled out by a local Butte official?"

"Indeed," Mrs. Wagner said. "Mr. Jonathon Matthews was the official who had the certificates drawn up."

"I'll be speaking to him tomorrow."

"I'm afraid that won't be possible either because Mr. Matthews is not in town. We were disappointed to learn he'd left because he's also the one who files death certificates at the courthouse. I was to meet him at the courthouse to officially file the certificates on the very day he was called out of town due to a family emergency." Mrs. Wagner settled a sweet smile on Eunice. "As I've already said, though, it's a blessing we weren't able to file those certificates since you're not, well, dead."

Given the looks of annoyance on everyone's faces, Eunice was certain they weren't finding the fact that the death certificates were never officially filed to be much of a blessing. She took a step closer to Mrs. Wagner. "Blessings aside, Mrs. Wagner, I find myself curious as to what you're doing here. I would have thought the memorial service would have been for family members only."

"Your grandfather always considered me a part of the family, dear, and I'm pleased to say that status has remained even after his death."

"And *I* attended your memorial service with Mother," Vincent Wagner spoke up, "not simply because I'm a doting son but also because I was your tutor for years and spent an immeasurable amount of time with you."

"You never seemed to like me."

Vincent smiled. "That's simply because I was your tutor. Tutors cannot allow their true feelings to show toward any of their students, especially a student as charming as you were. Why, if I'd not presented myself as a hard taskmaster, you would have had me wrapped around your little finger in no time. Your grandfather wouldn't have approved of that, and I'm sure he would have sent me packing. I would have hated for that to happen because I relished teaching such a brilliant mind and looked forward each day to the lessons I methodically planned out for you."

Before Eunice could respond to what was an unexpected and quite unbelievable statement, Aunt Hazel clapped her hands, drawing everyone's attention.

"I'm sorry to interrupt, but the thought has just struck me that Eugenia and Georgette must not be thinking very kindly of us right now. Here they've just arrived home after a long absence and instead of greeting them properly, we're letting ourselves become distracted with nonsensical matters."

It came as no surprise when everyone began looking at Aunt Hazel as if she'd lost her mind, not that she noticed because she moved to take hold of Eunice's hand. "To make amends for our serious lack of manners, I'd like to ring for some tea and then have a nice sit-down where you can explain to the family exactly what you've been doing all these years."

Even though Aunt Hazel had always been a rather dotty woman

who was slightly caustic with her tongue at times, she was far more intelligent than anyone gave her credit for. That she was trying to redirect the conversation from what was clearly nefarious actions taken by the family left Eunice wondering if Hazel might actually belong at the top of their list of possible suspects after all.

She gave Aunt Hazel's hand a pat. "And while recounting what I've been doing all these years would be a lovely way to spend the evening, I'm going to have pass on that. I have a lot of additional questions I need to ask surrounding the decision to have me declared dead."

"But everyone is turning downright dour with all the questions being tossed at them, and this should be a joyous occasion." Aunt Hazel gestured around the room. "We've only recently attended your memorial service, which was quite moving, although . . ." She stopped talking as her gaze sharpened on Eunice. "One of the first things you said when you entered the room was that you'd returned home to attend your memorial service. How did you know about the memorial service in the first place?"

"I think it'll be best if I explain that," Arthur said, striding across the room to join Eunice.

Aunt Hazel raised a hand to her throat. "Mr. Livingston. What are you doing here? I thought you were off on one of your mining investment trips and weren't expected to return to Montana for weeks, although Wyatt will be glad you've returned early. He's been pining for you, dear. I've had to take him extra apples to get him to leave his stall every day."

"And while I'm sure Wyatt has been refusing to leave his stall because he knows you'll bribe him with apples, I'm afraid I wasn't upfront regarding where I was going. There was no mining business to attend to. It was more along the lines of personal business."

Aunt Hazel frowned. "Did that personal business have something to do with Eugenia?"

"Indeed. I decided to make a last-ditch effort to find her, apprise her of the situation, and then convince her to return home to prove that neither she nor her mother were dead." Arthur nodded to Uncle Raymond, who was red in the face and looking furious. "I overheard you speaking with someone in your office a few weeks ago about planning a memorial service for Eugenia and her mother. From what I overheard, you'd decided they'd been gone long enough to where questions wouldn't be asked if you had them declared dead. Since I was relatively certain Eugenia was still alive, as the Pinkertons I hired years ago concluded she'd never left New York City, I thought it was only fair to her if I tried to track her down one last time and tell her about her impending memorial service."

"You never once told me about any Pinkertons you hired to search for my great-niece," Uncle Raymond snapped. "And far be it from me to point out the obvious, but the family received a telegram from Eugenia stating she was going to stay in Europe for the foreseeable future, which means whatever information those Pinkertons gave you had to have been false."

"Eunice didn't send that telegram. I did," Arthur said.

Uncle Raymond's face turned redder than ever. "Why would you have done that?"

Aunt Hazel cleared her throat before Arthur could respond. "Forgive me, but who is Eunice?"

"Oh, forgive *me*," Arthur began, "I'm sure that does need some explaining. Eunice is Eugenia, but she doesn't go by Eugenia anymore, so everyone will need to address her as Eunice from this point forward. Except Georgette, of course, who prefers Sunshine."

Before Aunt Hazel could say anything more than "How very curious," Uncle Raymond began making his way across the music room, every thump of the cane lending credence to the idea the man was furious.

"It doesn't matter what the girl is calling herself these days, Hazel. We have more important matters to discuss." Uncle Raymond stopped two feet from Arthur and shook his cane at him. "You're not a member of the family, sir, and you had no business taking it upon yourself to fetch my great-niece home."

"Arthur was honoring the word he gave to Grandfather before he died to look after my best interests," Eunice said before Arthur could answer. "Clearly, the only way for him to do that was to track me down. What I'm most curious about, though, is why you were planning a memorial service for Mother and me weeks ago when that investigator you hired brought you proof of our deaths just last *week*." She tapped a finger against her chin. "Could it be that you've taken to consulting with fortune tellers and they let you know that you'd be receiving word of my death within the month, which then prompted you to begin making arrangements to have Mother and I buried once and for all, although without our bodies, which I assume everyone believes are in India?"

"They were supposed to be burned," Mrs. Wagner said. "That's standard practice, or at least that's what I've been told, to dispose of the dead in India."

"And wouldn't leave a shred of evidence behind," Ann muttered from where she'd stepped directly behind Eunice.

"Indeed," Eunice said before she turned back to Uncle Raymond. "Explain the death certificates."

"There's not much left to explain. The investigator gave me his report and then Mrs. Wagner took that report to Mr., ahh . . ."

"Jonathon Matthews," Mrs. Wagner supplied.

"Right, Jonathon Matthews. Mr. Matthews decided everything was in order and signed the certificates. As has been mentioned, he was unable to officially file them because he was called out of town on a family emergency."

Arthur cleared his throat. "I'm sorry to interrupt, but I fear with all the disclosures being tossed about regarding investigators and Butte officials that I've neglected to mention something that's relatively important."

Given the gleam in Arthur's eye, Eunice was fairly certain he hadn't neglected to mention whatever it was out of negligence, but out of timing.

She refused a smile. "And what would that be?"

"Jonathon Matthews didn't leave on a family emergency. I sent him a telegram from New York." Arthur turned to Uncle Raymond. "I had a feeling you might begin taking steps to have Eunice declared dead before I had a chance to find her and bring her home. Since Jonathon Matthews is the Butte official responsible for death certificates, I decided he needed to be unavailable in Butte for the foreseeable future." Arthur smiled. "He's currently enjoying some fishing and is not due to return for another few weeks."

"You bribed him to go away?" Uncle Raymond asked.

"Without a second's hesitation, and I made the bribe large enough to where he couldn't refuse my fishing suggestion."

Eunice felt the distinct inclination to throw her arms around Arthur and kiss him soundly, and not on the cheek this time, but refused the inclination because that would definitely distract from the drama that was currently unfolding in the music room.

"It's probably fortunate those certificates weren't filed," Cooper said, moving across the room to join Eunice before he flashed his badge in Uncle Raymond's direction. "I'm Agent Cooper Clifton of the Pinkerton Agency, and while it's one thing to fabricate an investigator and an investigation report, it's quite another to file fraudulent death certificates, especially when there's reason to believe the persons in question are probably not dead."

"You're a Pinkerton man?" Howard asked, stepping forward and looking closely at the badge Cooper held out to him. He turned to his father before Cooper could do more than nod. "This is where you and everyone else in this room stops answering questions."

"But we were just uncovering all sorts of family nastiness," Eunice said. "If you ask me, refusing to answer additional questions is a clear mark of guilt if there ever was one."

The silence that settled around the room spoke volumes.

"I suppose I'm simply going to have to puzzle this out on my own," Eunice said, taking a few moments to pace around the room as she tried to sort through the jumble of tidbits her family had disclosed, which weren't many. She stopped pacing and frowned.

"What I think happened so far is this—when Arthur brought

in geologists to survey the old Green farm, it was discovered that there's a huge windfall coming to Mason Mines. Because of that windfall, you"—she gestured around the room—"my beloved family, turned greedy."

She began pacing again. "Clearly, plans were set into motion not long after that copper was discovered because I have to imagine word about the copper got out. A find like that would surely draw investors, so I needed to die, as did Mother."

"Alice and I didn't know anything about any copper find," Doris said, speaking up.

Alice nodded. "We don't even understand copper." She glanced to Cooper. "But to be honest here, Agent Pinkerton man, we didn't question the deaths, even if, now that I consider the matter, the timing does seem somewhat suspicious."

"Too right it does," Eunice agreed, arching a brow Uncle Raymond's way.

Uncle Raymond gave a tug of his tie. "Since those death certificates weren't filed, it seems to me that there's been no harm done."

"Only because I came home."

"But since you *did* come home and those certificates weren't made official, I say all's well that end's well, so there's no need for the Pinkerton to stay."

Eunice narrowed her eyes on him. "And I might have agreed to send Agent Clifton away since all of you are family except I didn't return home simply to save my inheritance. I'm also here to address some unfinished business from the past."

"Eunice . . ." Ivan said from where he was standing by the music room door, his voice brimming with an unspoken warning.

She pretended she didn't hear him. "That unfinished business pertains to Grandfather's death."

"There's nothing unfinished about that," Uncle Raymond said. "My brother's been dead and buried for the past seven years."

"Oh, there's no question that Grandfather is dead, but there *is* something unfinished about his death because, you see, I have reason to believe he didn't die from an accidental shooting."

Aunt Hazel raised a hand to her throat. "James would never take his life on purpose."

"I wasn't suggesting he committed suicide. He was murdered, plain and simple, and it's past time to bring his murderer to justice."

CHAPTER

Twenty-Five

"Just so you know," Ivan said, "it's now no longer up for debate that after we solve this particular case, you'll resign yourself to the fact you're far too direct to go out into the field on investigations ever again."

Pausing in the process of cinching Wyatt's saddle, Arthur smiled as Eunice sauntered into view, wearing not one of Phillip's dresses, but trousers paired with a gentleman's jacket, complete with riding boots that had seen better days. Ivan was at her side, exasperation stamped on his face, exasperation Eunice did nothing to temper when she rolled her eyes.

"My continuing to go out into the field is certainly still debatable," she argued. "Why, I imagine, what with how I blurted out about Grandfather being murdered, that our case is going to move forward at a rapid rate." She stopped in her tracks when Wyatt let out a nicker that sounded somewhat menacing. "You mark my words, the killer will be exposed within the week."

"Or you'll be dead within the week."

Eunice lifted her chin. "I didn't get the feeling last night that the family is going to cooperate with us, given the vast disappointment they didn't bother to hide over my being anything but dead. I figured they needed a shake-up. With the murder business out in the open, everyone knows there's skullduggery afoot. And," she continued even though Ivan had opened his mouth, clearly ready to argue against that, "because the members of my family aren't the type to take a bullet for anyone, I'm hoping we'll be inundated with clues the longer we spend time with them."

Arthur gave Wyatt's ears a scratch, earning a nuzzle from Wyatt in return, something that had Eunice settling a glare on the horse.

"It's obvious Wyatt didn't miss me."

"Or he was bereft without your company and is being ornery right now with you because it's his way of showing you how distressed he was," Arthur countered.

Wyatt tossed his head, released another nicker, then tossed his head in Eunice's direction, which had her backing her way into a stall. "He's ornery because orneriness is his normal nature."

Arthur smiled when Wyatt gave him another nuzzle. "Perhaps that's why he likes me. He senses a kindred spirit."

"You're nothing like Wyatt."

Arthur's lips curved into a grin, which faded when he realized Ivan was watching him far too closely. "Yes, well, that's very kind of you to say. But returning to your theory about being inundated with clues the longer we spend time with your family, that might be somewhat tricky to do considering all except Hazel fled from the music room last night after you added that bit about being certain your grandfather's killer was in that very room."

"They didn't flee directly after I said that," Eunice argued. "If you'll recall, Uncle Raymond didn't hesitate to throw suspicion on you, stating that you were the one to find Grandfather, so you were obviously the one to murder him."

"And you rose to my defense splendidly, telling them I wouldn't have ended up with the empire James was willing to hand over to me if he died before he got us married." Arthur frowned. "I have to admit, I was surprised when you disclosed everything about the day James died. I thought the plan was to keep the fact you were on the target field a secret."

Eunice took a step out of the stall, freezing on the spot when

Wyatt began pawing the ground. "That was an unintentional disclosure on my part, but I simply couldn't figure out how to sufficiently explain why you'd stage the scene without telling the whole story."

"Which led everyone to begin accusing you of murdering your grandfather," Cooper said, pushing himself away from the stable wall he'd been leaning against. "That's why I stepped in to explain that the Pinkertons had concluded neither you or Arthur were credible suspects, and then told your family I was prepared to sit down with each of them individually to do some interrogating." He rubbed a hand over his face. "Can't say I was expecting everyone to make a mad dash for the door after I suggested that. I'm surprised no one was injured in the stampede."

"It's obvious no one is going to willingly sit down with you," Eunice began, "hence the reason behind traveling into town today. I'm hopeful we'll be able to take Doris and Alice, as well as Howard, by surprise when we stroll into their respective businesses. Surprise appearances have been known to have people spilling a few secrets, or at least that's happened a few times on cases the agency has solved."

"And while all of you are off to town," Judith said, looking up from where she was sitting on a haybale, sketching Wyatt, "Ann, Georgette, Lloyd, and I will see if we can find some answers here with Hazel, Raymond, and Clarice. Hazel has agreed to sit for me this morning after I admitted to her that I admired her eyes. I'm not certain, however, that we'll make any headway with Raymond and Clarice, given that they're now sequestered in their suite of rooms and refuse to come out."

"A clear sign of guilt if there ever was one," Eunice said as one of the groomsmen appeared, leading a lovely mare by the name of Samantha and handing Eunice the reins once he reached her side.

"She's got a nice ride, Miss Howland," the groom said, smoothing a hand over Samantha's neck. "But don't let her get too close to Wyatt." He shook his head. "He's smitten with her, and that might make for an interesting jaunt to town."

After Eunice sent the groomsman a smile, she swung into the saddle, Arthur, Ivan, and Cooper doing the same with their horses.

"We'll be back soon," Ivan said, nodding to Judith. "Remember what we discussed—you have to remain vigilant. Don't let your guard down around Hazel, Raymond, or Clarice."

Judith closed her sketchpad and sent Ivan a flirty smile. "I'm sure Ann and I are more than up for dealing with two eighty-year-old suspects and Hazel. We are inquiry agents, after all—not that anyone knows that since, surprise, surprise, Eunice didn't blurt that out last night. And since the family thinks I'm one of Georgette's artist companions and Ann is Eunice's traveling companion, there's no reason for anyone to go after us because we're not a threat." She gave a wave of her fingers toward the stable door. "So, off you go, but know that I wouldn't mind a lovely piece of chocolate from Doris and Alice's candy shop. It's my very favorite treat."

"Then chocolate you shall have," Ivan said, returning the flirty smile. "And not just a piece, mind you, but your very own box."

"Come on, Romeo." Cooper nudged his horse into motion as he settled a grin on Ivan. "Time's a-wasting, and besides, I thought you and Judith were supposed to be limiting your flirting until we catch our murderer."

With Judith saying something about that being a difficult feat to maintain and Ivan's cheeks turning somewhat red, Arthur urged Wyatt forward, keeping a firm hand on the reins when the horse kept trying to sidle up next to Eunice's horse.

No one said much as they headed off for town until Eunice nodded to the Rocky Mountains rising up behind the town of Butte.

"I'd forgotten how lovely the mountains are," she said before her nose wrinkled. "Although I've also forgotten the smell from the mines and the smoke that seems to have increased from the factories since I've been away."

"The smoke can be overwhelming at times," Arthur agreed, pulling Wyatt a good distance away from her. "But it's a sign Butte is booming with business, that state certain to increase once Mason Mines begins mining operations at the old Green farm."

"And when are those operations set to begin?"

"That depends on you. You are the majority owner of Mason Mines now."

"But as we've discussed, and ad nauseum at that, I don't want to run the mines. As president of Mason Mines, you will make all those types of decisions."

Arthur stilled. "You never said you wanted me to take on the role of president."

"I'm sure I mentioned it at some point."

"You suggested it once, but we've not discussed it since and certainly haven't discussed it ad nauseum."

She tilted her head. "I didn't realize there was much more to discuss because I assumed you'd want to be president. Was I mistaken about that?"

Arthur rubbed his chin. "Well, no, but there's a lot left to discuss about the matter."

"I suppose there is, so if you'll present me with a written contract stating your terms, we can begin negotiating those terms."

"We're going to negotiate my terms?"

She grinned. "If you've forgotten, my grandfather forced me to learn everything there was about the mining business, including having Vincent instruct me on negotiation and contracts. As you pointed out to me recently, it would be a shame if I never put any of that education to use."

The thought of sitting across a table from Eunice and arguing over contract points left Arthur with a sense of anticipation he'd not been expecting. He smiled and inclined his head. "I'll look forward to that."

"As will I, but for now . . . to town." She urged Samantha into a gallop, Wyatt straining against the reins as he tried to gallop his way closer to his ladylove.

After they left their horses at Mason's Stables, Arthur took Eunice's arm and began strolling with her down the planked sidewalk, Ivan and Cooper following a few steps behind. Amusingly enough, many of the Mason-owned shops were sporting black bunting on their doors, which was only now being taken down by employees, suggesting word had gotten out that Eunice and Georgette had miraculously returned from the dead.

"Shall we go to Wagner's Bookshop first?" Eunice asked, stopping in front of a brick building that was owned and operated by Vincent. Vincent hadn't lingered the night before, rushing for the door along with his mother and everyone else when Cooper had suggested it was time to begin interrogations.

"I thought you wanted to see Doris and Alice first," Arthur said.

"Since Vincent's mother is Uncle Raymond's personal secretary and may be privy to family secrets, some of which she could have shared with her son, it wouldn't hurt to stroll around his store and engage in light chitchat with him. He might let something slip."

After following Eunice into the store, Arthur began browsing through a table of the latest history books, Eunice beside him, but only for a moment because Vincent came striding their way, smiling as he took hold of Eunice's hand and placed an unexpected kiss on it.

"How lovely you look today, Eugenia—or rather, Eunice," Vincent began. "I see you're back to wearing your preferred style of trousers instead of skirts."

"I wasn't sure there would be any sidesaddles available in the stables when I got dressed for riding this morning," Eunice said as she retrieved her hand from his. "But what a charming bookstore this is, although I don't recall you ever mentioning during our lessons that you longed to own a bookstore."

Vincent's smile turned rueful. "I must admit it was not a longing I knew I had." He gestured around the store. "This was actually a gift from Mother. After you left, I had no pupil to teach, and she grew concerned that I'd gravitate to the mining industry because of my engineering degree from Harvard." He shook his head. "Since I'm her only child, and she dotes on me, she decided to provide me with a different way to earn a living. Mother is very dear to me, so how could I refuse her generous gift, or worry her by pursuing an occupation that would cause her sleepless nights?

To my delight, I've discovered I have a knack for the book business, and sales have been robust from the moment I opened my doors."

"How lovely for you," Eunice said as she looked around. "You seem to have an extensive inventory, which does suggest your business is booming. And given the size of this building, I have to agree that your mother does dote on you because this must have cost her a pretty penny."

Vincent considered Eunice for a long moment before he inclined his head. "On a fishing expedition, are you?"

"Perhaps."

"I would expect nothing less, given what I know to be a keen sense of curiosity lurking in that astute mind of yours. However, if you're setting your sights on me or my mother, you're fishing in the wrong pond. Neither of us has anything to do with the Mason family saga."

Eunice frowned. "Your mother had a direct hand with the death certificates that could have seen my inheritance stripped away from me."

"She's Raymond's secretary. Of course she had something to do with the death certificates, but it was at his direction. Perhaps your time would be better spent fishing in Raymond's very large and, need I add, murky pond."

Given the way Eunice's eyes narrowed just a fraction, it was obvious Vincent's reply hadn't satisfied her curiosity, but instead of pressing him on the matter, she sent him a sweet smile that was so unlike her that Arthur found himself hard-pressed not to laugh. "Perhaps that's exactly what I should do. And since we've gotten that out of the way, I find myself in need of a good read. Would you direct me to your Jane Austen section?"

Vincent suddenly looked as if he'd smelled something rank. "This is more of a literary bookstore, and as such, I don't stock romantic drivel."

"And yet Jane Austen books sell remarkably well, and one would think, being a businessman, you'd be mindful of your bottom line—unless, of course, you and your mother are independently wealthy. If that's the case, it demands all sorts of questions, such as where your wealth came from, or more specifically, if any of that came from my grandfather."

Any hint of affability disappeared from Vincent's face. "I'm sure you've heard the rumors about my mother and your grandfather, but it's not a subject I've ever discussed with her, which means I can't speak to the terms of their financial arrangement."

"She wasn't mentioned in his will," Eunice said, the sweet smile remaining firmly on her face, which was in direct contrast to the scowl Vincent was settling on her.

"Something we also never discussed, but I'm going to caution you against speaking about the matter with my mother. She always claimed James was the love of her life, and she suffered greatly after his death—and not simply because she wasn't remembered in his will."

Before Eunice could respond, Vincent spun on his heel and stalked away, disappearing through a door at the back of the store and then slamming that door shut.

"Vincent and his mother definitely go on our list," Eunice said, taking Arthur's arm. "And I will be asking Mrs. Wagner where she got the funds to purchase this bookshop." Her lips curved as they strolled through the store. "And before you ask, Vincent should go on the list simply because there's something shifty about a bookstore owner who doesn't sell Jane Austen."

"I'm not going to argue with logic like that," Arthur said, walking out of the store and heading toward Doris and Alice's candy shop.

It took them far longer than it normally would to reach the store because they were stopped every few feet by Butte residents who recognized Eunice and wanted to tell her how delighted they were that she wasn't dead. Each and every resident would then launch into what a wonderful job the Mason family was doing with improving Butte, while also making sure to mention that they hoped she was going to continue with the improvements now that she was back and was the majority owner of Mason Mines.

"Word seems to have gotten out about my return as well as the contents of Grandfather's will," Eunice muttered as they made their way into the candy shop.

"The town always knew you were left the majority of Mason Mines," Arthur said quietly. "But after Hazel and Raymond began pouring money into the town to improve it, people stopped questioning where you were or if you were going to return and embraced your family because they were finally getting the town they always felt James should have provided them with, what with the fortune he acquired with his mines here."

"Do you think we're looking in the wrong place and it was a disgruntled miner or town citizen who could have killed Grandfather?"

"Let's hope not," Cooper said, moving up beside her after having kept a discreet distance from her ever since they'd reached town. "That would make our investigation almost impossible to complete. Seems to me, from what I've overheard people saying about James, your grandfather was not liked by many people in Butte."

"He was a difficult man," Eunice agreed before she waved to Doris, who was standing behind a counter and looking less than pleased to see her cousin.

"We've come for a tour," Eunice all but chirped, which was very unlike her and earned her a wrinkle of the nose from Alice, who'd just stepped out from behind a large barrel filled with lollipops.

"You came to snoop," Alice corrected. "Father told us you might, but we've got nothing to say about any murder because, if you've forgotten, Doris and I were attending boarding school when Great-Uncle James died." She shot a look to Cooper. "That's what's called an airtight alibi, or so my father said."

Eunice smiled. "I'll be sure to take you off the list of suspects straightaway."

"We were on a suspect list?"

"I'm afraid you were, but now you're not."

Less than five minutes later, Arthur found himself back on the sidewalk, escorted in a not-very-subtle manner by both Doris and Alice. "That went well."

"I should have known Howard would caution them not to say anything," Eunice grumbled before she took a bite of the chocolate Doris had thrust at her as she'd shoved her through the candy shop door. "Oh, this is heavenly. And while we didn't learn anything of worth about the murder, we did learn that Doris and Alice aren't married because they believe the suitor pickings are slim in Butte."

"We also discovered Hazel is the one who taught them how to make candy," Ivan added, tucking the large box of chocolates he'd purchased for Judith into the satchel he'd slung over his shoulder. "I never knew Hazel knew her way about the kitchen."

"Neither did I," Eunice said. "Although, according to Doris, that's simply because I was always spending my time with Grandfather." She frowned. "Did you notice the hint of resentment in her voice when she said that?"

"It would have been hard to miss," Cooper said, wiping a smear of chocolate from his lips with a handkerchief. "But I don't think they're viable candidates for the crime, unless they came home from boarding school and no one knew it."

"We'll keep them on the list, just in case," Eunice said before she set her sights on Mason's Dry Goods Store. "Shall we see if Howard is around?"

Arthur took Eunice's arm again, and together they began making their way across Main Street, dodging people and carriages as they crossed. "I'm not sure Howard's going to disclose anything of worth to us," he began. "It's clear the family is closing ranks against you, which means it'll be—"

Before he could finish the sentence, a shot rang out, and without a second's hesitation, he grabbed hold of Eunice and took her to the ground.

CHAPTER
Twenty-Six

"You were certainly right about the investigation moving along at a rapid clip considering someone has already tried to murder you, and we've only been in town a little over a day," Ivan muttered. "And not that I want to say I told you so, but if you wouldn't have divulged the fact we're here to find a murderer, you wouldn't now be sporting that lump on your head. Although I suppose it's better than you sporting a bullet hole."

Eunice lifted the ice pack Aunt Hazel had given her from the large lump on her head, compliments of hitting her head against the hard surface of Main Street. "I know, Ivan, you were right, but now we know for sure that we've gotten the murderer's attention, and we can whittle the list of suspects down simply because some of the people on our list have alibis."

"How delightful to learn I'm no longer a suspect," Aunt Hazel said, bustling into the library with a bowl filled with a fresh batch of ice. She took the towel Eunice was holding, dumped fresh ice into it, then placed the towel back on Eunice's head. "Keep that on for a good thirty minutes, dear. Thankfully, the swelling does seem to be going down, and at least you didn't mar that beautiful face of yours when you fell."

"I didn't fall. Arthur took me to the ground, and then Ivan

jumped on top of him, which sufficiently left me squished in the dirt and things best left unmentioned on Main Street."

"Seemed better than allowing you to be shot," Ivan said.

"I'm not complaining." Eunice leaned back against the fainting couch right as Howard burst into the room, Hester, Doris, and Alice rushing in after him.

"We got here as soon as we could," Howard said, moving to take a seat on the fainting couch beside Eunice and forcing her to scoot a bit to the right in the process. "The town's all abuzz. Dare I hope the miscreant who tried to shoot you was apprehended?"

"Agent Clifton is still in town questioning people who were on the street, but so far we've not had any word that anyone's been taken into custody."

"Well, at least the family can be ruled out," Howard said. "I was at Hennessey's Mercantile when I heard the shot, and Mr. Hennessey can testify to that. We were discussing inventory purchases because before I set up the Dry Goods store, I agreed not to sell anything Mr. Hennessey sells."

"Done so because the whole point of investing in businesses in town was to finally improve the Mason name as well as our standing in the city," Hester said, settling into a chair in a rustle of expensive fabric. She began waving a fan she pulled from her reticule in front of her face. "The gossip is going to be dreadful over this latest incident. I mean, it was bad enough, Eunice, that you and Georgette reemerged from the dead, and it's been a little tricky to explain why you're no longer Eugenia." Her waving increased. "Now that someone tried to shoot you, though—on Main Street, no less, and in broad daylight—well, it's yet another stain on the Mason name."

Eunice readjusted the ice. "I'm sorry my near death today has caused such an inconvenience for you, Hester. Perhaps it would have been best if I'd simply gotten up from the ground after Arthur and Ivan saved me and allowed whoever shot at me the first time to get a better shot."

Silence settled over the library, broken when Arthur strode into the room, looking rumpled and far too dangerous as he moved to the fainting couch. Howard jumped up from it to make room for a man who, clearly, was in a mood.

Arthur took hold of Eunice's hand. "How's the head?"

"Tender, but I'll live. How's your temper?"

"Under control for now." He glanced around the room. "I've been thinking a family meeting might be in order because obviously matters have escalated."

"I was thinking the same thing."

"Wonderful." He looked to Howard. "If you would be so kind as to fetch your father and mother from their room, we'll be able to get started."

"I'm afraid Raymond isn't feeling well today," Mrs. Wagner said, stepping into the library, Vincent by her side.

Eunice frowned. "I wasn't aware you were here, Mrs. Wagner."

"I'm here five days a week, dear. As your uncle's secretary, and as there's so much involved with keeping Mason Manor running smoothly, I'm needed every day except for weekends. I usually only stay until two, when Vincent comes to fetch me." She smiled. "And good thing for that, since he has an alibi for his whereabouts during the time of the shooting. He arrived here early today, at one to be exact, just about the time I believe you were under fire."

"And that would be fortunate if everyone actually needed an alibi," Cooper said, striding into the room and looking disgruntled. He caught Eunice's eye. "It was a false alarm. Turns out the shooting had nothing to do with you. It was a gambling argument between two cowboys that spilled onto Main Street. The man responsible has now been taken into custody, so no true harm was done."

"I have a lump the size of a goose egg on my head," Eunice couldn't help but point out.

Cooper winced. "Which is unfortunate, but at least you're not sporting a bullet hole."

"That's what I told her," Ivan said as Judith moved to join him, giving his arm a soothing rub.

"It sounds to me, Ivan," Judith began, "as if you were very gallant in your defense of Eunice, something I would have adored seeing. Just as I would have adored witnessing a cowboy showdown in the middle of Main Street."

"Cowboy showdowns are a dime a dozen in town," Aunt Hazel said. "I'm sure there'll be another one the next time a trip to town is planned, so no need to fret you missed a treat." She smiled. "On the bright side, though, if you'd have gone into town today, then you, Ann, and Georgette wouldn't have been able to oh so subtly question me about the family as I was sitting for my portrait."

Judith shot a glance to Ann, who grimaced, before she returned her attention to Aunt Hazel. "We weren't deliberately questioning you. We were merely curious about your life in Montana."

Aunt Hazel rolled her eyes. "Please, dear, give me a bit more credit. As I mentioned at one point today, I'm very adept with eavesdropping. James was never forthcoming with family information, so I became very proficient over the years with lurking around corners and pressing my ear up against doors. Because of that, I'm what I like to think of as the family secret keeper."

"You didn't share many of those secrets today," Judith muttered.

"That's because you didn't ask the right questions." Aunt Hazel switched her attention to Eunice. "Before I forget, darling, allow me to congratulate you on being a partner with a lady detective agency. The very idea of ladies solving mysteries fascinates me. You're simply going to have to tell me all about how your Bleecker Street Inquiry Agency came to be."

"You know about the agency?" Eunice asked, ignoring the look of outrage Hester was sending her and the fact that Doris and Alice's mouths were gaping open.

"Of course." Aunt Hazel smiled a far-too-innocent smile. "I was in the barn while you were getting the horses ready for the trip to town."

"I didn't see you in the barn."

Aunt Hazel gave an airy wave of her hand. "I was hiding out

in the loft, hoping to learn something interesting, and lo and behold, I heard you talking about the agency." She tilted her head. "I am curious, though, if you run an inquiry agency, why it took you so long to decide to investigate James's death. Might it have had something to do with the fact someone could very well want you dead as well, or at the very least, locked behind bars, framed for his murder?"

"This investigation is turning into a complete fiasco," Cooper muttered as he joined Eunice.

"I'm not going to argue about that, but since *everything* is out in the open now, and we've already called for a family meeting, we might as well take the remainder of the afternoon to try and sort matters out."

"Is it actually going to be a sorting out, or will it be more along the lines of a family interrogation?" Aunt Hazel asked.

"Interrogation," Cooper said without hesitation.

"How lovely" was all Aunt Hazel said to that before she waltzed toward the door, saying over her shoulder that she was off to fetch Raymond and Clarice and ring for coffee.

As murmurs sounded around the room, Hester muttering the loudest and saying something to the effect that it was scandalous that anyone in the family needed to be subjected to an interrogation, Lloyd moseyed over to join Eunice and Arthur, pulling up a chair and taking a seat before he leaned closer to her. "Interesting family you have, dear, but I must say, Hazel is a delightful woman, and I don't believe she had anything to do with murdering her brother. From what she disclosed today, she was rather fond of James, even if he did keep her under his thumb." He lowered his voice. "Raymond, on the other hand, didn't care for his brother at all, and Hazel mentioned in passing that he always resented James because his brother didn't believe he possessed the intellect needed to be an asset to the family business."

"I think it's fair to say that James did not possess a sensitive side," Arthur said, which left Eunice smiling as Aunt Hazel reentered the room, Uncle Raymond and Clarice trailing behind her.

Given that Uncle Raymond's face was remarkably drawn, it was clear that while he'd been keeping to his suite of rooms, he'd certainly not been resting.

Howard stepped forward and got his parents settled on a settee, then settled himself in a chair next to Hester, while Alice and Doris went to sit beside Mrs. Wagner, who'd apparently decided to join the interrogation without even being asked. Vincent had taken to looking at his pocket watch, his expression annoyed, quite as if he didn't want to waste his time dealing with Mason family matters since he wasn't a Mason.

Cooper strode to the middle of the room, which had silence descending over the library. "Since everyone is now here, I believe we'll start where we ended last night before the mad stampede for the door, which was . . . ?"

Doris raised her hand. "I believe Eunice explained how she knew her grandfather, my great-uncle James, had been murdered, and also how someone tried to set her up to take the fall, and then everyone voiced their innocence and the evening ended."

"What an interesting recap of the evening," Cooper said. "But yes, that's somewhat accurate, so I'm going to start with this—I'd like to hear thoughts on who all of you think would be the most likely to have killed James, as well as who would have then tried to frame Eunice for the crime."

"And let the games begin," Georgette murmured as everyone began glancing around the room, almost to see if someone would have the audacity to name a possible suspect.

To Eunice's surprise, Uncle Raymond suddenly stood up, his face ashen, but she quickly realized he hadn't stood up to announce a suspect. Mr. Crawford, the butler, had entered the library, along with a distinguished-looking gentleman.

"Begging your pardon," Mr. Crawford began, "but Mr. D. H. Loring is here to speak with Mr. Raymond Mason. He told me he's expected."

"I forgot all about Mr. Loring," Raymond said, taking a step forward. "In the hopes of sparing him our family drama, I'll just go and—"

Whatever else Uncle Raymond had been about to say came to an abrupt end when Georgette shot out of her chair and began stalking across the room, not stopping until she was five feet away from the man Mr. Crawford was standing beside.

"What are you doing here?" she demanded.

Mr. Loring stiffened right before his eyes narrowed on Georgette. "I could ask the same of you. When Raymond Mason let it be known he was interested in selling Mason Mines, I inquired about you and was told you'd died. You don't look dead to me."

"Oh, I assure you, I'm very much alive," Georgette said before she stepped closer to the man and slapped him smartly across the face.

For the briefest of seconds, Eunice found herself at a loss for what to do, because even though her mother possessed a temperamental nature, she normally refrained from accosting men, even when she was provoked.

"You should intervene," Uncle Raymond said, drawing Eunice's attention away from where her mother and the gentleman were now glaring at each other, neither of them saying a word.

She set aside the ice and rose from the fainting couch. "You're the one who decided to assume the role of head of the Mason household. That means this type of business falls under your jurisdiction."

"I have no idea how to intervene since I have no idea what could have possessed your mother to slap Mr. Loring. He's a distinguished man of business, and as such, he certainly shouldn't be treated in such a deplorable fashion."

"I'm sure Mother has her reasons, and I'm not comfortable intervening in whatever is occurring between Mother and Mr. Loring unless I feel the situation is turning concerning."

"That's not Mr. Loring," Lloyd said, moving closer to her.

"What do you mean, it's not Mr. Loring?" Uncle Raymond demanded. "I met the man less than a month ago when he stopped to tour the mines."

Lloyd darted a look to the man still glaring at Georgette, then settled a concerned eye on Eunice. "Do you remember me asking Georgette about Mrs. Edward Howland, one of my widow friends?"

"She didn't seem to be acquainted with her."

Lloyd rubbed a hand over his face. "Indeed, although because she just gave Mr. Douglas Howland, Mrs. Howland's son, a bit of a wallop, I'm beginning to believe she may not have been exactly truthful with me."

Eunice retook her seat on the fainting couch. "I'm sorry, did you say that man is *Douglas* Howland?"

Lloyd nodded. "Are you familiar with the name?"

She drew in a breath, released it, drew in another, then closed her eyes for the briefest of seconds as she realized what had been a well-kept family secret had most unexpectedly come to light.

She opened her eyes as temper began to simmer. "I am familiar with the name, and concerningly enough, Douglas Howland is my father, although the story I was told about his having died before I was born doesn't seem to be true, seeing as how he looks very alive to me."

She got to her feet again and took a step toward the door but found her path blocked when Aunt Hazel stepped in front of her.

"You're going to have to give them a few minutes without interruption," Aunt Hazel said.

"Do you know who that is?"

"I've never personally met the man, but I believe it's Douglas. I always knew this secret was going to come out someday."

"So that *is* my father?"

"If I were to hazard a guess, I'd say yes."

"You knew he was alive?"

Aunt Hazel released a sigh. "I did, and it's why I got you out of the house that day your mother disappeared. Georgette and your grandfather were having the most horrific argument, and I knew it was only a matter of time until your father was brought into the conversation because he always seemed to come into play whenever your mother and grandfather were arguing." She pulled a handkerchief from her sleeve and mopped at a forehead that was beginning to perspire. "Now is not the time to get into the full details of what happened, but the short of it was this—your father, I'm sad to disclose, really *was* a fortune hunter. He left your mother without a backward glance after your grandfather gave him ten thousand dollars to remove himself from Georgette's life and made him promise he would never contact her again. Your father took that money and ran."

Lloyd's brows drew together. "That makes absolutely no sense. Douglas Howland is from one of the wealthiest families in New York. Granted, he's a third son, but his father and oldest brother died years ago, and the second son, Stanley, was deemed unfit to run the family real estate business because he's an opium addict. I believe he's now attended to by a private nurse, his mind permanently affected by the opium he consumed in his younger days. That means Douglas is now in charge of the family's many investments as well as possessed of a fortune he amassed on his own before his oldest brother and father died. He would have never been a fortune hunter."

Aunt Hazel frowned. "Then why would he have taken that ten thousand dollars from James and abandoned his wife?"

"I'm sure I have no idea. But given what I've seen thus far of the Mason family," Lloyd began, "I wouldn't be surprised to learn that there's more to the story than what you've disclosed."

Dread settled in Eunice's stomach. "I suppose the only way to get to the bottom of this is to go speak to my parents, of which I apparently have two who are actually alive." She reached out and took hold of Arthur's arm. "You'll come with me?"

"Of course."

Thankful for Arthur's support, Eunice began walking across the room, trying to control emotions that wanted to splinter every which way. Stopping a few feet from her mother, she turned her gaze on a man she'd never expected to see.

Breath suddenly became difficult to come by because there was no question she bore a distinct resemblance to the man.

He was tall, lithe, and had hair that was almost the same shade as hers, although there were a few strands of white mixed in with the blond. His eyes were a brilliant shade of light blue, which went far to explain why her eyes were so unusual, a mix of her mother's darker shade, blended with the lighter shade of her father's.

Before she could think of a single thing to say, though, Georgette crossed her arms over her chest. "You've yet to tell me what you're doing here."

"I'm here to meet with Raymond Mason to discuss the terms of the purchase agreement he and I have been discussing."

"Purchase agreement pertaining to Mason Mines?"

Douglas inclined his head as Georgette released a snort.

"You would have me believe you have the wherewithal to buy Mason Mines, one of the largest copper industries in the country?"

"I do."

"Why would you want to buy it?"

Douglas smiled a smile that was so cold Georgette took a step back. "Because I thought it would be poetic, purchasing James Mason's lifelong obsession, and using a fortune I acquired from that ten thousand dollar bank draft he gave me almost thirty years ago."

Georgette's face flamed with color. "You're despicable, and I hope you don't expect me to be impressed with your fortune. In fact, it sickens me, although I hope it was all worth it for you, taking his money and abandoning me in the process."

The smile faded from Douglas's face. "I have no idea what you're going on about, Georgette. I remember quite clearly what transpired back then, and I certainly didn't abandon you. You abandoned me."

Georgette's hand clenched into a fist. "I fear your memory is faulty because you left me with only a letter that told me in no uncertain terms why you were leaving me. It was a cowardly thing to do, Douglas. Did you ever take into consideration how devastated I'd be, learning the man I thought was the love of my life had decided he'd made a grave mistake? That having his allowance and trust fund taken away and being cut out of the family will wasn't worth having me as his wife?"

"I never left you any letter," Douglas argued. "You left me one. But I only got to read that letter after I found myself abducted and thrown on a ship bound for the East Indies, compliments of your father."

Georgette's hand unclenched. "What are you talking about? Father told me you were taking the ten thousand dollars he offered you and heading off for a tour of Europe, wanting to put distance between us because you knew I wouldn't react well after learning you'd left me."

"I never left you."

"You went out to fetch coffee and pastries for us and never returned, as your trip to the bakery was an excuse to get away after you'd met with my father the night before and he gave you money. He told me you were only too eager to accept it and he gloated for years about how right he'd been that you were a fortune hunter." Georgette brushed a tear from her face. "For days afterward, I insisted on staying in that room we rented in that rather shabby house, knowing you'd come back, but . . . you never did."

"Because I was on a ship bound for the East Indies," Douglas said. "Your father hired men to jump me as I left that bakery. I was then thrown into your father's rented carriage, where he was waiting for me. He told me I was fortunate he'd merely decided to send me off on a little adventure instead of permanently keeping me away from you. He tucked a bank draft for ten thousand dollars into my jacket and told me he was doing me a favor. He actually felt he was being magnanimous when he suggested I look up a friend of his who worked for the East India Company. After that, he told me he'd make sure you got an annulment, then called for the carriage to stop, got out, and that's the last I saw of him."

Temper flashed through Douglas's eyes. "At first, I thought for sure that your father would change his mind about his decision to send me off to the far regions of the earth. But as the ship I'd been thrown on began sailing away, I realized your father was nothing more than a controlling tyrant who couldn't accept that his daughter made a decision without his input. He misjudged me, though, because he thought I was a wastrel and lacked ambition, which wasn't true. I proved that from the moment I reached the East Indies and decided I would look up that friend of your father's instead of trying to make my way home. I'd been accused of being a fortune hunter and was devastated that the woman I loved had evidently convinced her father to get rid of me. I decided I had no reason to return to the States. Your father's friend brought me into the East India Company, and I used the ten thousand your father gave me to make initial investments in that company. Those investments paid off, and I eventually returned to New York a good fifteen years later with a large fortune in hand. During my time away, my father and oldest brother had died, so I assumed the role as head of the family after I realized Stanley was unfit for normal life." He tilted his head. "I'm now one of the wealthiest men in America, which means you could have been married to one of the wealthiest men in the country if you hadn't decided to listen to your father."

"I didn't listen to my father."

"That's the impression I got from your letter." He pulled out his billfold, flipped it open, and retrieved a folded-up paper that was well-worn. "Sad as this is to admit, I've carried this with me for twenty-nine years, a remembrance of the mistakes I made in my youth."

"I never wrote you a letter."

"Just read it."

With hands that were trembling, Georgette unfolded the paper and bent her head, squinting at print that Eunice could see even from a distance was faded with age.

The library was completely silent as she read. A few minutes later, she lifted her head. "I know this looks like my handwriting, but I didn't write this. I never changed my mind about marrying you, and I definitely never thought about getting our marriage annulled."

"Your father told me he was going to make that happen the moment you got back to Montana."

Georgette nodded. "And I believe he intended on doing just that but was thwarted from those intentions because of certain . . . circumstances."

"What circumstances?"

Eunice drew in a deep breath and stepped forward, her gaze settling on Douglas, whose face began leaking color the moment he clapped eyes on her.

"I believe the circumstances were because of me—your daughter."

CHAPTER
Twenty-Seven

Even though Arthur was becoming accustomed to surprising Mason family disclosures, having Eunice's father show up on the scene was an unexpected circumstance he wouldn't have imagined in his wildest dreams.

"I think I'm going to need a detailed explanation about, well, everything, especially how a father I thought was dead seems to be very much alive," Eunice said, shooting a glance to Douglas, who'd not spoken a word since she'd told him who she was but had instead moved to the closest chair and taken a seat, quite as if his legs were in danger of failing him.

"I'll be back in a jiffy" was all Georgette said before she bolted out of the room, leaving Eunice frowning after her before she resettled her attention on her father. "Looks like it's up to you to explain."

Douglas ran a hand over his face. "I wouldn't know where to begin. Although I do have numerous questions I'd like to ask you—such as what you've been told about me."

"As I just mentioned, I was told you were dead—died before I was born. I believe a sudden illness was to blame."

"I suppose that was one way of explaining why I wasn't in your life."

"Death did seem to explain that rather sufficiently." She pulled up a chair next to Douglas and sat down, silence once again settling over the library, with Eunice not saying another word as she considered her father.

That she didn't appear distressed lent credence to the fact she was a woman possessed of a strength not many people had, especially after dealing with so many revelations in a short period of time.

There was no question left in Arthur's mind that Eunice was an exceptional lady, an incomparable in her own right, and that he'd overlooked that years before because of a nonsensical plan on his part left him filled with a renewed sense of regret.

It had taken him far too long to realize he would have never been happy living his life in the midst of society with a proper, demure, and well-connected lady.

He didn't want demure, proper, and well-connected.

He wanted direct, temperamental, romantic at heart, and independent.

In other words, he wanted Eunice.

How he was going to convince her that she wanted him in return was a bit of a mystery, but . . . she had kissed him on his cheek the day before, which seemed to suggest she was at least a little fond of him.

"Forgive me," Douglas said to Eunice, pulling Arthur back to the odd situation at hand. "But I've just realized I don't even know your name."

"This should be an interesting conversation," Hazel said, speaking up from where she was sitting beside Lloyd on a settee. "One doesn't usually get to meet a daughter one didn't know about in the first place, but it'll get even more unusual once Eunice starts trying to explain why she has so many names."

"You have more than one name?" Douglas asked.

"My birth name is Eugenia Sunshine Howland, but I prefer being addressed as Eunice these days."

Douglas blinked. "Georgette named you Eugenia?"

"I know, I know, it's an awful name," Georgette said, dashing back into the music room and waving a letter Douglas's way. "I found it."

Arthur slid a chair next to the one Eunice was sitting in, and after giving him a smile of thanks, Georgette plopped down on it, thrusting the letter she was holding into Douglas's hand. "There it is—proof that I did, indeed, receive a letter from you." She shoved a strand of blond hair that had escaped its pins out of her face. "I kept it in an old jewelry box that I found stashed in the back of my wardrobe. The jewelry I left here is missing, but this was still hidden underneath the lining." She quirked a brow Raymond's way. "Would you happen to know where my jewelry went?"

"Given that Clarice is currently wearing one of your necklaces, dear," Aunt Hazel said before Raymond could respond, "I think it's safe to say your jewelry stayed in the family."

"I'll expect all of my pieces to be returned" was all Georgette said before she turned back to Douglas, nodding to the letter in his hand. "Well, aren't you going to read it, or don't you need to refresh your memory because you remember what you wrote to me?"

"I didn't write this," Douglas countered, "and I will read it in a minute, but I'm in the middle of being introduced to my daughter. We've only gotten around to her name so far, but I have to say that Eugenia was an interesting choice. I thought we agreed if we ever had a daughter she'd be named Sophia because you adored that name."

"And I still do adore that name and was considering choosing it for her middle name, but then decided that was a horrible choice because it would be another reminder of you, the man who'd told me he loved me but then abandoned me."

"I didn't abandon you."

She waved that aside. "That remains to be seen. But returning to Eugenia, she goes by Eunice now, if she hasn't mentioned that—a name I always associated with a woman who is most likely surrounded by cats and lives a dull and uneventful life."

Douglas glanced to Eunice. "You don't strike me as a woman who surrounds herself with cats."

"Cats make me sneeze."

"Sunshine prefers dogs, although we never had any dogs because Father wouldn't permit it."

"A decision your father made after your dog Sparky died when you were ten, and he believed you were being overly sensitive about the death," Douglas said, which had Georgette drawing in a sharp breath.

"You remember me telling you that?"

"I remember everything about you."

Georgette's shoulders sagged a touch before she squared them. "How unexpected, but returning to your daughter's name, she kept the middle name I gave her—that being Sunshine—which suits her to a *T* because of her sunny disposition."

"I wouldn't take Mother's word about that," Eunice said. "I don't have a sunshiny personality, more along the lines of direct and annoying."

Georgette rolled her eyes. "You could have waited at least an hour before divulging your character weaknesses to him, Eunice. It would have been nice to at least allow him to think, if ever so briefly, that he had a daughter filled with sunshine and light."

"I've been disguising myself as a widow for years," Eunice countered. "And while it's true now that I've abandoned my widow's weeds that I do feel lighter, sunshiny has never been an appropriate way to describe my true nature." She crossed her arms over her chest. "And while I understand you're discussing my names to try to avoid starting what you know is going to be an unpleasant conversation, I'd like to know why you hid the truth about my father all these years."

"I wasn't going to tell you that your father was a no-good, lying rogue who left me when I was expecting you."

"I had no idea you were expecting, Georgette, and you know it, and again, I didn't leave you," Douglas argued. "Your father had me abducted. I mean, how could we have ever thought he'd go to those lengths simply because he mistakenly thought that I was a fortune hunter? Yes, I was a third son, and yes, at the time we married, I was given an allowance. But I know I told you I had a trust fund coming, and a rather substantial trust fund at that."

"Your family told you they were cutting you off from your allowance after you told them we'd married. I assumed your trust fund was to be taken away as well."

"My grandfather left me that trust, so there was no way for my family to deprive me of it, but I wasn't eligible to receive the trust until I turned twenty-five. I was in the process of seeking out a paid position when your father snatched me. As for his assumption that I was a fortune hunter, I didn't even know who your father was or the extent of his fortune when we married. Yes, I assumed you had some family money because you were attending an expensive finishing school. However, I had no idea your father was a copper mogul, but it wouldn't have made a difference to me. I fell in love with you the second I laid eyes on you, and I thought you'd done the same with me."

"I did do the same. You were the love of my life. It's the reason I never sought out a divorce, since I couldn't very well seek out an annulment or get married again, something that drove my father mad."

Douglas stilled. "You didn't divorce me?"

"I didn't have the stomach for it, but . . ." Georgette's eyes widened. "Good heavens, you're probably married, which means I'm the reason you're a bigamist."

What almost sounded like a laugh escaped Douglas. "I'm not a bigamist because I could never contemplate the idea of marriage again, seeing as how the one and only time I fell in love ended badly for me."

Georgette blew out a breath. "Well, thank goodness for that—I mean, not the part about matters ending badly for you, but that you're not a bigamist. That would have added to a situation that's quite complicated enough."

Douglas's only reply to that was to settle a smile on Georgette, one she returned right before she and Douglas began to simply stare at each other, quite like a few other couples had been doing of late. Not wanting to intrude, Arthur fetched himself a chair and sat down beside Eunice, who reached out and took hold of his hand, giving it a squeeze.

"This is certainly a peculiar turn of events," she whispered.

"Indeed, but are you all right? It's not every day one discovers a father one didn't know was alive."

"I'm not certain how I feel just yet," Eunice admitted. "However, I'll have to sort through my feelings later when I'm at my leisure. For now, I still have scads of questions to ask, and we still need to uncover the person responsible for killing Grandfather."

"What was that?" Douglas asked, tearing his gaze from Georgette's.

Taking a few minutes to fill Douglas in on what was transpiring and why an agent with the Pinkertons, along with agents from the Bleecker Street Inquiry Agency, were gathered in the library, Eunice finished with "And that's why Mother and I returned to Montana. And with all that out of the way, before Agent Clifton begins questioning the family again about Grandfather's death, I have a question for you. Why did you assume the name D. H. Loring when you began corresponding with my uncle about the sale of Mason Mines?"

"There's no mystery there," Douglas began. "Even with the time that had passed since my marriage and subsequent disaster with your mother, I was concerned that someone would remember that Georgette had once been married to Douglas Howland. I thought they might then refuse to entertain my offer to purchase Mason Mines, hence the reason for creating an alias with Loring as my last name, which is my mother's maiden name."

Georgette's nose wrinkled. "But I remember that your mother's maiden name was Loring, which means I could have put an end to your plans to purchase Mason Mines."

"Considering that Raymond told me James's daughter was dead, I wasn't worried about my alias. I did mourn far deeper than I expected, though, after learning you were no longer alive."

Georgette released a bit of a sigh before she turned and leveled a glare on Raymond. "You really should be ashamed of yourself, telling everyone I was dead."

Raymond didn't bother to respond, merely turned his head and began taking a marked interest in the vase of flowers next to him.

"Clearly, our family has been participating in a lot of shameful behavior," Eunice said before she nodded to the letter Douglas was still holding. "I believe you should read that letter so you'll understand what Mother must have been feeling all these years. After you're done, though, I'd like to look at both letters."

"Why?"

"As I recently disclosed to you, I'm an inquiry agent. Solving mysteries is what I do. I'm beginning to get a hunch about what happened to the two of you."

As Douglas began reading the letter Georgette had given him, Arthur couldn't help but notice how Douglas's face turned ashen the longer he read. He finally lifted his head, his gaze seeking out Georgette again. "Forgive me, Georgette. Here I've been less than charitable toward you since I arrived, but you obviously would have been devasted to receive such a letter from me. I promise you, though, that I didn't write this, just as I realize you didn't write the letter your father gave me."

Georgette's eyes glistened with unshed tears. "It's almost unfathomable that Father would pit us against each other in such a despicable manner, but obviously, that's what he did. The only question is *how* he managed to do it because we already know the *why*."

"He wanted control over whom you chose for a husband," Douglas said.

"He wanted control over everything and everyone," Georgette corrected, taking the letter from Douglas and handing both of the letters to Eunice. "Learning I was expecting Eunice must have been quite the wrench in whatever plans he'd made for me."

Silence once again settled over the room as Eunice began reading the letters, shaking her head a few minutes later. "Whoever forged these was very good at their craft."

She got to her feet and began pacing around the room, her family watching her every step. "I'm beginning to wonder if everything that's been disclosed today, as well as yesterday, is connected to Grandfather's death. This is a family with too many secrets to count, but I believe it's time for those secrets—all of them—to come out."

"We could be here for days," Hazel said from where she was still sitting beside Lloyd.

"If days is what it takes, then days it'll have to be," Eunice said. "We need closure in the matter of Grandfather, and I need to stop looking over my shoulder every other minute, wondering if whoever killed him is coming after me next. So, with all that said, if anyone would like to raise their hand and take responsibility for the transgressions that have occurred, it would save all of us a lot of time and drama, since I'm sure once we open this Pandora's box that can be labeled Mason Family Secrets, it'll be difficult to get those secrets back in the box."

Arthur wasn't exactly surprised when no one raised their hand.

"Ah, so we're going to have to go the difficult route," Eunice said before gesturing Cooper forward. "I believe this is where I turn everyone over to you, Agent Clifton. Would you care to set up an interrogation room in the parlor? It's relatively removed from the rest of the house, which means any noises the suspects you're questioning may make are certain to be muffled."

It really wasn't unexpected when Eunice's family, save Aunt Hazel, who was looking around the room with a small smile on her face, and Uncle Raymond, who seemed to have misplaced his cane, immediately made a mad dash for the door.

CHAPTER
Twenty-Eight

"I was worried I was going to have to pull out my pistol at one point to stop the mass exodus from the library," Ivan said, raking a hand through hair that was standing on end before he bent over and rubbed his shin. "And not that I want to sound like a whiner, but I think Doris kicked me."

"You got off easy, because Alice bit me," Cooper said, rubbing his arm. "I've often said a person needs to watch out for the most unsuspecting types, a sentiment that's now been reinforced because I never imagined those particular sisters would turn violent."

"And begs the question why they did," Ann said, narrowing her eyes on Doris and Alice, who were huddled together on a settee and looking sulky.

Cooper's lips curved. "I'm relatively certain the answer to that is a direct result of Eunice implying I use somewhat intimidating interrogation techniques."

Ann rolled her eyes. "They'll figure out you're not into torture a few seconds after you begin questioning them, but even without questionable interrogation techniques being an option, I have a feeling no one in this room is going to cooperate. They're family, and families are tricky, believing in loyalty and all. We need a different plan to get them talking."

A loud clearing of a throat drew Eunice's attention to the doorway of the library, where Aunt Hazel was standing, no doubt having been eavesdropping on them.

"If I may offer a suggestion?" Aunt Hazel began.

"By all means," Cooper said.

Aunt Hazel sent a fond look to Ann. "It is true, dear, what you said about family being tricky, so I'm going to suggest you have everyone write down who they believe might have killed James. Since no one will be required to sign their names, well, it might have the family being more cooperative."

Ann smiled. "Honestly, Hazel, that's a brilliant idea, and it may very well work."

"I do occasionally have brilliant ideas." Aunt Hazel gave a pat to her hair. "I also have another brilliant thought, but that will need to wait until everyone scribbles down their suspect." With that, she turned and moved back into the library, saying something about going to rejoin Lloyd, who, she added, was a most delightful gentleman.

Eunice turned to Arthur. "Your grandfather seems to be using his charm."

"In all honesty, I've been thinking Hazel is the one who has been doing the charming." He smiled. "It'll be interesting to see how that develops."

"Just another interesting aspect to our time in Montana," Eunice said before she sent Ann and Judith off to the office to fetch supplies, with Cooper and Ivan telling her they were going to take up positions directly inside the door in case anyone decided to make a run for it again.

"Anything you'd like me to do?" Arthur asked.

Warmth immediately tinged her cheeks at the odd response that suddenly sprang to mind—a response she didn't dare voice because what she'd really like for Arthur to do had absolutely nothing to do with their investigation.

Instead, what she felt an almost irresistible urge to tell him was that she'd really like him to kiss her, although not on the cheek as she'd done to him the day before, but on the lips, because the more she came to know Arthur Livingston, the more she was convinced he would, without question, know his way around a kiss.

She'd never actually been kissed before, which was a pathetic state given her age, but she'd been thinking about kissing quite often of late, doing so, no doubt, because there was a very good chance her life was in danger. How sad would it be if she were to depart the earth before ever enjoying a kiss with a handsome gentleman?

That type of thinking was exactly why she'd kissed Arthur on the cheek, even though what she'd really wanted to do was wrap her arms around him and kiss him on the lips, but thankfully, a bit of sanity had prevailed, and she'd not given in to that particular desire.

It would have been inappropriate to say the least, and besides that, what she'd always dreamed of when she'd dreamed of a first kiss was for a gentleman to take the initiative, pull her ever so close to him, and then cup her face in his large hands and linger on her lips as if he had all the time in the world.

Arthur had large hands.

"Perhaps I should guard the back door?" Arthur asked, pulling her abruptly from thoughts that had the warmth already settled on her face intensifying.

She forced all thoughts of kissing and large hands aside and managed a smile. "I beg your pardon, Arthur. I fear I'm somewhat distracted, but yes, guarding the back door would be appreciated because we certainly don't want anyone making a stealthy escape."

"I'm not certain your relatives are capable of stealth, given the mad rush earlier that was hardly discreet," Arthur said before he headed across the library, stopping in front of the back door where he crossed his arms over his chest and took to looking dangerous.

There was something incredibly appealing about a dangerous-looking man.

Thrusting aside that thought because now was hardly the time to become so thoroughly distracted, Eunice looked to Cooper, who was watching her with a hint of a smile on his face. "What?"

He shrugged. "You're an interesting woman, Eunice, and while I would love to know what you were just thinking because I'm not sure I've ever seen you blush, I think I'll save that type of questioning for a later date when we don't have an audience. For now, how do you want to proceed?"

She narrowed her eyes on him. "First, there will be no questioning me because, well, there just won't. And second, just be ready for the unexpected. There's no telling what might happen if the family actually agrees to write down their top suspects." She rubbed her hands together as Ann and Judith hurried into the room. "And now, let the games begin."

As Ann and Judith began handing out slips of paper and pencils, Eunice ignored the grumbling that was in full swing amongst the family and moved to the center of the room, drawing everyone's attention.

"Since it appears no one is keen to cooperate by admitting their . . . involvement, if you will, with Grandfather's death, I'm now going to try something different."

"It was my idea," Aunt Hazel said, earning more than a few scowls from the family, which she ignored.

"Indeed it was, and it's a simple enough task, so there's no need to fret I'm asking any of you to do anything overly strenuous. I simply need you to write down who you believe might have killed Grandfather."

"This almost sounds like one of those murder mystery games that I've heard are all the rage in the big cities," Hester began, a spark of what almost seemed to be excitement in her eyes. "If this goes well, I may have to introduce a similar game at the next dinner I'm hosting, which is three days from now."

"You were going to hold a dinner less than a week after you held a memorial for Eunice and me?" Georgette asked, pulling her attention away from Douglas, whom she'd been preoccupied with staring at, not even bothering to look away from him when everyone had tried to flee.

Hester bit her lip, evidently realizing she might not be up for the task of defending her decision to host a dinner when the family should have been in mourning, and slunk back against the chair, not saying another word.

"Shall we begin?" Eunice asked, and after much muttering, the family finally picked up their pencils and bent over their pieces of paper, Mrs. Wagner and Vincent the only two not bothering to write anything down.

"We're not family," Mrs. Wagner said when Eunice arched a brow her way.

"But yesterday you told me you were considered family, and Vincent made a point of telling me how he was my tutor for years, so I don't think it would hurt anything if both of you were to participate. I think the more suggestions we get, the better."

"Of course we'll participate," Vincent said, sending his mother a smile. "It might be fun."

"It's a peculiar way to have fun, but very well." Mrs. Wagner picked up her pencil, looked around the room for a moment, then began scribbling away.

It was rather amusing to watch everyone sneaking glances at one another every other second, with Doris and Alice even going so far as to mouth what name they were writing down to each other.

Less than three minutes later, everyone was done. Ann collected the papers and handed them to Eunice, who took a seat beside a small table and began placing the papers in piles according to the names written down, her sense of amusement increasing with every paper. When she was done, she shook her head. "I'll say one thing for the family, you're more loyal than I expected, because we have one vote for Georgette, two for Douglas, two votes for St. Nicholas, three votes for me—thank you very much—and . . . one other name."

Georgette released a snort. "It's ridiculous that anyone would believe Douglas killed Father. Yes, he was treated abominably by him, but Douglas would never resort to murder."

The fact that her mother was so quick to defend Douglas was quite telling, but before Eunice could dwell on it further, Howard sat forward.

"But he, out of anyone here, had a legitimate reason to want James dead," Howard said. "James sent him off to the East Indies. I know I would harbor a lot of resentment if something like that happened to me."

"And one can't dismiss the information that came back from the investigator who learned that Georgette and Eunice died in India," Aunt Hazel added.

Eunice resisted a smile. "Forgive me, Aunt Hazel, but the East Indies and India aren't in the same place."

Aunt Hazel blinked. "But they're similar names."

"True, but should I assume you were one of the ones to write Douglas's name down because of the connection you mistakenly assumed those places have?"

"I had to write someone down." Aunt Hazel shrugged before she smiled at Douglas. "Not that I think you murdered James, dear, but I wasn't comfortable writing down another name, although I do have a few thoughts."

"And we'll get to those thoughts later," Eunice began, "or perhaps sooner once I tell you that your name is the other name submitted as a prime suspect for killing your brother."

Aunt Hazel, instead of immediately denying the accusation, laughed. In fact, she laughed so hard that Lloyd fished a handkerchief out of his pocket and handed it to her because her eyes had taken to watering.

"Has Aunt Hazel gone mad?" Doris asked.

"Mad with guilt if I'm not mistaken," Alice replied.

Aunt Hazel gave a wave of the handkerchief. "I'm not mad, girls, merely amused that of everyone gathered in this room, I'd be the only suspect listed besides Arthur, Douglas, Eunice, and St. Nicholas—none of whom are involved, at least in my humble opinion, in James's death."

"You know you resented James for stifling you over the years, making sure you never strayed far from home," Uncle Raymond said.

"Oh, he definitely stifled me, but I wouldn't have murdered him over that," Aunt Hazel shot back. "And I'd be careful, brother dear, about hurling accusations at me. You've been resentful of James and all he accomplished, always whining about not being given your share of his vast holdings or a lofty title that came with no responsibilities."

"It's not a secret I resented James at times, but you'll notice that no one wrote my name down as a suspect," Uncle Raymond snapped.

"Which only means that everyone is anxious to keep all of our family secrets secret."

"But aren't you curious as to who threw your name into the hat?" Doris asked. "If someone wrote my name down, I'd be burning to know who did that."

"There's no need for me to suffer any curiosity about who pointed the finger at me, dear, because I already know." Aunt Hazel waved the handkerchief in Mrs. Wagner's direction. "Mrs. Wagner did."

Mrs. Wagner drew herself up. "Why would I, out of anyone in this room, want to throw suspicion your way?"

"Come now, Mrs. Wagner, you already know the answer to that," Aunt Hazel returned. "I'm the only one in the family who knows you've been perpetuating a rather large lie regarding how you've been able to insinuate yourself into the Mason family."

Mrs. Wagner's eyes flashed with something interesting. "I have no idea what you're talking about."

"Of course you do, but because it's a somewhat tawdry topic, you should simply admit you wrote down my name and leave it at that."

"Unless, of course," Cooper said, stepping forward, "this information could shed light on James's death. Then I'm going to have to insist it be disclosed."

Aunt Hazel tilted her head. "I'm not sure Mrs. Wagner lying

about being my brother's mistress has anything to do with his death."

Dead silence settled around the room until Hester jumped to her feet, snapped her fingers in her daughters' direction, and nodded to the door. "It's time for the two of you to leave. Now."

"Absolutely not," Doris argued. "We're Masons, Mother. Do you actually think anything is going to scandalize us after having been raised in this family?"

Hester stabbed a finger toward the door without saying a single thing, which had Doris and Alice exchanging mutinous glares with their mother before they finally stalked their way across the library and through the door, telling Ivan, who'd been blocking the door, that they'd be right outside.

After Ivan closed the library door, Eunice turned her attention to Mrs. Wagner, who was looking rather mutinous as well as she glared at Aunt Hazel. "If what Aunt Hazel says is true," Eunice began, drawing Mrs. Wagner's notice, "why did you allow everyone to believe something different?"

"There's no proof that James and I didn't share an intimate relationship."

Aunt Hazel released a snort. "Except that after the carriage accident that killed his wife and grievously injured James in the process, he couldn't share intimate relationships with a woman, nor could he father children." Aunt Hazel got to her feet and moved to stand in front of the fireplace. "James's condition wasn't well-known because, for obvious reasons, he didn't care to share the details of what happened to him. I only learned about it because I overheard a conversation he was having with his doctor."

She narrowed her eyes on Mrs. Wagner, who was now looking decidedly uncomfortable. "I've always been curious, though, why you would have allowed everyone to believe you were his mistress. Because you first came to work for James as his nurse after the accident, you were told by his doctor about his condition and then instructed in minute detail how you were to care for all his injuries because you lacked any nursing experience. Truth be told, I was reluctant to have you attend to James in the first place because of that and only relented because you were the only person capable of not dissolving into tears because of his surly temper."

Mrs. Wagner narrowed her eyes right back at Aunt Hazel. "Did it ever occur to you that your brother wanted everyone to believe I was his mistress because he was ashamed of his condition?"

"That would certainly explain your continued employment, because I know for a fact you didn't have any secretarial experience either before James offered you that role," Aunt Hazel said.

Cooper stepped forward, drawing everyone's attention. "I find myself curious what type of employment you held before you began working for James, Mrs. Wagner."

"I don't believe that has any relevance to anything."

"She came from Chicago," Aunt Hazel said, earning a scowl from Mrs. Wagner. "She worked as a maid in an established household but was fired when her employer learned she dabbled in theft on the side, more specifically, signing her employer's name to bank drafts she then deposited in her account." Aunt Hazel inclined her head in Eunice's direction. "That's why I suggested having everyone write down their favored suspect."

Eunice's lips began to curve. "You just may have a career in the inquiry agency ahead of you, Aunt Hazel."

As Aunt Hazel took to looking remarkably pleased with herself, whereas Mrs. Wagner began eyeing the door, Eunice plucked up the piece of paper with Aunt Hazel's name written on it before she gestured for Georgette and Judith to join her.

"I need you, Mother, along with Judith, because you're both artists with an eye for detail, to examine Mrs. Wagner's handwriting and then compare it to the notes Grandfather clearly had someone forge to keep you and Douglas apart."

"I *knew* I'd eventually become useful to the agency," Judith said, hurrying forward.

"You've always been useful," Ivan replied, settling a warm smile on Judith that had her face turning pink.

"This is a rather unusual time for that type of business, Ivan," Eunice muttered.

"There's never an unusual time for a bit of flattery," he returned with a wink before he sobered and began looking intimidating again.

As the minutes ticked away while Georgette and Judith pored over the letters, Hester hurried out of the room and returned almost immediately with Doris and Alice, who'd clearly been listening at the keyhole. To Eunice's surprise, Alice sent her a cheeky wink before she squished herself on a fainting couch between Doris and her mother.

"I think I found something," Georgette said, leaning close to Judith as she pointed something out.

"Yes, I noticed that as well," Judith said. "It appears, upon close inspection, that the person who forged these was good, except for with the letter *E*. There's a rather odd curve to the *E* on all these pages, which suggests they were written by the same hand."

As everyone turned their attention to Mrs. Wagner, Vincent rose to his feet, shock stamped all over his face. "Do not say they could be right about this, Mother. Tell them—tell them they're wrong."

Mrs. Wagner considered Vincent for a long moment before she reached out and took hold of his hand. "I wish I could deny everything but, darling, given that they're holding indisputable evidence because, well, I've always had trouble with the letter *E*, I'm afraid I've been found out."

"You forged those letters to Georgette and Douglas?" Vincent asked, pulling his hand away from his mother.

"I'm afraid I did, but I only did it because James told me to do so. How could I refuse? He'd provided me with a position that paid me a more than handsome salary, and James would have thought I didn't appreciate all he'd done for me if I'd turned down his little request."

Eunice frowned. "But how could Grandfather have possibly known you had a gift for forgery?"

Mrs. Wagner shrugged. "He was a very difficult patient while he was recovering from the carriage accident. I thought it would lessen his boredom, as well as amuse him, to show him how I can copy almost anyone's handwriting. He was a man with a memory like a steel trap and remembered my talent after learning Georgette had married without his express permission."

"You don't seem to me to be very remorseful about your actions," Douglas began, sitting forward. "You played a large part in ruining two lives, and for what? Because you couldn't say no to James Mason or because you knew he'd be generous to you if you complied?"

Mrs. Wagner turned her head, ignoring Douglas's questions.

"I'm curious how you were able to get a sample of Douglas's handwriting," Georgette said, her eyes hard as they never wavered from Mrs. Wagner, who turned her attention to Georgette.

"I traveled with James to New York. It didn't take much to pay a maid to have a look around that tiny little room where the two of you were staying while you were out in Central Park one day. She very kindly snatched one of those lovely little notes Douglas enjoyed tucking under your pillow. After I had that, I took a few hours to practice Douglas's handwriting, and that was it."

Cooper flipped to a fresh page in his notepad and arched a brow at Mrs. Wagner. "May I assume you're also behind the investigation report since I have a feeling no investigator was ever hired to look into Eunice and Georgette's whereabouts?"

Mrs. Wagner shot a look to Uncle Raymond. "I see no reason to deny it, especially since I'm sure Georgette and Judith will pour over that report next and find the same issue with the letter E. Raymond knew he needed proof of the deaths after someone pointed out that the discovery of all of that glorious copper on the old Green farm wasn't going to benefit the family much since no one except Eunice and Georgette had actual ownership of Mason Mines." She shrugged. "Georgette and Eunice had been gone without a word for over seven years. That seemed like a reasonable amount of time to assume they were dead, but Raymond understood, given the extent of the estate, that some sort of proof of their deaths would be expected."

"I don't think you should say any more, Mother," Vincent said.

She sent Vincent a small smile. "You may be right, dear. But for the record, I had relatively little to do with having Eunice and Georgette being declared dead." She nodded to Uncle Raymond. "That was mostly Raymond's doing."

Uncle Raymond's face began to mottle. "You know that's not true. You're the one who suggested I start taking steps so that the family would be able to access the money that was certain to be lining the Mason coffers once operations began at the Green farm. And"—he continued when Mrs. Wagner opened her mouth, cutting her off—"you're also the one who decided I should get an official investigation report made up to prove Georgette and Eunice were dead, and then"—he settled a glare on her—"you told me you'd be happy to write up that report because you have some ability with forgery."

"If you think for one minute you're going to put all of this on me," Mrs. Wagner spat, rising to her feet, "you're sadly mistaken. I'm certainly not going to stand here and wait for you to accuse me next of killing James, especially when you should be at the top of the suspect list for that." She nodded to Cooper. "You should ask him how he felt after he learned James had drawn up a new will not long before James died."

Cooper swung his attention to Uncle Raymond. "Were you angry about that?"

Uncle Raymond, surprisingly enough, shook his head. "I wouldn't claim I was angry, more along the lines of apprehensive. But I only found out about the new will because Mrs. Wagner told me. If anyone had reason to be upset, it was her, what with how she and James had been quarreling. Given that she was not left a bequest in that new will, something she could have very well learned while in the midst of that heated argument, it stands to reason that she, far more than I, had reason to kill him."

"Which is something we'll revisit in a moment. For now, I'm

more curious to learn how you felt about not being left a stake in Mason Mines," Cooper said.

"I wasn't thrilled about that, but in the spirit of transparency, I had an uncomfortable conversation with James directly after Mrs. Wagner told me about the new will. I asked him if he'd taken me out of his will. He told me I was still in it and then disclosed he was leaving me ten million dollars but I wasn't to expect being left a percentage of Mason Mines. He also told me that he was leaving Hazel one million dollars, and my son, Howard, five million dollars."

Mrs. Wagner sucked in a sharp breath. "You never told me James left you ten million dollars."

"Why would I mention the extent of my inheritance to you?" Uncle Raymond asked. "You're not actually family, even though you enjoy claiming differently."

As temper flashed through Mrs. Wagner's eyes, Cooper flipped to another blank page. "Since we're discussing the will, the next question I have is for you, Mrs. Wagner. Why were you taken out of James's will, and how did that make you feel when you discovered you weren't going to be left a bequest?"

"I believe this is where Mother and I should take our leave," Vincent said, moving to take hold of Mrs. Wagner's arm. "You may direct any further questions you have to our attorney, whose name I'll provide you with in a few days."

As Eunice's thoughts began to whirl with ways to keep Mrs. Wagner and Vincent from leaving, an idea, albeit a questionable one, suddenly sprang to mind.

"I think it may be time for *everyone* to take their leave," she said, drawing more than a few murmurs from her family in the process as well as confused looks from Cooper, Ivan, and Arthur, which she ignored. "I've just had the most curious memory flash to mind from out of the blue, and I need to act on that memory while it's still fresh in my mind."

Uncle Raymond thumped his cane on the floor. "Have you lost your wits, girl? Now is not the time to disband the family meeting. We're making progress here—progress that I'm sure is going to clear the suspicion surrounding my name once and for all since obviously Mrs. Wagner has been the guilty party all along."

"But if I can uncover the clues I just realized *were* clues given to me far too subtly by Grandfather on the night before he died, I believe we'll be able to unmask the guilty party once and for all," Eunice said.

"What clues?" Vincent asked, glancing to his mother before returning his attention to Eunice.

"Well, to be honest, I always thought when Grandfather sought me out to wish me well on my trip, it was somewhat peculiar, and definitely confusing. Now, though, everything he said to me makes perfect sense."

"What makes perfect sense, or better yet, what did he say to you?" Vincent pressed.

"He said if anything unexplainable happened to him that I should look in the spots where I keep my secrets because he'd left me a letter, one that held important information."

"What kind of information?"

Eunice shrugged. "I'm not certain. Frankly, at the time, I thought Grandfather might be experiencing a bit of an elderly moment because it was beyond peculiar. However, in retrospect, he was obviously telling me where I could find clues as to who killed him if, in fact, he ended up dead under suspicious circumstances."

Even though Eunice was relatively certain she'd just told a flimsy story if there ever was one, and one that clearly suggested she didn't have a future as a fiction writer, given that everyone was watching her with wide eyes and no one was scoffing at the tale she'd just spun, there was actually a slight possibility that everyone believed her.

Not wanting to leave time for any questions that might trip her up, she turned to Cooper. "Would you care to accompany me to search for that letter?"

Mrs. Wagner began fanning her face with her hand, her forehead, tellingly enough, beaded with perspiration. "You're going to search right now?"

"I don't see any reason to delay the inevitable, although . . ." Eunice caught Mrs. Wagner's eye. "If someone in this room wants to confess, it would save me the bother of going on, shall we say, a treasure hunt?"

Mrs. Wagner's gaze darted to Vincent, who was watching her with narrowed eyes before he shook his head ever so slightly. Mrs. Wagner squared her shoulders, dashed a hand over her forehead, and leaned closer to her son.

"Know that I love you more than anything, darling," she said before she turned to Eunice. "To spare my son the drama of what is certain to unfold once that letter is found, allow me to confess to what I'm sure everyone in this room, save my son, is already thinking. If there's a name in that letter, yes, it'll be mine.

"I'd been blackmailing James for years about what he'd done to Georgette and Douglas. He was more than willing to pay for my silence because while he wouldn't have cared overly much if Georgette found out, he would have hated for you, Eunice, to realize he was responsible for why you never knew your father." Her expression turned ugly. "The last time I approached him for money, though, he agreed to give me a sizable bank draft but told me it was going to be the last of the money from him. The next thing I knew, he'd gone to his attorney and redone his will, taking out the bequest he'd always promised me. And while I did have a nice nest egg saved from all the money he'd paid me over the years, the fact that he was trying to have the last word against me was maddening."

"You need to stop talking, Mother," Vincent muttered.

Mrs. Wagner sent him a sad smile as she took hold of his hand and placed a kiss on it. "It's too late for that, my dear boy. Everyone in this room, including you, now knows the truth about what happened to James. I killed him for taking me out of his will, and to be clear, I don't regret it in the least."

CHAPTER

Twenty-Nine

Arthur reined Wyatt in after allowing him his head, smiling as Eunice galloped up to join him, the look of disgruntlement on her face suggesting she was a bit put out that Wyatt had left her and Samantha in his dust.

"I'll give one thing to Wyatt," she said, drawing Samantha to a stop beside him. "He can move."

Wyatt tossed his head and began sidestepping his way closer to Samantha, which had Eunice nudging her horse a few feet away. "But simply because you can move, Wyatt, does not mean I'm going to appease your infatuation with Sam."

Arthur wasn't surprised when Wyatt tossed his head again and began pawing at the ground, quite as if he were considering appeasing his infatuation with Samantha whether Eunice was agreeable to that or not.

"Settle down," Arthur said before he swung out of the saddle and walked to the nearest tree, wrapping the reins around a branch. Eunice steered Samantha to a tree well removed from Wyatt and slid gracefully from the saddle. After looping the reins around a limb, she strode his way, her attire leaving him grinning.

"Phillip's most assuredly going to have a few things to say about how you seem to have embraced a fondness for trousers again over the fashionable wardrobe he designed for you, especially when he was so proud of that riding habit he made."

She returned his grin. "Since I have no intention of riding through the streets of New York in trousers once I return, what Phillip doesn't know won't hurt him. Besides, I was in no mood to ride sidesaddle today, even though I found a few of those in the tack room. Riding astride comfortably is next to impossible to do in a riding habit, hence the trousers." She gestured to the crystal blue sky rising above the ridge of mountains in the distance. "I needed a good race across the fields to clear my head, and I'm pleased to say that the view alone has helped me with my thoughts, so much so that I'm actually considering visiting the target field at some point today."

"The field isn't far from here. Would you care to take a stroll over there now, or would you prefer to visit it by yourself?"

She drew in a breath. "I suppose now is as good a time as any, and I'd welcome your company. Even with Mrs. Wagner admitting to Grandfather's murder, I'm a little wary about returning to the spot of Grandfather's death. I know I'm not going to find that complete sense of closure, though, until I confront the fear that still lingers whenever I think of Grandfather dying on that field."

Taking Eunice's arm, they began walking through a grove of trees, Eunice's pace slowing the closer they got to their destination.

"We don't have to visit the field today," he said, drawing her to a stop and turning her to face him. "It is your birthday, after all, and I'd hate to see your day turn melancholy, something that's certain to happen when you revisit the spot of James's death."

She waved that aside. "I'm not dragging my feet because I'm in fear of turning melancholy. I'm dragging my feet because I can't seem to stop revisiting the events of yesterday and Mrs. Wagner's disclosure." She shook her head. "I keep feeling something's off about her admission. Yes, I believe she was capable of shooting Grandfather, but didn't it seem odd to you that she up and confessed simply because of that letter my grandfather supposedly left me?"

"It *was* a rather abrupt ending to the discussion."

"In all honesty, I didn't actually believe when I made up the story about the letter that anyone was going to up and confess. But that's exactly what Mrs. Wagner did, which seems out of character for her. She strikes me as a shrewd woman, and I would think she'd realize there's a good chance that a letter could have been lost or destroyed over the years I've been gone."

"I'm sure after Cooper returns from questioning Mrs. Wagner again today he'll have information that will explain the reason behind her admission."

"Unless she refuses to cooperate. After her admission last night, she didn't bother to say another thing except to beg Vincent to forgive her before Cooper carted her off to jail. That she then didn't say anything more to Cooper or Ann on their ride to jail suggests she's unwilling to cooperate further."

Arthur moved to a fallen tree trunk and pulled Eunice to a seat beside him. "Even though Vincent can be an unlikeable sort at times, I felt sorry for him last night. He seemed dumbfounded over his mother's admission, and I couldn't blame him for making a speedy exit as Mrs. Wagner was being led away."

"I'm sure he *was* shocked by her disclosure. Frankly, I wouldn't be surprised if he ends up leaving Butte. The townspeople may not care to frequent his bookshop once they learn his mother is a murderess."

"Speaking of bookshops," Arthur began, reaching into his jacket pocket and pulling out a package wrapped in brown paper. He handed it to Eunice. "I got you a little something for your birthday, an occasion that should not go unnoticed."

"You got me a present?"

"Of course, but don't get your hopes up. It's nothing much."

"Honestly, Arthur, I'm hardly going to be disappointed with a present a friend took the time to get me."

He stilled. "You consider us friends now?"

"I would think so, given all we've experienced together of late, even though I could have done without being squished by you on

Main Street. Still, it was sweet of you to save me from a bullet that wasn't intended for me, even if I had to suffer a bump on the head in the process." With that, she untied the twine wrapped around the package, then tore the paper away, her mouth making an O of surprise. She lifted her head, her eyes sparkling. "What a beautiful copy of *Pride and Prejudice*, although I have no idea why you'd think I'd be disappointed because it's the perfect gift for me. Thank you."

His lips curved. "You're welcome. I was hoping to find a first edition, but I didn't have much time in New York before we left for Montana. I was then hoping Vincent might have a first edition in his bookshop, but since he doesn't carry Jane Austen, well, my hopes were dashed. However, if you already have a leather-bound edition, I could try to find you that first edition once we return to New York, if you've decided you're going to go back there soon."

"I haven't given it much thought, although New York feels far more like home then Montana does now." She traced a finger over the binding, opened up the book, then bent her head and drew in a deep breath. "There's nothing quite like the scent of a new book."

"Then you really aren't disappointed your present is merely a book?"

"'Merely a book' should never be said to an avid reader, and besides . . ." She hugged the book to her chest. "This is the most thoughtful present anyone has ever given me."

Warmth flooded through him, and he found himself leaning closer to her, wondering for what felt like the millionth time how he could have been so oblivious seven years before to the charms of the remarkable woman sitting beside him.

Eunice's eyes grew wide the closer he got, but then she closed her eyes and stilled when he pressed his lips against hers, the softness of her lips causing a groan to escape him before he pulled her closer, cradling her face with one hand while sinking his other hand into the blond mane of her hair as he caught a sigh from her against his lips.

Time seemed to stop as he drew her closer still, not wanting the moment to end, until a loud clearing of a throat had his eyes flashing open before he pulled away from her.

He blinked and then frowned when his gaze settled on Vincent Wagner, who was standing a few feet away from them, looking rather sheepish as he shifted from one foot to the other.

"I beg your pardon," Vincent began. "Clearly I'm interrupting a . . . ah . . . moment."

"That's a bit of an understatement," Eunice muttered before she got to her feet, set her book down on the tree trunk, and settled a frown on Vincent. "I wasn't expecting to see you at Mason Manor again."

Vincent blew out a heavy sigh. "I wasn't intending on coming here again, but I found myself at loose ends this morning. My house is far too quiet without Mother wandering around. When I found myself sweeping the kitchen floor for the third time, I decided I needed a better use of my time. I thought I'd come to Mason Manor and see if there's anything I can do to make amends for Mother's crimes against your family. The butler told me you'd gone riding, and I had a hunch you might head for the target field, perhaps to pay your respects to your grandfather in the place where he died."

Eunice cocked her head to the side. "You didn't care to wait at the house for me to return?"

"I thought perhaps if you'd gone to the target field that you'd enjoy the company of someone who admired your grandfather and could tell you stories about him that aren't unfavorable. I'm sure you've been disheartened by the disturbing actions perpetuated by the man that have come to light."

"Disheartened is putting it mildly," Eunice said. "And while your offer of telling me favorable stories about Grandfather is considerate, I'm not ready to talk about my grandfather with anyone just yet."

Vincent inclined his head. "Perfectly understandable, but allow me to return to the offer I mentioned earlier. Is there anything I can do to make the slightest amends for what my mother took away from you? Perhaps help you search the estate for that letter you mentioned last night?"

The hair on the back of Arthur's neck stood up.

Eunice stiffened for the briefest of seconds before she gave a casual shrug of her shoulders. "I wasn't intending on searching for that letter today. There's not much urgency to find it, not after your mother confessed to the crime."

"But if your grandfather named my mother in the letter, it can be admitted into court as evidence."

"And while that's true," Eunice began slowly, "such evidence could see your mother locked away for the rest of her life. I wouldn't think you'd want to lend your assistance to finding something that could see that happen."

"James was a mentor to me. I looked up to him, and that my mother murdered him leaves me feeling unsettled."

"And I'm beginning to find this conversation unsettling, because, again, she's your mother."

"Who murdered your grandfather. I think that's explanation enough for why I want to help you. With that now settled, shall we commence our search?"

Given the gleam residing in Vincent's eyes, there was little question that Vincent had an ulterior motive for volunteering to help locate the missing letter. What that motive was remained to be seen, but considering the hair on the back of Arthur's neck was standing at attention yet again, he knew danger had arrived in the form of Vincent Wagner, just as he knew he needed to get Eunice removed from that danger with all due haste.

"While I find it commendable you're willing to lend the Mason family your assistance," Arthur began, drawing Vincent's attention, "today is Eunice's birthday."

Vincent settled a smile on Eunice. "Allow me to extend my sincerest wish that your birthday is extraordinary. And to make certain you aren't distracted from experiencing that extraordinary birthday because of lingering questions you must have about what your grandfather wrote in that letter, allow me to offer to search the estate for you so you may go off and enjoy your day. I'll simply need to know where those secret spots are you mentioned last night."

Before Arthur could voice his approval to that because it would allow him to get Eunice far removed from a threat he didn't quite understand yet, Eunice shook her head.

"I'm afraid I don't recall all the secret places from my youth."

"Do you remember any of them?" Vincent pressed.

She tapped a finger against her chin. "There might be one in the barn."

"Then to the barn I'll go."

"I'll go with you," she said before Arthur could suggest they repair to the house, her decision leaving him arching a brow her way, something she ignored as she glanced around. "May I assume you rode out here? I don't see your horse."

"I left him past the target field on the chance you were enjoying some target practice."

"Behind that small grove of trees and over that slight hill that borders the target field on the right?"

Arthur bit back a groan when understanding struck.

Eunice had apparently figured something out and was now determined to ferret out answers to whatever questions were roaming around her brilliant mind, no matter that the ferreting could very well place her life in jeopardy.

Vincent narrowed his eyes on her before he smiled, although it seemed to be a forced smile with not a hint of amusement in it. "That's exactly where I left him."

Eunice smiled. "A prudent choice, especially if I had been practicing with my pistol, since it spares your horse being startled because the hill muffles the sound of a pistol firing."

Trepidation began crawling up Arthur's spine, but before he had an opportunity to give in to the urge to throw Eunice over his shoulder and dash off with her through the trees, she began walking in the direction they'd left their horses, looking over her shoulder.

"Arthur and I left our horses this way. We'll meet you back at the barn."

As Vincent turned and loped off in the opposite direction, Arthur strode to join Eunice, taking her hand. "Have you lost your mind?"

"Of course not. In fact, I'm remarkably clearheaded right now. Vincent's not here out of the kindness of his heart, and I intend to find out exactly why, although I have a few suspicions."

"I might need a little more to go on than that."

She didn't slow her pace. "He may have been an accomplice in Grandfather's murder and may believe his name is also included in that letter, along with his mother's name."

Arthur stopped in his tracks, pulling her to a stop as well. "If that's even a remote possibility, the last thing we should do is meet him in the barn to begin a hunt for a letter that doesn't exist. He won't react well when he realizes you don't have any secret hiding places."

"Oh, but I do have secret hiding places spread all over the estate," she said, her lips curving. "Granted, none of them are going to hold a letter, but we need answers. If Vincent had something to do with Grandfather's death, I need to know. And to relieve the worry that's now residing in your eyes, I suggested the barn because it's not that far from the house. There's every chance that Ivan will see us approach, because Judith's sketching him this morning in the backyard, which has an unfettered view of the barn. And," she continued, holding up her hand when he opened his mouth, "if Ivan doesn't see us, and after we don't find a letter in the barn, we'll move to the stables. I know for a fact there'll be plenty of people there, which should dissuade Vincent from doing anything rash."

"Such as shooting us?"

"Indeed."

"And isn't that reassuring," Arthur muttered as Eunice pulled him into motion again.

"If you need more reassurance, know that if Ivan doesn't notice us and matters turn concerning, he's only a pistol shot away."

"You're armed?" he asked as they reached the horses.

"Do you really think you need to ask that?"

"Sorry."

She released his hand and gave his arm a bit of a pat. "Just because I've begun dressing in the first state of fashion—well, not today of course—does not mean I've abandoned habits my grandfather instilled in me from an early age. He believed I should always be armed, and even if I wasn't, I can rely on my boxing skills to buy me time to escape."

"You should let me handle Vincent."

Eunice stepped away from him, swinging up in the saddle a second later and wrinkling her nose. "And while it's very gallant of you to want to protect me, I can't let you handle this for me because I need to find out why Vincent wants that letter. If I'm right in my assumptions and he is an accomplice in Grandfather's death, then, and only then, will I be able to put my past firmly behind me once and for all and get on with the business of living my life to the fullest."

CHAPTER
Thirty

Even though Arthur continued to mutter about the idiocy of prolonging their time with Vincent as they rode for the barn, he did assure Eunice that he'd have her back as well as tell her he wouldn't hesitate to shoot Vincent if he thought the man posed a threat to her safety.

There was something remarkably appealing about a man who would do whatever was needed to keep her safe, even if she knew he was rather annoyed with her for not allowing him to deal with the Vincent situation on his own.

Before she could do more than send him a smile, Vincent galloped into view, swinging out of the saddle and joining Eunice after she jumped to the ground. He immediately backed away from her, though, when Wyatt tossed his head and began pawing the ground the moment Arthur dismounted. That Wyatt didn't have his attention settled on Eunice and instead on Vincent almost seemed to suggest he sensed something about Vincent he didn't like, which had Eunice ever so discreetly reaching under her jacket to ascertain her pistol was easily accessible.

"I never liked that beast," Vincent said, stepping away from the horse when Wyatt tried to lunge closer to Vincent, an action that left Arthur struggling to hold the horse back.

"Maybe we should go into the barn so Arthur can get Wyatt settled," Eunice suggested, which earned her a look of disbelief from Arthur, one she ignored as she sidestepped around Wyatt, Vincent trailing behind her.

Striding through the barn door and into the shade of a large rectangular room that sported stacked bales of hay and stalls with goats, donkeys, and a few pigs, Eunice stopped and took a moment to look around before she nodded.

"If memory serves me correctly, I believe I stashed some of my most prized possessions in a toolbox." She strode into motion across the barn, snatching up a pitchfork that was leaning against a wall. Using the pitchfork to lift away the hay that was scattered over the floor, she lingered on the task, taking the time to gather her thoughts.

"You have a secret spot underneath the hay?" Vincent asked, interrupting what few thoughts she'd managed to gather.

"It's underneath the floorboards, but I can't remember where the loose floorboard is." She paused with the pitchfork as Arthur came to join her. "Did you get Wyatt under control?"

"He settled down after you and Vincent got out of sight," Arthur said before he held out his hand. "Allow me to do that for you."

"Always the gallant," Vincent muttered.

Eunice handed Arthur the pitchfork. "Arthur enjoys embracing a sense of chivalry. But while he clears the floor, allow me to take a moment or two to ask you a few questions I still have about Grandfather's murder."

Vincent shrugged. "I don't know why you think I'd be able to answer any of your questions about that. I was as shocked as everyone last night when Mother fessed up to her crime."

"I'm sure you were, but I'm curious as to whether you were just as shocked when Aunt Hazel disclosed the truth about your mother and my grandfather's relationship—that it wasn't as intimate as she'd always allowed everyone to believe."

Vincent's eyes flashed with temper. "I don't believe how I felt about that tawdry matter is relevant to anything concerning my mother."

"And I would have to disagree with that because I imagine there was some point in your life when you might have thought you were my grandfather's illegitimate son."

When Vincent released a laugh tinged with a slightly menacing air, the thought sprang to mind that she might have once again been a tad too direct, that idea reinforced when a blink of an eye later she found herself staring down the barrel of a pistol.

"You're going to want to put that away if you don't want me to shoot you," Arthur said, training his own pistol on Vincent, who laughed again, right as another laugh joined his, one that had Eunice swinging her attention to the right, blinking at the person who'd just entered what was clearly a concerning situation.

"And you're going to want to put your pistol on the ground, and then kick it Vincent's way, Mr. Livingston," Mrs. Wagner said pleasantly, holding a pistol in her hand that was trained on Eunice. "I assure you, I won't hesitate to shoot darling Eugenia, or whatever she's calling herself these days. I'm rather fond of my son and didn't just break out of jail to watch him suffer a bullet wound."

When Mrs. Wagner cocked her pistol, Arthur didn't hesitate to set his pistol on the ground and give it a kick in Vincent's direction. Vincent didn't so much as blink at the glare Arthur was leveling on him, instead moseying over to Arthur's gun and picking it up before he inclined his head toward Mrs. Wagner. "I wasn't expecting to see you today, Mother."

Mrs. Wagner settled a fond smile on her son. "I don't imagine you were, but I had this sneaking suspicion you were going to do something foolish, such as try to find that letter, so here I am, doing what mothers do best—saving our children from their reckless impulses."

When Vincent didn't have a ready answer to that, Eunice cleared her throat. "You were spot on about Vincent's reckless plans, but speaking of reckless, how did you get out of jail?"

Mrs. Wagner shrugged. "James wasn't the only one I black-mailed in this town, dear. Blackmail is a lucrative business, which is why I make it a point to uncover unsavory tidbits about everyone. Deputy Hanson, unfortunately, enjoys helping himself to items that don't belong to him in stores around town. Since he'd prefer to keep that information private, and since he realized I was serious about getting out of jail before that annoying Agent Clifton returned to question me, he was only too willing to let me go. I had to knock him over the head with a club to make it appear I'd overpowered him, something I don't believe any of the other deputies will believe. But that's not really my concern." She nodded to the pitchfork Arthur had abandoned. "Do continue, dear, with whatever it is you were doing, which I'm going to assume was recovering that ridiculous letter James had the brilliance of mind to leave." She arched a brow Vincent's way. "May I assume we're going to find your name listed in that letter?"

"Why would you assume that?"

"Because when you didn't so much as flinch last night when Hazel disclosed I wasn't James's mistress, I realized then and there that you'd already discovered that unfortunate truth on your own. I then remembered how furious you were when you returned home the night before James died. It didn't take much of a leap for me to realize what happened next. You confronted James about your parentage, didn't you, dear, and he, being James, was probably far too blunt telling you that you weren't his son." She sighed. "I was hoping the purchase of the bookshop would be enough to soften the blow when James died."

Vincent's eyes began to glitter. "You thought presenting me with a bookshop would appease me when for years you allowed me to believe that James would see reason and acknowledge me as his only son and thus the rightful heir to Mason Mines?"

"I didn't know at the time I purchased the shop that you'd discovered James wasn't your father, so I thought you'd merely conclude that I was unable to convince him to claim you as his heir."

Vincent darted a look to Eunice. "I'm not certain we should be having this discussion in front of anyone, Mother. What say we wait to finish the conversation until after I find that letter and we're far away from here."

"I have a feeling Eunice, being annoyingly astute, as well as Arthur, who's no slouch, have already begun to puzzle out what actually happened that day on the target field. It's highly unlikely they will be given the opportunity to tell anyone anything they hear us discussing now, darling."

"You're going to kill us in cold blood?" Eunice asked.

"I'm afraid it's unavoidable" was all Mrs. Wagner said to that before she moved closer to Vincent. "I am curious, though, how it came about that you confronted James. Was there a specific incident that occurred that caused you to seek out a confrontation with a man you were ill-equipped to argue with?"

"I wasn't so ill-equipped to deal with him when I shot him."

Eunice blinked. "So *you're* the one who killed my grandfather?"

Vincent shrugged. "I see no reason to deny it, and it's not as if he didn't deserve it. I'd spent years trying to convince him you weren't suited to run Mason Mines, and after I finally got through to him, does he offer to bring me on? No, and granted, I wasn't his son, not that I knew that at the time, but I know the mining business. Studied it at Harvard with the hope I'd be able to take my place in the Mason company. To secure that place, I even agreed to tutor you in the hope James would recognize my worth and react accordingly. Instead . . ." Vincent shot a malevolent look to Arthur. "Your grandfather decided to hand the mine to a complete stranger, and on a silver platter, since he offered your hand in marriage to really seal the deal."

"How did you learn about that?" Arthur asked.

"I think that's enough questions for now" was Vincent's only reply. "I may afford you a few more answers, but only after Eunice finds that loose floorboard and locates that toolbox she mentioned."

"I'll need the pitchfork back," Eunice said, earning another laugh from Vincent, who picked the pitchfork off the floor from where Arthur had dropped it when he'd gone for his gun.

"Nice try, but I'm very familiar with your proficiency with weapons. A pitchfork can certainly be considered that if it's in the right hands."

Refusing to allow her frustration to show over being denied a viable weapon, Eunice used her boot to shift around some hay, stopping when she stepped on a board that wobbled. She dropped to her knees and pried up the loose floorboard, sticking her hand in the opening that was revealed.

"And here I've been wondering if there actually were secret hiding spots or if Eunice had made that up to rattle the audience last night," Mrs. Wagner said.

"I bet that type of wondering left you feeling rather annoyed," Eunice said as she fished around under the floorboards.

"Of course it did, because if you didn't have secret hiding spots, well, I would have declared myself a murderess for no reason."

"Why *did* you declare that?"

"A mother will do anything to protect a cherished son."

Eunice's hand touched something cool, and a second later, she tugged out a rectangular toolbox. Setting it on the floor, she brushed aside the dirt covering the lid before she glanced to Mrs. Wagner. "Am I mistaken, then, in thinking that you had absolutely nothing to do with Grandfather's death?"

"I wouldn't call me blameless, not when I'm relatively certain my Vincent confronted James after he might have overheard me ranting to myself about being taken out of James's will." Mrs. Wagner sighed. "It's true that I had gone to James for more money, of course, but I'm afraid I may have been a touch too demanding. When I then learned he'd followed through with his threats and drawn up a new will the day after our exchange, I knew he'd taken me out of it. A bottle of wine later, I was talking to myself, unaware that Vincent was apparently within listening distance."

Vincent nodded to the box. "You're getting distracted. Open it." He turned to his mother. "I did hear you, which is why I decided it was time to have a chat with James about his being my father. I'd been putting that talk off for quite some time, building up my nerve to present him with the perfect solution regarding who should take over the running of Mason Mines once he retired. I'd just about gotten up my nerve when my plan was disrupted when"—he jerked his head in Arthur's direction—"he arrived in Butte. I knew right off the bat he was going to be a problem. Still, I arrived at Mason Manor fully prepared for my chat that would hopefully convince James I was the perfect candidate to be his heir, and discovered that James was having a meeting with Arthur."

"They were discussing marriage, weren't they?" Eunice asked, prying the lid off the toolbox and withdrawing a battered dime novel, which she immediately tossed aside.

"Indeed." Vincent sent a sneer Eunice's way. "Imagine my surprise when Arthur at first dodged James's suggestion—not that I blamed him since I had firsthand knowledge of how difficult you were. However, the tone of the conversation changed, and I realized that not only was James determined to turn the company over to Arthur, he was doing his utmost best to convince Arthur to marry you." He shook his head. "I missed a great deal of the conversation from there because I had to duck into a room when Hazel came wandering down the hallway. When I returned, the only other thing I overheard was James saying something about an unspoken threat, which I believe prompted him to ask Arthur to give him his word that he'd look after your best interests if something happened to him. After Arthur left, I felt it was still imperative to have that difficult conversation with a man I believed was my father. It did not go well."

Eunice pulled out an old slingshot from the box. "I wouldn't think it did, since James wasn't your father."

"Well, quite," Vincent said. "He didn't hesitate to tell me he'd never had relations with my mother nor hesitate to tell me that I was the son of some traveling salesman my mother took up with when that man was peddling his wares in town. He then told me he'd provided for me and Mother because of a debt he owed, but he wouldn't admit anything specific about that debt, which turned out to be more along the lines of blackmail. When he was finished, he told me he'd had enough of the Wagner family, that it was time for me and Mother to leave town, and if we didn't go voluntarily, he'd be making his own arrangements. That's when I decided to kill him."

Setting aside the slingshot, Eunice frowned. "But what benefit would you have derived from killing him, and why set me up to take the fall?"

"I believe the simplest explanation for killing James would be rage and then spite for trying to frame you."

Eunice set aside a necklace made of paste she'd won at a local fair before she continued rummaging around a box that was slowly but surely being emptied. "I'm curious why you think Grandfather named you in the letter he left for me."

"Because I lost my temper with him that night I learned the truth. After I left, I'm sure he was relieved he'd made plans to send you away, clearly having done so after he had that contentious exchange with Mother."

"James was quite enraged the last time I demanded money," Mrs. Wagner said. "And, because he knew full well what I was capable of, I'm sure he wanted to send you away, Eunice, in case I turned spiteful." She smiled. "James, being a ruthless sort, always recognized that same characteristic in me, so I'm certain he was worried I'd spill just one or two of his secrets to you in order to get him to agree to give me more money."

"Were you intending on using your ruthlessness to garner yourself an endless stream of funds through blackmailing Uncle Raymond?" Eunice asked.

"Raymond is an idiot and would have been far more easily manipulated than James ever was," Mrs. Wagner said. "I thought he'd be a plump pigeon for the rest of my days because he didn't exactly behave in an ethical fashion when he agreed to have you declared dead. Since Raymond wants to be remembered as the Mason who finally helped Butte turn into a cosmopolitan city, you can bet he wouldn't have blinked an eye over giving me whatever I demanded."

Eunice reached into the box again, trepidation flowing freely when she realized there were only a few items left, none of which was a letter from her grandfather. It was a stretch to think Mrs. Wagner was going to be agreeable to moving on to search for another secret place, which meant she needed to delay what was certainly going to be some type of showdown for as long as possible. Pulling out a rag doll that had seen better days, she began searching through the folds of the doll's dress, hoping Vincent and his mother would take her actions as a search for a letter, not a delay tactic.

"What are you doing?" Vincent demanded.

She pulled off the doll's dress. "Grandfather might have hidden the letter in the stuffing. You wouldn't happen to have a knife I could borrow to open her up, do you?"

"If I won't let you have a pitchfork, I'm certainly not going to hand you a knife."

"Probably a wise decision on your part," Eunice said, pulling a loose thread on the doll, which had it unraveling. "While I disassemble this doll stitch by painful stitch, I hope you'll humor me because I find myself curious as to how you set up the scene so well for Grandfather's death. Clearly, since you left my pistol on the field, you didn't know I was supposed to be at the train station, but I imagine my showing up turned out to be an odd twist of luck for you."

"It would have been lucky if you hadn't thrown a wrench into my plans by showing up earlier than I was expecting," Vincent said. "You normally didn't meet your grandfather until nine, but he always went at eight. That's why I struck when I did. I thought I'd shoot James, position your pistol to where it would certainly be found, then leave and return a few minutes after nine, catching you in the act, so to speak. Unfortunately, James was a tough old bird, and after I shot him, he actually staggered to his feet at one point, looking around to see if he could find who'd shot him. I was forced to huddle down in the tall grass, and then, while I was hiding, you arrived early on the scene. I was considering shooting you as well, making it appear like a murder-suicide, but before I could do that, Arthur showed up out of the blue." He cocked a brow Arthur's way. "I don't bet you were planning on Eugenia shooting you, but then I thought for sure that my plan would still work, which is why I crawled away into the trees while you were lying on the ground and Eugenia was running away. After you finally sat up, I was expecting you to return to the house, telling everyone you'd seen her shoot her grandfather. Why didn't you do that?"

Arthur shrugged. "I knew she hadn't killed her grandfather."

"Because?"

"She didn't shoot to kill me, merely slow me down."

"And while that's an unexpected explanation," Mrs. Wagner said, gesturing with her pistol at Eunice, "James clearly didn't hide his letter in the doll. What else is in the box?"

Eunice pulled out a tin pin and placed it on the floor, bracing herself for a confrontation she was convinced would soon come. "That's it. That's all that's in there, which means we'll need to move to my next secret spot."

"And draw attention in the process?" Mrs. Wagner laughed. "I think not." She nodded to Vincent. "I have a carriage waiting outside the barn. Wait for me in it, dear."

"But we don't have the letter."

"And we're not going to find that letter because the longer we linger here, the better the odds are that we'll be caught." She jerked her head toward the barn door again. "Go. I'll take matters from here."

As Vincent opened his mouth to voice an argument, Mrs. Wagner aimed her pistol directly at Eunice, but right as she cocked the trigger, Arthur raced into motion. Before Eunice could do more than grab her pistol from her pocket, a shot split the air, and a second later, Arthur and Mrs. Wagner were tumbling to the ground.

CHAPTER

Thirty-One

"Of anyone I thought might race to my rescue, you never entered my mind, Aunt Hazel," Eunice said. "Allow me to say that was a brilliant shot on your part and suggests you may be more proficient with a pistol than either me *or* my mother."

Aunt Hazel gave a wave of the smelling salts she'd fetched after Mrs. Wagner and Vincent were carted off to jail, Vincent moaning dreadfully about the gunshot wound to his leg Aunt Hazel had been responsible for and Mrs. Wagner complaining that she was bound to sport bruises all over after Arthur knocked her to the ground in his rush to disarm her. "It's no secret I found my life in Montana stifling at times. To stave off my boredom, especially after you left, I had to immerse myself in hobbies. Besides whipping up batches of candy, target practice became a predominant hobby of mine. And not that I want to brag, but yes, I'm a better shot than you or Georgette will ever be."

"That sounds like a challenge."

"A challenge I'll take up, but only after I get my nerves under control."

Exchanging grins with her aunt, Eunice returned her attention to her grandfather's last will and testament, wanting to review it again before she made decisions that had to be made regarding the Mason estate.

The moment she'd brought out the will, Uncle Raymond had repaired to his room, her grandfather's old room, telling Eunice he was going to begin packing because he believed his time residing at Mason Manor had come to an end.

His declaration had left Eunice facing a bit of a dilemma.

Yes, Uncle Raymond had plotted and connived with Mrs. Wagner to steal her inheritance, but he was an elderly man and he *was* her grandfather's brother, a grandfather who'd plotted and connived for most of his life. It really came as no surprise that Uncle Raymond had picked up a few tricks from his brother over the years.

"Anything you missed in the will that surprises you?" Arthur asked, pulling up a chair and taking a seat beside her.

"Nothing in the will, but the day has certainly been one big surprise after another."

"Probably not the birthday you were expecting."

"That's putting it mildly."

After Arthur had disarmed Mrs. Wagner and Aunt Hazel had shot Vincent, events had unfolded quite quickly.

Ivan, Cooper, Ann, and Judith had rushed into the barn, pistols drawn, Georgette and Douglas following them. After securing Vincent and his mother, and after Vincent's leg had been wrapped, Cooper had set about what he did best, getting confessions that Ann wrote down.

After drawing out all the pertinent details, Cooper and Ann had left to transport Vincent and his mother to jail, Ivan and Judith going along because it had certainly been proven that the Wagner family was not to be trusted.

Georgette and Douglas had decided to wander off to the stables to see the horses. However, given the way they'd been gazing at each other, Eunice was convinced they weren't going there because of the horses but instead to find time alone together. The fact that they'd taken to holding hands suggested there might be no talk of divorce in their future but perhaps a reconciliation.

Eunice glanced at the will again. "I've been left an obscene amount of money."

"I can't argue with that."

"I also seem to have been left as head of the family."

"Indeed."

She blew out a breath. "I don't know why that thought never settled until now, but with that title comes responsibility."

"Your grandfather did leave your relatives bequests," Arthur pointed out.

"True, and large bequests at that, but . . . still." She nodded to Aunt Hazel, who seemed to be enjoying a bit of flirting with Lloyd as they sat on a fainting couch together. "Aunt Hazel was the most loyal to Grandfather and yet he left her a mere million dollars, which is a pittance compared to what he left everyone else. But even being so obviously slighted by her brother, she used a great deal of her inheritance to improve the town of Butte and improve the Mason name. If you ask me, that speaks volumes about her continued loyalty to the Mason family."

"May I assume you're intending on rewarding Hazel for that loyalty?"

"I don't think I'd consider it a reward . . . more along the lines of finally acknowledging her importance in the family." She glanced at the will again. "I'm afraid I'm going to have to call for another family meeting, even though the last family meeting turned beyond contentious."

"It is still your birthday. Perhaps you should save further con-tentiousness for another day."

She smiled. "And while that's an intriguing thought, I can't put off the inevitable because it's time for me to get my past settled once and for all, and I can't do that until I make matters right with my family."

It took two hours to get everyone gathered at Mason Manor because a message had to be delivered to Howard at his mercantile store, and then he had to fetch his daughters from their candy shop as well as Hester from a social luncheon. Hester had been quick to inform Eunice that she didn't appreciate being summoned out of one of her events, especially not when she'd been doing what she'd called "Mason family damage control" after so many rumors had begun spreading about the family—none of which were favorable.

After assuring Hester that the meeting might result with Hester being able to quash those rumors once and for all, Hester settled down and even agreed to help Howard get Uncle Raymond and Aunt Clarice down to the library, something they'd been refusing to do.

Five minutes later, Uncle Raymond shuffled into the library, looking like a broken man. He went to sit behind James's old desk, then seemed to think better of it and took a seat beside his wife, who looked as if she'd been crying.

It was a sight that left Eunice's heart aching.

Yes, her family was capable of horrendous behavior toward one another, and yes, they seemed to thrive on secrets and holding fast to slights they felt they'd been dealt.

However, they were her family, and sometimes one needed to remember what family was all about.

After Georgette and Douglas finally wandered into the library after Lloyd had been sent to find them, a task he'd done reluctantly because he was convinced the couple wasn't going to be thrilled to be interrupted, and settled themselves on a small chaise that barely had room for one, Eunice strode to the center of the room as everyone fell silent.

"I think we can all agree that it's been a very interesting few days, filled with confessions I wasn't actually surprised to hear—well, except for who killed Grandfather," she began. "But with those confessions came the revelation of some truths, and all we can do now is accept those truths and try to move forward as a family. And speaking of truth," she continued, "I recently revisited some notes I jotted down during my stint at Blackwell's Island Insane Asylum."

Douglas sat forward. "I don't believe you've gotten around to telling me about a stint in an asylum."

Eunice's lips curved. "There's much you and I haven't gotten into, but that'll need to wait for another time. To return to what I was going to say about my notes, as I was looking through them, one note in particular caught my attention. It was a note to explore the topic of truth."

She walked over to a small table and picked up the old family Bible she'd found on a library bookshelf, the beautiful handwriting inside it belonging to her grandmother Mary. "When I found Grandmother's Bible, I opened it to where she'd marked a page with a faded ribbon and found exactly what I was looking for. It's in the book of John, and the verse states, 'And ye shall know the truth, and the truth shall make you free.'

"And while the meaning of the verse is clear—that we need to follow the path Christ laid out for us, to accept His teachings and live by those teachings—I was struck by how accepting my own personal truth could finally set me free. I also believe everyone in this family could be set free as well, if we move forward in truth and move forward by adhering to this verse and follow the path Christ expects us to follow."

She gestured around the room. "We, the Mason family, seem to have a very large problem with the truth, and we have that problem because of Grandfather and the vast fortune he used to control everyone. Some in this room have abandoned truth in order to get a greater share of that fortune, done so because Grandfather's actions encouraged that type of behavior. He should have freely shared his wealth with his family because family is important and should be treated with love. Instead of doing that, though, he doled out his money at whim, creating resentment and lies that have almost ruined this family. It's time for the lies to stop. It's time for truth to be the motto the Mason family embraces, and it's time to divide the Mason fortune in a way that's actually fair."

As those words settled, everyone began glancing around the room, expressions of disbelief on every face, except for Arthur's, who was smiling warmly at her, the warmth of his smile leaving heat settling on her cheeks. She sent him a smile in return and set aside the family Bible before she picked up her grandfather's will.

"As I'm sure all of you know, Grandfather left me seventy-five percent of Mason Mines, along with his entire savings, stock portfolio, and this house. The other twenty-five percent of Mason Mines he left to my mother." She arched a brow at Georgette. "Before I continue, do you have any desire to live in Mason Manor?"

Georgette shuddered. "Absolutely not. It reminds me of Father, and while I know I'll eventually get around to forgiving him for tearing Douglas and me apart, I'm not quite there yet. I certainly won't get there if I permanently return to a house where rounding every corner brings back memories of him."

"Where do you intend to go?" Douglas asked.

"I've been thinking about using some of my inheritance to turn my little artist colony into a resort," Georgette said. "I could invite artists from all over the country at no cost to them and paint to my heart's content, surrounded by artistic types. I would no longer worry about how I'm going to afford my next meal, or if I have to set aside my painting to milk a cow." She smiled. "I was thinking darling little stone cabins might be the way to house all the artists, the kind one always imagines in fairy tales, and the kind that would certainly spark some creativity."

Douglas's lips curved into a smile. "May I assume, knowing how you always adored those fairy tales, that you're considering building your very own castle to live in?"

"That would depend on whether or not you'd enjoy living in a castle."

"If it comes complete with my very own fairy princess, you may count me in," Douglas said before he leaned closer still and settled his lips against Georgette's, both of them seemingly oblivious to the fact they were in a room filled with curious relatives, most of whom had taken to sighing, except for Howard and Raymond, who were looking somewhat embarrassed.

"I bet that struck a chord in your romantic heart," Arthur said as he walked up to join her.

Eunice grinned. "Indeed, and I'm going to have to remember to tell Daphne all about what just happened with my parents. She'll be certain to want to include that in one of her books, now that she's been including more romance in her plots."

"Maybe I'll have to think of something she could include as well," Arthur said, not bothering to expand on that before he moseyed to take a seat beside his grandfather, who was sitting on a long couch beside Aunt Hazel. Lloyd looked completely delighted by the fact that he needed to scoot closer to Hazel to give Arthur enough room.

Having no idea what Arthur had meant but remembering she had a somewhat captive audience at the moment, or at least she might have a captive audience if her family could pull their attention away from Georgette and Douglas, Eunice took a step toward Uncle Raymond, who immediately began fidgeting.

"I'm going to start with you, Uncle Raymond," she began, which had everyone swinging their attention back to her. "You seem to be under the impression I'm going to boot you out of Mason Manor. But since Mother has no interest in living here, there will be no booting from me. In fact, I'm going to give you and Clarice the house, along with the grounds, so there'll be no more talk about your packing up and moving. This is your home, and this is where you're going to stay."

"You're giving me the house?" Uncle Raymond asked.

Eunice nodded. "I'm also going to give you an additional five million dollars, which combined with what you already inherited and what you've been taking as salary for your titled role in Mason Mines will see you living more than comfortably."

As Clarice dissolved into tears and buried her face in a handkerchief, while Uncle Raymond looked stunned, Eunice turned to Howard. "I'm also giving you another five million, and in addition to that, I'd like you to head up the Montana Mason Family Philanthropy Institute, which I'm going to fund but which I'd like you to run." She settled a smile on Hester. "I expect you to help run it as well because I have a feeling you, with your society connections, have the pulse of Butte, and know what additional improvements need to be made in the city."

Hester raised a hand to her chest. "Goodness, being involved with philanthropy like that could cement the Mason family as the reigning society family for years."

"Which is why I know you'll throw yourself into selecting the perfect charities to sponsor as well as choosing cultural improvements that could very well see Butte considered one of the most progressive cities in the West."

Hester smiled. "I've long thought a pavilion would be nice to hold outdoor concerts in the summer, and an art gallery would lend an air of sophistication to Main Street." She glanced to Georgette, who didn't notice the glance because she was staring at Douglas again. Hester returned her attention to Eunice. "We could hold a show featuring your mother's work, but apparently I'll need to speak with her later about that because she seems to be preoccupied right now." She turned to Doris and Alice. "You two can assist me as well."

Alice's eyes began to gleam. "Doris and I don't know much about art, which means we should probably schedule a trip to New York to view the galleries there before we're capable of lending much assistance." She caught Eunice's eyes. "Do you think there's any possibility that you could arrange for us to attend a society event while we're there, one that might include dashing society gentlemen?"

"I don't actually travel in society, but . . ." She glanced to Lloyd, who was already nodding. "Lloyd is a member of the New York Four Hundred. I'm sure he'd be able to secure a few invitations to some society events held this Season."

"Or better yet, perhaps I'll need to host a ball to introduce you to society," Lloyd offered, earning grins of pure delight from Doris and Alice as well as from Hester, who immediately pronounced that she'd adore seeing the big city too.

Switching her attention to Aunt Hazel, Eunice moved to join her on the couch, taking hold of her aunt's hand. "You, out of anyone," Eunice began, "were always the kindest to me. You also kept your brother's secrets, not that I'm sure he realized that, but he should have rewarded you for your loyalty instead of leaving you a pittance of what he left Uncle Raymond. That, and the fact that you've taken it upon yourself to improve the Mason name through philanthropic measures, is why I've decided to give you ten percent of Mason Mines, along with the ten million dollars your brother should have left you when he died. And because I'm certain you're wondering why I asked Howard to be in charge of the Mason philanthropy efforts in Butte when you're the one to have taken the initiative with that, I thought you might not want to take on such a responsibility and instead take time to simply enjoy yourself for a change."

Aunt Hazel settled a smile on Howard. "Howard is the best choice for that position, dear. He's far younger than I am, and I must admit the thought of no responsibility is vastly appealing." Her smile dimmed as she returned her attention to Eunice. "I'm curious, though, why you're giving me a percentage in Mason Mines when you didn't offer that to Raymond."

Eunice chanced a glance to Uncle Raymond and found him watching her warily. "He tried to have me declared dead, and while I'm certainly not going to hold a grudge about that, I'm also not going to reward him for his actions."

"I am sorry for that," Uncle Raymond began. "It wasn't well done of me."

"No, it wasn't, and I hope you realize that if you'd been successful, Mrs. Wagner would have plagued you for the rest of your life with blackmail demands. But since she's now going to be spending time behind bars, along with Vincent, who will be spending even more time behind bars for the murder of Grandfather, I'm going to put your duplicity behind me. But I'm not quite charitable enough to give you a percentage in the mines."

"But you're charitable enough to give Raymond this house and an additional five million dollars, which is nothing to sneeze at," Aunt Hazel pointed out. "And you're giving me more money than

I'll ever be able to spend, although I believe I might spend just a bit of it in New York City." She smiled. "I've always wanted to shop on the Ladies' Mile, and I'm really interested in meeting that Monsieur Phillip Villard. I'm hopeful he'll agree to design a few gowns for me."

"I can make arrangements for all of you to meet Phillip, and I assure you he'll be more than happy to have you attired in his latest masterpieces."

As all the ladies began exchanging smiles, Eunice rose to her feet and made her way over to stand in front of Douglas, who'd stopped staring into Georgette's eyes, but was now holding her hand while Georgette kept smiling, something Eunice had never seen her mother do so much before in her life.

"And now we're up to you," Eunice began, "the father I had no idea was alive."

"There's no need for you to give me anything," Douglas said. "I have no need of money since I have a remarkable fortune of my own."

"True, but you suffered because of the actions of my grandfather. He was mistaken about you, misjudged you, and proclaimed you a fortune hunter without learning the facts. He tore you and Mother apart, which was reprehensible of him. If he had not done that, you would have been capable of being the son he never had—the son he always wanted—but he didn't allow you an opportunity to prove yourself to him." She inclined her head. "I'm giving you twenty-five percent of the shares in Mason Mines, which means, given that you're still married to my mother, you now own fifty percent of the company." She glanced to Arthur. "I do have one condition, though. Arthur gets to be president of Mason Mines."

She walked across the room and took hold of Arthur's hand. "I know you were hoping at one time to have ownership of Mason Mines, but I think it would be fair if you were allowed to take as your compensation forty percent of any profits the company sees in the future. With the development of the old Green farm, profitability should be impressive, which will allow you to achieve that goal of yours of being one of the leading copper moguls in the country. It'll also allow you to return to society with an impressive fortune."

When Arthur opened his mouth, Eunice shook her head, stopping him before he could utter a single word. "I realize that we still have matters left to discuss between us, but I'd prefer to discuss those matters without an audience and after I get my life somewhat settled again."

Something interesting flickered through Arthur's eyes before he inclined his head. "That's fair, but allow me to say that I have much I need to discuss with you, so don't keep me waiting too long."

"I'll keep that in mind," she said before she moved to the center of the room, finding herself in front of a captive audience again, a circumstance that left her smiling.

"To end the family meeting, I'd like to reiterate the point I made regarding the Mason family moving ahead in truth. I'm intending to do exactly that from this point forward because I believe truth really can set you free and my truth is this:

"I'm going to retain some of my shares of Mason Mines, along with the rest of the fortune Grandfather left me, not because I have any great need of that fortune, but because even though Grandfather was clearly a conflicted man, and rather reprehensible to boot, I loved him, and I know he would expect me to honor his wishes and keep some of the fortune he spent his entire life acquiring. He probably wouldn't expect me to use his fortune to improve the plight of others, but that's what I've decided to do. I'm going to set up the Howland Philanthropic Foundation when I return to New York. One of my first orders of business will be to begin making plans to build an insane asylum, one where patients will be treated with the respect and care they deserve. I'll also devote funds to improving the conditions at Blackwell's Island Insane Asylum, along with other asylums in and around New York."

"What about your inquiry agency?" Georgette asked. "Are you going to abandon that and devote all your efforts to philanthropy?"

Eunice shook her head. "There's a need for the agency in the city. I intend to expand it as well, although I believe recent events have shown me that I probably shouldn't spend too much time out in the field. I may, as Ivan has suggested, be far too direct to successfully immerse myself in covert operations."

She drew in a breath and slowly released it. "I've also decided that it's time for me to live the full truth of who I am. I'm not fearless, but that doesn't mean I'm content to continue to live my life in the shadows. That's why I'm going to return to New York as Eunice Howland—no longer a widow and no longer hiding my identity from the world." She turned to her parents. "I'm not sure if the two of you want me to claim you as my parents since I'm not actually sure how you're going to go about handling a marriage that has been anything but usual for the past twenty-eight years or so."

"Of course we'll claim you as our daughter," Georgette said, dabbing a tear that was trailing down her check. "And don't you worry about how we're going to explain our estrangement. We certainly don't want to draw too much attention to how reprehensibly your grandfather treated us, but you let me and your father worry about that. We'll come up with something."

"Then it's settled," Eunice said, exchanging a smile with her mother. "I'm now Miss Eunice Howland, philanthropist and partner in the Bleecker Street Inquiry Agency." She turned to Arthur. "As was mentioned earlier, we still have much to discuss, but you, as the new president of Mason Mines, have matters you need to attend to here, while I need to get back to New York because I have a business to run. Before I leave, though, I need to make it clear that even though I'm now one of the wealthiest heiresses in the country, I have no intention of setting aside my work to become a part of the New York Four Hundred. Since you divulged your life plan to me, a plan that includes an incomparable and a place within society, you'll need to take that into consideration before we have any future discussions between us. Once you've settled things here and have decided what life you truly want to pursue, you'll know where to find me—behind my desk at the Bleecker Street Inquiry Agency."

Her heart did a bit of a lurch when Arthur stepped up beside her and took her hand, pressing a kiss on it.

"You may be sure that I'll be sitting on the other side of your desk from you soon, but for now, you should pack. I'll see to the business, but then, know this, Eunice—I'll be coming to have that discussion with you because I already know what I want from life."

With that, Arthur kissed her hand one last time, and with a charming smile, gave her a nudge toward the door. After sending her family a smile and a wave, she headed out of the room, feeling more at peace than she'd felt in years because embracing her truth had truly set her free at last.

CHAPTER

Thirty-Two

Even though a month had passed since Eunice had returned to New York, Arthur had yet to share a meaningful conversation with her, what with how he'd stayed behind in Montana to work out terms with Douglas regarding Mason Mines.

He'd only returned to New York City three days before, anxious to get home because he knew it was past time to get matters settled with Eunice—his incomparable, and a lady he knew he wanted to spend the rest of his life with. And while he understood why she'd wanted to delay speaking with him about their relationship or speaking about the kiss they'd shared, he'd not needed any time at all to consider the matter.

Yes, she'd obviously wanted him to know that she had no interest in reigning at his side in the midst of society, but what she didn't know is that a place in society held little appeal to him these days, not if it meant Eunice wouldn't be in his life.

However, during the month they'd been apart, he'd had a lot of time to ponder the matter and was actually thankful she'd asked for their conversation to be delayed because Eunice was a romantic at heart, and romantics deserved romantic gestures that would leave them breathless and anticipating a lifetime of romance ahead of them.

If he would have blurted out his affection for her at Mason Manor, it would not have been a spectacular gesture, which is exactly why he'd brought his grandfather into his confidence, Lloyd only too happy to help him set up what he hoped would leave Eunice breathless as well as hoping it would leave her, at the very least, realizing she held Arthur in some affection.

"Your mother told me to tell you she expects you in the receiving line on time tonight," Lloyd said, striding into the suite of rooms Arthur used at his parents' house whenever he was in the city.

"I see you've abandoned your cane."

Lloyd smiled. "Saw the doctor today. He says I'm fit as a fiddle."

"But you will be staying far removed from Wyatt, right?"

Lloyd's face fell. "I was hoping to take him for a canter around Central Park tomorrow. Hazel has purchased a delightful mare, and she asked me to accompany her."

"You're not taking Wyatt. But dare I hope things are progressing well with the only woman you've been squiring around town of late?"

"She refuses to marry me."

"You asked her to marry you?"

"I did, just last week. She immediately turned me down, telling me she's now a completely independent woman and she intends on remaining that way."

"And you're fine accepting that decision?"

"For now." Lloyd smiled. "I understand her point. Hazel was kept in line for most of her life by her brothers, and now she's free to do as she pleases. She's already purchased a charming home in the city and has settled Doris and Alice into that home with her, both of whom were perfectly willing to turn over their candy shop to Howard to manage. Hazel has decided her 'girls,' as she calls them, are going to take New York by storm, even at their advanced ages. They're also planning a trip to Paris because Hazel is convinced that city is home to dashing gentlemen." His smile widened. "I have a sneaking suspicion, though, given how charming Doris and Alice are, they might ruin Hazel's plans and find gentlemen they can love this Season in New York. I'm still hoping a trip to Paris will be in order because Hazel invited me to tag along with them. It is known as the city of love, and it could very well turn into the city where Hazel changes her mind about marriage."

"I wouldn't get my hopes up about that, Grandfather," Chase said, strolling into the room as he attempted to tie his tie, his hair still a bit damp from the bath. "Hazel seems perfectly content to remain independent, although it has been remarked upon by more than a few of your widow friends that she might be responsible for reforming you. Rumor has it that those widows are highly amused that she seems to be leading you a merry chase."

"Indeed she is," Lloyd said. "And truth be told, I'm rather relieved the widows aren't looking at me so unfavorably these days. I was concerned I might never be welcomed back into the midst of the elite, or that if I did travel in society, I'd be placing my life at risk during every luncheon I attended."

"Then thank goodness Hazel decided to come to New York," Arthur said before he turned to Chase. "You're cutting it close this evening, and Mother's not going to be happy about the damp state of your hair."

"I've already had a lecture from Mother about my hair, Arthur, but I made it home before the ball started." Chase continued to fiddle unsuccessfully with his tie. "I couldn't very well have left poor Mrs. Collins weeping into a handkerchief at the agency. It took me three cups of tea to get her settled down, although I suppose, in all fairness, I should give the credit for that to Eunice." He grinned. "She realized I was faltering and stepped in, using her standard no-nonsense approach to get Mrs. Collins's weeping under control. And by the way, Eunice will be late."

"What?"

"Again, Mrs. Collins was in a state. Eunice was going to accompany her home, then return to the boardinghouse to get dressed. I believe Phillip was meeting her there, so he'll have her dressed and presented in a timely fashion." Chase gave up on his tie and walked over to Lloyd, who immediately began tying it for him.

"I'm sure you're right about Phillip getting her here in a timely fashion," Lloyd said. "I've seen the creation Phillip made for Eunice, and since Phillip's attending our ball, there's little doubt he'll not want Eunice to arrive too late, not when he wants society to be given the pleasure of watching her in his gorgeous dress for as many hours as possible."

"He's going to be disappointed, then, because I have a plan."

"One you've been very stingy with disclosing," Chase grouched. "But even with Eunice arriving late, I say you're fortunate she's arriving at all."

"She wouldn't have missed a ball we're hosting in honor of her parents after they renewed their vows." Arthur smiled. "Mother's thrilled that every invitation we sent out was accepted, but I don't know why she thought anyone would decline to attend what's certainly going to be considered one of the events of the Season. Society is still all agog over what's being called the love story of the decade. It was quite clever of Daphne to write a lovely tale she gave to the newspapers to introduce Georgette to society. She really is a gifted storyteller, and I have to admit I got a little teary-eyed reading what is only a slightly fictitious tale about how Georgette and Douglas fell in love in their youth but were tragically parted due to a misunderstanding with James, which Daphne handled incredibly vaguely. The romantic ending, of course, is what made the story—that of them being unexpectedly reunited, realizing neither of them had sought out the expected annulment because they were too distraught to do so and are now free to embrace their love for each other forever."

Chase grinned. "It was quite the story and will all but guarantee that Georgette's paintings will fly off the wall when she opens the Howland Art Gallery next year."

Arthur returned the grin. "Her paintings would have flown off the wall even without the romantic story, since her gallery is going to be set in the castle she and Douglas are building in her artist colony. Every member of society is dying to get a personal invitation to tour the castle when it's done. Many of those society members are suddenly taking an avid interest in becoming patrons of the arts, or more specifically, patrons of Georgette's work."

"I have a feeling a lot of people are going to find themselves longing to become artists as well, what with how charming the plans for Georgette's improvements for her colony are shaping up," Chase said. "I got a look at them yesterday at the agency. It should look like a fairy-tale town once it's completed."

"Things going well at the agency?" Arthur asked, turning to his own tie.

Chase nodded. "Turns out I was right about understanding the human condition. Eunice has decided I'm good with handling our more emotional clients because I seem to have a knack for drawing out information that helps Daphne puzzle out solutions to their problems."

"Except for Mrs. Collins today."

"She was an extreme case. Turns out the gentleman her daughter agreed to marry might have some rather nasty skeletons in his closet, at least according to Alva Vanderbilt. I wouldn't be surprised if we find Eunice tracking Alva down at the ball tonight to see what's behind the rumors."

"An idea that's somewhat alarming, considering the plans I have for Eunice."

A light rap on his door had Arthur turning to see his mother standing in the doorway. "It's almost time, boys."

"We're coming, we're coming," Lloyd said, "and it's rather disconcerting for my daughter to be calling me a boy."

As Lloyd ambled out of the room, Chase joined Arthur in front of the mirror.

"May I assume you're going to ask Eunice to marry you tonight?"

"I'm not telling you that. It's a surprise."

"Please, you and Grandfather have gone to a lot of effort to plan this evening, all on the guise of having everyone believe it's to introduce Georgette and Douglas to society as a married couple— something I know Georgette wasn't keen to do and only agreed to cooperate with after you told her your plan. It hardly seems fair that she knows, whereas I, your favorite brother, do not."

"You're not getting it out of me, and here, let me fix your hair. Don't you own a comb?"

After getting Chase relatively put together, and after Arthur shrugged into his formal evening coat, they made their way out of his room and down the curved staircase to the first floor, where his mother, father, older brother Benjamin and his wife, and Lloyd were already in the receiving line.

Arthur had barely gotten to his spot when their guests began to arrive.

Bending over one young lady's hand after another, all of whom smiled brightly back at him, and all of whom had mothers who were only too willing to extol the recent accomplishments of their unmarried daughters, many of whom he learned were considered incomparables, Arthur found himself wondering time and again how he could have ever thought his life's plan should be to amass a fortune and then marry an incomparable. Now when he was meeting so many of them, he realized that he'd done each and every one of them a disservice. Yes, they were beautiful and accomplished, but they were each special in their own way, something he'd never thought about before, but something he'd never forget again, especially if he were fortunate to have a daughter or two of his own.

He would never allow a gentleman to pursue a daughter of his simply because of a title she'd earned or, worse yet, because of the fortune he had managed to amass.

"Arthur, I was hoping you'd be here this evening."

Waiting until the young lady he'd just addressed moved on to Chase, Arthur found Mitzi Jarvis, now Mrs. Thomas Gibson, standing in front of him, beaming a genuine smile at him.

He took hold of her gloved hand and kissed it. "Mrs. Gibson, it's lovely to see you."

She surprised him when, after he released her hand, she took hold of it again and gave it a squeeze. "It's Mitzi, Arthur, not

Mrs. Gibson. Honestly, we were always good friends." She glanced around before she tugged him out of the line and down a hallway that had relatively few guests milling about.

"Forgive me for pulling you away, but something has always bothered me about the way we last parted." She searched his eyes. "Do tell me you're not still cross at me for . . . ah . . ."

"Rejecting me out of hand?"

"Oh, I was right," she said with a sigh. "You did take our last encounter badly, and to be honest, I fear I made a muddle of it."

"You told me you wouldn't marry me because I was a second son and didn't have a large enough fortune."

Her eyes widened. "Is that what I said? Good heavens, I am sorry. I fear you simply took me by surprise, and it was just when I was about to tell you that Thomas had proposed to me and I was over the moon about it. I had no idea you had tender feelings for me, and not that this is an excuse, but because of my youth, I panicked and said the first thing to spring to mind, something that I thought would have you realizing you didn't love me at all."

"I thought I *did* love you at the time."

She released another sigh. "You were young as well and possessed of such a romantic heart. I should have realized you were considering me in a romantic manner, but I suppose I enjoyed the attention, because what young lady doesn't enjoy having a handsome, as well as charming, gentleman pay her attention? Again, it was not well done of me, but you would have grown bored with me in a fortnight. You were never meant to spend your life mingling in society like so many second sons do, with relatively few demands expected of you from your family. You were meant to forge your own way in the world, and that's exactly what you've done." She gave his arm a pat. "*I*, on the other hand, was meant to mingle in society and would not have wanted to go off with you in search of your destiny. That's why Thomas has always been perfect for me. His family business is well established, as is he, and he enjoys listening to me prattle on about the latest *on dit* or the latest fashions, something that would have bored you to tears."

It was fortunate Arthur had already concluded he'd been a bit of an idiot in his past, because what Mitzi said was nothing less than the truth and something she had realized about him even in her youth.

"May I hope you're happy, Mitzi?" he asked, pulling himself from his thoughts when he realized he'd been silent for far too long.

"Ecstatically so," Mitzi said. "I have two daughters and three boys who keep me on my toes."

"You have five children?"

She sent him a wink. "Proof that I do, indeed, love my Thomas." Giving his arm another squeeze, Mitzi hurried off, calling over her shoulder that she expected a dance at some point that evening.

Realizing he needed to get back to the receiving line before his mother noticed he was missing, Arthur spent the next thirty minutes greeting guests and checking the doorway time and again for signs of Eunice, but to no avail.

"I think that's the last guest," Lloyd said, taking hold of Arthur's arm. "Hazel told me to tell you not to worry about Eunice. She went through the line right after you disappeared with Mitzi." He arched a brow. "May I assume things were finally sorted out between the two of you?"

"If you're asking if I realized I was an idiot about all that happened with her, yes. But returning to Eunice?"

"Eunice arrived back at the boardinghouse before Hazel, Doris, and Alice left to come here."

"What was Hazel doing at the boardinghouse?"

"Making certain Eunice was going to show up, per my request."

"You are an extraordinary grandfather, you know that, don't you?"

Lloyd beamed. "Of course I do. So don't worry because she'll be here soon."

Exchanging grins, Arthur walked with his grandfather into the ballroom, spotting Daphne and her husband, Herman Henderson, standing next to a beautiful woman with black hair who was with

Mr. Nicholas Quinn, a gentleman Arthur was casually acquainted with because they'd once belonged to a few of the same clubs.

After getting introduced to Gabriella Goodhue Quinn, Nicholas's wife, and then watching her sprint out of the ballroom, saying something about time being of the essence, he turned to Daphne, who sent him a sad shake of her head.

"Unlike me, Gabriella still finds herself tossing up her accounts at the oddest of times."

After congratulating Daphne on her upcoming addition to her family, which Daphne said would arrive in the spring, Arthur excused himself to check on the other Bleecker Street ladies. All of those ladies had been given invitations to attend the ball as guests, but many of them had refused, instead agreeing to attend dressed as servants in order to preserve their identities in case a day came when they needed to infiltrate a society event and couldn't risk being recognized.

He stopped beside Ann, who had come as the companion of a society matron but who was, at the moment, in the company of Cooper.

"You're looking beautiful tonight, Ann," he told her, kissing her gloved hand and earning a scowl from Cooper.

"Don't mind Cooper," Ann said. "He's grumpy."

"Because?"

"I can't settle on a date for our wedding."

Arthur blinked. "You're getting married?"

Cooper rolled his eyes. "I asked her, she said yes, but now she can't pin down exactly when she has time to get married."

"I don't want to leave the agency in the lurch, and if I get married, I won't be able to be a paid companion anymore, which will limit the gossip I'll have access to." She leaned closer to Arthur and lowered her voice. "Phillip and Elsy, not that this is well known, are engaged and are planning on getting married in the near future. That means she'll no longer be able to be a paid companion, which means we're going to have to find more agents to take over roles we outgrow, but roles that are imperative to the agency."

"I'll be drafting an advertisement for more inquiry agents tomorrow," Cooper said firmly. "And it was hardly fair of Phillip not to give me adequate notice about what he was intending because then I would have asked you before he asked Elsy in order to avoid this particular problem."

"Since Phillip ended up abandoning his grand scheme after he realized Elsy was growing impatient and simply popped the question out of the blue one day, I doubt he had the foresight to give anyone adequate notice. I'm relatively convinced his proposal surprised him as much as it did Elsy." Ann smiled. "Elsy was thrilled, of course, and burst into tears, and Phillip had to take the reins because Elsy was driving the agency's carriage at the time and inadvertently let the horses have their heads. They apparently ended up a few miles from where they were going before Phillip was able to bring the horses under control again."

Arthur nodded to Cooper. "Perhaps you should add a position for another carriage driver in that advertisement you're going to place."

"Elsy would have my head if I did that because she enjoys driving the carriage," Cooper said right as Georgette and Douglas entered the ballroom, which immediately erupted in polite applause from all the assembled guests.

"I told my grandfather I'd help him present the lovebirds to everyone," Arthur said, exchanging grins with Cooper and Ann before he strode away.

He reached Georgette's side and gave her a kiss on the cheek.

"Where is she?" Georgette whispered in his ear.

"She's running late. Agency business."

"Honestly, that child," Georgette said before she took hold of Douglas's hand. "Let's hope she arrives within the next few minutes or she's going to ruin the spectacular surprise you planned."

"A surprise you haven't told me much about," Douglas muttered.

"It wouldn't be a surprise if I told you."

As Douglas sent Georgette a fond smile, Lloyd walked across

the ballroom floor and stopped in front of the assembled orchestra, drawing everyone's attention as he waved his hands and sent the guests his signature charming smile.

"Treasured guests," Lloyd began, "it's my honor to welcome you tonight to the Livingston house to celebrate the renewal of vows between Douglas and Georgette Howland. As you've undoubtedly read in the papers, they . . ."

Whatever else Lloyd said, Arthur didn't hear because Eunice took that moment to sweep into the ballroom on Phillip's arm, looking quite like a fairy-tale princess in a gown that Phillip had certainly outdone himself on.

Made of ivory silk with an overlay of lace, it flowed over her figure, the thousands of glass beads Phillip had attached to the gown sparkling underneath the light cast from the chandeliers. Her hair had been drawn to the top of her head and secured with a tiara that more than one young lady was gazing at in envy. A necklace dripping with diamonds encircled her neck and brought attention to charms more than one gentleman was eyeing with far too much interest.

He was in motion a second later, not stopping until he reached her side.

A trace of male satisfaction flowed over him when she gave him a bit of a perusal.

"You're looking quite dashing tonight, Arthur," she said as he took her gloved hand and brought her fingers to his lips.

After placing a kiss on them, which had her cheeks turning pink, he smiled. "And you're looking exquisite."

"Thank you." She nodded to Phillip. "Phillip was worried my hair was rushed, but I told him it was fine."

"She was covered in mud an hour ago," Phillip muttered, blowing out a breath. "We're lucky she's still not dripping wet from the bath I forced her to take."

"I wasn't covered in mud, just smeared with a touch of it, compliments of the large dog Mrs. Collins has little control of, which jumped out of the carriage before we reached her home. I was forced to chase after the beast because Mrs. Collins dissolved into tears the moment she thought her dog would be lost forever. But speaking of Mrs. Collins"—Eunice's lips curved—"I might have to reconsider my refusal to mingle in society because I just had a delightful chat with Mrs. Vanderbilt right outside this room. Turns out, she was mistaken about the name of the man she thought was up to dastardly business. It wasn't Samuel Medley, whom Mrs. Collins's daughter is engaged to, it was Samuel Morphine, so case solved, and with very little effort on the agency's part. Well, except that I was forced to rescue Mrs. Collins's dog, which did make me later than I expected."

"But you're here now."

"Indeed I am, but I seem to have missed Lloyd's speech about my parents." She looked past Arthur and frowned. "I wasn't aware the ladies from the agency were coming tonight, but there's Daphne, Gabriella, and, oh dear, she's looking peaked. There's Judith, Elsy, and I can't tell who else is here because guests are blocking my way, but . . . are some of the ladies dressed as the help?"

"They wanted to preserve their anonymity because of the agency."

Eunice frowned. "Why didn't I know everyone was going to be in attendance?"

"Because I told them not to tell you."

"Why?"

"You'll see" was all he said before Lloyd's voice boomed around the ballroom.

"Ah, and there she is. Finally." Lloyd sent Eunice a wave before he beamed his smile around the ballroom again. "As I mentioned, I'd asked Georgette and Douglas to open the ball with the first waltz, but they've decided to step aside and give that privilege to my grandson Arthur." Lloyd gestured Arthur forward, who took hold of Eunice's arm and tugged her into motion, ignoring that she seemed to be dragging her feet. He walked with her across the ballroom floor, stopping when he reached the middle and turned to his guests.

"While we're gathered here to celebrate Douglas and Georgette Howland, we're also here to introduce to all of you for the very first time Douglas and Georgette's daughter, Miss Eunice Howland, who was mentioned, but not by name, in the newspaper article penned by the extraordinary Daphne Beekman Henderson. Miss Howland has recently created the Howland Philanthropic Foundation, which I know everyone has already heard rumors about. I decided tonight would be the perfect night to introduce her to society, because I know many of you are going to want to contribute to the Howland Foundation since it already has plans for many improvements to our city."

Polite applause sounded through the room, and Eunice, after sending him an arch of a brow, quite as if to say she had no idea why he'd make such a production out of introducing her, dipped into a perfect curtsy and sent the crowd a wave right as the first notes of a waltz rang out.

Arthur presented her with a bow. "Miss Howland, would you do me the honor of opening up the ball?"

"You probably should have asked me if I know how to waltz."

He stilled. "I didn't even think about that."

She grinned and sent him the slightest hint of wink. "Clearly, but not to fret, I had dance instructors in my youth. With that said, though, I'm bound to be rusty, so I apologize in advance for what I'm certain is going to be a crushing of a few of your toes."

"I'll consider myself warned," he said right before he pulled her close and swept her over the ballroom floor.

To finally have Eunice in his arms, her closeness allowing him to breathe in the scent of her perfume, was something he'd dreamed about often during the time they'd been apart. He pulled her closer still, unable to help but wonder if he should have planned a more intimate affair when he'd been planning out the evening because he was hard-pressed to resist kissing her, something that would certainly set society agog.

He'd not kissed Eunice since her birthday, but he was fully

intending, if she cooperated with his plan, to kiss her whenever possible from that day forward.

"I seem to be leading, if you neglected to realize," she whispered in his ear. "You're letting yourself become distracted."

"And thank goodness you're capable of taking the lead," he whispered back, grinning as she led him in a turn before relinquishing the lead to him.

Before he knew it, the music came to an end, and with a bow to Eunice and then to the guests, he took hold of Eunice's hand, pulling her to a stop when she began walking off the ballroom floor.

"We're not done yet," he said.

"But the music stopped."

"It did, but the best part is just about to begin—or so I hope." He stepped closer to her. "Just remember, though, if this goes badly, it's all your fault for reminding me I'm a romantic at heart."

As Eunice blinked, he dropped to one knee, which had the ballroom falling silent. Taking her hand in his, he met her gaze, finding her eyes already suspiciously bright. Blinking a few times because his vision was turning blurry as well, he smiled. "Eunice, er, Howland." He winced and lowered his voice. "I almost called you Holbrooke, and wouldn't that have been tricky to explain to society, but . . . I'm getting distracted." He gave her hand a squeeze. "You were the most annoying young lady I ever met seven years ago, but even then, not that I told you this, I found everything about you fascinating, and that's still true today. I love how you can argue with me one moment and laugh with me the next, and I adore how you read dime novels and romances, and how straightforward and practical you are. But what I love most about you is your heart, one I believe you've kept hidden for far too long, but one you've now let into the light, which makes me love you so much more."

Eunice raised a hand to her throat. "I'm sorry, but did you just say you love me?"

"I thought you would have figured that out by now."

"Well, no. I mean, I thought you might hold me in a slight bit of affection, given the, ah, well"—she leaned closer to him—"kiss we shared, but I had no inkling you might love me, and I certainly wasn't expecting to hear that tonight."

"I thought it would be romantic to take you by surprise, while also thinking it would be romantic to have all your friends present to watch."

A single tear trailed down her cheek, one Eunice ignored. "You thought right because this is very romantic."

He smiled. "Thank goodness because, for a moment there, I thought I misjudged this, but now for the second surprise, although I'm not sure you'll find it a surprise since I am on bended knee." He withdrew a blue box from Tiffany & Company and opened it, revealing a brilliant circular diamond that was ringed with smaller diamonds. "And now, with all of your friends watching, as well as our families, Miss Eunice Howland, would you do me the very great honor of becoming my wife?"

She managed a whispered "yes," which had him on his feet, taking her hand in his and then placing a chaste kiss on her cheek, which was what society expected even if he knew he was going to kiss her more thoroughly once they repaired from the ball, which was going to be soon.

As the guests erupted into applause again, this time a little louder than was considered exactly proper, everyone crowded around them to extend their congratulations until Ivan edged his way through the crowd, picked Eunice up, and gave her a hug. He set her down, then nodded to Arthur.

"It's waiting for you out front."

"What's waiting?" Eunice asked.

Ivan sent her a wink. "You'll see."

Eunice caught Arthur's eye. "We're not staying?"

"You said you didn't care for society events so, no, we're not staying."

Her eyes began to sparkle. "Where are we going?"

"First, I'm taking you for a ride through the city, and then we're going to repair to the boardinghouse, met there by Aunt Hazel and my grandfather, who will act as our chaperones, as we're served a lovely dinner by Alma in the parlor. After we've enjoyed our meal, I'm then going to begin reading *Pride and Prejudice* to you because you once mentioned that would be romance at its finest."

"You remembered that?"

"I remember everything you've ever said." He extended his arm to her. "Shall we go?"

She shook her head. "Not yet."

"Why not?"

"Because I think I've neglected to tell you something. Something important."

"And you need to tell me that right now?"

"Indeed, in front of your friends and your family because . . . you're a romantic at heart as well." She smiled and stepped closer to him. "Before we leave this most lovely of balls, I want everyone here to know that I love you and have wanted you to ask me to marry you for a very long time, and that I am now going to kiss you."

A second later, Eunice kissed him, and not on the cheek, lingering on his lips for a good moment before she pulled away and grinned. "And now we can go."

Given the rousing applause that followed her kiss, Arthur was relatively certain if Eunice decided she wanted to enjoy society every now and again for philanthropic reasons, society would be more than receptive to welcoming her into their hallowed midst.

With Ivan clearing the way for them, they walked down the hallway and out the front door, Eunice stopping in her tracks before she made it to the front steps.

"You brought Wyatt tonight?"

"I was hoping you'd notice what I did to the carriage first."

Eunice glanced to the carriage, her eyes widening as her gaze traveled over the many roses covering it. She turned to him, took hold of his jacket lapels, pulled him close to her, and kissed him soundly before she tugged him down the steps. "It looks like a carriage straight out of a romance novel."

"Phillip designed a special cover for the seat of the open barouche. If you'll notice, it matches your gown."

"You really are a romantic," Eunice said before she flung her arms around his neck, kissed him again, then smiled as she looked the carriage over, her smile dimming when Wyatt gave a toss of his head before he snorted.

"That's not a good sign," she said, "and proves he still hasn't warmed up to me."

"You're imagining that. Wyatt adores you."

Less than three minutes later, Arthur was fairly convinced he might have been wrong about that because when he'd gotten distracted with kissing Eunice again after he'd helped her get settled on the seat, Wyatt had taken off, bolting down Fifth Avenue as Arthur tried to get control of the reins.

Instead of being concerned, though, Eunice's laughter drifted through the air as she reached out and helped him with the reins, partnering with him to bring Wyatt under control, just as he imagined she would always be, from that point forward, a true partner in life.

As Wyatt settled into a canter and they trundled down the streets of New York, Arthur knew they were riding off into their very own happily-ever-after because that's what always happened in fairy tales when two people who were meant to be together found each other, conquered obstacles that had been placed in their way, and then embraced the fairy tale that was certainly going to be theirs forever.

Epilogue

Stepping around a baby carriage that was blocking the door to her office, Eunice stepped over Winston, a one-eyed pirate dog who'd turned into somewhat of a mascot for the agency, and skirted around Precious, the poodle who rarely left Winston's side. Ducking when Pretty Girl, a parrot with a propensity for nicking sparkly objects, flew over her head, she finally made it to the chair behind her desk and sat down, jumping out of that chair when a lady dressed in widow's weeds and weeping veils moved silently into her office.

A second later, Ann pushed aside the veils and grinned. "I hope you don't mind, but I borrowed these from your wardrobe. I'm going undercover at a funeral later."

"The Tandler case?"

Ann nodded. "I'm taking Hazel with me. She's worried that Ivan's not around to provide me with proper backup, what with him and Judith being on their wedding trip. And even though I told her I'm capable of taking on the slightly disreputable Tandler family if they turn tricky, she thinks I need, and I quote, 'a hired gun' watching my back."

"But Aunt Hazel doesn't take a salary from us, which makes the 'hired gun' part somewhat inaccurate."

"I tried to point that out, but your aunt can be difficult. I believe it runs in the family."

"I'm not difficult."

"So says the woman who agreed to plan my wedding since I don't have time and has turned it into an elaborate affair at your mother's new castle."

"Mother wants to officially open the castle with a grand event. Your wedding is perfect for that."

"You only decided to hold my wedding there to appease the guilt you've been feeling over disappointing your mother when you and Arthur eloped a week after he proposed because he wanted to whisk you off to Paris before the weather turned nasty."

Eunice released a sigh. "It was a very romantic elopement and wedding trip."

"I can't argue with that, but because you disappointed your mother, I'm now going to find myself getting married in a spectacular castle when I was really thinking I'd get married in a small church with perhaps a small gathering held afterward in the Holbrooke boardinghouse parlor."

"A castle tops the boardinghouse parlor any day. Besides, since you and Elsy decided to get married on the same day, the parlor was not going to be an option because it would have been overly crowded."

"I didn't decide to get married on the same day as Elsy—she decided that. She's annoyingly difficult when she gets her heart set on an idea, even though I pointed out to her that she was going to have to delay her wedding to Phillip by months since Cooper got that promotion and was sent out on a case we knew was going to take him months to solve."

"But because of that delay, you're now going to be able to get married in a castle." Eunice smiled. "Add in the fact that Elsy was able to retain her position as a paid companion for a few extra months, months during which I was then able to find and train replacements for both her and you, and I believe everything has worked out to perfection."

"Rose Santana probably believes everything worked out well too since she was worried she might have to take on a companion role after learning Elsy and I were getting married."

"Rose is much too good at manning the reception room for me to have considered having her replace you or Elsy. She's formidable yet compassionate and knows a thing or two about how to console the distraught clients who seek us out, a skill I imagine she picked up at Blackwell's Island Insane Asylum."

"She's also very good with my darling Branson," Daphne said, strolling into the room while cradling her son in her arms. She stopped in her tracks the moment she caught sight of Ann and grinned. "You're looking rather frightful today."

"Tandler funeral."

"Ah, well, that explains it, and since they're a frightening family, you'll fit right in. Is Hazel going as your hired gun?"

"Of course. I'm just waiting for her to get here. She and Lloyd were having tea at Rutherford & Company and are expected to join me in the next hour."

"While you're waiting for her to arrive, would you mind watching Branson?" Daphne asked, handing her sleeping child over when Ann immediately held out her arms. "I have a client who showed up early and Herman seems to be running late. He's turning in a new book, so his tardiness was expected, but I can't very well have Branson in the room when I know Mrs. Jordan is not going to react well after I tell her she wasn't imagining things and that her husband has taken to gallivanting around town in the company of questionable women."

"Branson will be just fine with me," Ann said as she placed a kiss on Branson's forehead, a kiss that didn't have him stirring in the least. "You know I can never refuse an opportunity to hold this little darling."

"Does that mean you wouldn't refuse a request to spend time with him tomorrow afternoon, which would allow me time to polish off my latest novel?"

"I can be there by noon, after I help Cooper put our new recruits through his improved physical exertion lessons."

"I'm sorry I'll have to miss those because of my deadline," Daphne said with a grin, her grin fading when the sound of Mrs. Jordan's voice drifted through the doorway, the clear note of impatience causing Daphne to blow out a breath before she hurried out of the room.

"I see Mrs. Jordan is back again," Gabriella said, striding into the office a second after Daphne disappeared, looking striking in an afternoon dress that had, of course, been designed by Phillip, who'd had to hire on ten new dressmakers just to keep up with the business that kept pouring through his door. She dropped into the nearest chair and shoved an errant strand of hair out of her face. "Poor Daphne always seems to get the overly dramatic clients."

"Where's Prudence?" Eunice asked, setting aside a file on a potential client.

"Nicholas has her today. His father, Rookwood, has been dying to take Prudence for a carriage ride through Central Park, so Nicholas is meeting him there. I believe Professor Cameron is going as well." Gabriella smiled. "It's amazing how Prudence has those gentlemen wrapped around her tiny finger already."

"Nicholas is going to have his work cut out for him once she reaches her majority, because she is a beauty," Eunice said.

"She'll marry Branson, of course," Ann said, stroking little Branson's cheek.

As Gabriella and Ann began planning Branson and Prudence's futures for them, although it was completely likely the children would have minds of their own, given who their parents were, Eunice leaned back in the chair as thoughts of how everyone's lives at the Holbrooke Boardinghouse had changed so significantly ever since they'd had the audacity to take on the case of Miss Jeanette Moore almost two years before, a decision that had altered every lady's life in the most unexpected yet delightful of ways.

Before the formation of the Bleecker Street Inquiry Agency, she'd been a woman alone, except for Ivan and Alma, disguising the truth of who she really was beneath her widow's weeds and veils because she'd been afraid to live her life in the open, afraid of a nameless monster who'd murdered her grandfather.

But with the formation of the Bleecker Street Inquiry Agency, she'd formed real friendships for the first time in her life and had found a purpose in that life as well, that being helping others seek justice when no one else would. She'd also found the best thing in her life—a love that was forever in the form of Arthur Livingston.

He understood her, didn't expect to manage her, and filled her days with laughter and spirited debates, which always ended in the most delightful of ways, normally involving a great deal of kissing.

She'd been right that Arthur knew his way around a kiss.

"Did you see where there's been more reform at Blackwell's Island Insane Asylum because of that article Nellie Bly wrote?" Gabriella asked, drawing Eunice from her thoughts.

She nodded. "I found it interesting that a reporter was able to go undercover and not be detected after we'd done the exact same thing mere weeks before Miss Bly set out to get her story. But thank goodness she released that story. Now additional steps can continue to be taken to improve conditions there."

"Arthur told me you've been thinking about having the Howland Foundation break ground on asylums throughout the country."

Eunice nodded. "Now that development has begun on the old Green farm, Mason Mines is yielding more copper than ever, which means my fortune is increasing at an alarming rate. I can't bear to allow that money to go to waste like Grandfather did, hence the decision to build more asylums. Reverend Danford is thrilled with that decision and is excited to begin working with local churches to ascertain there'll be services offered at least two times a week at each asylum. He and I are in full agreement that providing the most vulnerable amongst us with a message of hope may very well see some of the patients suffering from acute melancholy improve through sermons devoted to good news and the power of healing through a loving God."

Gabriella smiled. "And while I agree that the country needs

institutions that actually care for the state of their patients' well-being, you might have to pull back just a little, especially when you reach the stage where you're tossing up your accounts all the time."

Ann's mouth dropped open. "Eunice, are you . . . ?"

"Shh . . ." Eunice said as she heard Arthur's voice in the hallway. "I haven't told him yet."

"We should go," Gabriella said, rising to her feet and walking with Ann toward the door. "We'll take Branson for a walk around the block." Grabbing hold of the baby carriage, Gabriella wheeled it out of the room, Ann following her.

Eunice heard them speaking with Arthur, and then he was walking into her office, a smile on his face and roses in his hand.

She got to her feet as he kissed her cheek, and then her lips. "I brought you flowers."

"So I see. What's the occasion?"

"I saw them and they reminded me of you."

Her heart melted, something she never thought she'd get to experience in life, but something she experienced on a daily basis with Arthur.

"I was hoping you'd have time to steal away and go on a picnic with me."

Even though she had a dozen files to get through, she didn't hesitate to take his arm and head out of the office, handing her roses to Gabriella, who was waiting for Ann to get Branson settled in the baby carriage.

After assuring Eunice she'd get them into water straightaway, Gabriella sent her a wink that Eunice returned before she walked out of the Bleecker Street Inquiry Agency and stopped beside Arthur's two-seated phaeton. Wyatt, of course, tossed his head the moment he caught sight of her.

"He's never going to like me," she muttered as Arthur helped her into the phaeton and picked up the reins.

"Of course he likes you. His surly attitude is simply his way of expressing his devotion to you."

Given the way Wyatt lunged forward, Eunice was relatively convinced Arthur was wrong about that.

"I thought we'd go to Central Park," Arthur said, steering Wyatt through a crowded Bleecker Street.

"Or perhaps we could drive down Fifth Avenue or take a turn through Gabriella's or Daphne's neighborhood. I've been thinking it might be time to find a house."

"I thought you loved living in the boardinghouse."

"I do," she began, "but it might be a little too crowded for us there soon."

Arthur brought the carriage to a stop, seemingly unconcerned that he'd done so in the middle of traffic. "Are you saying that our family might be going from two to . . . three?"

"That's exactly what I'm saying."

It came as no surprise when Arthur pulled her close and kissed her in the middle of Bleecker Street, right before he turned the phaeton around and headed for the boardinghouse. He then insisted on carrying her from the phaeton up the steps, through the front door, and then told Alma, who was watching them with a smile, that they weren't to be disturbed but she might want to start planning a feast because they had good reason to celebrate.

Striding into their suite of rooms, Arthur set her down on the fainting couch where he read a variety of books to her every night, told her she was his incomparable, and then all thoughts of looking for the forever home they'd share with the many children she was certain they were going to have were forgotten as Arthur drew her close and kissed her.

Named one of the funniest voices in inspirational romance by *Booklist*, **Jen Turano** is a *USA Today* bestselling author, known for penning quirky historical romances set in the Gilded Age. Her books have earned *Publishers Weekly* and *Booklist* starred reviews, top picks from *Romantic Times*, and praise from *Library Journal*. She's been a finalist twice for the RT Reviewers' Choice Awards and had two of her books listed in the top 100 romances of the past decade from *Booklist*. She and her family live outside of Denver, Colorado. Readers can find her on Facebook, Instagram, Twitter, and at jenturano.com.

Sign Up for Jen's Newsletter

Keep up to date with Jen's news, book releases, and events by signing up for her email list at jenturano.com.

More from Jen Turano

Daphne Beekman is a mystery writer by day, inquiry agent by night. She happily works behind the scenes, staying away from danger. But when Herman Henderson arrives on the doorstep, desperate for someone to investigate numerous attempts on his life, Daphne finds herself in the thick of a case she's determined to solve—and finds her heart in jeopardy as well.

To Write a Wrong • THE BLEECKER STREET INQUIRY AGENCY

You May Also Like . . .

Gabriella Goodhue thought she'd put her past as a thief behind her . . . until a woman is unjustly accused. But when Nicholas Quinn, a former friend against whom she holds a grudge, catches Gabriella looking for evidence to exonerate her friend, he insists they join forces. But their feelings for each other are tested when danger follows their every step.

To Steal a Heart by Jen Turano
THE BLEECKER STREET INQUIRY AGENCY
jenturano.com

When Beatrix Waterbury's train is disrupted by a heist, scientist Norman Nesbit comes to her aid. He soon finds himself swept up in the havoc she always seems to attract—including the attention of the men trying to steal his research—and they'll soon discover the curious way feelings can grow between two very different people in the midst of chaos.

Storing Up Trouble by Jen Turano
AMERICAN HEIRESSES #3
jenturano.com

A very public jilting has Theodore Day fleeing the ballrooms of New York to focus on building his family's luxury steamboat business in New Orleans and beating out his brother to be next in charge. But he can't escape the Southern belles' notice, nor Flora Wingfield, who is determined to win his attention.

Her Darling Mr. Day by Grace Hitchcock
AMERICAN ROYALTY #2
gracehitchcock.com

◊ BETHANYHOUSE

More from Bethany House

A birthday excursion turns deadly when the SS *Eastland* capsizes with insurance agent Olive Pierce and her best friend on board. After her escape, Olive discovers her friend is among the missing victims. When she begins investigating the accident, more setbacks arise. Finding the truth will take all she's got to beat those who want to sabotage her progress.

Drawn by the Current by Jocelyn Green
THE WINDY CITY SAGA #3
jocelyngreen.com

On the surface, Whitney Powell is happy working with her sled dogs, but her life is full of complications that push her to the edge. When sickness spreads in outlying villages, Dr. Peter Cameron turns to Whitney and her dogs for help navigating the deep snow, and together they discover that sometimes it's only in weakness you can find strength.

Ever Constant by Tracie Peterson and Kimberley Woodhouse
THE TREASURES OF NOME #3
traciepeterson.com; kimberleywoodhouse.com

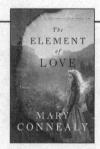

After learning their stepfather plans to marry them off, Laura Stiles and her sisters escape to find better matches and claim their father's lumber dynasty. Laura sees potential in the local minister of the poor town they settle in, but when secrets buried in his past and the land surface, it will take all they have to keep trouble at bay.

The Element of Love by Mary Connealy
THE LUMBER BARON'S DAUGHTERS #1
maryconnealy.com

BETHANYHOUSE